V. J. & . Flynn
got at J'ck Market charity stall
baskers, A lupila Territory
October, 2011

POOR
MAN'S ORANGE

AUSTRALIAN CLASSICS

POOR
MAN'S ORANGE

RUTH PARK

ANGUS & ROBERTSON PUBLISHERS

ANGUS & ROBERTSON PUBLISHERS
London • Sydney • Melbourne • Singapore • Manila

First published by Angus & Robertson Publishers, Australia, 1949
Reprinted 1950, 1952, 1955
This A&R Australian Classics edition, 1980

© Ruth Park 1949

National Library of Australia
Cataloguing-in-publication data.

Park, Ruth.
  Poor man's orange.

  (Australian classics)
  First published, Sydney: Angus & Robertson, 1949.
  ISBN 0 207 14290 4

  I. Title. (Series)

A823'.3

Printed in Hong Kong

CHAPTER

I

AND then the queer sounds would begin again, heavy, rhythmic breathing, and muffled whimpers as though someone had his head pressed hard into a pillow, afraid he would be heard.

Charlie lay awake for a long time listening. He became aware he had often heard it before in his dreams, a penetrating sound that had half-pierced the veils of sleep. He awakened Roie.

"What's the matter?"

"I don't know. Listen."

Roie listened. "Oh, it's only Mr Diamond. He's talking in his sleep. He always does it."

"Wonder if he's crook? He looks funny these days."

"Oh, go on. He's getting as fat as a porker." Roie was cross. She scrambled out of bed to see if Motty was covered, scolding the sleeping child in a whisper when she found the bedclothes in a tangled scarf at the bottom of the cot. Mr Diamond's bed creaked, and the floor shuddered as he walked across it. They heard the pop of the gas-ring.

"He's got indigestion again, that's all. Shut up and go to sleep."

Charlie laughed and drew her head down on his shoulder. Her fragility and slenderness charmed him, as he might be charmed by the delicate slightness of a gazelle. He stroked her cheek, and once again drowsily thought his way through the litany of his love for her, for they rarely spoke of love.

In the next room Mr Diamond waited for the kettle to boil. He waited with the fixed and avid stare of a drug addict, and all the while the pain crept downwards through his abdomen in a trembling, undulatory progression till even the bones of his legs seemed to twist and grow brittle under its impact. He knew he couldn't hold out much longer. His teeth clamped together, his face built into a square mask of determination and

1

agony; he knew that one night he would give way and start screaming.

The kettle boiled, and he poured some water into a cup, filling it to the brim with thick, black pain-killer. Its opium smell, thinly disguised with aniseed, filled the room, and Mr Diamond snuffed it like the odours of paradise. He tossed off the filthy stuff, vomiting against the taste, and while his throat was still numb, he filled a hot-water bottle and lay down again with it on his stomach.

He started to pray, "Our Father Which art in heaven . . ." mumbling the line over and over again, for he was exhausted into stupidity with pain and sleeplessness. Slowly the agony subsided. It was as though he had an animal inside his body, and it gnawed and clawed until he fed it with the pain-killer. But it wasn't an animal, it was a fish. Mr Diamond moved the hot-water bottle aside, and once again, for the thousandth time, he felt the thing that lay across his stomach. Unbelievingly, astoundedly he felt it, the shape and solidity of it, and wondered at the alien, incredible thought that this revolutionary bastard creation of his body tissue could really exist.

It was the shape of a fish, not very large, but firm and well-defined. As though in protest all the rest of his abdomen had grown soft and spongy, bulging out his trousers as though he were an alderman puffed with expensive living.

"It just can't have happened," thought Mr Diamond, and once again he felt piteously hopeful that it was just a nightmare, and he would wake in the morning to find it gone.

Then he knew that it wasn't, that he really did have a growth and sooner or later he would have to die, and go to another world even lonelier than this one, and at that appalling, certain thought, Mr Diamond began to cry harshly and loudly—he who had never wept since he was a little boy in Ireland, and his feet so chilblained he could hardly walk.

He tried very hard to stop crying, but he couldn't. The terror and the despair rushed in and seized him, and out of the past came the old cry for his mother, his father, anybody who could take the responsibility of it all off his shoulders and make him better.

"Ma, Ma," he babbled, "where are you, Ma?" The memory of her—the big, bony woman with the red splash on her cheek-bones, her black petticoats turned up and tucked in at the waist, gutting fish so fast the knife was a flicker of silver—came at him so alive and real that it was almost as though he were a little boy again, and in trouble about something that was small, and yet seemed to fill the whole world.

"Maybe this is small, too," thought Mr Diamond, "but oh, God, I don't feel it that way."

He fell into a nightmarish doze, in which he wandered again through the old days that came up thick and fast as though someone were flicking them out of a card pack. An uneasiness and foreboding fear ran through them all. He chased the black bobtail pup, but never caught it. He fell into the weedy lagoon, and never came again to the surface. He fled the brindle boar, but was caught for ever suspended upon the moment when the froth-flecked snout was just behind him. The pain suddenly surged up and shook him out of his sleep, and Mr Diamond sat up and stared into the darkness, which was hot and prickling with panic. Not all his fortitude and courage could stop the terrific groan from bursting through his lips, and almost at once he heard movement next door, and the young man Charlie Rothe called softly, "What's up, Pat? You sick?"

The door handle turned, but it was too late for Mr Diamond to curse. He could see the tall shadowy figure in the dusky doorway, asking again, "I heard you call out. Do you feel crook?"

"No," gasped Mr Diamond. "Just dreaming."

He closed his eyes, sweat streaming off him with the effort of speaking normally, but when he opened them again Charlie was still there. A sickening, trembling rage seized him.

"I told you I was all right. Coming into a man's room, you bloody nigger! Go on, clear out." He sat up and shrieked, "Get out! Get out! Get out!"

The door closed. Mr Diamond lay back, fainting with the pain and thought of the hours ahead of him, the long minutes, the endless seconds that would have to be borne in silence.

In the morning Charlie said privily to his father-in-law, Hughie Darcy, "I reckon you ought to go up and see if old Patrick's all right, Pop. He was making a lot of noise in the night."

So Hughie, buttoning up his blue shirt and stuffing it into his pants as he went up the stairs, barged into Patrick's room, singing as he went, for it was pay-day, and already his tongue was hanging out like a length of red flannel with the delicious anticipation of the pub.

Mr Diamond was lying half out of bed, a grey greasiness on

3

his face, and his eyes fallen into blue pits. A cold hot water bottle grumbled beside him.

"Goddlemighty," said Hughie. "And the night last night like a furnace."

It seemed quite plain that Mr Diamond was drunk, and Hughie lifted him to put him back into bed. A hoarse croak came from Mr Diamond.

"Don't be touching me, Hughie."

Now Hughie was alarmed. He hurried to close the door in case one of the girls should pass and see Patrick's nakedness.

"You know me indigestion, Hugh?"

"Like an old pal," said Hughie, puzzled.

"Well, it ain't."

Mr Diamond motioned Hughie to pull up the old shirt in which he slept. It was grimed with dirt, and so was Mr Diamond.

"Put yer hand on me here."

Hughie did so, and felt the fish. For a moment appalled horror held him motionless. A cold tingling feeling ran over him from top to toe. It was almost as though death had breathed over his shoulder. He said in a small voice, "Christ, Patrick."

Mr Diamond hoisted himself up a little. Often the daylight brought surcease to him, and now the pain was ebbing with the onward march of the morning. He seized Hughie's arm.

"It's got me, Hugh. If I go to a hospital they'll carve me up, and it won't do any good. I'm done, Hugh. You got to stick by me."

"Whatever you say, Pat," promised Hughie, his eyes averted.

"I won't go into a home for the dying. I been on me own all me life, and I'm not going to be mucked about with now. I don't want anyone praying over me."

Hughie swallowed hard. "There might be some chance . . . you don't want to drop your bundle . . ." he said feebly. Mr Diamond lay back.

"Don't tell anyone, Hughie. You're me mate, and I trust you. I want to stick it out by meself, that's all."

"I'll bring you up a cuppa strong tea," muttered Hughie. Mr Diamond opened an eye in which was the ghost of an old twinkle.

"It'd suit me better if you've got a drop of muscat under the bed, mate."

All day long Hughie pondered on Mr Diamond. He moved

4

in a dream, his lips moving silently, his eyes focused on the inner problem and not on his work. Predominant in his mind was astonishment that Patrick should have had this thing so long, and yet no one had guessed. A growth! Hughie shied away from the real word. It was as obscene to him as some of his commoner expressions would have been to a nun.

And Patrick, who was so tough he never even got a snuffly nose in winter! How did it happen, this terrible secret process that uncurled in a man's vitals as softly, gently as a rosebud, until it was a dam of the life-force itself, strangulating and suffocating?

Trembling, Hughie stopped the machine. He couldn't trust himself to carry on. The sinewy strength of his own robust body, the deep chest of which he was proud, the short, strong arms, the legs like little tree-trunks were forgotten. All at once he felt that he was a cardboard man, for God alone knew whether within his own structure he was not carrying such a seed as Patrick had carried. But under his fear there was deep grief for Patrick, and indignation that this should have happened to such a good man.

"He ain't ever done anything to You!" Hughie cried to God. "Why didn't You pick out some rotten warmonger, or stinking politician raking in the chips, instead of an old bloke like Patrick, living decent on the pension, and not doing anyone any harm?"

His eyes stung, and his throat ached. He wanted to rush up to the hospital and hammer on the door of some big specialist and cry, "You gotta come and fix him up! I don't care if I have to work the rest of me life to pay you. You gotta save Pat's life."

It made him feel sick. He had to go to the pub for the warmth and companionship there, and it wasn't until he had had half a dozen beers that the keen edge of his pain was blunted. Even there he couldn't do anything about it. Cancer wasn't a thing you could shape up to, and knock silly. You couldn't even sneak up behind it and slam it with a bottle in a sock. Hughie felt so bad that he had to leave the happy buzz and go home. He pleaded once more with Mr Diamond to see a doctor, but Mr Diamond only became angry and told him to go to hell.

He went downstairs and sat silently at the table, waiting for his tea. Mumma peeped round the door at him several times, for she was alarmed at his un-Friday-night-like lack of rum-bustiousness. Finally she said timidly, "Feeling sick, Hugh?"

5

Hughie longed to tell her, but it seemed to be so much Mr Diamond's property, this terrible secret, and he had promised solemnly not to tell.

"I'm tired," he grunted.

Mumma came a little closer; all the love in her heart springing upright like grass after the heavy weight of a building has been removed.

"I got two bob if you'd like to shout me to the pitchers," she said

"I can't," said Hughie awkwardly. "I said I'd go up and have a yarn to old Pat."

Mumma's love retreated like a turtle into its shell. She flamed, "That's right! Spend the night boozing instead of letting people know I've got a husband. For all they know you're only a boarder."

And so she went on, pounding around the table and slapping down knives and forks and fuming about old booze artists like Mr Diamond who would only have to breathe on a naked flame to cause an explosion.

"Shut yer mouth!" roared Hughie. He looked at her with real hate, for it was just like a woman to berate a dying man, even though she didn't know he was dying. All at once his eyes began to sting, for at last he had put the thought into words. He rose hastily and went into the bedroom, and Mumma looked after him, amazed. She went out and spoke severely to Motty, saying, "Your gran' pop's a bit tired. Don't you go roaring round the house like a grampus, now."

CHAPTER

2

In this narrow-gutted, dirty old house, squeezed with its elbows flat against its sides between two others, there lived seven people. There was Mr Diamond, the Orangeman, and Hughie Darcy and his wife. Also there was Dolour Darcy, who was sixteen, and her elder sister Roie, who lived in one of the attic rooms with her husband, Charlie Rothe, and their little girl, Moira, who called herself Motty. There had been two others—Thady, who had been born between Roie and Dolour, and who was stolen off the street when he was six and never seen again; and Grandma, dead a long time now, and yet curiously a part of their daily life, a shuffling little ghost, pungent as a whiff of pipe smoke, and Irish as the words that were all she had to leave them.

The Irish in these people was like an old song, remembered only by the blood that ran deep and melancholy in veins for two generations Australian. The great tree, kernelled in the rich dust of Patrick and Columbanus, Finn and Brian, and Sheena of the unforgotten hair—the tree whose boughs had torn aside the mists of Ultima Thule bore in this sun-drowned southern land leaves in which the sap welled sharp, sweet, as any on Galway quay, or the market at Moneymore. The great music that had clanged across the world, of lion voice of missionary, of sword and stylus; the music that spoke aloud in the insurrections, in the holds where the emigrants sweltered in vermin and hunger—this music was heard in Plymouth Street, Surry Hills, and was unrecognized.

For how could Hughie Darcy, stumbling up that street in the dusk, with the wind blowing dead leaves about his feet, and in his heart the helpless, defenceless despair that comes after drunkenness, know that what he sought his forefathers sought, and equally misdirectedly? The rainbow that never ended anywhere, the unbeatable conviction that somewhere, sometime, things would be better without his bothering his head to make them so.

And how could Mumma, flapping about the house in her old slippers, turning the mattresses and exclaiming at the clouds of dust in old, apt, unique phrases that came to her tongue unbidden as birds, know that those same phrases had been used for centuries, rising out of the brilliant logic of the Irish? She only knew that her mother had used them, and standing there amongst the settling curds of dust she remembered that wicked, invincible little mother who had made them Australian, and said a Pater'n'Ave for her peace.

Only in the little girl, Dolour, lying on her stomach and picking her face before a yellow corner of looking-glass, was the fierce positivity of the Celt, a surging energy that made her long for the world she did not know, for thoughts she could not yet comprehend, for experience she could not yet encompass. In her was the infinite delicacy of feeling of the Irish, the very halt of the raindrop before it rolls down the stem, the spin of light on the knife-blade, the tremble of the wind harp's string as the blown air touches. She was on the threshold of articulateness, and did not know it.

All the discomforts, the vulgarities, the harsh jovialities of her little world broke against her as repeatedly and unavailingly as a wave breaks against a rock; her real life was in school and in the church.

The church in Surry Hills was no fountain of stone, no breaking wave of granite like some of the great cathedrals. It was foursquare, red brick, with a stubby steeple as strictly functional as the finger of a traffic cop; it humped its sturdy shoulder into the schoolyard, and the children rewarded it by bouncing balls off it.

It was as much a part of Surry Hills life as the picture-show or the police station, the ham and beef or the sly-grog shop. Its warm brick wall was there in winter for the old men to sun themselves against, or for the feeble-footed drunk, staggering home in the dim, to lie beside. Its steps were seats for the old ladies who'd walked too far with their marketing, and them with their feet brittle as biscuits with the rheumatism. The church in Surry Hills had achieved the innermost meaning of Christianity; it was the commonplace of life, like a well-loved old coat, worn, ordinary, sometimes a little drab, but essential to living.

On Sunday Father Cooley mounted the pulpit, rather slowly, for he had lumbago. He stared full into the eye of the microphone they had installed while he'd been sick, and contemptuously clouted the thing aside. He'd always been able to blast the ears off the back-benchers, and he had no intention of giving way to new-fangled inventions at his time of life.

"We're going to have a mission," he said.

The congregation moved like grass in the wind. Mumma hurried home afterwards as excited as if someone had told her she was going to be taken to the circus. For a mission was like a tonic. It stirred the 'possum in the people, and for months afterwards they could still feel the enthusiasm, and the re-awakening of faith that had become a little monotonous and habitual.

"I'll get out Grandma's old beads and have them blessed again," she thought. For Grandma's beads, which were wooden, and big enough to have come out of a clam, had come over with Grandma from Derry in the seventies, and had had so many prayers counted on them that each bead was a little hollowed, like an old doorstep.

Mumma rushed straight into the house and dragged them out of the drawer where they lay entangled in old hairnets and tram tickets.

"Gawd, it's come again!" proclaimed Hughie, for he had seen this scene so many years in succession that at the very jangle of the beads his knees ached.

"This year I ain't going!" he bellowed, and he jammed his face into the pillow with the tea-stains on it, and stuck up his rear and registered ferocious determination.

"All right," said Mumma carelessly. "I'll pray for you."

Now, if there was one thing more than another that mad-dened Hughie, it was being prayed for. He was not good friends with God, and with the things that had happened to him, Hughie thought it was no wonder. He stood on his dignity, and the Lord stood on His, and Hughie's innate sense of justice revolted at the thought that Mumma was everlastingly trying to be a go-between.

For the woman in her innocence often said her prayers out loud as she lay in bed of a night, and Hughie would writhe in anguish as he listened to, "He's a hard worker, Lord dear, and it wouldn't be You who'd send him to everlasting fire for missing mass, when it's the only chance he's got of a bit of a snore-off", or, "There's some that don't take their duty seriously, and he's one of them, St Teresa love, and nothing but a pin in his bottom would stir him to it."

"It don't do any good," pleaded Hughie feebly. "All the good resolutions go west as soon as I get the breath of a bottle of plonk."

Mumma stuck another safety pin into the dragging hem of her old house dress.

"It's different this year, love," she reminded. "You got Mr Diamond to think about, poor man, and him looking so crook lately."

So Hughie went to the mission, getting over the first great and awful hurdle of going to confession to a shadowy hump that was the visiting missioner, and explaining why he hadn't been near the church for a year. Afterwards he felt curiously airy, as though the wind might well blow through his pores, or a sneeze whisk him over the telegraph wires. And he said to himself, forgetting all the other times, "This time I'll keep it up. What with the traffic the way it is, and the crook wine burning a man's innards into holes, you never can tell what's due next." Then he thought of Patrick Diamond, and a deep, painful melancholy settled on him. He stared at the stable will-o'-the-wisps of the candles, and hardly saw them; he got up and sat down mechanically, and while his lips moved along the old worn path of the Hail Marys and Our Fathers, his heart was saying, "Don't take it out on Pat, Lord, for all he is an Orangeman, and that bitter against the Church. But he's me mate, and as solid as a rock, and they don't come like Pat often. I'm the man who'll stand black for him."

And all the many things Mr Diamond had done for and with him came to him, the shared bottle when they were both on the dole, and how Pat came across with the two and a zack when Dolour was a kid with a tooth that needed to come out, and the way when, in the depression, they'd only had one shirt between them, and it hairy as an ape around the collar with the frayed threads.

"I been a worse man than Pat many and many a time," said Hughie, "and I swear I'll stick by You more than I've done if only You make him get better."

The organ mooed out a breve, and out of the dusty rafters came floating Mrs Siciliano's strong, throbbing Neapolitan voice. Mrs Siciliano was the wife of the fruiterer down Coronation Street. Every year she had a new baby, which was awkward for the choir, for it meant that for a good part of every twelve months she was not able to squeeze up the narrow stairs.

"Faith-a of our fathers!" roared Mrs Siciliano, and the congregation rose to its feet with a deafening clatter and joined in the hymn with such tempestuous emotion that you would have thought they had parked their shillelaghs in the porch but a minute before.

"In spite of dungeon, fire and sword!" cried Mumma, looking round her as though daring anyone to deny it. She saw the mouths of her family open and shut unheard, and Hughie, slouched on one leg, singing out of the corner of his mouth in case anyone noticed. Down the front were the nuns, Sister Theophilus with her straight back, and Sister Beatrix bowed under a little black shawl, and all the little postulants in their funny hats, their clean rosy faces shining with happiness and soap. And there was Jacky Siciliano, with his stomach eight inches in front of him, his head back, each candle-flame reflected separately in his glossy scalp, bellowing about it as though they were his fathers they were singing about. Mumma gave him a look.

The warm air enveloped them all. Dolour flowed backwards and forwards on the great gushing waves of sound. It was like a sea beating again and again on a beach. Her pulse was cognisant of the rhythm, but her mind was away, away. She looked at the walls, whose every crack she knew. She looked at the statue of St Patrick with the tiny church in his big capable hand, his thumb curled over the steeple; and the sad dark Byzantine Christ with the long nose and pure gold halo. When she was little Dolour used to crawl round the back of the statues to see how they did their dresses up. She found that inevitably they were like Superman, with no buttons, no nuttin's. It was a blow, too, to find that the gentle angels were afflicted with great knobs on the back of the neck to hold their haloes on.

"Oh, dear Lord," prayed Dolour, "let me get my examination, and make Sister pleased with me." Then she put her head down on her hands. "And please, if I can't be a nun, let somebody like me, the way Charlie likes Roie, only nicer."

For Dolour spent a great deal of her time praying for a vocation, though not at all sure what she would do with it if she got it.

As they went out into the hot darkness, ducking shyly past one of the missioners who stood at the steps, Dolour looked around for Suse, her friend. Anxiously, bewilderedly, Dolour yearned over Suse Kilroy, the sulky, impudent child of the dirty little house down Chapper Lane, a house overflowing with unwashed whining children, begotten by a drunken father of a wife so worn down with worry and work that she was as stupid as a cow.

There was Suse, leaning back against the fence, staring at the people as they went past. She didn't care that there were holes in her black stockings, insufficiently blacked-out with ink, or that her greenish gym tunic was ripped at one side.

Dolour thought, "Gee, ain't she pretty!" Aloud she said, "Watcher waiting for, Suse?"

Suse was disgusted. "I thought some of the boys might have been to this turn-out. Suppose they got more sense."

Dolour giggled. Suse's forthrightness always filled her with shocked amusement. Even when Suse went mincing up the corridor behind Sister Theophilus, mocking her every move-ment, Dolour, who worshipped the nun, felt an extraordinary impulse to laugh. It was impossible for her to condemn or resent anything Suse did.

"Come on," said Suse. Dolour hesitated, looking back at her mother, who was gossiping on the steps with Mrs Drummy, of the ham-and-beef.

"Oh, get out. She's old enough to find her own way home," said Suse impatiently. Dumbly Dolour trotted after her down Coronation Street, which was splashed with the green and livid pink of the picture-show neons, and filled with an odour of hamburgers and terrible coffee and dust but recently laid with a sprinkle of wet tea-leaves.

"There's Ro," said Dolour, relieved. "I could ask her."

"My God!" said Suse. "What you want to ask her for? You're sixteen, ain't yer?"

"She could tell Mumma I'm with you," stumbled Dolour weakly.

Suse snorted. Charlie and Roie were looking in a shop window, and she bowled boldly up to them. "Hiya."

"Hullo, Suse," Roie said shyly. "How's your mother?"

Suse was about to say, "Patching up the old pram for a bit more work", but she saw that it wouldn't do. She looked quickly at Charlie. Gee, he was a looker, in that dark foreign way. She looked at his mouth and thought it a pity he had to waste his kisses on a crumby little mouse like Ro Darcy. Then she looked down and said in a low voice, "She's not too well, poor old Mum. I got to stay home a good bit to look after her. You know how it is."

Roie was a little afraid of Suse as a rule, but now she said eagerly, "It'll do you good to have a little walk, Suse. Why don't you keep her company, Dolour?"

"Here, buy yourselves an ice-cream," said Charlie, pulling his hand out of his pocket.

"He's nice, ain't he?" said Suse as they went down the street.

"Who, Charlie?" Already in her mind Dolour was buying the ice-cream, piled in soft rosy whorls in a cone. Her tongue was out to lick it, the saliva came into her mouth at the thought of it.

"Ever caught 'em making love?"

Dolour blushed in astonishment. "Ah, hold on."

"Aw, fooey! I'll bet he's a stinger. I wouldn't mind getting up close to him."

Dolour said angrily, "Aw, shut your mouth! Don't you ever think of anything else?"

"Course not," said Suse, sidelong. "Do you?"

"I just been to Benediction," burst out Dolour. She sought for words to defend Charlie and her sister and herself. She floundered in a morass of indecision, of shyness, and a dreadfully definite feeling that Suse knew much more about everything than she did. She said helplessly, "It's awful, talking like that about a fellow who's married."

"Oh hell, what do you think he talks about?"

Dolour gaped. "Charlie?"

Suse prised her hand open. "Two bob! Jumpin' joey, we could sneak in to the pitchers at half-time with that."

Dolour badly wanted to ask what it was Charlie talked about, but she didn't get a chance. The swinging doors of the old theatre burst open, and out poured a crowd that seemed to be fleeing from a fire, but was in reality only dying for a smoke. There was a spout of music, the cry of a trampled usher, and interval was on.

"Come on!"

There were the boys, huddling in a group like a ring of mushrooms, dragging on queer cigarettes either rolled funnel-shape and showering the smoker with bits of burning tobacco, or screwed as tightly as a straw and resolutely refusing to burn. Now and then raucous shouts of laughter came from the boys, and one, pushed from behind, shot out of the group and staggered flap-armed on the edge of the gutter. They were dressed in clothes that seemed too roomy, trousers belted tightly about their slender waists, and colourful shirts with starched collars sticking up in wings round their cheeks. They were desperately self-conscious and not at all cognisant of why they were.

For this reason they gave cheek to passers-by, waddled after fat ladies, and woo-wooed at girls sailing past in trams.

"Jeepers . . . no!"

But it was too late. Suse was already strolling over towards them. She had pulled in her belt tightly, so that her bosom showed, and opened the neck of her blouse. Dolour followed, shy and excited, wanting to run away, and feeling the pimple on her chin come up like a Matterhorn.

All the boys knew Suse. Out of the corner of her eye, too excited to think about it yet, Dolour saw that they dug each other in the ribs, rolled their eyes, and one hung out his tongue and panted like a dog. Suse didn't seem to mind.

"Hiya, Nipper. Howsit, Joe."

Behind her glowing russet face, Dolour looked like a cold potato. She was so shy she didn't know which way to look, but she wanted very badly to be there, in this strange and exciting atmosphere, with the theatre blaring music at her, and brilliant light and dark furry shadow everywhere, and the air filled with the exotic odour of hair-oil, minties, and young men. She wanted to say something smart, to draw attention to herself, and she looked timidly round the group to find someone who wasn't staring at Suse. But there was no one.

They all looked furtively at each other, embarrassed and delighted. Conversation did not come easily to any of them. Their verbal range was limited to three or four hundred words, and the spaces were filled up with profanity, gestures, and inarticulate squawks of laughter, derision or protest.

"Well," said Suse, "ain't anyone going to ask us inside?"

"We got our own two bob," said Dolour helpfully.

"Oh, nuts!" glared Suse. "You know where you can put it."

Deeply mortified, Dolour stammered, but her words were drowned in the sudden stampede for the theatre as the warning bell shrilled, and the crowd was sucked back into its vortex like dust motes. Dolour was borne along with the crowd, struggling to get beside Suse, and being left behind. She rushed forward and squeezed in amongst the boys, ducking down as they jammed past the doorkeeper in a mass. In a moment she found herself in the back row, with big feet kicking all round her, and before she could take off her hat or pull up her stockings or anything the lights went out, and a great peanut-perfumed darkness surrounded her on all sides.

"Suse! You there, Suse?"

"No, I've gone home," answered Suse. Dolour craned to see

14

her, wondering what she was cross about. She sat back in the seat as the picture came on the screen, and a large moist hand groped around in her lap and picked up her own grubby, surprised one. Delightful shivers of excitement ran up and down her back. To be holding hands in the pitchers, just like Charlie and Ro!

"Aw, come on, snuggle up," said a voice in her ear.

"Go and bag yer head," retorted Dolour haughtily. An arm crawled along the back of the seat and hooked around her shoulder.

"I been chewing musk. Like the smell?" A warm puff of breath gushed into her face. Dolour snorted. She tried to see her companion's face. There was indication of a beaky profile, and long hair marked with the inch-wide channels of a recent combing. He was not the sort of boy she would have picked out for herself, but anyway he was a boy. In a flash she transported herself into the next day, and was telling the other girls all about it, and being mysterious and maddening, like Suse. Awkwardly she tried to kink her thin, rigid shoulders into a compliant shape, and relaxed against the boy's sleeve. It was hard, for she was taller than he, but by humping her back she managed it. It was the very first time she had ever been cuddled.

"I've started," she thought with relief and joy. "He must like me, or he wouldn't do it." Proudly she hoped that Suse had noticed, but all kinds of queer things were going on down Suse's end of the seat. Sometimes the whole row shook as though it were going to topple backwards, and there were the muffled reports of feet striking the backs of seats in front, and the unmuffled voices of patrons rearing round and crying, "Aw, quit it, you big-booted bludgers!"

Suse gave a whispered squeal, and a fusillade of peanuts came out of the dark like a swarm of meteorites and rattled about them. Though the screen showed Chinese refugees pinned beneath toppling walls, not one of the young people in the back row saw a thing. Their world was there, and they enjoyed it, even though they had to pay an admission fee for the privilege of darkness.

Now Suse was giggling, and the seats shook all over again. Dolour's companion was getting restive. He had turned almost completely round, and was squinting at her from a distance of two inches. His breath fluttered on her cheek like a fan, with the most curious melting feeling. Dolour's heart gave a jump. He didn't look like it, but maybe he was the one. The very first

15

boy to fall in love with. She half-turned, and an extraordinary kiss, like a clout from a damp hairbrush, landed on her lips.

"Gee!" said Dolour feebly.

"Come on," he said.

"Where to?" asked Dolour.

"Is this the time to give with the wisecracks?" he asked. Now his voice was hoarse, suddenly breaking in the middle into a squeak that he hastily suppressed. The audience burst into a roar of laughter. Instinctively she craned to see what she had missed, and at the same moment a hand pulled up her skirt and slipped between her knees. For a moment Dolour was so astounded she did not move, or even think, and the hand, encouraged by her stillness, slid up her leg.

"Stop that!" hissed Dolour. She seized a hairy wrist, but it was too strong for her.

"Cut the capers," said her cavalier roughly. "Watcher think you're here for?"

Dolour had no arguments, no psychology, no tactics of any kind. Indignation and resentment flared in her, and without a thought for the hundreds of people there, the usher prowling uneasily in a circle of torchlight, or anything else, she seized a bit of loose flesh on the boy's arm and twisted it as far as it would go. The hand dropped from her leg, and an oath rent the darkness.

"You bitch!"

Dolour kicked out and connected with a shin. Her friend gave a cry of anguish. From somewhere in the theatre came a roar, "Quit the row, or you'll get thrown out!" But Dolour hardly heard it. Blind with rage and tears she heedlessly trampled on legs in an effort to get out. She fell sprawling between their boots and the back of the next seat.

Now the audience rose almost in a body. The events on the screen went their way unheeded. Two ushers pounded down from the door, and the wandering star on the other aisle dived down from the ceiling and slid rapidly across.

"Watch it!"

There was a stampede from the back seat. Dolour was shoved down again. Somebody stood on her hand. Sobbing with fury and fright she stumbled after them, following the sound of feet running down to the side exit. The light from a torch bobbed at her heels, and a voice yelled for her to stop. Precipitated into the night, she raced down the rutted lane and out into the street.

"Suse! Suse!"

16

The boys had deserted Suse. Disconsolate, she was leaning up against the empty hamburger shop, where the dirty papers blew and spun in the wind.

"You're a bloody beaut."

She felt in the pockets of her coat and pulled out the bent stub of a cigarette. "And no matches, either." Suse sent the stub whirling into the gutter.

"Oh, Suse!" sobbed Dolour, suddenly aware of her barked knuckles, the knees out of her stockings, and bruises all over her. The greater pain and shock in her soul were still too unresolved to manifest themselves.

"Ah, you're mad," said Suse, and before her contempt Dolour shrivelled. "Go on, get back to your mother and ask her to change your nappies for you." She turned away.

Piteously Dolour said, "You don't know what that boy wanted to do."

"I can guess," said Suse.

Tears rushed out of Dolour's eyes, and she was dissolved in shame at this, her greatest humiliation, of being sixteen years old, and howling like a baby in public.

"O, wake up," snarled Suse. "What do you think boys are like?"

"They ain't all like that!" protested Dolour.

"Oh, shut up, you make me sick! Break down and be human like everyone else. You only got one life, ain't you?"

Dolour turned away and ran up the road. She was astounded to see, as she passed the post office, that she had been away barely an hour.

"They ain't all like that!" she said passionately to the clock.

She wanted badly to go home, but she was not ready for that. How could she dissemble before Mumma's eyes? How could she explain the torn stocking and the blood on her hands? She had to go somewhere, to quieten down and think up a story. There was nowhere but the church. But it was already shut up. A dark block of stone it stood there, stocky within its own shadows. Only the tall pointed sanctuary window showed dim red with the light burning behind it. The locked door seemed symbolic to Dolour. She pelted towards it, and stopped short. The confusion and shock in her soul hardened into shame. Before the penetrating gaze that pierced the door and went straight to her heart, she dropped her eyes. It wasn't possible that only an hour ago she was in there, feeling peaceful and chaste, and so sure of everything, singing her head off with the rest. She wiped her mouth hard.

17

"Dirty stinker," she said savagely. "And they aren't all like that, either."

But she could get no reassurance from the church door, any more than she could get from her thoughts. Where were they all, the young men who wanted and tried to be clean, just as she did? Was Charlie like that? Was Roie like that, in the days before she married, willing to go any way a boy chose to lead her? Was Mumma?

Sick with disgust Dolour flew into her own doorway. Charlie was standing at the kitchen door, rubbing his arms with a towel. She glared at him, daring him to say anything about her disarray.

"Where's Mumma?"

"She went to bed."

"Oh, well . . ." She turned away. Then she remembered something. She brought out the two shillings. "Here. I didn't spend it after all."

He looked at the coin lying in the dirty, blood-streaked palm.

"You can spend it another day, Dolour."

"I don't want it!" choked Dolour, and she banged it down on the table, and pelted up the stairs to her room.

The thud of her door woke Mr Diamond from an uneasy, nightmare sleep. His mouth had hung open, and was so dry that he could feel the constriction of the tissues within his cheeks. A sickish smell of decay came from his lips, and hung about him like a miasma so that he could smell nothing else. He lay there, not even his eyeballs moving, his skin pulsing to succeeding waves of hot and cold. He was terrified lest the pain should begin again, frightened to move a muscle, willing to lie like a log for ever rather than be subjected to that unutterable torment again.

The little sounds of the night, the girl sniffling in the bedroom next to him, the whimper of Motty in her sleep, the rattle of a garbage-tin lid knocked by a prowling cat, the whine of Lick Jimmy's loose clothesline, passed over his head. They were part of his consciousness and that was all.

Into the orbit of his sight reared his stomach, huge and unsightly. It did not have the firm rotundity of Jacky Siciliano's, a healthy and hearty stomach. It was a flabby bag, obscene and meaningless.

Lying there, in the quiet and objective tranquillity that comes between bouts of terrible pain, Mr Diamond knew what he must do.

18

CHAPTER

3

ONCE he had made up his mind, things became easier for Mr Diamond. He was a brave man; he was not afraid of death as he was of disgracing his manhood, of becoming a shrieking, gasping wreck of a human being whose every breath was an unbearable torture. Mr Diamond wanted to finish his life with dignity.

He waited till Saturday, when they were all at mass, except Hughie, who, exhausted by Friday night's devotions, privily known to the faithful as the holy-hour-and-a-half, was snoring his head off downstairs. Mr Diamond had washed all his clothes, and folded them in a neat pile. He stripped his bed and tidied up the blankets. He did not have many belongings, and anything worth money had long ago been pawned. His pension book and his butter and tea coupons he put on the table, together with his mother's wedding lines and a postcard from Belfast bearing the news of his father's death forty years before.

Mr Diamond had always thought that a great sadness must come to a suicide when he was making preparations for the act, but he felt nothing but a little excitement as one might feel upon entering a railway station before a journey. Yet he found himself looking for little jobs to do so that he might be delayed. He cleaned his kettle and saucepan, and put all the chipped cups and plates in a row. He looked about, and there was nothing else to do.

Mr Diamond drew a deep breath. Well, no use dilly-dallying. Soon they would all be home from church, and it would be too late. He looked out the window, at the sun gilt on the top fans of the phoenix palm, and Lick Jimmy's chimney-pot trimmed with a row of sooty bobbles that were sparrows warming their toes in the smoke. It had been a wonderful world, and there had been happiness in it, though not much of it had come to him. He thought, "It's for the best, and I've been square, in me own way. God won't be minding it, if He's the man I've always thought Him."

He had already stuffed up the crack under the door, and made the window air-tight with paper. The gas-ring was on the floor, stretched to the limit of its greasy reptilian pipe, and Mr Diamond lay down beside it and put a blanket over his head. As he stretched out, the thing in his stomach seemed to shift in its net of connective tissues, and fell back with a heavy dragging sensation. Almost at once the pain began, sweeping into the innermost recesses of his body and brain. The gas came hissing down the pipe, stinging his nose. Greedily Mr Diamond sucked it in, feeling the membranes at the back of his throat swell and grow taut. It seemed to take a long time for anything to happen. He rolled closer to the jets and inhaled fiercely, but with a mournful sigh the supply of gas ceased.

Mr Diamond cursed bitterly. Black specks were swimming before his eyes. He seized the gas-ring and thumped it, but only a gasp or two came out. Only too well he knew what had happened. He was always running short of gas in the middle of cooking, for he had never accustomed himself to the use of the penny-in-the-slot meter. Now, with a desperate urgency, he hurried over to the table and scrabbled amongst the coins there. No pennies! He would have to go downstairs and borrow one from Hugh. Mr Diamond almost laughed. It was a joke that Hughie would appreciate. He had a temptation to call the whole thing off and go and tell Hugh all about it.

Like the galloping of far-away horses, the pain increased in intensity, and with a sudden savage desperation Mr Diamond knew that he must not be cheated. He began to tear one of Mumma's greyish sheets into long strips.

Downstairs Hughie snuffled his way out of sleep. It was dreadfully hot in the little bedroom, and sweat lay in tiny pools round his collar-bone and in the creases across his stomach. He opened his eyes and looked dizzily into the shimmering air. There was a loud crash upstairs. Hughie was too fatigued even to swear. He lay glaring at the ceiling.

Then a muffled knocking began, a regular tapping on the wall, or perhaps the floor, so strange and unusual a sound that Hughie sat bolt upright, though he felt he had left the top of his head on the pillow. Maybe Patrick had taken a bad turn, and was banging on the floor for help. Without another thought he leaped out of bed and up the stairs.

"Everything all right, Pat?"

20

The door was locked; the tapping went on, and Hughie, standing on the landing in his patched underpants, felt cold with the strangeness of it.

"Patrick?"

Now the tapping was slower, and Hughie, drawing off to the limit of the landing, crashed against the door and tore the flimsy bolt from its socket. A wave of gas-tainted air flowed out to meet him.

It was for a long frozen moment that he stood there and watched Mr Diamond swinging from the old gaslight jet, his toes tapping against the wall. Absolute horror transfixed him. He had no idea what to do. Chittering, he rushed to Mr Diamond, lifting his body and holding the weight on his own shoulder.

"Christ . . ."

Mr Diamond was a heavy man, and Hughie buckled beneath the strain. He jerked the fallen chair towards him with one foot, and half-supported himself and Mr Diamond while he yelled, "Help! Hey! Help!" forgetting that the house was empty

"I'm gonna be too late."

There was no other way. He had to let Mr Diamond's swollen body dangle while he dashed for the knife on the table. For endless seconds he sawed at the sheet, cursing and praying in one breath.

He dragged his friend to the bed. Mr Diamond was not far gone at all. The dark grape colour of his face faded, and round his eyes the puffiness subsided into yellow waxy circles. Blood dribbled down his chin from his bitten tongue.

Hughie watched him, distressed beyond measure. The pity of it all ate into his soul. He wanted to bawl like Motty over a stubbed toe. Mr Diamond opened his glazed eyes and said in a croak, "Why don't you mind your own bloody business?"

Those were the last words he spoke in that house. The doctor came, and in a little while the ambulance, and Mr Diamond was carried down the rickety stairs to the dark musty hall. Hughie was waiting at the door.

He said, "You'll be back again before you know where you are, and me and you'll split a bottle of red ned."

But Mr Diamond only turned his face away.

The whole house was silent with the shock. Roie wept. "We should have got the doctor before, no matter what he said, poor old man."

Mumma picked up Motty and stood quietly, as though protecting her. In her heart she was saying Hail Marys for Mr Diamond, and lashing herself for all the times she'd been rude to him and said hard things in return for those he'd said to her.

"For even though he did call me a pope-worshipper, I might have turned the other cheek," she mourned, "and him all the time with the pain on him perhaps, and it enough to get anyone's rag out."

It was only a week or two afterwards that they heard he was dead. Though he had been expecting it, Hughie felt as though a great weight had been lowered upon him. On the top of his head and across his shoulders he felt it. It pressed his feet into the ground and made it a labour even to open his mouth.

"Hughie," pleaded Mumma, "come down to mass this morning and say a prayer for his poor soul."

But Hughie only looked at her with sunken, despairing eyes, and went down to the pub and stayed there until he was thrown out at lock-up time.

So Mumma, who had been Mr Diamond's enemy, put on her old hat and went to the funeral, the only one to follow the coffin. She stood at the graveside and waited till all the perfunctory, black-clad men had gone, then she said her rosary furtively, for she didn't want Mr Diamond to know, realizing that he would bitterly resent any popish prayers being said for him. And after she had finished she stood there staring at the raw clay mound and the coarse, white-striped grass which blew over the edge of it. She wanted to say something; something in her chest was struggling to be expressed, but all she could say was, "I'll keep your mother's marriage lines, Mr Diamond. I'll put them away amongst me things, and they'll be safe."

CHAPTER

4

CHARLIE came home early one afternoon, and there was
Mumma sitting at the kitchen table with half-shelled peas
all round her, and Motty sitting at her feet eating the pods with
the rapidity and precision of a machine. Mumma had her
glasses on. She had bought them at Woolworth's long before,
and when one of the ear-handles fell off she had replaced it
by a handy piece of wire that had to be wound round her ear
every time she put them on.

She looked up at Charlie with the gaze of a condemned
woman.

"Oh, Charlie," she said, "it'll drive a chill through your
stomach to read what's written here in the paper."

Mumma loved murders. She read them with shrinking horror
and prawn-eyed eagerness, her lips moving in Hail Marys for
the deceased as she did so, and interrupting herself with little
cries of, "Jesus, Mary, and Joseph, he cut off his own mother's
head!" or, "God help her, the poor young thing left with four
children, and their father getting hung for sure."

So Charlie said, "Is it a murder again, Mumma?"

"It's murder all right," said Mumma gloomily. "They're going
to knock us down, Charlie boy, and make flats of us." And with
this remarkable statement Mumma got up and stood on Motty,
who yelled blue blazes.

Mumma took no notice, she was so distraught. "It's them
parlimenticians!" she cried. "I'd like to see them tossed out of
house and home and the very places where their mothers and
fathers were brought up turned into factories and communist
laundries and the dear knows what! Stop yer ballyhooly! You're
making such a noise I can't hear me ears!"

She gathered Motty up and marched off with her to the
stove, where she held the child with one arm while she
gathered up the washing that was draped round Puffing Billy's
meagre black flue.

"Come and help me hang out the airing, Motty love, and

I'm sorry I stood on yer little foot with me big clumsy hoof."
At the door she turned. "I won't go," she fired back at Charlie.
"They'll have to haul me out with ropes first."

Charlie sat down quietly and read the paper. He was tired
and dirty, his hands grained with ink, for he was a printer's
machinist. There was a soft step, and Roie's hands came down
over his throat and dived into the front of his shirt.

"Like me a bit, Charlie?" A kiss landed at the corner of his
mouth.

"No, you're a little stinker. Shut up, look what's in the paper."

Together they read the page. A little chill touched Roie's
heart.

"It's just a lot of rubbish, isn't it? I mean, fancy pulling Surry
Hills down!"

"They've been talking about it a long time." His black nail
traced the map. "Coronation Street, Cornwall Street, Plymouth
Street, Murphy . . . and all those little alleys running down to
Elizabeth."

Roie gazed at him, disbelieving. "But people live there. Where
would they go? It's our home. They can't go pulling people's
homes down. What about those that own their own places, like
Mr Drummy's ham and beef?"

"Ah, you don't want to get all boxed up about it." He rose
and stretched. "Nothing'll happen for twenty years. You know
what councils are."

But in the laundry he bent over the tub with the soap in
his hand, motionless. So they were going to pull the old place
down. Almost Charlie could hear the squeaks and groans in
the ponderous machinery of city-building, as though it were
tuning up for the job. No more web of dark alleys lined with
hostile ochre walls? No more lurching lanes of corrugated iron
fences, each with a little box of a peak-roofed lavatory peering
over? No more tall tenements with lacy iron balconies and
strings of grey washing flying like flag day?

Though home was to Charlie where his wife was, he often
thought of green places, and a yard where he could go out
in the cool of the day and sit and think, or play with Motty,
and not have to conduct yelled conversations with a Chinese
fruiterer on one side or an iceman on the other.

He scrubbed the ink out of his nails, slowly, thinking.

As the paper boy whooped his way up Plymouth Street, one
house after another broke into a loud confusion of comment,
and before very long heads were nodding over back fences.

Soon the story was in Coronation Street, too, and Mrs Siciliano screamed and beat her breast, for she and her husband had recently put a deposit on the fruit shop, and they feared that they would lose everything.

"So they're going to put up dirty big flats," said Mrs Campion, next door to the Darcys. "Won't that be nice for them that live on the top floor, up and down all day. And me with me various veins that bad I can hardly lift a hoof without fear of them blowing out on me."

"Fancy Roie pulling the pram up to the top floor!" mourned Mumma.

Mrs Campion shrieked like a cockatoo. "Oh, no, dearie! We'll all have lifts!" She roared with laughter. "Can't you imagine the kids hacking the ropes through, and the louts riding up and down and leaving the doors open? Oh, it's a scandal, that's what it is."

It was all right to be funny about it, but in their hearts the people were uneasy. What did they want flats for, all herded together like rabbits with no privacy for a bit of a fight or anything? Most of the tenement people had roomers in their balcony rooms or attics, but roomers were like members of the family. It wasn't the same as sharing a dirty big building with forty other families.

"It's the washing that'll worry me," confided Mumma. "They say there'll be a big laundry downstairs, and we'll each have a day."

"Maybe we'll boil all our things up together," shrieked Mrs Campion, beating her red arms on the top of the fence in her mirth. "I can jest see me bloomers on the line alongside Lick Jimmy's flourbag underpants."

"Go on, yer scout!" Mumma blushed as she waddled indoors.

Roie was sweeping the crooked stairs, the broom handle almost as tall as herself. Mumma looked at the pale face of her daughter, and her slender body, and all at once she forgot about the housing problem, and remembered something she had been meaning to ask for a long time.

"I was wondering why you don't have more children," she said, and as soon as the words were out felt upset, for they sounded angry. Roie brushed carefully at dirt that wasn't there.

"You don't need to sound like that, anyway."

"I just thought Charlie might have made you use something," blurted out Mumma. Roie flew into such a fury her little body shook like a bough.

"You've got a nerve, Mumma! You've always had it in for him, as though he wasn't good enough for us or something. Pity you couldn't have picked out a husband for yourself as good as he is."

"I'm only warning you for your own good," pleaded Mumma, swallowing her indignation. "Because if you're doing anything to keep the children back. . . ."

"Well, I ain't!" cried Roie tearfully. "You can talk, anyway; there was nearly four years between Thady and Dolour."

"There was something the matter with me inside," retorted Mumma defensively. She had forgotten all about her long wait for her children.

"Well, maybe there's something the matter with mine, too," said Roie triumphantly. She whisked inside her door.

"Then you ought to go to the doctor about it and not go worrying people with the wrong ideas," said Mumma angrily, after her. Roie went into her little room and sat on the bed. She giggled to herself, for she knew that Mumma suspected she was pregnant again and was using this method of getting the truth out of her.

"And I am, I am," said Roie to herself. She could hardly believe it, it had been so long. She was twenty-four, and felt as though she had been a woman for a century. The summer of her fertility was all about her, warm and glowing. She was married to a man whom she loved in the true way so rarely comprehended by the civilized. He was breadwinner, protector, lover and beloved, and, more than that, he was the giver of children, the fertilizer of what would be without him a fallow field. Her pride in and adoration of her lover sprang out of her inarticulate recognition of him as her only bridge to fleshly immortality in her children. When he possessed her she worshipped him not only as the delighter of her body, but as the miracle-worker, the dear, familiar thaumaturgist in whose arms the new soul flashed into human clay.

Roie did not think these things; she felt them. The good simplicities of life were hers, and it would have been illogical to feel otherwise about Charlie.

The next day Dolour came bursting into the house at lunchtime. "Oh, Mumma, come quick! There's a newspaper man down the road, and he's taking Delie Stock's picture."

Everywhere people were galloping down to Little Ryan Street. Most didn't know what it was all about, hoping that it was a good brawl or a fire. There was already a crowd in the lane outside the sly-grog shop. Women stood there, arms folded over their aproned chests, slippered feet turned outwards at right angles, looking shyly at the young photographer with the hat hooked on the back of his head, and the elderly, disillusioned-faced reporter who accompanied him. A couple of carters, who had hopped off their trucks to see what was happening, were there, the leather carrier's pad on their naked shoulders, great beefy hands resting on invisible hipbones five inches below the natural ones.

"Oh, glory!" cried Mumma to Mrs Siciliano, who was there, a potato still in her hand, for she had run out while serving a customer. "And is it all over?"

"She's changing her dress," whispered Mrs Siciliano, spitting contemptuously and then looking round to see if anyone noticed, for she was a little afraid of Delie Stock.

And there she was, the worst woman in Surry Hills, hastily dressed up in a black dress that had been a model in the shop and now looked like a sequined bag. Delie's hair had been set and lacquered about three weeks before, and now it was like a doll's wig, growing in thick clumps, some in waves and some in a fuzz, all stiff and greyish with cracked lacquer.

"I ain't changed me slippers," she called, beaming at the photographer. "But you won't want me feet when you can get me pan."

A ripple of approving amusement ran over the crowd. "Ain't she a one!"

"Been up before the beak more times than you could count."

"She's got a good heart, that's what I say. More than you can say for some of the toffs."

Near by a woman began a spirited account of the flourishing brothel, one of Delie Stock's chain, which carried on business near her home, and in a fluster Mumma drew Dolour aside.

"Now, Mrs Stock," said the reporter, "you're a well-known citizen of Surry Hills."

"I'll say," chuckled Delie. "Had me dial more times in the paper than I can remember. Got a scrapbook that'd stiffen out an elephant."

"Well, we'd like a statement from you about the proposed resumption of Surry Hills by the—"

"Stinking mongrels!" said Delie strongly.

Somebody called out, "What about them electric stoves they're going to give us, but?"

"Can't put yer head in an electric oven when you've had enough of life!" called somebody else.

Delie put her hands on her hips. "That's what I mean," she said. "Nobody asked us if we want to be chucked out of our houses. We got along all right for years here. I spent a lot of money on my place, too. Only last week I got the kitchen kalsomined a lovely blue, real pretty and only a bit streaky round the sink. Now the bloody Council comes and wants to put up flats with private fishponds or something we don't want. Where'm I going to go, that's what I want to know. Where are they going to put us while they put up these bloody beehives?"

"The Potts Point people are going to take us in," jibed someone.

"Yes, we're all going up to the Point," said Delie, who wouldn't have lived there amongst the gardens and the blue-bayed streets and the dignified houses if you'd paid her. For what was there in Potts Point that you couldn't find in Surry Hills, except enough quiet to give a woman the splitting headaches?

"This is where we belong," said Delie definitely. Thus, while the rest of Sydney was reading the papers and thinking how nice it would be for the poor Surry Hills people to live in decent places at last, the poor Surry Hills people were fuming, and pitching all that was within and without the City Council to the seventeen devils.

That night as Roie sat brushing her hair before the spotted mirror that reflected the room as a dim cavern, Charlie leaned out the window. Now and then fountains of red sparks shot up out of Lick Jimmy's backyard, where he was letting off crackers in some solitary celebration, and from somewhere came the bad breath of a garbage can with no lid.

"What are you doing, Charlie?"

"Just thinking."

She went and leaned her head on his arm, listening to the pulse of the blood in his arteries. She didn't know how to begin. All at once a gush of love in her heart made her skin tingle and tears fill her eyes.

"Oh, Charlie!"

"What, darling?"

"I dunno. It's just . . . I'm going to have another baby." She hid her face against his shirt and laughed, not being able to express in words her joy and excitement. "You're not sorry?"

"No. I'm glad. I've been praying for it for months."

"Me, too. All the mission."

They laughed together.

"Do you reckon prayer did it?"

"I helped a bit," said Charlie. He held her close. "It's funny to think of—all that, all over again."

"Yes." She sat down on the bed, longing with a vast longing for the months when she would feel the child tremble within her, and the knowledge that life was there.

"Mumma will be glad. I bet she's been putting in her spoke with the saints."

"Embarrassing the tripe outa them."

They rolled about the bed in their mirth, until Charlie stopped his wife's laughter with his kisses. Next door Dolour heard the laughter, and the silence, and blocked her mind quickly to the thoughts that flowed into it. She put her head under the bedclothes, thinking, "I hate them! I hate them!" savagely and falsely, for all she hated was her own ignorance and jealousy. Then she hopped out of bed and said a prayer for her sister to make up for her thoughts, of which she was bitterly ashamed.

Mumma was complacent about the baby, and only a piercing glare from Roie prevented her from saying that she'd known all about it. Hughie was embarrassed. He could never get used to the fact that now his daughter knew almost as much about men as he did.

"I thought we'd call it Brandan, if it's a boy," said Roie shyly. Mumma nodded.

"It's a good Irish name, and the church and everything."

None of them thought it was at all strange to call a child after a church, nor to thank God that their parish was not that of the Holy Sepulchre.

"You can't go putting the name of demon drink on a child," bellowed Hughie. "They'll call him Brandy for short."

Roie blushed crossly, for she hadn't thought of that, and Hughie burst into song, "Mr Booze, Mr Booze, you've got me where you want me, Mr Booze!"

They slammed the door on him, but they could still hear him proclaiming, "Think of all the huzz-*puns* you have stolen, Mr Booze!"

"Never you mind, love," comforted Mumma. "It'll be real nice to see the pram out in the yard once more."

"Charlie," confessed Roie, "he wants us to find a place

29

somewhere else to live." She saw the distress creeping pinkly up her mother's neck and cried, "If they're going to pull down Surry Hills we'll all be out on our necks, and, well, Charlie wants us to start looking now."

Mumma wanted to say a lot of things, that she'd lived most of her life in Plymouth Street, and Dolour had been born there, and Thady gone from her sight. A tumult of thoughts rushed through her mind, Mr Diamond coming down and scrapping with everyone on St Pat's day, and Grandma pigeon-toeing about and taking on the world right and left, and in the end dying in there on the old stretcher with a candle beside her. All these things came up in her mind and she wanted to say, "This is your place, and no man's got the right to take you away from it and from me, because no matter what he is to you he's never a part of you, like me." But instead she said dully, "It'll be nice for Motty to have somewhere clean to play, and the children that cheeky about here."

The joy of the new baby was all spoiled, and she went out to the kitchen and kicked Puffing Billy in the firebox and poked a block of wood down to his cherry-red tonsils. All at once sharp tears sprang into her eyes, so she leaned over Puffing Billy and coughed at his smoke, just in case Roie should come in.

Now Roie had to screw up her courage to go to the hospital and be examined. Mumma, who had never been to a doctor in her life, and had no idea what went on in hospitals, could not understand her reluctance. And she was ashamed to explain it to Charlie.

"They're only doctors," he said. "You're just another woman having a baby to them."

"Yes," stammered Roie. "But I'm not just another woman to me."

Like her ancestors who had preferred to die of consumption rather than have some stranger listen in to the protests of their bubbling chests, Roie shrank from having the dark, innermost secrets of her body probed, and written about on index cards. But at last she went to the great brick building, into the out-patients' department, where the merry, black-stockinged nurses flitted to and fro, and the air was full of the tingling tang of antiseptic. Almost at once the feeling of being lost and completely at sea descended upon her. There were so many strangers to meet, so many cards to sign here or there, so many details simple in themselves to attend to that she recovered the feeling she had had at school, of being dumb and stupid, slow to catch the meaning of things, desperate lest she should miss some important word.

"It's not like that really," she assured herself as she took off her clothes and put on the long calico wrapper like a zombie's. From the cubicle next to hers came a loud crash of glass, and a voice was raised in a lament, "My Gawd, I've dropped me speciment!"

She sat and waited for a long time on the hard wooden forms, amongst the rows and rows of shapeless women. Some had drawn yellow faces, and others had blossomed with a ripe mellow beauty. Roie looked at their shining, ill-kempt hair, the mysterious glow in their skins. "I'm like that, too," she thought, and wondered. And a little shiver ran over her as she thought of all the others in that room, the mysterious hidden ones in whose hands the future was already held tight. Over and over it happened, a million, million times, and yet its wonder remained.

At last she was in the examination ward. As she clambered upon the high white table, sickness and terror nearly overcame her.

"Oh, God, I wish I didn't have to do this."

For who could express the delicacy that filled her mind about this? The shyness and modesty that desired to keep her body for those who possessed it, her husband and children?

"He's only a doctor," she kept saying to herself. "I'm nothing to him. I'm only a card with me name and weight and age on it."

Now he was here, the kind dark-eyed man with the gentle hands and crackling white coat. Roie tried to smile at him. It wasn't his fault she felt like this. It would be all over, very soon. She closed her eyes, bracing herself as she felt the cold air on her body.

Then she heard another voice, and another. To her appalled horror she saw five or six young men, hardly older than Dolour, dressed up in white coats, and crowding in behind the screen round the bed. They were medical students. She half-raised herself up, but the doctor gently put her down again.

"They—what are they doing here?" she whispered.

"They're going to be doctors some day," said the doctor. "They have to learn."

"Yes," whispered Roie. She kept her eyes closed tight, hearing what the doctor said to the students with a shame too great to bear. She felt no resentment or anger, nothing but terrible humiliation, of uncleanness and violation of her innermost womanhood. Her soul crept into a dark corner.

31

"I'll never feel the same again. Whenever Charlie touches me I'll think of this."

The cubicle was empty. She got down from the table, putting on her shoes and picking up her clothes with frozen hands. Her teeth were chattering.

Then a hearty indignant voice spoke from the next cubicle. " 'Ere!"

She heard the end of the doctor's reply, ". . . this is the only way they can learn."

"Oh, it is, is it! Well, they ain't gonna learn on me! Why, I've got a son as old as that feller there, and if I thought he was going around in a fancy white coat staring at naked women and calling it learning he'd get what for! Look at the face on 'im! Eyes sticking out like boiled onions! Yes, you oughta go red. The nerve! Give me me boots and lemme out of here!"

Roie clung fast to the table. She heard the doctor explaining that it was public hospital experience that taught these young students most.

"It's for the good of all women, you know."

"Yeah? Then why not use all women for guinea-pigs, eh? Why only public hospitals? Do you ever go into a posh private hospital out Vaucluse or Point Piper with your tribe of pop-eyed young louts and let them have a squint at one of them pampered poodles of women? Nice stinkeroo if you did, eh? But us, we gotta come to public hospitals because we're poor, and so we can be pushed around without so much as a kiss-me-foot. We can't kick. Get outa me bloody way before I let you have it in the eye!"

Roie escaped. There was nowhere to go to hide her shock and shame except in the church, and there she hid her eyes even from God.

"They took Your clothes off and hung You up where everybody could see You, but it's worse for a girl. Let me forget it, soon. Please let me forget it."

She went out from that dusty shadowy place into Coronation Street, where the light beat glassily down and the heat shimmered from the asphalt. She looked furtively at the women, laden with shopping baskets, with screaming children, always carrying or pushing or dragging something. These citadels of strength, of endurance, of deep undemonstrative dignity were deemed by authority to have no dignity at all. No one would dream of subjecting a rich man's wife to clinical rape, but the poor man's wife was different.

5

Mumma could never think what to have for tea. In Australia
the meals of the ordinary people are not varied. Though occasionally a woman turns out to be a God-inspired cook, usually
the housewife serves meals as though they were on a travelling
belt. No sooner has the chop disappeared over the horizon than
the stew looms up, and always both are accompanied by peas or
beans or cabbage, and potatoes, just as the boiled custard keeps
company with the packet jelly.

Every afternoon Mumma sat down with a stub of pencil and
worked out what she could buy on the little money daily
allotted to her. Even before she started, her forehead wrinkled
into a preparatory frown, and a dim, hopeless feeling assailed
her.

"What'll we have?"

Roie leaned her chin on the handle of the mop. She considered. "I dunno. Maybe we could get some of them minces
from the butcher's."

Mumma scoffed. "It'd be all right if you knew what he puts
into them. Catsmeat most likely. And I'll bet he rolls them
in ground glass."

Roie mopped round the chairs adeptly. "I know. Let's have
sausages."

The tension in Mumma's housewifely heart disappeared.
Good old snags. They were always there to be fallen back on.
She wrote down the things she wanted, and yelled up the
stairs for Dolour to go out and get them.

Dolour drifted out into the butter-yellow sunshine. It was
so hot that the tiny imperceptible gush of sweat to the skin
was like a cool shock. Dolour held her hair like a horse's tail
and lifted it to the top of her head, to let the air blow about
her neck. Motty was swinging on the gate.

"Hullo, fishface," she chirped.

"Hullo, pieface," returned Dolour unsmilingly. She blew the
child's nose, pulled up her grubby grey pants, pushed a strand

of hair out of her eye, and returned her to the gate. She drifted onwards till she came to the sausage shop. In the midst of a hundred shops with grease-ringed doorways, floors scrubbed down to the splinters, and high, pallid ceilings, the sausage shop stood out like a glittering box of glass. Its window bulged in a water-clear bow, boasting the rosy coils of tomato sausages, the puffy white pork, the suet-blotched Yorkshire, the giant grey horseshoes of the liverwurst, all shuddering away from the unsocial garlic. Dolour stood there for a long time, breathing in the wonderful smells and making a large misty patch on the glass. Then she passed in and bought two pounds of beef sausages, and a solitary frankfurt, which she chewed on the way home. She arrived at the gate with a pink ring from the skin surrounding her mouth. Mumma was there, her face pale.

"Where's Motty?" she called. "Ain't she with you?"

"She was on the gate when I left," replied Dolour, a qualm entering her soul.

"You musta left it open!" accused Mumma. "She's got out, and there's all that traffic. Roie's gone haring off up the street looking for her. You better go that way, Dolour."

She snatched the sausages from Dolour's grasp. Already the roar of the five o'clock traffic was funnelling deep and hollow into Plymouth Street. Dolour and Mumma stared at each other wordlessly, the same dread in each remembering heart. Then Dolour darted up the road.

"I didn't leave the gate open. I didn't!" Already into her mind rushed the words of excuse. Her swift imagination already had the child run over, enticed away by a stranger, found dead in a culvert, and before she had gone twenty steps she was in her mind confronting Roie and Charlie with fluent denials of her complicity. "It musta come open by itself."

The children of that district, accustomed from earliest days to play in the street, were independent and self-sufficient. But Motty was not allowed to play on the street. The wilderness peopled by the wheels and fenders of trucks was something she did not know. But she was a friendly child, whom some prowling pervert would find easier than usual to entice off the gate. Dolour began to breathe fast. She questioned children playing in the road, women leaning over gates. She went farther and knocked on doors, thinking that the child had slipped through a broken fence to look at a lovebird in a cage, or play with a puppy. But Motty was nowhere at all.

34

The shadows crept longwise over the pavement, and mothers began to call their children in to tea. She wanted to run back to the house to see if Motty had been found, but she felt a mournful certainty that she had not. Almost desperately she ran across the road, dodging the cars that followed nose to tail, honking impatience.

In the meantime Charlie had come home, grimy and tired. He met Roie, running along on her swollen feet, flaring-eyed panic on her face. She stared at him a moment, almost unrecognizing, then a croak came out of her throat.

"Motty's gone, Charlie. She wandered off somewhere, a whole hour ago." A little whimper came out of her, and her face collapsed like a child's.

"You oughtn't to be running about," he said roughly.

"Oh, my baby, my baby!" she sobbed. Charlie took out his handkerchief and wiped her face. He felt solid and strong and he smelt familiar.

"If anything's happened to her I'll die!"

"Nothing's happened to that rapscallion," he soothed. He walked her home, slowing her uncertain, hurrying steps, trying to be calm and unperturbed, though he was far from feeling it.

"Why, when we get inside, she'll probably be right there at the table, with Mumma feeding her bits of cake, and her spitting it out like a machine gun."

Roie tried to laugh. They went into the kitchen, where Mumma was poking the sizzling sausages with her long fork, and wiping her red eyes with the back of the other hand. She looked up eagerly as Charlie and Dolour came in, then turned away and said, "God wouldn't let anything happen to her, darling. Not after Thady. You lie down and let Charlie take care of it."

Meanwhile Motty had gone a long way. As soon as Dolour had disappeared she had ventured out into the street, a very small Christopher Columbus with a dirty pinny and one leg of her pants already falling down. For a moment she had ideas of following Dolour, then a lizard flashed up the fence and halted at eye-level, its heart beating perceptibly in its brown silk breast.

"Wizard," said Motty, grabbing at it. It was gone in a wink. She indulged in the unique pastime of looking through the wrong side of her fence. She saw the rank overgrown grass, the door gaping wide, and the little yellow square of window at the end of the hall. She went right round the fence this way, looking through each crack.

So she came to Lick Jimmy's shop. She stood on tiptoe and ate some of the peeling green paint that ran round the window. She wandered into the shop, eyeing the cliff-high counter, and sniffing deep breaths of the rich fruity air. Lick Jimmy was out the back, doing something domestic, so she picked up a fallen pea-pod and began to eat it. Lick Jimmy's cat sat up, bounded lightly to the floor and walked outside. Motty followed it down the alley. The cobblestones were hot to her small feet. In the niches beside tumbledown back gates grew tall thistles, which she tried to pick.

"Blast," remarked Motty, sucking her finger.

From a low point of view, the alley was peculiarly enchanted. The high tin fences were mottled with patches of rich rust, and here and there an unbeatable larrikin creeper had sprouted up between the cobbles and plucked with all its frail fingers at the tin. Here snails lived, too. Motty picked off four systematically, and hammered them on the stones until they gave off a green, indignant froth.

"Pooey," commented Motty. She wiped her hands on the back of her bloomers and went on. After a while she met a drunk, a faltering benevolent fellow who had crept into the alley on an urgent mission. Motty stood behind him and watched gravely as the puddle crept across the stones. He gave a long sigh, and suddenly burst into song.

"You're a dirty man," said Motty with quiet firmness. The drunk jumped and whirled round in a wavering arc, during which his feet remained on the same spot of ground. The dismayed look changed to a flush of relief. He doddered forward, carefully pulled up the knees of his indescribable trousers, and hunkered before Motty. The little girl looked unblinkingly into his rheumy eyes.

"You sweet little bastard, where did you come from?" He stretched out a hand and stroked her jetty hair. "Ah, I wish I had a li'l girl like you. Wish I had, honest. You know what, ducks?"

"You talk funny," said Motty.

He disregarded the interruption. "You know what? If my wife would have kids 'stead of going to work when there ain't no need, I wouldn't waste me time getting drunk. I'd be takin my beaut little kid to the soo to see the tigers and the hipposamus. Honest truth. Here, li'l beaut."

He stood up and endeavoured to wangle his hand into a pocket that had grown extraordinarily tight. He propped himself against the fence and fought to get his hand over the curve of his hip. Motty watched with great interest. Now and then he nodded gravely to her as though to assure her that all was going well. Finally he brought out a banknote. He put it close to his eyes to see what it was, nodded, and beckoned Motty closer.

"You smell, too," she said.

He looked muzzily at her dress, winked, and tied the note into the corner of his aged handkerchief. He wadded it into a ball and tucked it down the front of her dress, where it was securely held by the semi-circular curve of her stomach.

"There's one thing I got to tell you." he cautioned, wagging an erratic finger. "You muzzn't ever talk to strange men. Plenty of polecats about. And don't you never take money from them neither. Uncle Doug knows. Uncle Doug knows his onionses."

He waggled his hand from the wrist. "Goo'bye now." Motty waved hers casually and went on. She looked back, and saw him feather-stitching away in the opposite direction.

The alley was a long one, and all sorts of queer little runnels of back lanes and pathways debouched there between the broken fences. Now, as the horizon darkened, though the sky was still bright, a figure detached itself from a fence and moved after Motty, keeping close to the long shadows, and placing its polished toes carefully on the stones. A narrow-ridged nose jutted out under the turned-down hat-brim, and a narrow, reddish chin jutted out over the butterfly bow of a pale blue tie. These were the only signs of elegance about the figure; its tight blue suit was stained and frayed about the cuffs, and its fingernails were long and blackish. It kept its eyes on Motty with an extraordinary expression of eagerness and excitement, which made its pale eyes water and its mouth move as though rehearsing enticing words. It dug in its pocket and fetched out a shilling, and then, as Motty reached the end of the alley, it darted forward and hovered a yard or two away, looking at the child's fat legs and arms.

Motty looked out into the street. A moving forest of legs hurried past, pillars in trousers, hairy bare legs with traces of yellowish leg make-up, and fleet brown ones that Motty observed with most interest. She heard the staccato clang of tram bells, and the plaintive Indian love-calls of car horns. She wondered whether she should join the throng, then she became aware that an eye was watching her through a seam in the fence.

"Pieface," said Motty tentatively.

"Garn," retorted the Eye hospitably. It was replaced by a stubby black toe that protruded through the hole while its owner clambered to the top of the fence. A voice sounded from on high.

"Gah, what are you hanging around for, Burgess? Clear out before I tell Ma."

Motty looked round in surprise, and saw a dark figure melt into the shadows, creeping along the fence away from them. Then she looked up and saw a coal-black face looking down at her. She noticed the blackness, but did not think it interesting enough for comment.

"That dirty old cow, always making up to kids. Only been out of boob a few weeks," explained the face carelessly. A hand appeared, holding an ice-cream, which was systematically licked into a tall triangle.

"I'm free," announced Motty.

"I'm a nig," said the face. " 'Ave a lick?"

Motty beamed like the sun. The little boy shinnied down from the fence, and popped through the gate. He was about seven, tall and thin, with his long skinny arms sticking out of a spotless but ragged white shirt.

"You can finish it," he said magnanimously. "I've had three today." He turned and stared at the slinking figure, which was still hovering there, only a few yards away from them.

"Just look at that dirty ole secko, will you?" he said disgustedly, and scooping up a stone he ran after it, yelling, "Merv, Merv, the rotten old perv", throwing stones at its feet until it skipped into invisibility at the alley end. Motty had finished the ice-cream and was now licking her hands as far as the wrists, for they felt hopefully sticky. She and the little boy sat in companionable silence, just looking at each other.

"Lexie! What you doing out there?" cried a voice from the upper regions inhabited by adults, and Motty looked up to see a dark, beautiful face above her. A crow's-wing plait dangled downwards over a grubby pink frock pinned with a large mother-of-pearl map of Australia across an olive bosom.

Motty said, "You've got red shoes."

The girl picked Motty up. She smelt strongly of clove carnations.

"My, you've got pretty hair. Where do you come from, you little twirp? Who's this kid, Lex?"

"I dunno. Old Burgess was hanging around."

"I'm lost," said Motty amiably.

"Ah, like fun. Never mind, you come inside with me and I'll give you a cream cake."

She hoisted Motty across her hip and went inside. A thickset, sallow woman stood at the stove, stirring a pot, in which, every so often, the scarlet of pepper floated up like specks of red silk.

"Florrie's gonna give the little girl a cream cake," cried the black boy, dancing on the tips of his long slender toes. The woman looked dourly at Motty.

"Who's she?"

"I dunno. Where's the cakes?"

"Picking up kids! Yer mad," said the older woman, jabbing at the bottom of the saucepan.

"You can talk," said the other lazily. She jerked a thumb at the black boy and laughed. The boy laughed, too, and the older woman burst into a flood of passionate Italian, thumped him on the ear, and screamed furiously at her sister, who only giggled, took up a greasy paper bag from the dresser, and went out with the children to the tiny iron-framed balcony that faced the street. She spread herself comfortably on the wooden seat that had been built across the gas meter.

"Cake," demanded Motty, stretching out her pink, licked paw.

Passers-by stared curiously at the little group on the balcony, the slovenly, beautiful girl, the tear-stained black boy, and the white child peering through the railings and painting her face with cream. This was the scene that Hughie saw as he passed by on his way home from work. He stopped, astounded at the resemblance between the small child and his granddaughter.

Motty nodded amicably to him. "Hullo, nice old Pop."

The girl Florrie looked over the child with her soft, sultry eyes. Her smile was slow, revealing her glistening teeth, and the tip of her pink tongue. She was no more than seventeen.

"This your little girl?" she asked. "I found her in the alley."

"Christ!" gasped Hughie. "She musta run away. Her mother'll be off her head. You little devil, I ought to skelp yer hind-shoulders."

"Ah, no!" The girl put her arm around Motty, lifting her over

39

the railings, and the strong clove scent came to Hughie's nostrils. He became suddenly aware of his dirty working clothes, his grease-stained boots, and his unshaven chin. He stammered, and some strange nostalgic feeling came into his heart, so confusing and disturbing that he said brusquely, "I gotta thank you, miss."

"Oh, that ain't nothing," smiled Florrie. He looked away from her, unwilling to stare, and yet unable to control himself.

"Her name's Motty—Moira, that is."

"Mine's Florentina. But everyone calls me Florrie."

"Yeah? That's an Italian name, ain't it?" Hughie was even more confused. "I better be getting the little devil home."

"Yes." Hughie walked off, squeezing Motty hard.

"Oho." She was tired. In a moment her head drooped on his shoulder and she was fast asleep. Unnoticing, Hughie walked past the pub on the corner, the good winey smell following him up the road, but beyond a twitch of the nose he took no notice. It was late. The pure fields of the sky were darkening, and no longer did the gable windows of the old houses twinkle and burn in the sundowning light. Mumma was leaning over the gate, saying Hail Marys for the return of her darling. When she saw Hughie she gave a squawk, and blessed herself in four rattling good thumps.

"Roie!" she yelled. The attic window sprang open with such a bang it shivered in its sash, and Roie appeared like a ghost. The next moment she flew out of the door, snatched the sleeping child from her father's arms, and burst into tears.

"God bless us, it's all over," said Mumma, trying to take them both into her arms and glaring at Hughie. "And you sauntering up the road as though you had all the time in the world. You oughta be ashamed!"

"Keep yer hair on," began Hughie, but she interrupted, "No more feelings than the boots on yer feet! Where's that Dolour?" she fumed, turning towards the house. "A lot she'd care if Motty was run over. I dunno!"

Gladsomely she returned to the sausages, now dark, fossilized oblongs in the pan. The potatoes were dry, and the eyes, which Mumma in her agitation had forgotten to remove, stared out of the pot in black dismay. But Mumma was so happy she did not care. Breaking into the militant strains of "Hail, Queen of Heaven", she slapped the flour in the pan and made some gravy, to the accompaniment of the peevish gruntings of

40

Puffing Billy, who was making heavy weather of a mouthful of coke.

Dolour helped Roie to undress Motty for bed. The moment her sister's back was turned, Dolour put her arms round the child and kissed her with loving eagerness. She glanced up to see Roie looking at her.

"I did leave the gate open, Ro."

"I guess it's the kind of thing anyone could do," said Roie.

"If anything had happened to her," cried Dolour, "I would have killed myself."

"Me, too," agreed Roie. They looked at each other and giggled.

"Funerals all over the place," choked Dolour.

"Imagine how busy Mumma would be," snorted her sister. They laughed hysterically, and so Charlie found them as he came leaping up the stairs. He regarded the scene, the two girls laughing, and Motty playing peacefully with the soap, and all the anxiety and terror of the past two hours came to the top in an explosion.

"Of course no one thought to come and tell me she was found!" he shouted, wiping the sweat from his face and leaving it striped with a broad black streak. "I musta travelled six miles. And here are you two laughing your silly heads off."

Motty waved her soapy paw like a sceptre at her father and said, "Dogface!"

He pounced on her and turned her bottom upwards. "This is the last time you're going to run away, young lady."

"Ah, Charlie!"

He turned up her singlet. "By gosh, what's this?"

They stared as he pulled out a large and grubby handkerchief. In the corner was a rough lump.

"She musta found it. What on earth is it?"

Charlie untied the knot, and there was a screwed up five-pound note.

"Jeepers!" Dolour's eyes nearly popped out.

Roie, improving the moment, took the child from her husband's unresisting grasp and put on her pyjamas. "Here, would you take her downstairs and give her a bit of a lick, Dol?"

Charlie and Roie sat staring at the miraculous five-pound note.

"Just think of the days I've got to work for that, and this zack-sized brat goes out and picks it out of the air."

"What are we going to do with it?"

They began to remind each other of all the small necessities they and the family needed. They laughed together, and in their joy and relief at the finding of Motty loved each other all the more.

Downstairs Hughie was in the laundry, in an atmosphere of yellow soap and wet firewood and tomcats. He pottered from tap to candle-lit mirror, half-heartedly rubbing a wash-cloth round his neck. He lifted the candle and looked searchingly into the mirror. He saw there a good ruddy face, with bright and blue eyes of the clearness of glass. His hair was still thick, and hardly grey at all, standing straight up from his forehead in the Irish style. He lifted a lip like a snarling dog and studied his teeth. They weren't the best, having cost him eight pound the set back in the days when dentists measured the spaces between the teeth with ruler and T-square.

A deep restlessness had taken possession of him, a terrible distaste for his life, his work, the pettiness of his existence that added up to nothing at all. He hadn't even been to a war, having been in an essential occupation in one, and too old for the other. There was something he wanted to do, but he didn't know what it was. Get out and change his name and become someone else, perhaps.

"Guide of the wand-her-rer hee-yar below!" roared Mumma in her happiness. "Hughie! Hughie love," she bellowed through the closed door.

"Good-oh," he answered surlily. He went into the kitchen. It smelt of stale food and smoke and a dirty floor, yet, even though its own peculiar smell was so strong, he could catch the whiff of burning rags and rotten fruit from Lick Jimmy's backyard. He stared at Mumma, slopping round in her slippers, each with its heel trodden down to a pancake. Her shoulders, weary with the years, were bottle-shaped, and her hips so square her dress was hitched up on the corners.

"Save us from per-her-il and from woe!" implored Mumma.

"Oh, shut up," growled Hughie. "Watcher got?"

"Sausages."

Hughie groaned. "Not snags. Not again. By God, I won't eat them, so there."

All the trouble in his soul rose like a bubble and burst. Anger made him shake. He jerked open the oven door with such force that Puffing Billy spat a surprised little jet of soot from his flue. There, sluggishly reclining in their greasy dish, were the sad and sorry sausages, far past their prime.

42

"Look at 'em!" he roared. "Dirty little frizzled-up bastards! I won't eat them, I tell yer."

"I can't help them being dried up, dearie," explained Mumma reasonably. "Tea's about two hours late."

But Hughie raged up and down the room, explaining to the walls how much he hated sausages, and how many times he'd eaten them in a month, and why he was sworn off sausages for life. Finally he jammed on his hat and surged out of the house.

"I'll go and pick up some tucker at the Greek's!" he shouted.

"And good riddance," quavered Mumma, who was very upset, but too spirited to show it. She bent over the stove, and the tears in her eyes made the rejected sausages look twice as big.

Out in the cool evening Hughie paused. He looked forlornly this way and that, for he had nowhere to go now that Patrick Diamond was dead and the pubs were shut, and in spite of his proud boast about the Greek's he had no more than a shilling in his pockets. He was tired, and hungry, but more disturbing than these was the new feeling that had him in its grip. What was it? He wanted to fight someone, or to get drunk, or talk to an old friend—or to go into a quiet place and weep a little for his childhood, and the old days that were gone for ever. For the first time in years he thought of his mother and father, and his brothers, the way they used to be, sitting round the big table, and saying grace, and the boys kicking each other in the shins like full-backs.

He wandered along the street. Now that the dusk was coming into the air a lighted kitchen window popped into view here and there, and he heard the chatter of family talk, banging on a piano, a radio bellowing out a song. A pleasant, melancholy loneliness settled over him.

So this was what happened to a man. He found a lost child, and brought it home, and they abused him, and gave him his most hated food for tea, and after a long day's work, too.

"For it's not as though there's any nourishment in snags," muttered Hughie. "Any more than there is in sawdust."

Coronation Street was long and bare, and beyond it the street lights of Redfern were a scanty nebula. Hughie crossed the road and pottered along under the verandas, where already silent figures were bulked in doorways, shopkeepers enjoying a smoke in the cool.

When he was opposite the house where he had found Motty,

he stopped and stood in the shadows. He did not know why he was waiting, but he waited, and after a while one of the upper rooms was lighted, and a window flung up. He saw the figure of the girl outlined for a moment, leaning over the sill, as though she, too, were breathing gratefully the chilling air. Then she turned away. He saw a blue wall, a hanging globe that shed a harsh light, and the uplifted arms of Florentina as she brushed her hair.

For a moment a strange incomprehensible pain seized Hughie, something so revolutionary, so without words that he was at a loss to describe it, or know how to face it.

He pulled down his hat and fled away up Coronation Street, cursing as he went.

6

Now that Charlie and Roie had decided to leave Surry Hills, a most extraordinary civil war of the spirit went on within the Darcy household, so that the saints in far Paradise were put to the pins of their heavenly collars to decide who wanted which. There was Mumma, getting in first with the early morning mass, and asking God to keep her daughter where she was, and she with a child coming, and needing her Mumma, not some old rajah of a landlady that wouldn't lift a finger to wash a napkin, and the girl perhaps weak with the confinement.

"Your Mother will tell you how it is," Mumma chided God reproachfully, when no still small voice spoke up in her soul. And she kept her eye sternly on the Tabernacle, until peace came to her, and she felt that faith and the housing shortage would get her her own way.

And Dolour prayed ardently, "Oh, please let Ro get a nice little flat somewhere in a quiet street, and let me go and visit her, and I'll take the baby out and look after Motty at night so that Charlie and Ro can go to the pitchers. Dinkum I will."

Hughie said nothing, either way, but he often looked wistfully at his daughter, her small pure face, and the thickening body, and wondered why it was that kids grew up and wanted to leave their homes, and why it was that parents didn't want them to go, and so on, round and round in circles, until he had to go and scrabble amongst the defunct shoes in the bottom of the cupboard to see if, by mischance, he had left a bottle there with an inch or two still to be drunk.

For now Charlie and Roie became aware of the great, silent, seething battle which was going on under the roofs of Sydney. The city lay in the sun, careless and indolent under its banners of smoke, its glitter of windows, its tiger stripes of black shadow and sunshine-drowned streets, and it gave no indication of the savage fight for survival that continued amongst tens of thousands of its inhabitants. They were like birds, squeezed out of a too-crowded nest and scrambling to get back into haven. They were rabbits fighting at a hole in a rabbit-proof fence, biting and suffocating and killing in their mad desire for self-safety. They were people looking for roofs in a city where every roof already sheltered too many.

Now there was another tyrant in the land, the house-owner who ground the last possible penny out of his tenants under threat of eviction. The little old ladies who put pound notes in the plate at church, and who owned rows of tenement houses, lightless, damp, and smelly; the fat profiteers who came from other countries and bought up every available property and re-let at fraudulent rents; the hard-headed business people who let houses to the tenants who could slip them a little something for the key—something sometimes amounting to the life's savings of some desperate man who had to get a sick child, a tubercular wife, or an old and dying father under cover— these were the lions in the street, preying on the needy, threatening the weak, cracking the whip with Nazi arrogance.

Day after day Charlie got up and bought the morning paper, still damp from the machines. There, in the clear light of six o'clock, with the milk-carts waggling past and some lone hawker crying, "Close prarps! Close prarps!" through the quietness, he would read the three or four "to let" advertisements, and the scores of "wanteds". And sometimes he put in advertisements himself, ringing up the office for days to see if any answers had been left for him, and finding none.

"The only way to get a place is to knock on every door and ask if they've got a spare room," said Roie. She eased her shoes off her swollen feet, for she had run out at seven o'clock that morning to a place down by the park, advertised as having a balcony room to let.

When she got there, she found a queue of a hundred or more, most of whom had been there since the paper had slapped off the press that morning. She dawdled shyly along them, looking for some familiar face. And the faces were familiar. They all bore the same look of desperation, almost panic, and a dogged determination to outbid the other fellow.

The house was an ancient, clay-faced one, its paint covered with a velvety black bloom of dust, and wet-stains like stalactites coming down from each gable window. It was easy to pick out the balcony flat—just a veranda boarded up roughly with asbestos, which had a square cut in it for a window. There was probably a kerosene stove in the corner, and a tin dish on a bench for a sink. Nothing more uncomfortable, squalid, or makeshift could be imagined, and yet the hundred people, and a hundred more whose telegrams the postman brought to the door in a huge stack at eight o'clock, were prepared to fight to the death for it.

Roie said timidly to the woman in front of her, "Have you heard how much it is?"

The woman gave her a brief look that took in the shabby coat, the cheap shoes, and the scarf over the head. "She'll take what she can get, like the rest of 'em. But I'm prepared to go to four pound a week."

"Four pounds!" gasped Roie.

The woman shrugged. "I'm paying that now, and all I've got is a stretcher bed on a curtained-off landing. I might as well be paying it for a place of my own, even if it's only a rat-hole."

When the woman wasn't looking, Roie went away home. She said to Mumma despairingly, "We won't ever get a place. I know we won't. They're only for people with lots of money."

"Never mind," said Mumma. She wiped a rag that smelt like an old dishcloth over Motty's face, and Motty's face bloomed like a rosebud out of the vanishing dirt. "You've always got a room here." Roie felt comforted, knowing that not even the woman who could pay four pounds a week had a room to herself as she and Charlie and Motty had.

Mumma yearned over the girl's tired face, wanting to say something to get Roie on her side against Charlie in this scheme which to Mumma had all the absurdity of a proposed trip to a foreign country.

"It's not as if they've started to pull the roof off over our heads," she said. "And anyway, it's only them old, tumbledown shanties they're going to get rid of. This is a good house, if it wasn't for the roof and no bath, and the floor a bit gone here and there."

Roie's lips trembled. She wanted to confess to her Mumma how she felt about things, but her loyalty to Charlie held her back. That afternoon they were going over to Pyrmont as soon as he got off work, and at the very thought nausea rose in her stomach and the backs of her legs ached. For already, and the child still four months away from its coming, she had been to so many places. Up and down strange streets, following clues given by workmates and strangers in trams and shops, bearing little slips of paper from reluctant estate agents, Charlie led her, and whenever they came to the right gate he would say,

"Cross your fingers and pull in your stomach", and Roie would slump down in her coat to conceal her pregnancy. For eagle-eyed landladies never failed to give her figure the once-over. They always suspected young couples who came after a flat, in case that young couple had the best possible reason for finding a home, and were for that reason to be avoided like the plague.

They had not been to Pyrmont before. It was on the other side of the city, and might as well have been in another town as far as Roie was concerned, for to her the city was a vast wilderness, looped by familiar tracks, and a little dangerous to investigate in its remoter corners. As they crammed into the bus, rich with the smell of petrol and fat ladies, the rain started, drops, drips, beads of quicksilver slung diagonally across the windows. Down they swooped to the old Pyrmont Bridge spanning the grey stream of Darling Harbour. Once it was prodded by windjammer masts, and now was blackened by rude gusts of smoke from steamer funnels, crowding into that industrialized waterway of Sydney until it was like a ships' highway, with no traffic officer. And now the bus rattled up the road that sweeps into Pyrmont village, lined with tall flat-faced houses, and queer little dumpy ones like old women resting beside the road awhile.

Roie, who had been feeling sick, woke up. The place looked familiar. The women went shopping in slippers, and the younger ones wore curling pins, and pushed prams piled with mountains of groceries. There went a hawker with a horse just cobbled together, the bottles in his tilted cart jinking musically. There were the same little shops, all crowded together, all stuffed to bursting point with foodstuffs and overspilling in piles of baskets and straw brooms. Red geraniums grew in tins on some of the balconies, and even as she watched an old Chinese came out on a veranda and fed a canary in a cage, just as Lick might have done. Roie felt almost happy. It was like home here, and close to the shops and everything. It was sort of exciting with the wharves so near, and the big ships blowing their horns just beyond the factories and silos. But before she could open her mouth Charlie said, "It's not much of a place to live, maybe, but it'll do for a start."

So Roie did not say anything. Silently she followed him along a crooked-elbow street where the houses, two feet behind their fences, preserved a down-at-heel, old-maidish dignity with rows of potted ferns, a yellowish passion-vine, and a dwarfish,

48

deformed acacia, whose tender almond-shaped leaves had burst up through the asphalt itself.

"This is it."

Roie, to hide her shyness and reluctance, looked intently at the fence, and the way the tops of its pickets had been cut into mitres, crowns and spade-shapes. She huddled forward into her coat.

"Pull your stomach in!" Charlie hissed.

"I'm pulling it in as far as it will go," wailed Roie resentfully. The door opened, and a small dark woman with a moustache and a strange poultry-yard odour appeared. She looked at them both with watery eyes, inquisitive and scrutinizing. While Charlie talked, Roie peered past the woman into the little stuffy hall, where the source of the odour was pecking along the wainscot, crooning to itself and occasionally erecting a bright greenish-yellow crest at the sight of the strangers.

"What a lovely parrot!" cried Roie falsely, for she detested parrots. They went inside, Roie pressing shyly behind her husband, for she felt uncomfortable in strange houses. Almost instantly a pink galah scuttered out of a dark doorway and pecked her ankle.

"Oh, don't be silly," the woman reprimanded, at her startled squeak. "It's only a dear little galah." Roie smiled feebly, keeping an eye upon the rosy creature that circled her feet, fluffing out its quills and clashing its cherry-picker beak with malicious expectation.

"I'm Miss Moon," said the woman. She brushed off a couple of olive budgerigars that came fluttering down from the curtains, and Charlie made a sudden embarrassed dive for his handkerchief.

"Oh, really!" said Miss Moon crossly. "The dear little things have to follow nature. And anyway, her coat will dry-clean, won't it?"

"It's nothing at all," said Roie hurriedly. "Have—have you really got a flat to let?"

The woman gave her a long look, cryptic to both the young people, then she said, "It's upstairs."

They followed Miss Moon up the dim stairs, Roie thinking, "Oh, I couldn't get used to all them birds . . . that smell every-where, like a chicken-house . . . and Motty would pull their feathers out, I know she would. And she's a queer sort of a lady. Mumma would never get on with her when she came to see us."

"It's never been let yet," said Miss Moon proudly. The top of the house had been converted roughly into a kind of a flat, furnished sketchily and yet with infinite fussiness with bamboo and rickety, useless bits of pre-Boer-War specimens of the cabinet-maker's art. From one window could be seen the parting curtains of rain, shifting like veils over the pewter glimmer of the sea. There was no kitchen.

"You'll have to share that with me, and carry the food upstairs, but of course it's no trouble," said Miss Moon. "The last people didn't mind at all. I had them put out for other reasons."

"But she said—" thought Charlie.

"Up all them stairs!" thought Roie.

From under the bed waddled another parrot, a brilliant scarlet and bottle-green creature with one blind opal eye. Miss Moon picked it up, cradling it so that the long tail-feathers spilled over her dress.

"Poor Lucky! She wants to nest somewhere, and she does like it under the bed."

Charlie sent Roie a glance which said mutely that Lucky would be lucky to be alive if she survived their tenancy.

"It's three guineas, and cheap at the price," said Miss Moon.

Roie gave a quickly suppressed gasp.

"It's cheap for these days," admitted her husband.

"You've only got to share the kitchen and the laundry, and there's a bath in the laundry," said Miss Moon proudly.

"Yes," faltered Roie. She dodged away from a gas bracket, where two budgies cuddled together, their little snub noses together.

"It'll be nice to have a man in the house to fix things," said Miss Moon. "The last man . . . it's time some of the garden was replanted, and the tap's gone wrong in the kitchen."

She suddenly gave Charlie a beaming smile, and with fascinated distaste Roie watched her Adam's apple disappear beneath her collar and bob up again. She conceived a terrible dislike for Miss Moon. She felt that at any moment the woman was going to edge up to Charlie and stroke his sleeve.

"I don't suppose we could . . . sort of . . . discuss it?" asked Charlie shyly. Miss Moon was indignant.

"Discuss it! I don't know what you're going to discuss, I'm sure. Why, I could get eight guineas for that flat any time! And I'm only asking twenty pounds for the key."

"Twenty!" breathed Roie.

"It's small enough," said Charlie hastily. "But—if we could just walk round the block—we wouldn't be five minutes, would we, Roie?"

The woman was reluctant. Her lips moved angrily. She plainly considered their hesitation a slap in the face. Roie reached out timorously and stroked the ruffled head of the ponderous parrot.

"Well," said Miss Moon, "only five minutes then. Other people will be coming, you know."

They escaped from the house almost at a running pace. The air of the street, stale as it was, struck them like a blow after the fetid atmosphere of the house. They hurried up a door or two, and Roie looked hopefully at Charlie.

"Fancy asking for twenty pounds!"

"Yes, but we got to make up our minds to pay extra wherever we go," pleaded Charlie. "And we've got that money put by."

"But it's for the baby," wailed Roie. "The hospital and everything."

"We could save it up again. Look, Ro," he said urgently, "isn't this better than Plymouth Street? Look how quiet it is. And we could put the baby's cot by the window up there and we'd get the breeze straight from the harbour. And evenings we could go for walks down by the wharves," he said eagerly.

"Three guineas is an awful lot for two little rooms, and sharing the kitchen with that woman," faltered Roie, almost weeping. It was the first time they had ever differed about anything. "And we ain't said anything about Motty yet!" she added.

"I don't know how she'll take that," admitted Charlie.

"Or the baby."

"Oh, we won't tell her about the baby."

"I don't like her," said Roie obstinately. Her lips trembled. All at once she felt weak and unable to think. "I suppose you know best, Charlie."

"I just want you to be happy, that's all."

They stood indecisively, looking at each other unhappily. Her hand went into his. "You want to take it, don't you?"

"I want to get away from Surry Hills, that's all," said her husband. He had never before voiced his hatred of the place that was so great that anything at all, provided it were in some other part of the city, looked better to him. Now they were at the gate.

51

"Pull your stomach in!"

"Oh, shut up!" said Roie angrily. The door opened as though Miss Moon had been waiting behind it, and the galah and the cockatoo appeared, rolling over and over with claws entangled.

"Well?" demanded Miss Moon over the screeching.

"We'd be glad to take it," said Roie.

An extraordinary change came over Miss Moon. Her dark eyes took on the appearance of melted toffee, and she looked with a strange, greedy look at Charlie.

"My, that's nice," she said. Roie thought, "In another moment she *will* stroke him.'

"So nice to have a young man in the house," said Miss Moon. They sat down gingerly in the little lounge.

"The last tenant," said Miss Moon, mechanically stroking the galah's round, downy head, "he wouldn't keep me company." She stared into space with a concentrated look. "Of course the flat has never been let before."

"Will you want your rent in advance?" asked Charlie, nervously flashing a look of appeal and puzzlement at his wife.

Suddenly Miss Moon tipped the galah off her lap, and said briskly, "Of course, I must insist that you take the utmost care not to have children while you're here. Children make me ill."

She looked piercingly at Roie, with dislike and suspicion, as though Roie were obviously the kind of girl who would have children whether her husband wanted them or not.

"Loathsome, disgusting creatures," shuddered Miss Moon. Her fingers plucked tensely at her skirt. "Filthy little savages. I detest children."

She looked as though she were appalled at the very thought of them. Roie felt a surge of anger and indignation at the idea of this queer little woman calling her beautiful Motty loathsome and disgusting, but she didn't know what to say, looking furtively at Charlie and leaving the job to him.

"We've got a little girl of three," said Charlie.

Instantly Miss Moon flew into a rage, her voice growing as needle-shrill as a bird's, so that the smell of the room, the feathers lying round on the carpet, and the croonings and croakings from corners behind the furniture—all seemed to emanate from her.

"Get out! Get out of here! If you think I'm going to have a disgusting, smelly little beast of a child in my house—"

"Motty doesn't smell," flamed Roie, half-rising from her chair,

52

so that her coat fell open. Miss Moon stared at her, looking as though she were going to have a fit.

"You're pregnant!"

"Yes," said Charlie, "we were going to tell—"

Miss Moon's face was purple. She dragged at her collar, beating on her breast and going "huh-huh-huh", the expression on her face as terrified, as appalled as that of one who had seen a serpent.

"Bringing your spawn in here . . . breeding all over the place . . . just like all your sort . . . those last people . . . I used to hear the talk that went on . . . oh, how I hate you filthy women!"

Roie felt sick. She wanted to get out of the place before she fainted. She said, weakly, "Charlie, it isn't any use."

She wanted to speak loudly in defence of the nobility of pregnancy, of the fact that she was proud and exultant to be carrying a child, and to have already borne one. She wanted to be scathing and rude to Miss Moon, as Grandma could have been rude, even on her deathbed, but she felt too sick to be bothered.

"It's a pity you haven't had a child of your own, and then you'd know what a silly old tart you are," she said to Miss Moon.

"She's probably had one, and buried it under the rhubarb," said Charlie, trying to be calm and self-contained and only succeeding in being pure Surry Hills. Miss Moon began to breathe in stertorous grunts, like an asthmatic dog, and her face turned darker and darker.

"She's sick," said Roie, as she was hustled out the door.

"She's mad!" said Charlie. "A whole lot madder than you think."

He banged the door thunderously, and every bird in the house broke into a tin-whistle shrieking.

"I'd rather have Surry Hills than her," began Roie in a small voice.

"Old cow! Did you see the way she looked at me?"

"No," said Roie innocently. He was annoyed at her obtuseness.

"I don't know what she expected along with the rent," he said, half proud, half embarrassed. Roie was silent, a giggle bubbling up from her soul, and dispersing in a moment all her weariness and nausea and relief at escaping from that horrible house. She went into the warm, slovenly, familiar atmosphere

53

of her own place with deep pleasure. If Twelve-and-a-half Plymouth Street smelt, at least she knew where the smells came from. If it was rowdy, the row came from those she loved.

"We ought to get the place first, and tell them afterwards that we've got kids," said Charlie.

"That wouldn't be fair," said Mumma virtuously.

"It's as fair as they are," growled Hughie, "letting their rooms only to people who'd murder their kids rather than let 'em be born. Pretty funny, with Australia yowling out for migrants, and not making provision for new Australians."

"Italians, Gyppos, anything but Aussies, that's what they want," agreed Charlie.

"I suppose the Government knows best," said Mumma helplessly, for she had a great awe of authority. Then she burst out, "But you'd think anyone would be glad to take a little newborn baby in."

"They weren't glad back in Joseph and Mary's time," said Roie with unaccustomed bitterness.

From then on all the landlords and landladies took on, in Dolour's mind, a sort of callous, Oriental look, and most of them appeared to her vision clad in striped burnouses, with plugs of coral in their noses. She hated them vigorously, until she discovered that, deep in her heart, Roie didn't mind very much.

"What do you go along for, Ro?" she asked her weary sister. "Let Charlie do all the looking."

"He might take something I didn't like," said Roie evasively, and Dolour looked at her in astonishment, for she knew that in all their months of looking the only chance they had had of taking a flat was during their visit to Pyrmont. She and Roie were not used to looking into each other's eyes. They accepted each other's face as something that was inevitably on top of a body as familiar as the furniture. Now Roie turned away before the penetrating gaze of her sister.

"You don't want to get a place," marvelled Dolour.

"Oh, smart, ain't you!" mocked Roie, angry at the discovery of her secret.

"You want people to see you're having a baby, so they'll turn you down."

"Well, what about it?" asked Roie defiantly. She quavered suddenly, "I don't want to go away, it's just that Charlie's keen, that's all."

Dolour ruffled up her hair. "I dunno. I would have thought anyone would like to get out of this dump. Anyway, what's up with you? You don't have to go just because Charlie wants to."

"Oh, well." Roie was angry at the look on Dolour's face. "I'm married to him. You wouldn't understand. You're just a kid."

She had thought the look on Dolour's face was contempt, but it was envy, and at Roie's words she turned away to hide it.

7

ONE day Mumma told Dolour to clean out the scullery shelves, and grumbling she obeyed. Outside it was a clean, windswept day, with russet leaves whirling up, up in loose-spun willy-willies to the chimney-tops, but within the kitchen was a dismal grey light, spiked with the ruby square of Puffing Billy's toothless mouth

Dolour slowly passed a wet cloth over the soot-blackened tops of the baking-powder and jam tins. She worked as though she were at the bottom of the sea, with two hundred tons of water pressing on her, lifting her arms with the heaviness of an old woman, and moving her feet as though they wore leaden boots. Her hatred of the task drained her very blood away. By the time she came to the golden-syrup tin, with an imprisoned cockroach feebly waggling his legs in the puddle on the lid, she felt that she could fall over with sheer ennui.

"Gah!" said Dolour, lifting the cockroach with the tip of a knife and flicking him out the window. She leaned desolately on the sill, looking at the bare quadrangle of the yard, and a pair of Hughie's terrible underpants hanging forlornly under the yellow vanes of the phoenix palm. The wind, flowing over the rusty roofs like an invisible river, swooped down into the yard, brushed a wing into the alcove of the window, and swooped off again. Dolour sniffed. The wind was laden with the smells of a near-by factory, burnt sugar, and vanilla, and something foreign.

"Cinnamon!" breathed Dolour. She had never seen cinnamon. To her the word connoted a pile of transparent yellow crystals like topaz. It breathed of palaces with onion domes, and brown canals where little shoe-shaped boats floated. She lifted her wrists and shook them, and heard the jingle of bracelets. She sighed, for she had been imprisoned in the harem three years, and every day was whipped for her refusal to submit to the Sultan. Suddenly she spun round. A stranger was there, a fine handsome stranger with no shirt on, like Alan Ladd, and a striped tea-towel on his head. At his waist was strapped a gold-handled scimitar.

"How did you get here? It is death for you if you are discovered!"

"For you, my princess, death would be a small thing." He came closer, she felt his warm breath on her cheek, his lips came down on hers. . . .

"What the diggings is the matter with you?" cried Mumma, standing in the doorway and glaring. Dolour looked stupidly at her.

"Prancing around like a skitterbug. Sometimes I think you're a bit soft in the head," went on Mumma unpleasantly. She came closer. "And you've been picking your face again, too!"

It was the end. Dolour flung down her dishcloth, gave a sharp high wail like a knock-off whistle, and bolted from the kitchen. Mumma heard the retreating drum of her feet on the stairs and sighed. "I dunno. The kid's got a bug. Too much school, that's what it is. She oughta get a job." She looked at Puffing Billy threateningly as he belched. "Don't you start, now, or I'll beat your black brains out with the poker."

Upstairs Dolour beat her fists resoundingly on the iron rail of her bed. For a long time she had felt she couldn't put up with Mumma any longer, or her inspired talent for bursting in on the most luscious dreams. But underneath her impatience with her poor, down-to-earth, bunion-toed Mumma, Dolour knew that the real cause of her sorrow was that she couldn't put up with her face any longer. She propped the speckled old mirror up against the rail, and lay on her stomach staring into it, counting spots. She found fifty-two. It was hard to believe that one face, and not a fat, expansive one, either, should have room for fifty-two spots.

Suddenly she gave a squawk of despair, dragged her hair up, and close to the hair-line, found another one.

"Fifty-three!" said Dolour in a hollow, contralto croak. Fifty-three spots! What was the use of dreaming, and wishing, and planning when she had . . . . Dolour sobbed broken-heartedly. It was no good. Romance, accompanied by the skirl of flutes and the twang of harps, would never come into the life of a girl afflicted with fifty-three spots at one time. The terrible realization of it came again to her, as it had come a thousand times before, and been forgotten in the swift changes of mood that assailed her.

"No one will ever fall in love with me," groaned Dolour.

Her face hurt, too. It burned, and the skin, stretched tightly over the eruptions, felt as though she had been out in a high wind. But this was nothing to the pain she felt when people stared at her. She translated their casual gaze into contempt and pity, not knowing, in the intensity of her self-consciousness, that most often they saw nothing but a lanky, half-grown girl with a sullen expression

"They think I'm dirty," she said, and in passion and fury cried to the ceiling, "I will get my skin clear! I will! I won't let them laugh at me and make fun of me any longer." And then, because none of her family ever made fun of her, she crumpled again into tears, the hopeless, helpless tears that were her only defence against this humiliation.

She heard Motty's little footsteps on the stairs, climbing laboriously from one to the other, and Roie making little chirping sounds of encouragement. Dolour ran to the door and stood behind it, but Roie, who had heard the creaking of the bed, fooled her. She put Motty into her own room and closed the door, then popped her head round the edge of Dolour's. Dolour stood there, looking silly, and unable to find a word to say for herself.

"What's the matter, Dol?" asked Roie. It was no good. She began to cry again, till her face was red and swollen and plainer than ever. Roie sat quietly, stroking her lank black hair.

"Why don't you go to a doctor about it then?" asked Roie.

"I can't," choked Dolour. "He might find out something awful was the matter with me and send me to a hospital, and I can't miss school." She scowled at her sister to hide her embarrassment. "I wish you didn't look like that."

Roie did not become angry. "I don't mind. You sort of feel different about things when they're really happening to you. It seems pretty silly to think about the way you look when there's a new life coming into the world, and no one but you can have it." So she faltered for words while in the next room Motty hammered on the door with her stubby shoes and roared.

Roie felt in her shabby purse. "Look, I've got ten shillings here. I've been putting it aside for one thing and another, but you can have it. You go down to the doctor, and he'll give you an ointment or something . . . you just see."

"I don't want any money," said Dolour sulkily and ungraciously, but Roie just smiled and put it down on the bed and went out.

Immediately Dolour decided she would go to see Sam Gooey.

Sam Gooey had a shop in Coronation Street. In its window were two jars, each containing a tapeworm of unprecedented length and adhesive power, four bottles with swollen bellies full of emerald liquid, and very many tiny pottery trays containing powdered herbs. Every time you passed Sam Gooey's doorway a gush of hot pungent air whiffed out. It bore the fumes of concoctions that Sam Gooey was cooking over the charcoal stove in his cellar, or perhaps the savoury smell of a stew, the chief ingredient of which was, according to neighbourhood gossip, the humble puppy.

There was no doubt that, even among Chinese herbalists, Sam Gooey was a bright and shining star. Had he not cured Mrs Campion of an indigestion that made her rumble day and night like a traffic bridge? And Mr Siciliano's old brother Bep, whose rheumatics were so bad he creaked when he bent— Sam Gooey and a bottle of black medicine with leaves floating in it had made a new and younger man out of Mr Siciliano's old brother Bep.

She was so upset that her normal diffidence about visiting a strange Chinese and letting him look at her face had entirely gone. She hurried up through the gathering shadows in Coronation Street. It was not six o'clock yet, but the sun had long gone over the rim of the winter world. The dust-laden wind whipped back her coat and blew into her eyes. Her teeth gritted, and all her nervous system quivered with irritation and distaste.

To make it worse, she met Charlie, coming home from work. He looked taller and thinner and darker in the twilight, and his familiarity to her was as hateful as the rest of the world which surrounded her.

"Hullo, where are you off to?"

She looked at him sulkily. The uneasy dislike he aroused in her had never quite been dissipated since the day Roie married. He looked at her with his clear hazel eyes, and she felt he saw all the discontent and hopelessness that lay within her; he was ill-educated, and she had had more years at school than he, yet she felt small and young and unripe when he spoke.

"Just for a message."

"Where?"

"Oh—" She gestured irritably up Coronation Street, implying that it was no business of his, anyway.

"I'll wait for you."

"Oh, for gosh sake!" she burst out. "Nobody's going to hit me on the head with a bottle. Go on home. Tea'll be ready."

"O.K."

His smile as he gave her a dismissing wave of the hand maddened her all the more. He never got angry, never treated her as though she were worthy of provoking anger.

"I'm only a kid to him," she thought forlornly, and knew that in this was her resentment of Charlie. Outside Sam Gooey's window, lit with a bilious green globe, she stood for a moment. Was it worth it? Ten bob wasted perhaps, and God alone knew what he'd put in the medicine.

"Slugs and snails and puppy-dog tails," murmured Dolour, diving inside before anyone saw her.

But Charlie had seen her. He heard the protesting murmur within the corner pub as time was called. The bar bellowed out a roar of voices as the doors flew wide, and drinkers stepped reluctantly, and drunks doddered protestingly forth.

They stood about, arguing, pushing each other affectionately, and slowly peeling themselves away from the bee-cluster and dawdling away home. Charlie decided to wait for Dolour. He saw her go into Sam Gooey's, and wondered with amusement what Mumma could want there.

He waited a little, and Hughie appeared from the pub door, obviously the last, loneliest, loveliest of the drinkers who had refused to be hurried. He stood there a moment sticking out his stomach and wiping his mouth with the air of one who owned the place. Charlie gave him a whistle. Hughie was pleased to see him.

"Whatjer doing?"

Hughie said he'd wait, too, so they waited, walking slowly up towards Sam Gooey's shop and dawdling under the cold, windswept veranda, turning up their coat collars and poking their chilled fingers down into the dust-crumbs of pocket seams. Neither of them thought of looking inside the shop.

It was cold and dusty inside the shop, and an odd smell, even stranger than that ascribed to the puppy stew, curled up out of the many cracks in the floor. A hundred jars, each inscribed in red and black sabre characters, stood on the shelves, and on the counter a purple-veined wart-like thing as big as a fist swam in a bottle of spirit. This proclaimed itself as "Cancerous growth removed from liver". Dolour shied and was about to leave hurriedly when she saw an eye looking at her from a rent in a canvas screen pasted with pages from a Chinese calendar. Sam Gooey himself instantly appeared, smiling welcome. He was short and fat, with good health shining from his persimmon-glossy face and pouting red lips, which seemed to have been made of wax and applied after the rest of his face was made. He looked much too clean for the rest of the shop. He wore a collar and tie, a pink shirt with a white starched collar, and neatly tailored dove-grey trousers that clung companionably to his lunar stomach.

"Yes, yes," he chirruped in his clear, lark-like Chinese voice. "What you want, miss?"

In his hand he had a piece of buttered bread. He put this on the shelf and turned to Dolour, ready for business. But shame had overcome her, and she could not frame the words.

"My word," he said helpfully, "that's a bad case of acne you've got there, miss."

Dolour blushed with pleasure, for she knew she had acne, even though the rest of the world called her trouble plain pimples.

"That's what . . . I was wondering if . . ." she said.

"I have a look. Eh?"

He trotted round the counter and had a good look at her face. Dolour had to bend down like a hoop, he was so small. With the bright dark eyes so close to her, she was compelled to close her own, and inwardly she writhed with embarrassment at the picture she would present to anybody peeping in the door.

"Many, many things cause this acne," said Sam Gooey. "Sometimes one herb cure it, sometimes another herb. You come upstairs to my surgery and we have good look under proper light."

Without thought Dolour followed him, almost treading on his heels.

"Do you think you can make up something to clear it up, Mr Gooey?" she asked eagerly.

Behind the screen they came out into what was apparently Sam Gooey's living-room. A light with a red paper shade hung in the middle of the ceiling, and through the slits in the paper showers of light fell in slivers and drop-dapples on stiff black hair that grew straight upwards, like tea-tree, or swept back like polished leather from low brows. There were, in fact, five Chinese, young and old, all busily eating, not with chopsticks, but with spoons and forks and fingers and other prosaic European implements.

On one side lay an old man with his shirt open, so that his withered mound of stomach showed. He seemed to have the toothache, for he held a poultice of some sort to his face and moaned. His little eyes, sunken in a myriad diamond-shaped wrinkles, stared resentfully at Dolour.

"Come along, come along," chirped Sam Gooey. The Chinese looked up, unsurprised. They were eating something dark and glutinous, with green, spinach-shaped leaves floating in it. They sang something, and Sam Gooey jovially sang something back. The old man peevishly got up, did up his shirt and shuffled into the shop, still holding the poultice.

Dolour was embarrassed, but not alarmed. The intimacy of family and neighbourly affairs in Surry Hills had conditioned her mind to many things that would alarm a girl from another suburb. Admittedly she had never seen Lick Jimmy's stomach, but she had often conducted a conversation over the fence with him while he was cutting his toenails. So she followed Sam Gooey up the rickety angular staircase into the semi-darkness above.

Before she knew where she was Sam Gooey pushed open a door, and there was a quite clean, airy room, with the window open, and the air flowing in chill and crisp from the dark street. There was a barber's chair in the middle, under a strong spotlight, and all around hundreds of jars, and little saucers with seeds and leaves and chipped wood drying aromatically.

"My surgery. You sit down," invited Sam Gooey kindly.

He went to the door and called down into the darkness. The sound of feet on the stairs immediately answered him. All at once an extraordinary feeling of expectancy and fright started in Dolour's feet and travelled clammily up her legs. She felt acutely sixteen, in a strange house, with a great many Chinese downstairs, and no one of her own to call to. It was the sort of place where Fu Manchu might have lived.

Then a young Chinese girl poked her head round the door. She had a smooth moon face, the features but the merest ripple on that placid circle. Her hair was done in great puffs like a black meringue.

"This is my daughter, miss," said Sam Gooey. The girl smiled shyly at Dolour, who gawked back. She sank into the chair. Her hat was removed with a touch as light as a feather. Sam Gooey turned the blinding white light upon her, and she closed her eyes in self-defence. He studied her skin with an eyeglass.

"I know it's awfully bad," said Dolour, in shame and guilt, as though it were the signature of some shocking crime.

"No, no," he tweeted soothingly. "Don' you worry. We fix."

He sang a long psalm at the girl, who shrilled back an antiphon. So it went on, barking nasal syllables, and words obviously based on the note of a loose guitar string, flickering above Dolour's head, while Sam Gooey's gentle pretty hands rubbed and patted and painted. The girl stood by with a smile, and when Dolour winced from the stinging antiseptic she gave a little whistling note of encouragement.

Meanwhile downstairs Charlie and Hughie waited. The street was emptying fast, and Hughie was hungry. A reproachful rumble like distant thunder sounded under Hughie's breastbone, and he smote himself petulantly.

"My God, I woulda thought the beer would keep the works quiet for a while. You sure that kid went in there?"

"Sure."

He lounged over to the door. The tapeworms were there, and the cancer in the bottle, as well as an incredibly old, crumbling Chinaman, but there was no sign of Dolour. Charlie was astounded. The old Chinese lifted a lip, tenderly felt a solitary tooth as brown as tea, and winced.

"She went in here all right. And she didn't have a chance to come out without me seeing her."

They stared at each other, anxiety creeping on to their faces.

"What would she want to go to Sam Gooey's for?"

Hughie lifted a shoulder. "You know she never says anything to anybody about what she wants to do. Something comes up her back, and she just does it."

They entered the shop with such concerted determination that they jostled in the doorway. Hughie was puzzled and distressed, and his crest of hair bristled like a poll parrot's. If Dolour had gone into Sam Gooey's and was nowhere to be seen, then she had plainly gone into the dwelling behind, and Hughie was prepared to pull the place down to get her out.

"Hey!" He thumped the counter, and the old Chinese opened his eyes and shot filmy blue sparks at him. The vibration had jarred his tooth unbearably, and he scrabbled for the cooling pudding of the poultice and clumped it against his jaw.

"You! You see a young girl come in here about ten minutes ago? Young girl with dark hair, eh?"

"She had a blue coat on," supplied Charlie, who had one ear cocked to the laughter behind the screen.

The old man shook his head. Quite plainly he could not understand a word of English. He buried his trembling sallow chin deeper in the poultice, and plucked at the long coarse grey hairs that grew out of his cheek. He was so old his temple bones were round white bosses pressing the tight skin.

"What's the matter? Got toothache?" asked Hughie, interested in spite of himself. "Toothee go bang-bang, allee same horse kick you on head?"

The old man emitted a quavering whinny.

"Where's Sam Gooey?" demanded Charlie. "He's the one we want to see?"

He banged on the counter, and Sam Gooey's piece of bread fell on the floor. The old man picked it up, blew the dust off, and put it back.

"Come on out of there, Sam Gooey," bawled Hughie, "or by the living Hogan I'll pull the little yeller daylights outa you and wrap 'em round yer neck."

He ramped up and down the shop, talking at the top of his voice, frightening the old Chinese into such a fit of terror that he scuttled away into the back wailing like a tomcat. There was a great commotion behind the screen. First a flat Chinese face popped around, stared open-mouthed, and disappeared; then an older, withered one protruded, much higher up, as though the owner were standing on a chair. A lot of shrill cheeping went on, and the screen shook as though in a southerly buster.

"Where's Sam Gooey?" asked Charlie. "We want to speak to Sam Gooey."

"Yeah, and tell him if he's done anything to my girl, I'll roll him out and cut him into fancy patterns," bawled Hughie, now in the full swing of his beer-flavoured rage.

The screen shook violently, and the cheeping retreated. Feet thudded on stairs, and the fat flat face popped into sight again, and said timidly, "One moment, please."

"I'm going inside," said Hughie violently.

"There she is." They heard the quick rattle of heeled shoes down the steps, and in another moment she was in the shop, looking astonished and aghast and pleased.

"What's the matter? How did you get here? Gee, you've no idea, Dadda. Mr Gooey says he can make my complexion better!"

64

They were dumb as she showed them a pot of waxy black ointment.

"I got that much of a surprise when they said you were here. He said it's just my age. Doesn't it smell good? Come on, they'll be wanting to close the shop. Mr Gooey's that nice when you get to know him—" She hustled them out of the door, and before they had gone two steps it closed stealthily. She was oblivious to their stares, sniffing at the ointment, and feeling her face tenderly, for it was sore from the preliminary treatment.

Suddenly Hughie said, "You got no business going inside."

Dolour giggled. "I didn't know he was going to take me inside. And, Dadda, it was full of Chinamen, and one old type had his shirt undone right down to here."

Charlie and Hughie looked with alarm at her indicating finger.

Hughie cried, "I got a few things to say to you, young lady!"

And he said them all the way home, loudly. Dolour dragged her arm away from him, her eyes blazing.

"You shut up, you old nag. Nothing happened to me, did it?"

"It might have," said Charlie reasonably.

She swung on him. "You shut up, too. Following me round. Mind your own business!"

"End up in the gutter, that's what you'll do," prophesied Hugh. "Walking into a den of Chinks as though you owned the place. Wonder you didn't get raped, and serve you right if you were."

Dolour resolutely squashed any fears that she had had on the same subject. "He had his daughter there," she flared. "I didn't think . . . I just wanted to get my skin clear, that's all. I suppose you think it's funny, me having pimples."

She pelted ahead of them, and Hughie scratched his head. "Do you remember if you were peculiar like that when you were her age, Charlie?"

Charlie laughed. But Hughie was worried. He shut himself in the laundry to think about it, and was only enticed out by Mumma's kicking the door and asking irately whether he'd like his tea passed in through the keyhole.

That night Dolour applied the black ointment, as she had been itching to do all evening. Sam Gooey had said that she was to leave it on for an hour, but Dolour knew that if a little is good more is splendid, so she slathered it on to her hair-line, and left it on overnight.

In the morning Mumma called her several times, and Roie rapped on the door and reminded her of the time.

"All right, keep your hair on," a muffled voice replied.

The men went off to work, and still Dolour had not appeared. Then a figure, with bowed head, flashed through the kitchen into the laundry. Mumma heard a block of wood crash against it as a makeshift lock. She listened at the door, and heard a voice lifted in what was apparently anguished prayer. The tap ran interminably, and then there was dead silence. Mumma rattled the door, and a snort from a grievously wounded soul answered her. Mumma nearly went mad with the suspense.

"Oh, Dolour, whatever you've done, I'm on your side," she cried, and the door was flung open and Dolour bounded out, whimpering.

Mumma's eyes popped like blue marbles. Her hand flew up to her mouth and stayed there. Dolour's hair was tied up on top of her head, and her face was thickly covered with a hideous black mask which had set into a kind of cement. Out of this stared, in wild surmise, Dolour's desperate eyes. On the end of her nose the cement had cracked, so that the tip, bright pink, peeped through.

"Glory-lory," stuttered Mumma. "Holy Mother, what have you done to yourself?"

"It was Sam Gooey," moaned Dolour. "I bought some stuff to put on my face, and now it won't come off." She stood in front of the looking-glass on the mantel and thumped herself on the cheeks in an effort to crack it. Around her mouth it had set into circular furrows, where she had smiled or spoken before it had gone quite hard.

"I'll go mad!" she cried, seizing herself by the ears and working them violently up and down. A small chip fell off, and she picked it up tragically.

"Oh, Mumma! Mumma!"

Motty wandered in from the yard, looked casually at her aunt, got her red truck from under the table and wandered out again. She saw nothing different about Dolour, for to Motty, adults were composed of shoes, legs, skirts and trousers. Only other children had faces. Meanwhile Mumma had come out of her trance and begun to laugh.

"That's right," cried Dolour, "laugh. Oh, I wish I was dead!"

And she smote herself on the nose and was rewarded by another small chip. So Mumma, suffering in her heart for her poor child, and suffering even more from strangulated laughter, shut the door so that not even Roie should see, and with hot water and methylated spirits they laboured to get the mask off, Mumma clucking all the time about little heathens who ought to be thrown in the cooler for the things they did to innocent kids who knew no better.

"No," confessed Dolour, and she told Mumma that if the mask took all her skin off it would be her own fault. Then Mumma stopped laughing, and got very angry, and they flew at each other like cats and argued interminably, until Roie banged on the door and asked what was happening, and why she couldn't come in. So she had to be told, too.

"Serves you right," said Mumma grimly, as she put on her hat and went out to do the shopping, and tell Sister Theophilus that Dolour couldn't come to school that day. "And I got a good mind to tell her the truth, too," she threatened.

Dolour sat melancholy, staring at Roie. But Roie, who well remembered her own extreme and terrible sensitivity during her adolescence, did not laugh.

"The bits of skin that are showing through look clear already," she said helpfully, perjuring herself through love of her sister.

So Dolour lurked the whole day in her room, part of the time longing to be at school and stamping with impatience at the break in her studies, the rest of the time sitting at the window lost in a golden dream wherein Sam Gooey's ointment peeled off and left her with a skin like Motty's.

"I wish . . . I wish . . ." It was the whole theme of her living, and at the very words a warm flood ran over her body and released the burning, yearning for love. Her heart opened like a window to the world and cried, "Love me! Love me!" in so intense a voice that it seemed every passer-by must hear it.

By the next day the black cement had peeled away, taking most of her skin with it. Raw and bright pink gleamed her face, as though she had been badly sunburned.

"You can't go to school like that. You look like a peeled sausage," groaned Mumma. But Dolour heroically packed up her books and went. She saw indications that her skin was going to be a good deal clearer when it healed, and she was making an act of self-sacrifice as a slight return to God for His kind consideration.

Dolour believed in being business-like with Them Above.

CHAPTER

8

As the year wore on, Sister Theophilus called Dolour out into the corridor, and stood by the big rope of the Angelus bell. She seemed uneasy, and again and again her thumb rubbed lovingly over the worn brass figure on her crucifix. Dolour stared at her, her heart sinking, she knew not why.

"About Susan Kilroy," began Sister, and then she was silent. Dolour waited. The clear brown eyes looked at her without embarrassment, and yet the fastidiousness and delicacy of the woman hesitated before what she had to say.

"Dolour, you're Susan's friend. You must have heard . . . certain rumours about her . . . conduct with young men. Is there any truth in these stories?"

A dreadful cold tingle crept down Dolour's backbone. She looked imploringly at the nun. She blurted out, "People say nasty things. Just because a girl goes out with boys sometimes. People make me sick."

Sister Theophilus sighed. She might have known better, she thought, looking at the scarlet, sulky, stupid face of Dolour Darcy, determined to die rather than tell on her friend.

"Is it I?" she asked inwardly. "Have I made goodness too austere and chilly a thing to these children?"

It was not the first time one of her pupils had gone to the bad, but each time the blow on her heart had been almost physical. Anxiously, desperately, she had watched the developing body of Suse Kilroy, conscious that any moment now would come the temptation and the fall.

She sent Dolour back to her class-room, and on the day when Susan Kilroy was fifteen, and told her she was leaving school, she took the girl into her shabby study and talked to her a long time about the duty of the Catholic girl in a world corrupt with materialism. Suse listened silently, shifting from one foot to the other. She wanted to say something, to tell this silly old coot that what she knew about life could be written on a tray bit. Such scorn and fury rushed into her mind that

68

it was all she could do to prevent it from rushing out in an incoherent torrent. Silly old biddy, babbling about chastity and virginity, pleading with her not to go off the deep end! Suse looked at the straight and simple habit of Sister Theophilus and unconsciously arched her chest, proud of her own unconcealed and voluptuous body.

So Sister Theophilus said good-bye to her, knowing that she had lost the battle, and no one but God could reclaim Suse Kilroy. Dolour was waiting outside the gate. She said, "Gee, you were a long time. What did she say to you?"

"Nothin'."

They walked on in silence, then Suse exploded, "Old bag! What's she know about anything, anyway. Been in that convent since she was old enough to spit."

Dolour protested, shocked, "You don't want to talk like that about—"

"I will talk about her any way I like. Old cow. Thinks she can talk to me any way she likes just because I'm only fifteen and she's a hundred and eighty. Who're you gawking at, you bloody old hippo?"

This was to an interested woman who leaned arms like hams on a nearby fence. Dolour quaked with agony. The woman drew back as if Suse had shot her. "Nice thing for convent schoolgirls," she shrilled. "Oh, yerss, I can see the ties you got on. Think I won't report it to yer teacher!"

"Ah, stuff it," replied Suse concisely. "Go tell the bacon factory they need yer."

They walked on, Dolour writhing in shame and fear lest she should be involved.

"I'll never go near the damned school again, nor the church, neither," said Suse, and she ripped off her felt school hat and sent it sailing over the post-office fence. She combed out her hair with her fingers, and the short, silky black curls sprang up. Dolour gazed open-mouthed at her beauty, the delicate hollowed cheeks, and the satin shine on the mouth. A workman passing stared, too, and Suse gave him a wink.

"You little ber-yeaut!" said the man. Suse swaggered on with renewed confidence, with Dolour pattering at her side, asking anxiously, "You going to get a job, Suse?"

"If I gotta," answered Suse carelessly. Dolour burned to ask more, but she dared not, in case Suse told her. Already she was sliding into an insignificant position as a girl who was still at school, while Suse blended into a glamorous and unknown world.

"Suse," she implored, "wouldn't your mother go crook if anyone tells her that . . . you know . . . about the fellers?"

Suse's eyes flashed. "She'd better say something, that's all. I'll tell her a few things. She can talk. What about her?"

"I think your mother's nice," said Dolour shyly.

The other girl snorted. "She tried everything she knew to get rid of me before I was born. My auntie told me. But I beat her. I ain't got no time for her, and you wouldn't neither, if you was me."

Dolour looked at her with the shocked tragic gaze of one who has been wounded. She became aware of the sinister subtle battle that had gone on from the moment of Suse's conception, and wanted to run from the knowledge.

"What's she ever done for me but land me with one stinking baby after another to wash nappies for, and give bottles to, and put to sleep. Gawd, if I ever have to put another kid to sleep it'll be for good. She can go to hell. Just wait till I leave home. I wouldn't come back if she was dying."

"Oh, Suse!" Dolour trembled. "You don't mean it."

The other girl turned on her like a leopard. "What do you know what I've had to put up with? I remember when I was ten, and Dad was in the peter and she was having another nipper. She had it too soon, and I had to run up to the hospital and ask them to send an ambulance. They wouldn't come. Thought I didn't know what I was talking about, I suppose. So Mum had the baby right there, with her biting holes in the blankets and me screaming me head off. It was dead, all shrivelled up and blue. Know what she did? She made me put it in an old tin dish, blood and everything, and carry it up to the hospital."

Dolour wanted to be sick. "Whaffor?" she gasped.

"How do I know? She said it was their fault it had been born dead, so they could take care of it now. All she thought was getting her own back on the hospital She didn't care what I felt about it. How'd you like that when you was ten and didn't even know how babies were born?"

Dolour mumbled something. Her pinched pale face looked yellow in the ripe afternoon light, and with an exclamation of scorn, Suse turned and left her. Dolour went home in a trance-like state. No sooner had she reached the kitchen than she burst into hiccuping sobs, and only replied to her mother's exasperated questions by saying, "I hate everyone! I wish I was dead!"

"Oh, is that all?" said Mumma cheeringly. "Here you are, then," and she presented the kitchen knife to Dolour. "Not in here, though, alanna, because I've just scrubbed the floor."

Dolour gave a wail and fled upstairs, and Mumma looked after her and sighed.

Dolour did not see Suse for a fortnight, then, one evening as she was coming home from Benediction, she saw a familiar figure wavering along in front of her. Her heart jumped with pleasure.

"Hullo, Dol." Suse's voice was high and chirrupy. She tried four times to flick the glowing ash off a cigarette with her little finger, and the cigarette fell to the ground. She stood gazing at it with surprise and sorrow.

"Lookut, Dol, gone and got away on me."

"Jeepers, you're drunk," said Dolour, awed. Suse looked at her owlishly.

"I been drinking orange cocktail. Ain't no good, tastes like salts. Met such a lovely boy, Dol. Big blue eyes. This big." She tried to extend her hands, but they collapsed as though they had been made of wax. She tried again and sighed. "Gotta go home now, Dol. Right now."

Dolour caught her by the arm. "You can't go home, you dill, your dad'd knock spots off you."

Suse squeaked, and was suddenly sick. Dolour held her stationary, looking up and down the road in wild anxiety lest someone should come. She was consumed with desire to shelter Suse.

"Come home with me, won't yer? You can stay up in my room till you feel O.K. Mouthwash . . . I'll borrow Charlie's toothpaste to take the smell away . . . your dad'll belt you, you know he will," she babbled.

Suse jerked away. She began to walk with ridiculous caution down the dark alley. Dolour followed, pleading. "Gosh, you're mad. The cops could put you in a reformatory or something. Come on, Suse. I'll go down and tell your mum you want to stay the night with me. Come on, Suse."

"Shurrup!" yelled Suse, flapping her hand at her. There was a hot glazy look in her eyes, and at each step her ankles buckled. Half-weeping, not knowing whether to run and fetch Mumma or what, Dolour followed, feverishly making up explanations in her mind, in case they should meet someone they knew.

71

"Oh, God, don't let her father be home. She's only a kid. She don't know what she's doing. Oh, God, make him not be home!"

The Kilroy house was like a cardboard box in the dusk, a dark square slotted here and there with the light that peeped from the brown-paper-covered holes in the windows. Out of the open door flowed a peculiar smell of unwashed baby, of badly-rinsed napkins strung in a steaming row before the kitchen fire, of dirt and squalidity and congestion. Dolour had a confused impression of children, big-eyed and half-naked, scurrying from under her feet, to peep like elves from behind the door and under the chairs. Blinking in the light, she came into that tiny room and its all-pervading odour. Mrs Kilroy was there, standing in her run-over slippers, with a whining baby slung across her hip. She was a little, shapeless woman with all the width in her body across the hips and buttocks. She gaped uncomprehendingly at the two girls, showing her snaggled yellow teeth. The baby whimpered, and automatically she shifted it over her other hip.

"Suse doesn't feel well," said Dolour imploringly.

"Ah, fooey," chirped Suse. "I'm drunk."

"Your father ain't going to like that, Suse," said the woman in a voice as flat as a hammer on wood. Suse made a sweeping melodramatic gesture at Dolour.

"Watcher know! She's got the old record on again. Yer father ain't going to like that!"

She poured out a flood of filthy words about her father, and not even when she saw his huge, hairy-armed shadow standing in the doorway did she cease.

"Now, Harry—" It was the mother, a feeble squeak of protest. Dolour looked from one to the other of them, her heart thumping.

"I been waiting for you to come in," he said. "Tom Phelan told me he seen you going into the park with that dago from the shirt factory."

"Now, Harry," said the mother timidly.

"Shut yer mouth, you."

He unbuckled his heavy leather belt. He was a gigantic man, with a bald head too small for the rest of him, so that to Dolour, looking upwards with fright-blurred eyes, he seemed a malformed creature, pin-headed, with bushy brows and a face carved in deep vertical grooves. Suse's had gone white, but a piteous sort of defiance still remained on her face.

"Can't I go and sit on a park seat in the cool?"

72

"I was there, too," said Dolour, piping up suddenly in a voice like the sparrow's in the wilderness. He took no notice, but reached across the table and grabbed Suse by the hair. She had it pinned up in some elaborate grown-up way, and he tore the ribbon out of it, and it fell about her face. In a moment the illusion of the woman was gone, and she became a child, in whose face terror and a blind determination were fighting. He jerked her across the table, which tilted upwards. Dolour caught a glimpse of a dirty freckled leg underneath, which was swiftly withdrawn.

"You're a whore."

Suse said nothing. Her black eyes were fixed on his face with the dumb hatred of a conquered animal.

"You're a whore!" he shouted. With blazing eyes and face dark as a grape with passion, his immense height and hairiness, he seemed like a demon, and Dolour froze with a paralysis of terror.

"How many men 'a' had you?"

Suse's scarlet lips were pressed tightly together. He shook her violently. "Answer me, you bitch!"

She said nothing. Once again the mother squeaked, "Harry, you don't want to lose yer temper . . ."

Suse gave a sudden twist from his grasp, leaving his sweaty paw coated with fine dark hairs. Her escape seemed to madden him. With a bull-like roar he twisted the table out of the way, exposing two small boys, frog-eyed, huddled together like possums. They disappeared like magic into the shadows behind the dresser.

Now the man had hold of his daughter. He pushed her head down between his knees and thrashed her across the back and buttocks with the heavy strap, hitting with all his strength, a sort of demoniac lust on his face. At first she did not cry out, then she began to shriek each time the strap landed. Beside Dolour the mother whimpered as Suse screamed, as though it were her flesh that was cut. One of the smaller children began to wail loudly.

"You beast! You beast!" shrieked Dolour. She snatched up a tomato sauce bottle from the dresser and belaboured him about the shoulders, which were as far as she could reach. "You swine! I'll kill you!"

She sobbed in great hoarse gulps, her eyes blinded with passion and only the desire to murder in her heart. If she could have reached his head she would have smashed the bottle on his skull.

Mr Kilroy reached round a huge hairy arm and swept her across to the wall. "You pimply-faced little runt! Get out or you'll get the same!"

Whimpering, hysterical, Dolour retreated, holding the streaming bottle.

"You better go, love." The woman pushed her towards the door. Tearlessly and expressionlessly she looked at Dolour, with a face as waxy as the baby's.

Suse lay still on the floor. Only her gasping told she was still conscious. Her father thrust his hand down the front of her torn dress and pulled out a dirty handkerchief wadded into a ball. Inside were two pound notes. He put them into his pocket, and, sitting down at the table, pulled some betting slips out of his pocket and began to study them. The mother moved timidly towards Suse.

"Leave 'er alone or you'll get a belt on the ear, too," he growled.

The woman vanished out of Dolour's sight. For a long time she watched from the shelter of the darkness outside the door, until she saw Suse crawl to her feet, half-dazed, and limp towards the stairs. The man looked after her, then, with an expression which Dolour could not read, he shook out a newspaper and hid himself behind it.

Sick with shock, hatred and fright, Dolour ran and stumbled up the road, her face bleared with tears. She was crying loudly before she came into the kitchen of her own home. When she saw the scarlet stains on her dress, Mumma reared up with a shriek, "Jesus, Mary, and Joseph, what's happened to you?"

"It's only tomato sauce," hiccuped Dolour, and she hurtled into her mother's arms and blurted out the story. "Oh, Mumma, why is everyone so dreadful? If I was Mrs Kilroy I'd put bits of light-globes into his porridge. I'd wait till he was asleep and cut his throat with the razor. I would! I would!"

"Hush, darling," soothed Mumma.

"I'd be bad, too, if Dadda was like Mr Kilroy. I'd be bad just to show him. Oh, I wish I'd stood on a chair to hit him with the bottle, and he'd be dead now."

Mumma rocked her to and fro. She was much too big a girl to be tucked on to her mother's knees, and bits of leg kept falling over and trailing on the ground, but Mumma tried to enfold all of her just as she had done when Dolour was little.

74

"Come on, you get into bed now before Hughie comes home and starts asking awkward questions. And we'll say a decket for poor Suse and Mrs Kilroy and all the little children."

Soothed and pampered, Dolour lay back in the narrow creaking bed and fingered her rosary beads, while Mumma knelt beside.

"The Descent of the Holy Ghost," said Mumma. She had said half of the decade before she noticed that Dolour's responses were becoming mumbled and erratic.

"What's up with you? Where's yer respect for the Holy Rosary and Our Blessed Mother?" demanded Mumma sharply. Dolour looked at her with angry eyes.

"He said I was a pimply-faced runt, too, the big bonehead."

"Never mind your boneheads," said Mumma, and she squashed down her laughter and went solemnly on to finish the decade.

Suse Kilroy stayed home until her bruises were faded and the scratches where the belt buckle had torn her legs were healed, then she went out one day after a job in a powdered milk factory and never came home. Her mother whimpered a bit, but not too loudly, for she was afraid of her husband. The other children took up all Mrs Kilroy's time and she didn't have much time to think, but sometimes she dragged a port out from under the bed and took out a shrunken green woollen dress that Suse had worn when she was small, looked at it for a while, and then put it back.

9

IT was nearing examination time, and Dolour worked early in the morning and late at night by the light of a candle to save the light bill, soaking up knowledge so eagerly, so gratefully, that Sister Theophilus was touched. She alone knew what the girl's family only suspected, that of all her pupils Dolour Darcy was the only one who wanted to get a decent job in the great world outside Surry Hills.

But one morning Dolour awoke to find her eyelids stuck together. She opened them painfully with her fingers, and the slant of light from the attic window struck them like a blow.

"Musta got a cold in them," said Hughie, who was golloping down his breakfast. "Looking through keyholes. Better change your bedroom."

Dolour went a dark red for, though she had never looked through the keyhole at Roie and Charlie, she had often listened at the wall to hear what they spoke about in their private moments.

Mumma wiped her hands on her apron. "Let's have a look at you."

She peered into Dolour's eyes. Pink-rimmed, blinking painfully, they filled with thick syrupy tears almost instantly, but not before Mumma had seen the pearly spots on the eyeball, each surrounded by a suffusion of cloudy pink.

"You stick at them books too much. You better stay home, love."

"I can't!" cried Dolour. "Every day means something when you're getting near exams." She peered in the mirror but the stinging tears gushed out and she had to turn away.

So they got something from the chemist's. The chemist is a big man in Surry Hills. People are for ever going to him and describing other folk's symptoms, and going off with bottles of medicine and boxes of pills in which they have a complete and lovely faith. Mumma got a little vial of black eye-drops for Dolour, which she put in clumsily, so that great tattoo marks ran down either side of the child's nose. And all the time her eyes became worse, so that at last she just sat with her head in her hands, a burning band behind her forehead, and prickling acid in the eyes themselves. The water that ran down her cheeks was part discharge and part tears of anguish.

"Let's have a look, Dolour." She felt Charlie's hand on her cheek. Though he had worked hard all his life, his hands were warm, with a good smoothness. Gentle and capable, they lifted her chin.

"Maybe I'm going blind or something," choked Dolour. "Oh, Charlie, I'm missing such a lot of school!"

He turned her face into the half-light, and cautiously she raised her lids. He saw that the pearly spots were now much larger, like minute patches of sugar on the eyeball, surrounded by a map of tiny veins like distended scarlet threads.

"You poor kid," he said. "I bet they hurt."

Dolour tried to be her usual casual and aloof self with Charlie, but the ache in her heart and the scorch in her eyes was too much. She put her face into the middle of his shirt and sobbed.

"Let's go to the doctor, Dol. You can't play round with your eyes."

"All right," choked Dolour.

But while Charlie was getting ready, Hughie was hastily shaving, and suddenly appeared at the door and said gruffly, All right, boy. I'll take over", and took Dolour's arm and marched her out the gate. Mumma was very annoyed, but Charlie just laughed, and took Motty for a walk instead. Dolour was able to open her eyes a little behind the smoky shelter of dark sun-glasses, but Hughie took her arm as they went across Coronation Street. His hand felt strong and fatherly, and Dolour sank with grateful relief into the comfort of it.

They waited for a long time in the dingy waiting-room. Hughie creaked up and down, sucking his teeth furiously, and the old women who were the other occupants of the room knitted and chatted in loud voices of their intimate complaints. Dolour sat with her head down, her tight-gripped hands shaking with nervousness.

When it was her turn, Hughie went into the surgery with her. She sat down and took off her glasses, and in the stinging white light of the window the doctor looked at her eyes. A short, fat, hard-eyed man, he looked pitilessly into them, while they swam and involuntarily jammed tight.

77

"Open them wider," he commanded.

"I can't," gasped Dolour. "They just won't."

He seized her face and opened her eyes forcibly, and in face of the overwhelming pain Dolour tried to co-operate. There was a pencil in his other hand, and he lightly flicked at the mark on the eyeball with it. Dolour gave a squeal of agony, and the doctor spun backwards, with Hughie's infuriated hand on his shoulder.

"I got a good mind to send you through that window! What kind of a doctor do you call yourself?"

"Take your hands off me," commanded the man. "Any nonsense from you and I'll have you up for assault, quick and lively."

"I bet you would," agreed Hughie. "But you won't be a witness, boy. You'll be in hospital with a broken jaw and a shirtful of cracked ribs."

He let the doctor go so suddenly he staggered backwards. Hughie jerked a head at Dolour, "Come on, you." She crept after him, fumbling to put on the protective glasses.

"You'd better go down to the hospital with those eyes," called the doctor. "I wouldn't treat them, anyway."

A callous man, he had been momentarily touched by the shrinking misery on the child's face, but a moment later he had forgotten all about her.

Mumma thought that prayer might do some good, but it didn't, so a week later Dolour went to the hospital, she and Mumma together. The most terrible despair had settled into her soul. Day and night she was tormented by the pain in her head, for, like all head-pains, it was impossible to escape. But worse than that was the knowledge that all her desperate work during the year, her efforts to beat her natural dreaminess and inattention, her ambitions to succeed and get a good job— all were sliding away from her.

"You don't want to take it hard, darling," soothed Roie. "Why, them specialists down there might fix up your eyes in a day or two, and then you'll whizz through that exam like no one's business."

Dolour shook her head. She knew she would never catch up now.

At the hospital Mumma went through all the form-signing, her brows wrinkled in distress above her crooked glasses, and her clumsy fingers clutching the pen with a death-like grip. Then they waited, endlessly, in corridors and rooms, in surgeries and wards, in dusk, in blazing daylight, always with the smell of cleanliness round them like a new kind of air. Mumma was terrified of doctors and the very crackle of a starched coat was enough to reduce her to stupidity. When the nurse appeared and finally beckoned to Dolour, Mumma rose, too, but Dolour gave her cold hands a squeeze and said, "You stay here. I'm big enough to look after myself."

"It's going to be a long job," said the doctor. Somebody held her head in a grip of iron, and her eyes were swabbed out with fluid fire. Thrust into sudden blindness, with water pouring down her cheeks and pain knifing into her eye-sockets, Dolour staggered drunkenly at the side of a nurse back to Mumma. She heard a gasped "Glory be to God" from Mumma, the rustle of a prescription passing from one hand to another, and the nurse saying, "Has to be done three times a week . . . ten in the morning . . . no improvement . . . operate later . . . ulceration . . . no, certainly no school . . . no reading . . . no sewing . . . no pictures."

Something bubbled up in Dolour, and she was astounded to discover it was a laugh.

"Will I cut my throat here or outside?" she asked.

She entered into a strange world of semi-blindness, a world of passionate mutiny against her affliction, and long silences during which she found in herself the beginnings of self-discipline. Sometimes she stood by the window in Patrick Diamond's empty room, leaning on the splintered sill and looking out into Plymouth Street, which she could see but dimly through the black glasses she had to wear as a defence against the light. There was a flaw in one of the glasses, and it made everything look slightly crooked, so that the trees were lop-sided, and the houses as though set on a hillside.

She saw her schoolmates go down the street, day after day, and after a while she lost interest in them. A dull fatalism entered her heart. For a long while, all her life perhaps, she had wanted to get out of Surry Hills. But that was all gone. She belonged to Surry Hills; she was from it and of it, and God had made up his mind that she was going to stay there.

Roie said, "Maybe I could read to you, Dolour. Your schoolbooks, I mean—history, and things. Then when you go back to school—"

But Dolour shrugged. "I won't ever go back, Ro. What's the use of bothering about it?"

Though she obediently went back and forth to the hospital,

her eyes grew gradually worse, and at last she spent half the night in the kitchen, bathing her eyes with cold water, which was the only thing to relieve the pain. Sometimes Mumma got up and sat with her, huddled in her old coat, her weary feet thrust into Hughie's old cobbled socks.

They talked. In the unaccustomed silence, broken only by the far-off rattle of the tram, and the trickle of the water as Dolour pressed the cloth to her eyes, Mumma, who had nothing else to talk about, spoke of her childhood.

"Would you like to know how I met your father, then?"

Dolour nodded. Out of their swollen red rims her eyes looked, seemingly sly and cunning, their clear blue turned to nothing but black dilated pupils in the blood-red ball. She knew they looked monstrous and terrible, and she hated to let anyone see them, but Mumma never seemed to notice.

"Well, it was at the icemen's picnic. You've no more idea than a hen has teeth how many people were there. It was 'way back in 1918 just after the big war was ended, and I had on a black silk skirt. Moyry, we called it. And a striped fuji blouse with the stripes going round and round as if I was a barrel."

Dolour laughed eagerly, for she had the child's capacity of enjoying a story told a hundred times over.

"And what sort of a hat did you have, Mumma?"

Mumma spread her knees wide and put a red puffy hand on each. "Like a saucepan lid with a little crown in the middle. White straw it was, and it had three big yellow roses along here in front, and a whole bunch of green stalks, like parsley. And me hair down me back with a big black ribbon bow just here."

There was an agitated creaking from the bedroom, and Hughie stuck his head, ruffled like a mop, round the door. He blearily surveyed the two of them, sitting silent and guilty like children caught in a nocturnal orgy of bread and jam.

"Gawd, I could do a cuppa." His tongue came out and poked around his lips thirstily. "And a nice fried egg."

"Perhaps you'd like a few prawns, too," said Mumma sarcastically, as she lumbered over to Puffing Billy, gave him a ringing kick in the fire-box, and blew his slumbering coals to wakefulness. She was delighted at the thought of a little midnight supper.

Hughie sat down beside Dolour, his strong hairy chest showing where the buttons should have been on his old flannel.

He caught Dolour looking at it, and said heartily, "Don't worry, kiddo. It's warm in the winter. Ask yer ma."

"That's enough from you, you dirty old man," remonstrated Mumma. "Frighten the girl off marriage for life."

She cracked an egg smartly on the edge of the frying-pan, and the yellow globule slid out into the fat.

"Mumma's been telling me about the icemen's picnic," said Dolour shyly.

"Did she tell yer about Herbie?"

Mumma couldn't believe that Hughie would be so treacherous. Red-faced she turned, and the egg spat and danced unheeded. Dolour's eyes would have sparkled if they hadn't been so sore.

"Who was Herbie? Mum's boy-friend?"

"Herbie took her to the icemen's picnic," said Hughie with traitorous pleasure. "A great big yob with teeth that stuck out so far they looked like a white moustache."

"Hugh Darcy—" Helpless, Mumma waved the egg-turner at him. "And me cooking eggs for you, too, you devil. He was a real nice gentleman, Dolour, and played in the band, and don't you take any notice of your father."

"Real nice gentleman!" said Hughie, warming to it. "Sure he wore a collar so high it cut a groove in his chin, but does that make a gentleman?"

"At least he didn't career round like a madman after the greasy pig," flared Mumma. Unheeded behind her the egg reared up in the pan and flapped a charred wing. "With his pants rolled up showing six inches of red underpants, like you."

"What do you know about his underpants, eh?" bawled Hughie, twinkling a wink at Dolour. Mumma slid the egg on to a plate with such force that it skidded across to the rim. She slapped it down in front of Hughie and stood glaring at him.

"You or not, he was after me, Hughie, and if it hadn't been for him you might never have come up to scratch, God rest him. Died in the big 'flu he did, Dolour, and only twenty-five, poor Herbie."

Hughie dreamily looked into the haughty face of the egg. "Yeah, that's the place I lost me freedom, all right. What came over me, do you reckon, popping the question like a great big softy?"

"Ahhh!" snorted Mumma, grinning back at him, and buttering a slice of bread for his delectation and the egg's company.

Dolour sat still, the dripping cloth in her hand, forgetting to hide her eyes from them, anxious and delighted to hear how Dadda had proposed to Mumma. For proposals were the most wonderful and romantic thing in the world, and distant music and incense went with them, she knew, for that's the way they were on the pictures.

"Aw, go on," she beseeched.

"I can just see your old man sitting there," ruminated Hughie through a mouthful, "with his eyes popping out of his head with the heat and the beer."

"No wonder, after he nearly broke a blood-vessel in the hammer-throw," defended Mumma. Both of them sank into a reverie, fixing in their minds' eyes the long-gone figure of Old Man Kilker, with his double-breasted waistcoat, and his stiff collar with the turn-over points.

"Your mother didn't have any call to go slinging off at me moey, anyway," complained Hughie suddenly, and from thirty years ago steamed up a resentment that had never really gone off the boil. "She always did have a tongue in her head that would scare the hair off a coconut."

"Don't go poking borax at the dead," remonstrated Mumma, then she added softly, "It was that nice, too, all black and silky."

" 'Pardon me, you got something stuck on yer lip', that's what she said," simmered Hughie, and he was so annoyed he didn't even bother to chase the last of the egg round his plate with a crust. "Stuck on me lip! And me rubbing candle-grease into it every night for six weeks to get a decent bit of scrub going."

"Ma always spoke her mind," said Mumma admiringly, flopping down and staring into that long-ago day, where she saw her mother, neat as a flea, wearing her waist round her hips and her boots round her calves, sitting in the shadow of the great pudding and drinking beer out of a pannikin with her little finger cocked, maintaining at the same time a brisk rat-a-tat of repartee with Hughie and Herbie, who stood near by, crumbling the edges of their straw lids and showing the whites of their eyes at each other.

"The great big ugly moosh on him!" said Hughie, whose thoughts had been pursuing the same course.

"He beat you all the same," gloated Mumma, "and if it hadn't been for your weak stomach, he mighta got me after all."

Dolour, whose mind had been leaping from moustaches to

stomachs in pitiful bewilderment, implored, "But when did you ask Mumma to marry you?"

But she was unheeded. Her parents had left that room and were back on the show-ground in the little country town where they had grown up, back amidst the ripe smells of orange peel and sap from the wood-chops, and countless family parties chewing sandwiches, and old Quong, the Chinese storekeeper, wandering round with a tray of greyish chocolates and streaky pink ice-cream.

"I wouldn'ta done it if I hadn't thought I was dying," said Hughie.

"And I wouldn'ta accepted you if the doctor hadn't frightened the dear life outa me with the stomach pump, and him with the lip so long he was nearly tripping over it," retorted his wife. With sparkling eyes they glared at each other.

"What happened? What happened?" wailed Dolour. Her mouth opened. Surely her father hadn't taken something? She gazed at him with shock and reverence. He'd taken poison, and then the doctor had come and saved his life, and Mumma had married him, scared lest he did it again. Jeepers! She could see the scene, down by the river bank—no, under the willows— with the sunshine dappling down, and Mumma so pretty in her hat with the parsley, and Hughie pale and stiff, with the silky black moustache, and Grandma saying prayers for him. For the sake of that romantic moment she almost forgave Hughie everything, his Friday nights and all.

"I never heard such nonsense, hiding a diamond ring in the puddin'!" suddenly cried the hero of the story. "And leading everyone on to eat it until it came outa their ears."

"It was all in the luck," said Mumma dreamily.

"All in the size of the belly," scoffed Hughie, "and the endurance of a man, seeing the puddin' was the biggest sod God ever allowed to come out of a cloth."

"Fifteen dozen eggs," marvelled Mumma, "and a whole little keg of butter. And the women taking it in turns to do the stirring with a copper-stick."

"Don't tell anyone what you're talking about, will you?" snarled Dolour. Hughie and Mumma took no notice of her whatsoever, stirring their tea crossly and looking back in wonderment at the unbelievable boneheads on that Town Council, who had thought it a good idea to have at the annual picnic a pudding big enough to stuff everyone present to the eyebrows. They could still see it, like a monstrous wet mess of black mud, with currants and dates sticking out in dreadful anonymous knobs, being scraped into the pudding cloth, which was made of four sheets sewn together.

"Cooking it in the tank wasn't the best," said Hughie.

"That's what gave it the taste like old forks," agreed Mumma.

Hughie looked a little pale round the gills. "Just thinking of it gives me a stirring in the guts, after all these years," he confessed, and with averted eyes shoved his greasy plate away.

Mumma was reluctant to let the occasion pass without a preen. "I was the one to get you and Herbie on the move," she said complacently. "I'll never forget poor Herbie trying to eat with the front of his teeth, so he wouldn't taste it, and Ma fanning him with her hat, and cheering him on for Ireland and the Revolution.'

"Was he trying to get the ring, like the charm in a Christmas pudding?" cried Dolour, desperately grasping after what appeared to be the last vestige of sanity in the conversation. Hughie snarled.

"That's what we were after all right, poor mugs that we were. 'I could fall in love with the man who give me a diamond ring,' she said, sticking out her great paw and seeing the ring already there in her imagination. So me and Herbie went hell for leather for it, poor goats that we were. And him with a tight collar on, too."

"He always was soft on me," said Mumma smugly.

"Gah!"

"Eight helpings he had, anyway!" cried Mumma defiantly.

"So did I!" roared Hughie. Mumma sniffed.

"Oh, yes, but Herbie was ready for a ninth, and you down on the ground undoing the top of your trousers in front of everybody, and groaning for the priest," she sneered. "And when the Father came he said, 'It's not God's grace that boy's wanting, it's a good lift in the tail-end for making a hog of himself.'"

"Well, you couldn't expect him to know what a man would do for the love of a woman," growled Hughie, with reluctant loyalty to the priesthood.

Mumma blushed. "Ah, well. You looked that pale, after the stomach pump, my heart bled. And when you said, 'I'm a dying man, but you got to make me happy before I go', it was the finish of me," she said softly. And for a moment all the years between vanished, and they stared at each other, Hughie seeing the round-faced girl with some sort of yellow splodge on her hat, and the fluffy hair, and sweet pink coming and going in her

84

cheeks with the anxiety and love in her heart. And she saw him, with hollow blue eyes and eyelashes like soot on his pale skin, lying there amongst the peanut shells with the towel tucked round his neck, and suffering so much for her.

"Wish I coulda gnawed me way to that ring," he said sincerely.

"Shut up! Shut up! Shut up!" shouted Dolour, standing up so suddenly their tea sloshed over. Her poor swollen eyes blazing, she glared at them.

"Now what?" demanded Mumma.

"I'd think you'd be ashamed—why don't you keep all this stuff to yourself! Oh, you're awful!" cried Dolour, stammering in her disgust of the down-to-earthiness that destroyed every dram of romance in her conception of her parents. There were many things she wanted to say, but there were no civil words for them. She ran upstairs blinded with tears and passion.

The quick soft tattoo of her feet awoke Roie. The door next to hers wumped into its ill-fitting lock, and Roie sighed. "Poor kid."

She was sad for her sister, but the sadness did not affect her essentially. The ultimate contentment that filled her heart did not leave room for any deep sorrows, as long as its origin and propagator remained untouched. She lay in the quietness, hearing the two all-important things in her life, the breathing of her child and the breathing of her husband. Warmth radiated from the man, warmth and peace. She put her arm over him, feeling the arch of his chest, the smoothness of the flesh over his ribs. Her wordless wonderment at the miracle of his body came to her again. In her idolatry of her husband, Roie acknowledged her reverence and awe of the fleshly edifice of mankind, the dust-built, incredible temple that in its ceaseless repetition found immortality.

"Charlie, my boy," she murmured, not alone for his ear, but for the assurance of her own heart. Out of his sleep, he murmured in answer, inarticulate, wholly-comprehensible, the primitive language of unworded sound. He pulled her closer to him, and in the complete contentment of their love they lay, their breaths mingling, sleep flowing over them resistlessly as a dream.

Dolour heard their voices and knew them for what they were. Unformed, hardly understanding, her whole being reached out for an experience that seemed to belong to everyone in the world except herself. Her body was ready for love, and her mind was not, and in the boiling confusion only one thought emerged. Desperately she needed someone who would comfort and protect, who would belong to her alone, and who would above all love her. Love? What was it? Did she know?

"Yes, yes!" thought Dolour. She clung to the window-sill, staring into the moonlight-flooded yard, where the deep shadows welled up like splashes of Indian ink. She trembled with the force of emotion within her. No one would ever want her, with her disfigured eyes, and perhaps blindness ahead of her. Ill-educated, she would be good for nothing except slavery to the factory machines, like all the others. She would never know anybody except the Surry Hills boys, the good-hearted morons of the dance-halls, the scorchers on motor-bikes, the dills who frequented the corners and developed lips like cornet-players whistling after girls.

"Oh, what's the use? What's the use?" she groaned, and dragging off her clothes she fell into bed and closed her burning, stinging eyes.

1 O

AFTER a while it became accepted in that house that Dolour had bad eyes, just as they accepted the stairs that twisted in the middle, and the skylight that let in the wind and wet of heaven in the winter. Soon Dolour felt as if she had been at home for ever, and there would never be anything else for her but wet cloths, and darkness, and doctors, and searing swabs, and all the misery and loneliness of uselessness. The small pleasures of youth blew up like balloons before her, always unattainable. Sometimes she begged Mumma to let her go to the pictures.

"I'll just keep my eyes closed all the time, dinkum I will," she said eagerly. "I'll just listen. Honest I will."

"The doctor said—" remembered Mumma doubtfully, but Roie begged, "Aw, come on, Mumma."

So Dolour went to the pictures, her small thin face half-hidden behind the round black windows of the goggles. As the old smells—the peanuts and dusty plush, and rotting timber, and pressing, flurried crowds—swept up round her, she trembled with excitement. The trumpeting music, spouting out of a sound equipment worn down to a nub, seemed to her to be the essence of liveliness and sociability; the squirming, shouting children, wandering back and forth to the Ladies and Gentlemen which were placed with homely convenience on either side of the screen; the women with their hair in curlers; the battalions of babies asleep in their prams behind the seats. . . .

"Oh," said Dolour, in an outburst of childish joy, "ain't it lovely!"

When the lights went down she was plunged into almost total darkness. Dimly she could see the greyish flickerings on the screen, so she shut her eyes and tried to concentrate on the dialogue. She kept them shut conscientiously, but when the audience laughed, and no dialogue fitted the laughter, she surreptitiously pushed her glasses up on to her forehead, and gazed through slitted eyes at the screen.

She saw there the well-loved figures of her friends, the movie stars, the legendary shadows who brought laughter and quickly-soothed tears to the millions caught in the web of their monotonous and over-familiar lives. But it was only for a moment. Almost instantly her eyes began to water, and Roie leaned over and gave her a poke.

"You know what the doctor said," she reminded.

"Yes," said Dolour forlornly. She saw that Charlie and Roie were holding hands, and in a jealous rebellion she slid away to the further side of her seat and glowered there. But Charlie reached out, took her unresponsive paw, and squeezed it. His touch was different from that of the beaky boy in the back row when she had gone with Suse. It was calm, and comforting, and not at all clammy, so after a while Dolour giggled and squeezed back.

"Don't let my wife know," whispered Charlie. She sat there in contentment, listening to the disconnected dialogue, laughing with the laughter, and swaying to the same music that swayed Ginger Rogers. She was happy, pretending that Charlie was somebody else, who belonged to her.

When she had been away some weeks, Mumma said, "I think you'd better go and tell Sister Theophilus you won't be back for a bit."

Dolour was glad of the glasses that hid her lack of resignation at this final, bitter blow.

"O.K."

Going up the narrow, shabby corridor, with the buzz of classrooms on either side, she felt strange, as though she were a new girl. She knocked on Sister Theophilus's door, and a girl she had never seen before opened it. She saw the familiar files of desks, the blackboard with the coloured chalk scroll, the maps, the pictures of lobsters and shells and the Laughing Cavalier round the walls.

A little titter of surprise and welcome and pleasure went round the room. Sister Theophilus closed the door gently behind her. Dolour felt clumsy and awkward, all big bony legs that stuck out in every direction. She put out a hand and took it back. There was so much emotion in her chest that her voice was difficult to manage.

"I just come--came--to say I won't be coming back to school, Sister."

Sister heard the ache in the child's voice. She had heard it so often before. Most of her girls were so glad to get away from school they couldn't go out fast enough into the world of mystery and hardship and responsibility which yet called with so alluring a voice. But now and then she had had some promising pupil like Dolour, in whose breast burgeoned a desire for things better than those with which she had grown up.

Just a little while ago Dolour had been a child, grubby-finger-nailed, with cobbled holes in her stockings and scuffed shoes; now she had retreated into a girl who wore someone else's ill-fitting clothes, bobby socks, and sandals, and goggles that hid her sore, weeping eyes so well an onlooker could read nothing from her expression.

She sighed, knowing that she had lost yet another to the smoky maelstrom of Surry Hills.

"Dolour—" She hesitated. "Don't feel your life's ended. Things may look very black now, but—there must be a great deal of happiness for you in the future, you've been such a good girl. I'll pray for you, and perhaps when your eyes are better we can arrange some extra lessons for you, out of school hours."

"Yes," mumbled Dolour. She avoided the nun's eyes. She wanted to say, "Thank you, I've always loved you, I like the way you talk, and how you never get angry or loud-voiced and rude. I want to know what you think about, and whether it's a good thing for a girl to be a nun, and . . ."

Somehow she said good-bye, and stumbled away down the stairs where the banisters were notched and chipped with the initials of the daring.

Grey and disillusionary and hopeless the world stretched before her, with no avenue of escape. She passed up Coronation Street, and the boys on the corner, chewing their sandwiches and spitting out the crusts, turned and looked at her curiously. At most girls they whistled or called out ribaldries.

And that was how it was always going to be, thought Dolour. Her developing body, taking on the aspects of womanhood, seemed to her to be an insult and a reproach, an intolerable burden, for she wanted so much to return to the safety of childhood.

But there was too much Irish in her to keep from laughing long. Often the comical and the ludicrous that lay so close to the surface in their lives, sometimes a bedfellow of tragedy itself, cropped up in her path.

One day the cat plague descended upon Plymouth Street, which had always been a dispersal ground for strays of all sorts. It was a street with a faint, pervasive odour of tomcat, harsh and masculine and arrogant, and every patch of neglected grass outside a gate harboured its basking, knife-ribbed cat. The only fat cats in the street belonged to Lick Jimmy; aloof, unsociable cats they were, not speaking English, very conscious of stomachs lined with all the fantastically hacked titbits from the Chinese butcher shop, wherein nothing even remotely resembles a joint from an Occidental butcher.

But the stray cats were different. Like loose bits of fur slung over a backbone, faces shrunken into Tartar-cheeked triangles, their narrow paws and paltry tails poverty-stricken beyond description, they haunted the alleys, an army of the lost and unwanted. They came and went in bands, for if one picked up a full stomach somewhere, the others haunted that place until they were stoned away. Those at an attractive stage of growth, or with a pretty hide, were taken in and given a home; kindhearted folk sent others away to be painlessly destroyed; but always and always there were cats, producing kittens even in the midst of their starvation, living on and on, hanging to a thread of life so wispy a breath seemed sufficient to sever it.

Roie's gentle heart could not bear it. She was for ever picking up cats and bringing them home.

"I'll just give it a saucer of milk and then we'll put it outside the fence," was her excuse, knowing that she could not send the thing on its way empty-bellied.

Mumma stumped to the door and flung it open. "Look!" she commanded. On each step sat a cat, and there were eight steps. Eight rusty necks turned, and eight pink mouths opened feebly.

"That's the way they go away," commented Mumma.

"I'll put the lot in a bag and throw 'em over the bridge," roared Hughie. "I'd push the lot down the lavatory, if they weren't so big they'd choke the pipe."

Roie had a battle with herself. Finally she said, "All right, I'll take them away tonight."

"I'll go with you," said Dolour quickly, anxious to get in before Charlie, for she so rarely had her sister to herself. When she went outside she found Roie feeding the cats for the last time. They ate everything, meat, fish, vegetables, bread, even a piece of half-cooked pumpkin.

"Eat up big," commanded Dolour. "Lizards and rats for you tomorrow."

"Oh, shut up!" cried Roie.

Dolour held a sugar-bag, and Roie arranged the cats within, each with its head sticking out. They wriggled and squirmed feebly, all except a small dwarfish creature with a perpetual wet patch on its back, which Hughie had christened Dirty Dick. Dirty Dick didn't want to go into the sugar-bag. He had been in too many sugar-bags. He sprang to the table, fluffed up his fur, and spat from a mouth where malnutrition had formed teeth as pigmy as himself, like minute white needles.

"Oh, can it, Dick!" Dolour thrust him, with his legs sticking out rigidly to the four winds, into the midst of the mewling bouquet of cats. There was an agonized upheaval, but she held the sack in a grip of iron about their necks.

It was ten o'clock, a dark windy night with few people in the streets. Even the stars seemed wind-blown, like flames in a draught. The two girls walked slowly down the street, Dolour adapting her long strides to Roie's lagging ones. A continual soprano wail of complaint came from Dolour's bundle. They traced an irregular and difficult course through the alleys and streets, so that the cats would not find their way back.

Roie was hesitant about plunging into many of the pitch-black lanes, but Dolour was completely fearless. Brought up in Surry Hills, she felt there wasn't a drunk in the district she couldn't have handled if he bailed her up. But they met nobody, and saw nobody except lovers crammed into doorways whispering to each other.

Dolour hated the sight of their shadowy bodies, the sound of their urgent, secretive voices.

But Roie understood. "You got to go somewhere when you're like that. Lots of boys and girls live in residentials and they ain't allowed to have their friends there."

"Ah, fooey!" cried Dolour angrily. "Kissing and mugging and hugging, don't they ever think of anything else?"

"Wait till you fall in love," said Roie. "Wait till you want to get married."

How could Dolour reveal that dearest wish, that she wanted to get married more than anything in the world? She knew only one way to shelter it, and said in a scornful voice, "I wouldn't get married if all the fellers in the world were after me."

The forlornness was so apparent in her voice that Roie laughed. "Oh, Dolour, you are funny!"

Anger seized Dolour, "All right, so I'm funny."

They had come out into a little street on the edge of a high embankment, along which ran a high tin wall. Down below there was a wilderness of bricks and pieces of rusty tin, where two old tenements had been demolished in the slum rehabilitation programme. At intervals along the fence, crouched like images, squatted seven tomcats, each fixing the other with a loathing eye. Dolour ran along beside the fence, pushing them off one after the other. Diminishing wails came up from the dark hollow below, evoking cooing notes from the tabbies in the sugar-bag.

"This is a good place." Giggling like children, their disagreement completely forgotten, they hurried along the street, popping cats over the fences. One house had a large garden, so Roie generously presented it with two. Finally, over a high brick factory wall, Dolour shook the clinging, malodorous Dirty Dick.

"Quick!" They scampered along for a little, then Roie tired, and loitered heavily, the weight of the child bearing down her whole body. Dolour wanted to ask her questions that she was too shy to ask anyone else, and after a struggle with herself she burst out, "Did Mumma tell you anything—you know—before you were married?"

Roie giggled. "Yes, she did. She told me that lysol is good for perspiry feet."

"Ain't that just like Mumma!"

After a little while Roie blurted out, "If there's anything you want to ask . . . about boys . . . or anything . . ."

So much embarrassment seized Dolour that she said rudely, "What's there to know about boys, anyway?"

Roie was half angry, half relieved, but she understood her sister too well to take any notice of her. "It's just—well, when your eyes are better you'll be going out with boys, and if you know a little bit first . . ."

"Such as what?" asked Dolour with obstinate obtuseness, for she was too embarrassed to display anything else. Roie sighed.

"Well, I knew a girl once like you . . . I mean, a nice girl with . . . well, good ideas about everything . . . and she went around with a fellow and one night he asked her . . . you know."

"She should have hauled off and thudded him on the ear," said Dolour briskly.

Roie was exasperated. "Yes, that's all right, but when you love someone you don't feel like that."

"I would," said Dolour scornfully. She felt herself like Joan of Arc, clad in pearly armour, virginal, unconquerable. She could just see herself breaking her own heart to thud her lover on the earhole.

"Well, say you didn't," wailed Roie. "Say you loved your feller so much you wanted to please him, no matter what it was."

Dolour snorted, and Roie glared. They both struggled with their inarticulateness; Dolour because she was shy, and yet desperately eager to know, Roie because her vocabulary was so small, her powers of self-expression so limited.

"I want to tell you that it isn't worth it, never. That no matter how much you love a man he won't like you any better because you give in to him. He might even think smaller of you for it. This girl I knew—well, her boy took her pretty cheap afterwards, and when she was going to have a baby he cleared out and left her. That's how much he thought of her."

"Who was she?"

"A friend of mine."

"Rosie Glavich?"

"I'm not going to tell you. Course I'm not."

"What did she call the baby?" asked Dolour, her unconquerable interest in babies cropping up even in this angry and uncomfortable moment. She was astonished when Roie turned away from her and said, "It never had a name. It died . . . before it was born."

After a little while Dolour said, "I guess that was lucky for her."

"Yes, I suppose it was," said Roie. Dolour was staring at her, so she forced herself to stare back.

"Why did Rosie Glavich tell you all these things?" asked her sister suspiciously.

"I told you it wasn't Rosie," flared Roie.

"Who then?" jeered Dolour. She was going to accuse Roie of making it all up when she saw to her amazement the look on Roie's face, of sudden transfixation, as though she were looking in shocked horror at some memory almost forgotten.

"Thanks, Ro," she said, awkwardly. "I—you don't need to worry about me."

She thrust her hands into her pocket, and to her pleasure she found a piece of chocolate, dry and powder-streaked, wrapped up in golden paper.

"Gee, look! You can have it, Ro, it gives me pimples," she said gladly, and Roie took it gratefully, knowing it was Dolour's recognition of her desire to help.

They were near the house. On the steps crouched a small, humpy form.

"It can't be!"

"Oh, Lord!" Roie picked up the little creature by its soggy scruff, and the dwarfish figure, a perpetual frown against the hateful cruel world grooving the skin between its eyes, showed its malformed teeth and hissed. "It must have beat us home by a short cut."

They took it in and gave it a feed, which it ate, snarling furiously, gulping down the meat in an uncatlike way, slapping meantime with a savage, sixpence-sized paw at a flapping edge of the paper. The world had united against Dirty Dick, and Dirty Dick was going to give it a run for its money.

"Gern, I'll get rid of it once and for all," said Hughie, bending down to grab the animal, but Mumma, fat and rheumaticky and all as she was beat him to it. She interposed her plump leg between Dirty Dick and her husband, and Dirty Dick answered in gratitude by slashing his claws across it.

Mumma gave a sharp yelp, which slightly marred the effect of her defence. "No, you don't, Hugh Darcy. The poor little cow deserves to stay. It won't be me that can't find a skerrick of meat for him once a day."

So Dirty Dick became part of the household, a malevolent spirit that spent half its time being pushed off the table, slapped out of the butter, and bitten savagely on the tail by the loving Motty. Not even instinct told him what affection was. When a hand was stretched out to stroke him he crouched, flat of ear and glittering of eye, a sound like a vacuum cleaner deep down in his throat. No one ever picked him up without a wound. The smell of meat drove him completely mad, and he instantly climbed up the nearest object to the source of supply. Most often this was Mumma's patient back, and many and many a time she went roaring round the kitchen begging and pleading for someone to take the devil off the back of her neck.

"I hate to think of anyone in this house who gets a bloody nose," said Hughie, direfully. "He'd wake up to find himself nothing but bones."

Dirty Dick was a fine advertisement for mankind.

But Dolour was comforted by his prowling over the roof at night. He liked to sit, for ever licking at the sodden patch on his rusty back, on her attic window-sill. She never ventured to touch him, for she felt that their lonely, solitary quality was the same.

Dolour never prayed that her eyes might get better. The disease was her hostage to fate; the pain and discomfort and deprivation her cupboardful of treasure, to be swapped in the future for felicity. She had the good Celtic practicality about spiritual things and saw nothing niggling in God's demand to be paid for what He might give. It was just. She gave him her fortitude and resignation under suffering and misery; in return He would give her an overflowing measure of happiness that might start any day, any hour. Sometimes in her soul she had dark, despairful suspicions that He was overdoing it a little, but she kept this from Him.

But she considered her emotions were her own, and in the privacy of the dark she often gave way, weeping with her face tightly jammed into the pillow, so that she nearly suffocated. Sometimes Charlie heard muffled clangs as her feet, drumming on the counterpane, missed and hit the end of the bed. He grinned, for he was saving up for a surprise for her.

Finally it was bought. Mumma felt abashed that she had never grown to like him quite as she should, and she said gruffly, "It's real thoughtful of you."

"Listen," said Charlie. Mumma put the black earphone of the crystal set to her ear, and Spike Jones made her hair lift. An astonished, delighted grin spread over her face. "Ain't it clever! Lord, fancy that!"

Dolour was overcome by the sight of her present, but she did not know how to thank Charlie. She put her ear to the black plastic circle, and a minute budgerigar voice assured her of everlasting glamour if she used R-O-S-E-B-U-D soap.

"Jeepers, Charlie," she croaked. To hide her emotion she jammed the earphones over her head, and beamed at him, looking grotesquely like a refugee from the War of the Worlds, with the horned black muffs over her ears and the large round goggles flashing heliograph signs.

Now her life was strung on the vibrating whisker of the crystal set. Every night she went to bed early and lay in the darkness to listen in. She listened in to everything, and went to sleep with the earphones on, so that she woke to the gay canary chirp of an announcer whose great cross was that he had to sound like noon at six in the morning.

Without the fretting, and the tears, her eyes improved a little. There was something to look forward to now, the heterogeneous, noisy entertainment of the radio world. She was still not of the world, but at least she could hear its voice. When she was down the road doing the messages, Mumma often went up and picked up the earphones, holding them at arm's length, and bending her neck towards them like a flamingo; they seemed to her much more wonderful than the wireless itself, and much more likely to explode. And probably if she had been left with them long that was just what they would have done, for Mumma was the sort whose very instinct was to do things wrong. She put patches on the wrong side of the rent in Hughie's trousers, wore her hats backwards, and could never find the dotted line she was supposed to sign on. There was no mechanical contrivance on earth Mumma couldn't hurt herself with, feeding her fingers into egg-beaters and shutting her skirt into the ice-chest along with the milk. If anyone had ever given her an electric iron she would have electrocuted herself with it the first hour, by doing something to the defenceless thing that no one else would ever have thought of.

Dolour could not find words to thank Charlie, so she went to mass for him instead. And Roie, slowly and laboriously now, went with her, getting up in the early summer morning so often that Charlie became used to waking up and finding the short body of Motty beside him instead of his wife's. She was a thoughtful, self-possessed child, and liked to put her face within two inches of his, so that he opened his unfocused eyes to find them staring into two unwinking circlets of blue, which had obviously been committing every line and feature to memory.

"How did you get here?" he groaned, turning his face into the pillow.

"Mummy put me here," said Motty calmly, which was a lie. She poked her fingers between his teeth and pried his mouth open.

"What are you looking for, for gosh sake?" mumbled her father.

"Things," said Motty. She clambered on to his stomach, lay back against his knees, and looked peacefully at the ceiling.

"Flies have whiskers," she said. Charlie, coming slowly out of the sleep of exhaustion and discomfort that a slum night can bring, surveyed his daughter. She was a ceaseless wonder to him, this little being who had been nowhere, nowhere at all until he had loved Roie. He looked at the perfection of her body, the completeness of her eyelashes and teeth, and marvelled. The number of generations that had gone to make her, the lines of blood and bone and nerve that converged in her —he tried to count them and failed. The great-grandmother who had been black, who had given him golden eyes and long sinewy hands—she was manifest in Motty in the wet polish of her hair that was no more like Roie's soft, sooty Irish hair than metal was like silk. And her blue eyes, with the dark thumbprints about them, were Irish. So he stared and wondered, until he heard Roie climbing clumsily up the stairs.

At first Dolour's tender, inflamed eyeballs protested with furious tears that they could stand no light, but gradually she became used to the evening light without her goggles, and even in the noon she could bear it, inside the house, for a few moments. The pearly spots, which had been swallowed up in the bloodshot conjunctiva, became apparent as the red faded into pink, but instead of being swollen white excrescences on the eyeball, they were fading into a transparent mucus.

"They're going to get better, Ro," she breathed. "Oh, I don't mind if I have to wear goggles for years if only they get better a little!"

Roie was silent, not knowing what to say in case Dolour were to be disappointed. But Dolour said herself, "I'll be able to get a job to help Mumma out a bit."

She said not a word of her lost ambitions, and Roie wondered pitifully if they had been put away on a shelf for ever. She was glad when they met little Mrs Drummy on the church steps. Mrs Drummy did sewing, it was plain to be seen, for her hair was covered with odds and ends of cotton, as though she were a mop that needed to be shaken out the window.

"Oh, love," gasped Mrs Drummy breathlessly, "ain't it a lovely morning! It's that nice to see you around again, Dolour. I been saying a prayer for you, don't you worry. Dear St Martin de Porridge, the black man, he's that good." And she beamed as a gardener does when an unexpected seed pops up and produces a blossom. "Oh, Lord, I gotta skip outa mass before it's finished again. We're that busy in the shop with the races on. I never see Bert at all, he's that busy with the S.P."

She beamed and trotted into church. Dolour and Roie looked at each other, then without a word Dolour hurried after Mrs Drummy. Somewhere in her heart tears were rising, for the lost knowledge, the lost opportunities that would never be hers now. Then she squashed them down. Yes, they could be hers, some day. She was raised to be a worker, to take the amount of schooling the Government decreed was necessary, then to scuttle out as fast as possible to get a job to help out in the family. But somehow she could put by a little every week to educate herself later on. Some day she'd leave, and do what she wanted to do, and never come within the shadow of the Hills any more.

She marched down the aisle to where Mrs Drummy, a

humped, shabby little figure, was conducting a loud conversation with St Theresa. Dolour crashed in without an apology.

"Could you give me a job, Mrs Drummy?" she hissed. "I could serve in the shop and help you out a bit."

Mrs Drummy's eyes shone with pleasure, and Father Cooley, who had been watching willy-nilly their reflected conversation in the shining brass door of the Tabernacle, turned round, glared, and coughed thunderously. Dolour slunk back to her seat.

This was how she got her first job, down at the ham and beef.

II

W HEN Hughie learned that Dolour was going to work at Drummy's, a tiny pang entered his heart, and he ate his lunch hurriedly and went off to the pub. He boasted for a while to his old mates—of his girl's smartness, and how she had had eye trouble and had to leave school. Then he was silent, remembering Dolour's passionate and tender spirit that had taken all the humiliations and rough hardships life had imposed upon it, and yet retained enough energy to bud forth in little ambitions of its own.

"She wanted to get a posh job," he said.

"Nobody out of Surro ever gets a posh job," said one of the old mates, a melancholy fellow with a face like a goanna.

This was manifestly untrue. Surry Hills citizens had become priests, politicians, and police-sergeants. They had soared into the heavy income-tax division of factory-owners, black-marketeers and garage proprietors. But in his uneasy disappointment for Dolour, Hughie accepted the dictum of his miserable friend. The beer went off, and Hughie retaliated against the unfeeling publican by pouring a pint or two of harsh Australian sherry into his stomach on top of what he had there. It made him feel even worse. He barged off home, through a world which had dislocated itself from its horizon and was floating some feet above the ground.

The heat was so intense, and the beer and sherry hated each other so furiously, that Hughie felt he might die any moment. Sweat soaked the back of his shirt in a huge irregular grey patch. His hat was obviously made of iron, drawing down the rays of the sun like a burning-glass focused unerringly upon his brain.

In his distress he missed his way, and blundered down the wrong turning towards Darlinghurst. He stood staring dizzily round, wondering how he had got there, but he was too sick to bother retracing his steps. He saw a desolate fig-tree leaning over a fence and casting a thick oval of shade. There was already a panting dog lying there, but Hughie pushed it out of the way and collapsed against the fence.

He lay there, scratching frequently, for two or three hours. No one went past on that lazy Saturday afternoon. All the windows hung open, washing drooped its spiritless legs and arms from sagging lines, and there was no sound save the muffled squawk of a radio belching out the races. Already, so early in the summer, the sun was like golden syrup, dripping languidly off a spoon. Hughie tried to remember what he had been so upset about, but he was too dizzy. His eyes felt as though he had been crying, but he hadn't.

Somewhere above him, roosting in the tree perhaps, a voice said, "Hey!"

Hughie, unable to move his eyes for the pain in them, lolled his head and looked into the upper air.

"I'm 'ere," said the little voice, and, upside down, Hughie saw a face protruding over the fence. A peculiar face it was, something like a Pekinese's, with a bulging, wrinkled forehead, pathetic eyes, and a nose fair in the middle like a push button.

"Like a cuppa?" invited the face. Hughie groaned. There was a scruffling sound, and a finger poked him through a hole in the fence. He turned painfully, and there was a bluish eye staring at him through a knot-hole.

"I been watching you," the eye informed him. "You been looking as though you got heat-stroke, moaning away there, and sweating yourself into a puddle. 'Ere, you come inside, and I'll give you a cuppa and a powder."

Hughie needed an A.P.C. powder. He needed anything that would turn the fermenting solfatara out of his stomach and the thumping pain out of his head. He swayed to his feet, and magically at his right hand a door in the fence creaked open, and he was ushered inside.

By the smell, he thought the large building at the end of the yard was a garage. The yard itself had plainly been used as a parking lot, for the stains of old grease blotted the soil, and a serpentine heap of inner-tubes lay in a corner like unimaginable offal.

Along the fence was a curious building of asbestos sheets, plywood, and hammered out iron. It was shaped like a fowl-house, with sloping roof patched with tacked-on pieces of boxes and petrol tins, and it was divided into many little cubicles seven foot square.

"Whazzat?" asked Hughie, politely.

100

"Oh, that's the flophouse," replied his new friend, a baggy, miniature creature like a full-sized man whom someone had allowed to deflate. Hughie was no giant himself, but the little man came only to his breastbone and this in some mysterious way made him feel a lot better.

He realized, as they went towards one of the cubbyholes, that each cubicle was occupied. Here sat an old man on a chair at his doorway, cutting his toenails with the slow, cautious preoccupation of one who could not trust his own toes to stay twice in the same place; on a stretcher in another sibilantly slumbered an old woman in a hideously advanced stage of debilitation and neglect; and in yet another two aged crones quarrelled feebly.

"'Ere." Hughie sat down on the rickety bag bed. The air within the cubbyhole was sickeningly hot, and the sweat popped out on his brow again. He sat looking at a large glossy brown teapot on the table, surrounded by a bead-like ring of flies. He moistened his lips and felt an overwhelming urge to hang his tongue out.

"Take sugar?" The host raised his face inquiringly from a sticky brown paper bag. Hughie nodded, dry-mouthed, as he unfolded to his feet.

"Scuse me. Won't be a jiff."

"Sure," said his little friend cheerily.

After that Hughie felt better, the uplifted, garrulous feeling of one who has been sick beyond all mortal calculation.

The interior of the cubbyhole was not very clean, and each leg of the stretcher stood in a jam tin of water. This did not amaze Hughie, though their bugs at home took no notice of such precautions, falling down from the ceiling or throwing themselves off the walls to get at their sleeping prey. A thin grey blanket, obviously at three bob a shot from the Army Surplus Stores, and a depressed, dirty pillow were on the bed, along with three racing magazines and a tobacco tin with a butt in it transfixed by a pin. This did not surprise Hughie either; he had often taken a butt about half an inch long, stabbed it through its malodorous middle and got a few more puffs out of it.

"'Ere's yer mike," said his host, shoving over a pannikin of stewed and boiling tea. Hughie blew on it gratefully. It did not enter his head that it was odd for this stranger to have invited him in; he had often done the same for those who seemed under the weather or the influence. It had never occurred to him that he was throwing bread on the waters of charity. The poor cow needed a helping hand just as other cows needed a boot in the jeer, and he was just as free with the one as with the other.

Soon he felt almost himself. "Watcher mean, flophouse?"

"Ain't it a flophouse?" inquired the little man.

"My oath," said Hughie, looking around distastefully.

"Got rats, too," said the little man. They drank their tea in silence.

Then Hughie said politely, "How much they sting yer for it?"

"Half a frog."

"Strewth!"

"Jest leaves yer enough to starve on," said the old man with a sort of perverted pride.

While the tea in the pot sank lower, and the sunlight crept up the wall to disappear in a burst of twinkles under the iron roof, Hughie learned the history of the flophouse, probably only one of many in that city. Each cubbyhole was the home of an invalid or old-age pensioner, most of them once good hard workers, who had committed the mortal sin of living too long. Unable to find anywhere to live for the sum they could afford, they dragged out their lives in cold, misery, and squalidity in places such as this, erected hastily by landowners who saw a good opportunity to clean up regular small profits by charging these people ten shillings a week each for rent.

The man who owned this Surry Hills flophouse made eleven pounds a week clear profit out of his pensioners.

"What's up with you, anyhow?" asked Hughie.

The old man smote his chest. "I got angela pectoris. It's a heart trouble. Serious."

"Not serious enough to be worth more than a coupla quid a week though," growled Hughie.

"Well, I got me roof," said the old fellow peaceably. "After you've slep' out of doors for a few nights you change your mind about the sorta roof you like best."

"Yeah." Hughie brooded. He wanted to go out brandishing a cudgel in defence of these poor, ragbag creatures who had no homes of their own to sleep in, or cut their toenails in. Two pound two and six a week, and they hadn't been getting that much a short while ago. That meant they had about three bob a day to feed, clothe, warm and amuse themselves. Hughie quickly translated it into beers, and in horror translated it back again even more quickly. It was plain that a pensioner could never have a beer.

"Ain't so bad for me," said the old man placatingly. "I got this little kerosene burner to cook on. Everyone else has to eat out, and it takes your money that fast!"

"Haven't you got any children you could stay with?"

The old man seemed suddenly to shrink, and Hughie was alarmed in case he should disappear altogether into an empty heap of clothes.

"I 'ad a boy once. But he was killed in the fust war, at Gallipoli. That's all the kids I ever 'ad. And me wife, she died on me close on twenty year ago." He brightened up. "You mightn't know, but I was a jockey once. Bumper Reilly they called me. Fust-rate jockey. 'Ad me name in the papers more times than I could count."

He rummaged eagerly in the pockets of an old coat spread-eagled on a couple of nails. It was his cupboard and storehouse. He took a piece of yellow soap out of the breast pocket, two nails, and a bundle of clippings with stained, rat-nibbled edges.

"There!" The black-nailed finger pointed to the almost illegible print. Hughie held it close to his eyes, then at arm's length.

"Hum."

"Good, ain't it?" asked Bumper Reilly, delighted. "Look where it says Bumper Reilly rode such a race as has not been seen on the Australian Turf."

Hughie spread a pleased grin over his face like butter. "Fine to have things like that to look back on in yer old age," he assented. Instantly the pathetic Pekinese look took its place on Mr Reilly's face. He wrapped the clippings round the soap, and put it back in the pocket.

"I'd like to slip yer a coupla bob for a drink, seeing you sorta came to me rescue," said Hugh in embarrassment.

"The soap keeps the mice away, I always think," said Mr Reilly with an indescribable look of proud rejection. Hughie sneaked the two bob on to the table. The old man saw it, but his pride had been satisfied, and he left it where it was.

There was a squall from the next cubby, and one of the old women, like a grey old mangy cat, hardly human in her poverty and raggedness, hobbled past, weeping. She was a little old animal, as unwanted and as smelly as Dirty Dick, who, having ridden the tides of life, was thrown up in this yard like flotsam of the worst possible quality.

103

"Never stop fighting," observed Mr Reilly gloomily. "Yah, yah, yah, all night long. When one dies, the other will commit suicide."

"Look," said Hughie impulsively, "we gotta spare room in our place."

The wine, oozing triumphantly up through the tea, sent forth a great warm fume of generosity and good feeling towards this poor old wreck.

"Sure," he said, "the missus wouldn't be objecting if we rented it to you. The roof's all in one piece, and there's a gas ring for cooking on, and there'll be plenty of tucker floating around," he added largely, "which we wouldn't miss, just to help you out a bit like. Seven and six would do for the rent."

"But maybe the missus wouldn't take to me," quavered the old man. "I got all them parcels, you know."

Hughie noticed what he had not noticed before, that under the table were stacked dozens and dozens of small parcels, all neatly tied with string, and clothesline, and bits of red wool.

"Aw, what's a parcel or two between mates. A man can't help collecting a bit of luggage, and he can't always be buying ports on two quid a week. Tell you what, Bumper," he said, beginning to feel dazed again, but in a soft-headed, happy way, "you come round on Monday, and see the missus, and don't let her give you any cheek. Mrs Darcy's the name. Anyone who comes up all friendly the way you did and asks me in just like an old cobber is going to get what's coming to him. Me mother never raised a squib."

"What's the address?" asked Mr Reilly feverishly, in case Hughie should change his mind. He licked a stub of purple pencil and stood waiting.

"Twelve-and-a-half Plymouth Street," said Hughie, undecided whether he wanted to cry at his generosity or not. It was one of those moments when you leaned against your cobber and your cobber leaned against you, and you slapped each other's backs feebly and benevolently, and swore never to part. But Mr Reilly was much too small to lean against unless you were a dwarf.

He tottered home, enveloped in a golden mist of good fellowship, and it wasn't till he saw Mumma that he realized what he was in for, when Bumper Reilly and his parcels arrived.

"Ah, don't worry your head, Hughie man," he chided himself. "Sure, he's an old man, and that shaky a good thump

104

on the ear would blow him over. He might be dead by
Monday."

That Monday morning Dolour had to start work. She had
spent most of the Sunday learning the ways of the shop, which
was one of those that open at dawn to catch the headache-
powder, chewing-gum, soda-water trade, and close as late as
the inspectors allow. There was a great sensation among the
Drummys when it was known that Dolour Darcy, their old
schoolmate, was to work for their mother. A careless, roaring
crew, they thundered in and out of the shop almost without
ceasing, and never a can of ice-cream in that place was emptied
without their grubby fingers scooping up the last blob.

Dolour had chosen to take the early shift, opening the shop
at six, when the milkmen clashed and clattered down the road
with their cans. Then she was supposed to sweep and scrub
it, fill the refrigerator with soft drinks, clean the counters, and
freshen up the window. She was to learn that trade was so
constant there was almost no time to do these things. The
shop was in a good position, the focal point of a dozen poor
streets. It sold milk and bread, butter and groceries, and deli-
catessen goods of a strictly utilitarian kind. The pickled
cucumber, the olive, and the black walnut found no resting
place there; but corned beef, pressed ham, and various kinds
of dreadfully pink or miserable grey sausage, which could be
sold at a "frippence-worf" and a "zack's worf", filled the glass
window of the refrigerator.

The little shop was well aware of its prosperity. Drab of paint,
its window decorated with curly strips of coloured paper hung
up two Christmases before, nevertheless it appeared to bulge
and burst with its contents. Straw brooms and sacks of onions
and boxes of eggs and pegs gushed out of the doorway as though
they were just about to leave, and inside cases of tomatoes and
tins of biscuits provided handy steps and stairs to the counter
for the children who were too short to see over the top.

It smelt of bacon and cheese and long-vanished tobacco, and
Dolour hated it from the moment she entered it as its slave.

She unlocked the flimsy door, which was cracked with the
efforts of a thousand drunks shoving each other affectionately
against it. The milk carters, great husky whistling fellows,
charged down the almost empty street like knights in armour,
whirled into the shop, sloshed the milk into the cans, chyacked
Dolour about her goggles, and charged out again, leaving

105

behind them such an atmosphere of arrant masculinity that it was almost an odour.

She peeped timidly into the room behind the shop, in case any of the Drummys should be sleeping there, but, hollow and twilit, it was empty save for the headless form of Mrs Drummy's dressmaker shape, which stood in a corner, its pure calico bosom cruelly studded with pins. Here, too, was the sewing machine, and the little table where Mr Bert Drummy made out his S.P. books. Upstairs she could hear the stirrings of the Drummys, groans from Bert, querulous chitterings from his wife, and all the piggish snorts from the boys' bedroom. She quickly got the broom and swept out the shop, sprinkled down the pavement, and looked longingly into the sunrise that blossomed in the clear morning sky above Coronation Street. Fresh and pure, it was a fan of light reaching out of the vast chalcedony spaces and focusing like a searchlight on the city that was, after all, but an irregular red and grey speck on the vast tawny continent.

Now smoke was tufting the chimneys, for most of the houses in this street had landlords who hadn't heard of the invention of gas or electric power. She saw Lick Jimmy appear, trundling a little handcart, and trot off towards the vegetable markets. The little noises of stirring people, the little smells of breakfast, rose up in a perceptible wave.

"Ah, gee!" Dolour went inside, and put on the old pink overall that had been left over from Roie's box-factory days. Of course it did not fit her, and her long legs stuck out like a heron's. She took off her glasses and cautiously peered into her eyes. They were weak and pinkish, but no longer savagely inflamed. The lids were thickened and she had lost any looks she had ever had, but . . .

"Thank You, God," said Dolour. She put on some lipstick. It made her pasty, unhealthy face even pastier, but it made her feel better.

Somebody pounded on the counter, and a harsh voice shouted, "Sharp!"

Dolour scurried out, feeling nervous, for she was not at all good with change. She was out of luck, for her first customer was the Kidger.

The Kidger was an alcoholic who nightly slept with the snakes. A tall, emaciated creature, he was so bowed by his indulgences that he was bent in the middle like a fish-hook. A face as stony as a turbot's was the Kidger's. He drooled almost continuously, and his filthy coat, double-breasted and long-draped in a piteously slick spiv fashion, was streaked with the snail tracks of saliva. The Kidger was the pet and mascot of the street. He was so far gone down the path to physical and mental ruin that no one had the heart to refuse him a drink when he came begging for one; anything came well to the Kidger, plonk, plink, metho, bombo, or just ordinary whisky. He was never known to eat.

A protégé and employee of Delie Stock, the procuress, he received a small salary and a bed for doing nothing at all. It was commonly believed that Delie sent the Kidger out to cause a commotion when the Vice Squad was getting too close, and used his arrest as a distractive measure. But she liked him, and protected him, and whom Delie protected you did not offend, if you didn't want your ribs in splinters.

This was the creature that Dolour found, lolling over the counter at half-past six in the morning. He had plainly been on the booze all night, and a cheesy pallor was added to his dreadful face.

"Why'n't yer starp in the sharp?" he demanded, his bleared eyes not even distinguishing between Mrs Drummy's dumpling face and Dolour's thin sallow one.

"Boll milk!" he demanded. She handed him a bottle, and he tore off the foil cap with his teeth, tipped it up and flooded it in a white stream over his face and coat.

"Gah!" A stream of profanity spouted out of his gaping mouth and joined the milk. He dropped the bottle on the floor and reached for another.

"Go easy," protested Dolour, rescuing the other bottles, which teetered before his restless arm. He snatched another from her grip and stood with his hand over it, looking at her over the neck of the bottle he had in his mouth, like a dog defying all comers to take his food from him.

"That'll be elevenpence," said Dolour, taking the mop and dabbing at the pool of milk on the floor.

Now the Kidger was feeling happier. Something like a smile made an effort to alter the concrete grooves of his face, and failed. He began systematically on Dolour, giving her detailed, filthy information about herself, what had happened to her, and what was likely to happen.

In spite of all the drunken flip-flap she had heard from her father, she had never before witnessed the stirring up of such a pool of slime as this creature's mind. For a few moments she

107

pretended not to hear, not knowing whether to yell for Bert Drummy, or burst into tears, or what. The shock and horror of the Kidger's words had such an effect on her that it was years before she forgot them.

"That's elevenpence," she said weakly.

Now the Kidger saw that he was talking to a bit of a girl, and he was delighted. In her pale face and awed eyes he saw the good world he hated, the respectable world he despised. He came a little closer and said a lot more, the running commentary of the brothels during the drink-sodden, nightmarish nights.

All at once Dolour lifted the mop and charged. It was so swiftly done that she had thudded him in the solar plexus before she realized she had moved. Using it like a lance, she bore him out of the door. He slid in the pool of milk and landed on his back, whereupon Dolour, unconsciously using the technique of her ancestors, reversed the mop and stabbed him with the handle under the chin.

"Gulk!" said the Kidger. He rose upon hands and knees and scuttled down the footpath for home and Delie Stock, but Dolour pounced after him, cracked him across the skull with the handle, and shoved him violently into the gutter, where he lay on his back crying, his hands and legs up like the paws of a beaten dog.

Dolour was shaking with fury and distress. She went back into the shop and washed the mop conscientiously, then soaked up the milk on the floor without being at all aware of what she was doing.

The whimpering outside lasted for quite a long time, for the Kidger was hoping for someone to come along and listen to his story and be sympathetic. But everyone hastening along Plymouth Street on the way to work was in too much of a hurry even to look at him, and at last he crawled out of the banana skins and lolly-papers and filth, and wandered off, spouting such a ceaseless stream of disgusting obscenity about Dolour that it made even the citizens of that street wonder what had upset him like.

Dolour served the early morning customers for two hours—the young girls who had a threepenny ice-cream for breakfast, the drunken woman who choked her way through half a siphon of soda water, the man who, she was to learn, bought three boxes of headache powders every morning. In his way he was a dope addict, but his strings were tied to the unusual horses of anacin, phenacetin and caffeine. And there were the endless

108

cheerful, sooty-pawed children, who even at that hour were having penny glasses of the gaseous, sweet-syruped contents of the soft-drink bottles. Dolour did not wonder why it was that these children, improperly fed, never provided with nourishing school lunches, always had plenty of pennies to spend. She knew only too well the way of an overworked mother or surly father with a penny. It was one sure way of getting a kid out of the road.

She was feeling accustomed to it, even interested, when Harry Drummy came lurching into the shop, wiping grease off his mouth and slicking down his hair in the same motion. He leaned himself against the counter on the extreme tip of one elbow, which seemed to have a nodule on the end, as a pumpkin does. Harry Drummy, whom Dolour had once fleetingly loved in their schooldays, had grown into a large youth with a pear-shaped face upon which pimples struggled to get a foothold. His hands, his feet, his wrists and knees were a matter of ceaseless confusion to him. He felt like a small boy wearing a very large suit, and this suit was his all too solid, unpredictable, unmanageable body. His manner was a mixture of shyness and rudeness, and he tried to cover it up by adopting the veneer of a larrikin, as though to demonstrate to the world that he didn't give a deener for its regard. His hair, swept straight back, was marked with savage combing.

"Howya?"

He dived into the box of stale cakes and stuffed one after the other into his face as though he were posting letters.

"Hullo, Harry." Dolour was acutely conscious of the length of leg protruding from her overall.

"You've got lipstick on."

"So what?"

He peered at her critically, and hung out his tongue and licked a crumb off his chin.

"Wrong colour. Brunettes shouldn't wear that colour."

"Fat lot you know about it," said Dolour crossly.

"Sure I do. I'm a tiger with the tomatoes. Take yer glasses off and let's have a look at yer eyes."

"I certainly won't," said Dolour. "I gotta wear them all the time," she added lamely.

"Certainly make yer look a crumb."

He fished in the refrigerator, found a raw sausage, and ate it. Dolour marvelled how she had ever found him romantic. She watched fascinated while he stuck out his tongue and squeezed the greyish-pink sausage meat on to it in blobs from the ruptured skin. He held out the stump of the sausage.

"Have a bite?"

"Ah, you turn me up!"

"Like to go to the pitchers tonight? If you gotta coupla bob you can shout me," he offered casually. Dolour was thrilled in spite of herself. Nobody had ever asked her to go to the pictures except Charlie, and he was so old, and married, anyway.

But she answered carelessly, "Oh, I dunno. It hurts my eyes."

"You needn't look at the screen," he said helpfully. "We can just sit and cuddle."

"Get out!"

In such graceless conversation did they pass the time until Harry went off to work. Mrs Drummy popped in for a moment to see how things were going, commended Dolour on the orderliness of the shop, and went out to the kitchen to get the children off to school. There was an avalanche of kiddies in to spend their pennies before the bell rang, and Dolour nearly drowned under the cascades of orangeade and lime juice 'n soda.

Then, in the lull that followed, the Kidger returned, with Delie Stock. At the sight of them, Dolour's heart turned over like a fish and fluttered its fins. She had seen Delie Stock only from a distance, but she knew her reputation stone by stone. And it was quite clear that she had come down to the shop to avenge the beaten Kidger.

The Kidger had sobered up a little. He had changed his double-breasted coat for a pale yellow shirt, which had the collar turned up so that it flapped its sharply-starched wings on either side of his chin. His soulless face was completely consumed by a hyena-like triumph; he wanted to stand by and watch while his owner and mistress whaled the tar out of this upstart who had gone for him with a mop.

Delie came in as though she owned the place, looked contemptuously round as though this were the kind of dump where she'd expect to find a girl like Dolour. Dolour stood behind the counter trembling; she was frightened that if she opened her mouth Delie would give it a backhander.

"That's 'er!" said the Kidger helpfully.

"Shurrup," commanded Delie. She leaned her elbows on the counter and stared at Dolour. Dolour stared back, paralysed, overcome by the legend that surrounded this woman.

"Slugged me with a mop, she did, and all for nuthink," said

110

the Kidger with the meaningless ferocity of a wounded child. Delie Stock took no notice of him.

"Didjer?"

Dolour opened her mouth and a squeak came out. Hastily she tried again, and a weak, placatory little voice explained, "He swore at me."

Delie Stock had been taken aback by Dolour's presence in the shop. She had expected Mrs Drummy, who could always be bullied into tears and cajoled into smiles, a process that pleased the curious mind of Delie Stock, who liked to feel her authority and be commended for her humanity. She tossed back the mangy fur collar of her coat.

"Gawdelpus! You're old enough not to mind a bitta bad language! Chrisake, if you go round bashing up everyone who swears at you you'll spend yer life in the boob."

Delie sounded so reasonable, and the Kidger glared at her so unblinkingly that Dolour could not say a word. Her youth prevented her quick thinking; she stood there and blushed and gaped.

"Jabbed me in the belly, too," whined the Kidger, "and me liver's as tender as a boil on the neck."

"I don't care," blurted out Dolour. "He came in here and made a mess on the floor, and he took two bottles of milk and wouldn't pay for them. Then he called me everything he could think of." Her lips trembled. This was the limit of her defence, and she could think of nothing else.

Delie turned slowly and looked at the Kidger. "That's true, ain't it?"

"I was gonna pay," defended the man. "No one's got any business taking a broom to a customer, specially when he's a sick man."

"Gerrout," said Delie.

"Stuck-up little bitches think they're the only one on earth just because they're on the other side of a counter. Listen to the way she talks, stinking little bitch," he mumbled, staring off at a tangent over Dolour's shoulder.

"I said gerrout!" bawled Delie suddenly, and the Kidger hurriedly got, executing a pathetic stagger on the threshold as though to impress his implacable mistress with his frailty.

Delie slapped a shilling on the counter. "I'll pay his bill," she said, "and any time he comes in here giving up the breadth of his tongue you pop up to Little Ryan Street and let me know about it."

111

Dolour took the shilling silently. Delie prepared to be chatty. "Whassa matter? You look as pale as a sheet."

"I'm fine," said Dolour.

"What's the matter with yer eye? Got a pig-sty?"

"They've been bad," said Dolour. "I've been at the hospital lots of times."

A warm feeling came into Delie's heart. She knew that a few moments earlier she would have slipped this kid a fiver to pay the hospital bill, but, after all, it was only this morning that she'd passed out three quid to someone who'd snapped off an ankle like a stick of celery down the street. A woman had to be business-like. A glowing weakness overtook her limbs at the thought of her generosity, for with the passing years, Delie Stock had become more and more sentimental.

"That's crook," she said, nodding her head, and Dolour saw in the gesture the old woman who stood like a humped shadow behind Delie Stock, the old woman she was going to be. "I ain't too well meself these days. Dunno why."

"Fancy," said Dolour awkwardly, feeling that she was to be treated to the details of some loathsome occupational disease, but Mrs Stock only said, "I feel sorta all-over. Tired, kinda. Maybe I ought to take a holiday somewhere." She pressed a hand to her flabby, sequined green bosom. "Sorta heavy feeling in here."

"Maybe you work too hard," said Dolour mechanically, then burned scarlet. But Delie Stock did not notice anything.

She went on, heavily, "That Kidger, you don't want to take any notice of him. He's low. Even talks that way when I'm around sometimes."

"Gee," said Dolour.

"Ignorant. *You* know," said Delie, including Dolour in the ladylike circle to which she herself belonged. She looked querulously at the girl. "Why'n't you use a bit of rouge? You're terrible pale."

"I guess it's the light in here," said Dolour feebly.

"You wouldn't be so bad if you put on a bitta colour." Delie grew confidential. "You know what? You got a nice little figure coming up there."

Dolour did not know which way to look. She was terrified lest Delie Stock should offer her a job, for she had no idea how to refuse tactfully. But the woman did not. She touched her bosom again, tried to say something, and went heavily away, sinking down inside her dirty and neglected finery as though she were a bird in another's feathers.

There was silence in the shop. Dolour said shyly, "Hullo, what can I do for you?" though there was no one there. What the Kidger had said was true. She did speak differently. The harsh chirpiness of the Surry Hills girls, the raucous laughter, and the slurred, twanging vowels of that district's argot were absent in her voice. She wondered at it, not knowing that she had grown up with Grandma's purling Irish tones her criterion, nor realizing that ever since she had been at school she had been unconsciously imitating the speech of the sisters there.

She was pleased, but disturbed, for she was enough of a Surry Hills girl to dread comment on any form of personal superiority. Almost unconsciously she began to put away her manner of speaking, and to talk in the same lazy, ungrammatical way as the rest.

Meanwhile, at home Roie and Motty had gone up to the hospital for Roie's pre-natal check, and Mumma was dawdling through her housework. Mumma liked to think she was going through "the change", which she had actually passed through peacefully and without song five years before. Now and then she pampered herself, blaming every physical disturbance upon the mysterious upheaval that was supposed to be going on in her body, and thinking up a lot of new ones. It was an education to Roie and Dolour to hear her talking across the fence to old Mrs Campion, who, having abused and cruelly punished herself for over-fertility for a period of twenty-five years, was now suffering in real earnest.

"Twelve misses I had, love," Mrs Campion would say, "counting the one I had when the mister let fly with his boot when I was three months gone and him seeing snakes with God-knows-what. And now the doctors down at the hospital say I'm all in rags inside and operations wouldn't do a bit of good."

And Mumma would look at her with her innocent eyes and say, "It's downright cruel on a woman, that's what it is. Do you have flushes?"

"Flushes!" Mrs Campion would scream like a crow. "Why, dearie, I have pricklings!"

And Mumma would make a concussive sound with her tongue and retreat hurriedly inside, dying to ask more, but forbidden to do so by her chaste soul. She would ruminate, silently, in

113

her way, on pricklings and sure enough by the end of the week she had them even worse than Mrs Campion.

So this Monday she doddered about the house, sweeping here, and dabbing with a duster there, for Roie had already done the washing-up, and there wasn't much to do in that small crowded house where tidiness was not considered a virtue, anyway. She went out and looked at the step and sighed, for it had been done only yesterday, and now it was freckled all over with purple where Motty had been squashing a beetle. Mumma hated to bend, for bending brought on not only flushes and pricklings, but what Mrs Campion cryptically referred to as whirligigs.

"You see black specks floating round in front of you," she explained. "And when you straighten up again, yellow flashes and whirligigs in front of your eyes, something awful. But it's only to be expected, and I suppose a woman's lucky that it only lasts five years."

Mumma got the sandsoap and the floor-cloth, and cursorily wiped the step. She straightened up cautiously. The black specks were there all right, and she waited patiently for the yellow flashes, but they were apparently off plaguing someone else.

"Oh, well, they'll come in their own good time," murmured Mumma, "please God", for she was a little disappointed. Then she gave a squawk of horror for something worse than whirligigs was standing there—a strange, peculiar little man with a face like a Pekinese dog and so intense an expression that she almost expected him to burst into tears.

"You the missus?" he quavered, over the armful of brown paper parcels he held.

Mumma relaxed. "We really don't want nothing today," she said.

"Mr Darcy sent me," said the little man. "I'm Mr Reilly."

"Oh, yes," said Mumma civilly but uncertainly, for Hughie had mentioned sending no one.

"He said you'd show me the room," said Mr Reilly, his Adam's apple tremulously bobbing. Mumma gaped. Which room? Was he here to mend Roie's gas-ring? Or the roof in the kitchen? Or the leaking copper in the laundry? While she turned over the questions in her slow mind, wondering which one to ask first, Mr Reilly piped up, "The spare room he said I was to look at."

Mumma was completely bewildered. It was clear that Hughie

had said something to her about Mr Diamond's room that she had forgotten, but nothing came to her recollection.

"Well," she said doubtfully. "I suppose . . ."

She stood aside, and Mr Reilly flitted past on the sandshoes that had been so carefully whitened with window cleaner. The dark hall, haunted by cabbage and fish and onions, seemed to him beyond compare, and he looked eagerly at Mumma.

"Mr Darcy said it was upstairs."

"That's right."

Mumma eased her hips past him and stumped laboriously up the stairs. Half-way up she held on to the banister and tried to see whirligigs, but they were not for her. She turned, further questions about his business with the room already on her lips, but Mr Reilly was pressing behind her like a small excited dog, and in embarrassment Mumma hurried up and flung open the door of Pat Diamond's room. It had the forlorn air common to all empty rooms; its windows tufted with dirt, and the tenuous, delicate fabric of dust-strung cobwebs draping the corners of the roof. The old bed was there, dipping in the middle, its legs splayed out, and there was the picture of a racehorse tacked over the mantel by Patrick's own hand.

The smell of the place, its emptiness, and its dank airless coldness brought a lump to Mumma's throat, remembering the nightmare that had been here. She looked down at Mr Reilly.

"Well, this is it," she began dubiously. "Now, what—"

Mr Reilly darted past her into the room. He saw the gas-ring standing rusty and unused on its grease-stained table, the window that could be pushed open to air and sun, and the bed that was perhaps not so much more comfortable than his own little trestle with its legs in the jam tins for fear of bugs. But it was a bed with space about it, so that he would not be afraid to fling out his arms and legs without crashing into the wall.

Tears came into his weak old eyes. He fumbled for his glasses and hid behind them, then he looked at the woman peering and frowning at the door.

"It's lovely, missus," he said. "Lovely."

"I've done me best with it," agreed Mumma, mollified. She waited for a little while, but Mr Reilly did not seem to be going to say anything, so she prompted, "Now, what did you say Mr Darcy sent you along to see me for?"

Mr Reilly unloaded his parcels cautiously on the bed, as though they all contained rare and brittle china, then he straightened up, and a look of humility, joy, and disbelief that

115

could not be duplicated by anyone except a homeless, family-less man who had just found a comfortable room at a rent he can afford flamed all over his face.

"I'll take it right away, and I'll pay you the rent as soon as pension day comes round."

A dreadful procession of emotions moved over Mumma's face as she realized that in spite of her delight in her home with no strangers in it, Hughie had gone and let Pat Diamond's room under her very nose, and to this peculiar man who looked like a dog. He wasn't even clean, and for all she knew he would bring things into the furniture, to join the starveling bugs.

"Oh, no you don't," she blurted out. "This room isn't for rent. I dunno what that Hughie's thinking about. He made a mistake, that's what he's done."

Mr Reilly's Adam's apple disappeared beneath his collar. Tears trembled on the pink rims of his eyes.

"But Mr Darcy said——" he croaked.

"I don't care what he said," exploded Mumma, suddenly feeling pains in the back of her legs, and flushes and pricklings and whirligigs all at once. "He might wear the pants in this house, but he isn't going to let my rooms over me head. The nerve of him! Go on, get out of here this blessed minute."

"But I ain't had a home for years," wailed Mr Reilly. "Oh, missus, you don't know what it's like! And Mr Darcy said——"

Mumma hardened her heart. "Teach him a lesson, the straddy. Come on now, out of that!"

Sorrowfully, his head bent, Mr Reilly began gathering up the parcels. Mumma hovered for a moment, then stumped down the stairs. When she was half-way down there was a bang, and the staircase was blotted into darkness. Mumma felt herself go hot as fire all over, the very worst flush she had ever had.

She rushed up the stairs and hammered at the door. But Mr Reilly had shot the bolt. She could hear him breathing heavily.

"Oh, you fladdy-faced little tripehound!" roared Mumma, rattling the knob so loudly she could not even hear herself. "You did that very knacky, but I'm not the one you can put it over! Open this door! Oh, I'll knock the priest's share out of you when I see your face again. I'm going to get the police this minute!"

A little voice squawked, "I'm going to wait for Mr Darcy, that's all, and if he says I've got to get out, I will."

Mumma would have liked to take a running kick at the door, but the landing was too small. She stood and rattled and pleaded and roared for a long time, but not another sound did she hear. Then she stooped and put her eye to the keyhole. Judging from the darkness within, Mr Reilly was doing the same thing.

"Snoop!" said Mumma haughtily, and she lumbered downstairs, talking to herself and making all kinds of fantastic plans for luring Mr Reilly out of his fortress. First she thought she would let Mrs Campion in on the secret, and ask her advice, but at the fence she paused. Mrs Campion was such a gab-bag, and only the Dear knew what she would make of a strange man in Mumma's spare room. It almost seemed like evidence for a divorce.

So she went to the other fence and hooted for Lick Jimmy, but Lick was not back from the markets, where he had got into a dice game and lost all his oranges and bananas at one throw.

Mumma couldn't even enjoy a cup of tea.

"I'm bothered," she admitted, and sat down on a chair at the foot of the stairs like a fat old watchdog, waiting for Roie to come home.

After a little while she heard the creak of the gate, and Motty shrilling some incomprehensible song.

"Good heavens, Mumma," cried Roie, "what ever are you doing there?"

She looked waxen, and breathless, and her little feet bulged out of her shoes as though she had dropsy.

Mumma gasped out the story. "I'm that upset, Roie, and I haven't a stirring in me head what to do. Do you think we ought to get the police?"

"I dunno." Roie considered. "You know what people are like, seeing coppers come in here. Dad'll be home early, and anyway, this Mr Reilly can't steal anything or hurt the room even if he does stay there."

"But the look of him, Ro!" moaned Mumma. "He might be queer in the head, and come down and let us all have it with the axe."

So they cooked up a great plan. Roie went quietly up the steps and placed a chair in a strategic position just where the architect had made a slip with the pencil and caused a sort of kink in the straight flow of the steps. It was a mantrap for anyone sneaking down to give his landlady the axe.

"There'll be such a clatter we'll have plenty of time to run," she assured Mumma. Roie did not take it very seriously. She gave Motty her lunch without a qualm, while Mumma roamed up and down like a caged tiger, addressing Hughie as though he were present, and informing him that the dogs wouldn't pick his bones after her.

Suddenly Roie hushed the chatter of her daughter. "I heard something, Mumma."

There was a stealthy sound. Mumma's face went pale as a candle. Roie grabbed Motty. The next moment there was the sound of a crashing chair, the thud of a falling body, and an eldritch scream.

"We got him!" cried Roie jubilantly.

"Run, quick!" cried Mumma, but Roie bravely went into the passage, peering into the semi-darkness for the stricken form of Mr Reilly. She gave a shriek.

"I should think you oughta scream," remarked her sister severely, painfully unwinding herself from the newel post. "Of all the barmy tricks! You and Mumma ought to have your heads read." She came limping out into the light, rubbing her elbows.

Roie started to giggle. Dolour glared at her and Mumma, whose face was inscribed all over with guilt and consternation.

"You ought to be more careful," she snapped, heaving some of the blame on to Dolour's shoulders.

"How would I know that some bullet-headed calonkus would leave a chair on the stairs?" shouted Dolour. "Wonder me glasses weren't smashed."

All the nervous strain of the morning, of Delie Stock, and the Kidger, and a too-early breakfast, and the disappointment of not being able to sneak upstairs and privily try the rouge she had just bought, made her temper flare. But they took no notice of her at all, but poured out the story of Mr Reilly and the bailing-up in Mr Diamond's room. Dolour was delighted. She was all for going up straight away, climbing along from her window to his, and overpowering Mr Reilly by force.

"After all, he's only little," she said reasonably.

"No," said Mumma ominously. "We'll wait for your Dadda, and if there's anything left of him after I've finished with him, he can get rid of his friend Mr Reilly."

By the time Hughie arrived home he had forgotten entirely about Bumper Reilly, and when Mumma confronted him with the locked door and a torrent of accusing words, he felt quite sick. For once his wife had caught him at a loss. He stammered out an explanation of Mr Reilly's kindness, and the terrible situation at the flophouse.

"After all," expostulated Hughie pleadingly, "he's a clean old bludger, and you often said yourself that—"

"Clean is one thing he isn't," stated Mumma. "Sure you could grow enough potatoes to tide us over a strike in his ears."

"Well, what's ears?" exploded Hughie, losing his patience. "What are you doing gawking into his ears, anyhow? Hasn't a man got any privacy?"

He banged on the door. There was silence, and Hughie looked around to see the four pale faces of his womenfolk grouped at the bottom of the stairs.

"Hey, Bumper, you old cow," he bellowed. "It's me. What are you doing bailing us out like this?"

There was a muffled gasp from someone very near the door on the other side, and the lock clicked. Hughie pushed inside, and Mumma and Dolour began to inch cautiously up the stairs.

"Oh, Mr Darcy!" cried Bumper. He stood in the middle of the floor in the piteous condition of one who had been through terrible hours of nervous strain. "You did mean it, didn't you?"

"Well, I—" stammered Hughie, wishing to hell he'd never seen the man, let alone been bound by chains of gratitude.

"You didn't say she was yer wife, you just said the missus," babbled Mr Reilly. "How was I to know? She was going to throw me out into the street, and I already guv up me place at the flophouse and I got nowhere to go now."

"You took it pretty much for granted," growled Hughie.

Mr Reilly's throat moved convulsively. "I won't never make a noise. I swear I won't. You won't even know I'm in the place. I don't drink and I don't smoke. Everyone will tell you I allus pay my rent and don't never rampage around. And it's such a beaut room."

A little placated, Mumma snorted out of the dusky stairs. She and Roie and Dolour began a heated controversy.

"I don't see why he can't stay, poor old coot," began Dolour.

"But maybe he's one of those nasty old men who look through keyholes," protested Roie, who hated the idea of having a listening ear on both sides of her room.

"If he looks through mine I'll jab a knitting needle in his eye," promised Dolour heartily, taking no notice of Mr Reilly's audible gasp at this information.

119

"I'm not giving way to Hughie, I don't care what he says or promises," said Mumma sulkily.

Meanwhile Hughie was wondering what all the fuss was about. Mumma had been glad enough to receive a little extra money from Patrick Diamond, and what was the difference in this poor little dingbat except that Pat had been big enough to roll out into two of him?

He began to think pleasurably of a place of refuge where he could go when he had a few in and Mumma was being a bit obstropolous, somewhere where it was possible to shoot a bolt and have her safe and sound and steaming on the other side. He looked critically at Mr Reilly. There was nothing the matter with him that a scrubbing brush and soda couldn't fix.

"I knew that if I could only hang out until you came I'd be right," babbled Mr Reilly. "I knew you was the boss."

Tired as he was, and confused as he was, Hughie knew that his new lodger had hit the nail on the nob. Give way now, and there was no knowing what liberties Mumma would be taking. He had to make a stand, even if he didn't particularly like the ground. He winked at Mr Reilly.

"You can take yer coat off, boy."

He went downstairs and told them Mr Reilly was staying.

"If you was going to let it you could have picked someone nicer," said Roie. "There's Tonetta Siciliano looking for a place so she can get married, poor kid."

"She could have had it, and welcome. Better than that old ratbag," backed up Mumma.

Hughie looked defiantly at the pair of them, then bent his fierce blue gaze on Dolour. "Well, what you got to say for yourself?"

Dolour was sulky. The first excitement of Mr Reilly's advent over, she had remembered that he had stolen all her thunder. Her first day at the new job, and all the things that had happened, and nobody had even asked her how she had got on. A fat lot they cared if she had to beat off rotten old drunks with brooms. No one would even think they were her family. She hated them all.

"Oh, go to hell!" she blurted. She glared at the astonished faces and bounced out of the room.

"Now what's up with her?" wondered Roie wearily.

"She's growing up all within herself, and I can't say I like it," agreed Mumma. "Raving like a cat in the measles one minute, and on with the day-dreaming the next."

120

"Ah, yer makes me sick, every goddam one of yer, picking and poking, scroogin' and scrabblin'," growled Hughie. He stamped out to the lavatory, and after five minutes of futile wrenching at the door, remembered that his home was no longer his own. He had to go inside again and go through all the strain of preserving a stony silence while Mumma, tight-lipped and offended, got a cuppa tea ready.

12

So Mr Reilly became an inmate of that house. He was an irritating shadow whose ways took a lot of getting used to. Because he was terrified of meeting anyone and annoying them by his very presence, he was always peeping round the edge of his door, waiting for the strategic moment to streak down the stairs and into the yard or the street. This unnerved Mumma, and she began doing the same thing, sneaking round her kitchen door to make sure she would not catch Mr Bumper Reilly in the act of flying past.

Daily she placed the broom and dustpan at the foot of the stairs, and daily they disappeared as though pixies had swooped upon them, to be followed half an hour later by the slight clang of the garbage lid as the dirt was interred. It was like having a ghost in the house. Twice Charlie had reported seeing his face suspended on the darkness under the stairs, where he had retreated when he heard the younger man enter the house. And Dolour, who went off to work so early, had never seen him at all.

She began to develop a dreadful curiosity about Mr Reilly, and desperately thought up excuses for going across the landing and hammering on his door. But either he wasn't in, or he wouldn't answer it, for it never opened, though once, seven shillings and sixpence slid on a sheet of paper underneath it, as though to infer that her knockings could only be for the rent.

"But what does he do all day?" wondered Mumma.

"Rattles paper," answered Roie. "He makes noises like a rat in a paper bag all day and all night."

"Ah, it's the poor old cow's parcels," said Hughie comfortably. He had finished his tea and was sitting in his Jackie Howe, which is a singlet with the sleeves out of it, and called after a famous shearer of the blade days.

"Parcels? What of?"

"How would I know?" asked Hughie. "He had a lot the day he came here."

"And he's always got one under his arm when he comes into the house," added Roie.

Hughie frowned at her. "And what business is it of yours, always sticking your nose into other people's parcels?"

He shook out the paper, making a white wall between him and the family, which immediately went into an animated discussion on what the parcels might contain. Dolour thought he might be a dope-peddler, and briskly prophesied a police raid, and Mr Reilly getting hauled off to the pokey by the scruff of his little neck, a vision that gave Mumma such a fright that she sat quite silent and yellow for some time. In spite of her big talk about policemen, Mumma was dead scared of them.

Very slowly and solidly, like a blancmange setting, a conviction formed in her mind that she must find out the contents of Mr Reilly's parcels. Once the decision was made, she felt quite differently towards the old man. From a spirit-like creature who haunted unoccupied portions of the house, he became a man. He was a human creature who ironed his collars with a flat-iron disastrously heated over the gas-ring; a man who stayed an unconscionably long time in the lavatory; who was too timid to come and ask Charlie for a hammer when a nail came out of the wall and his coats fell down, but knocked it in with the heel of his shoe instead.

Like Dirty Dick, Mumma felt that God had made him to be put up with, so she adapted herself round his presence like an oyster round a pearl, though Mr Reilly was no pearl. In time she even thought how tough a go he must be having on his little allotment of weekly money, because he was obviously putting out a shilling a week in insurance for his funeral, in the decent, dignified way of the poor. So she went out and slapped down an enamel plate at the foot of the stairs, with such a loud emphatic bang that Mr Reilly couldn't help hearing. On the plate lay sheepishly some warm potatoes, a cold chop, a hard boiled egg, and a tomato that Mumma had thought twice about. She bellowed for Mr Reilly, and as she waddled back into the kitchen she heard the upstairs door open stealthily.

Within ten minutes there was a musical clang from the garbage tin, and Mumma hardly waited for Mr Reilly to skip back into shelter before she went out and investigated. She was confronted by the polished bone of the chop. Mumma felt that was satisfactory, and ever after that all the odd bits went to

Mr Reilly, silently, without even an overture of friendship. In this way Mumma salved Hughie's conscience about his rash promises.

The last weeks of Roie's pregnancy passed in a dream. The days were like a calm golden river flowing down to a heavenly sea. Such contentment filled her as she could not explain, nor did she want to. Sometimes she sat for an hour not thinking, not doing anything but breathe, a rich, wonderful delight welling inside her. Sometimes she would hold Motty and just stare at her, soaking her senses in the child's silken brown skin, the plum bloom of her lips, the warmth of her hair. At night she lay quietly in the curve of Charlie's arm, lost in a haze between sleeping and waking, so rich, so ripe a tranquillity emanating from her he could feel it like a perfume or a flavour.

"Asleep, Roie?"

"No."

"What are you thinking of?"

"I dunno. Us. Motty and you and me."

She was like a tree at the prime of its harvest, a creature that had withstood storms and the bare lonesome winters, that had flowered delicately, felicitously, and now stood drooping, laden, lost in a delicious dream that nothing could break.

He leaned over her, seeing the white triangle of her face on the pillow, the shadow of her eyes, and the glossy gleam of her eyeball. He traced the outline of her mouth with his own, feeling her lips relax and smile under his.

"What's the matter, darling?"

He wanted to tell her that he loved her, that he worshipped her, that she was his life-spring and his end and beginning, but he was dumb. The two races that met in him—all their powers of fiery and passionate articulation that had poured themselves out in place-names and chants and laments of unequalled beauty—were silent before this need to speak.

"You know, don't you, Ro?"

"I know you, that's why."

And so the days and nights went on, fluidly bearing her closer to the birth.

One night about a fortnight before her confinement was due, she was alone in the house except for Motty and Hughie, who had come home dead drunk and was snoring on the bed, still fully clothed, with a trickle of spittle down his chin, and his dirty shoes turned upright at right angles.

Mumma did not like going off to Benediction, for Charlie was working a late shift, and Dolour was helping Mrs Drummy to clean out the shop window, but Roie laughed away her fears.

"Don't you worry, Mumma. I won't put a fast one over you."

She liked the unaccustomed stillness of the house, the way the street noises seemed to vanish down a long corridor, till she felt that the old house had drifted out to sea and was rocking quietly there on the fathomless quiet. She sat for a while trying to brush her hair, for now she found it difficult to lift her arms above her head. Twice she toiled up the stairs and caught the bugs that had scuttled out in the darkness to feast on Motty's soft skin. And once she went in and looked at Hughie, wistfully hoping that he would wake and speak to her. His mouth was wide open, showing his teeth, and with every snore his cracked tobacco-stained lip fluttered like a leaf in the wind. Roie put a blanket over him so that he would not be chilled.

She went back to the kitchen, and suddenly she was paralysed by a piercing scream from Motty upstairs. It gave her so much of a shock that even the child in her womb leaped and shuddered.

"Motty! Motty, I'm coming! It's all right!"

She scrambled clumsily up the stairs where once she had bounded two at a time. The screams were ringing one after the other now, interspersed by a gabble of cries and sobs.

Roie burst open the door and flicked on the light. She saw Motty sitting up in her cot, blood on her cheek streaming down in a blackish map. Her eyes were screwed up tight, but she was beating with both fists at the thing that crouched on the blankets in front of her.

Roie dragged Motty out of the cot and retreated a step, but the rat merely scuttled to the end of the bedding and sat there, its teeth bared. It was as big as a kitten, an old, scarred warrior with one ear and a dozen shining cicatrices on its hide. Its eyes gleamed like garnets, and its teeth seemed all bunched together in the front of its mouth. It snarled with a kind of self-possessed ferocity that petrified Roie, as she stood with the howling Motty over her shoulder.

Suddenly it leaped out of the cot and flashed across to the door, but it had swung shut after Roie. It bounded against the panels, as though it knew the way to liberty, and the rattle of its filthy claws on the wood made the girl shudder. It slowly turned and looked at her with an almost human intelligence and defiance, then it darted into the old fireplace and squatted in the ash-pan.

125

Motty had stopped yelling, so Roie put her down on the bed and wiped away the blood. There was a ring of toothmarks on her cheekbone, but only one had penetrated the flesh. At the sight of the wound a deep, devouring fury seized Roie. She panted with rage. That this carrion prowler should bite her baby! She glared at the rat, and out of the duskiness its garnet eyes glared back.

If Motty had been younger, she might have died as other babies had died in that locality, awaking in the night with a feeble cry, and dying with the same cry, their throats torn into holes, their faces gnawed, and even the tiny bones of their fingers exposed through the nibbled flesh.

For all those babies Roie was enraged to a savagery unknown to her gentle nature. She slammed shut the window through which the rat had come. Then she went to the door, and, keeping her eyes all the time on the fireplace, screamed down the staircase to her father.

"Dadda! Dadda! You got to come!"

But Hughie was unconscious in his methylated sleep, and not even a whisper penetrated.

Roie shut the door. She cautioned the wide-eyed Motty to remain on the bed, and Motty, already recovered from her fright, sat there motionless, her bright eyes following her mother. Roie scrabbled in the corner, where there was an old walking-stick of Patrick Diamond's, kept as a sentimental souvenir by Mumma.

It was a heavy stick, with a broad, splayed rubber point.

She approached the fireplace, holding it like a hockey stick. She gave a sharp poke at the half-seen body of the rat, and the thing scampered out across the floor. It was a small room, and the rat ran along the wainscot, leaping up and falling back every few inches as though looking for an opening. But Roie knew it had come over the rooftops and through the window. She had it imprisoned. Quietly she followed it. It flew into the shadow of the bed and crouched against the wall. But there was a little opening between the bed and the wall, and Roie leaned across and looked down. The eyes shone up at her, like cigarette ends. She stabbed downwards with the stick, and the tip hit something soft. There was a squeal, and Roie made an inarticulate sound of triumph.

The rat pounced out now, between her feet, and Roie stumbled backwards and nearly fell. It whisked under the narrow base of the dresser, and she got down on her knees and slashed about with the stick, muttering to herself an unheard chant of, "I'll get you, you swine, you beast. You won't get away."

Once again there was a squeal, and the rat rushed out and began to dart round and round the room on an endless orbit, eluding Roie's frantic swipes with the stick, and tiring her to a standstill. She sat down on the bed, wiping the sweat from her face. Motty's face was bleeding again, and she wiped away the blood, saying to the child, "Lie down. Keep still. It'll be all right soon."

She waited till her breathing grew easier, then with a quiet, vicious determination she went after the rat again. She had hurt it. Tiny bubbles lay spattered on the floor, and the sight of that blood made her crazy to catch it and beat it into pulp.

The chase went on for twenty minutes more. Once she caught the rat glancingly with the point of the stick and threw it off-balance into a corner. She gave it a savage whack across the back, and it squealed piercingly, opening its mouth wide and vomiting dark blood. But it was alive as ever, and flickered into the fireplace and jumped agilely up against the flue, knocking down a cloud of soot.

She was sobbing with frustration and weariness now, scared that the beast would elude her and get away somewhere. She poked and slashed in the fireplace, and the rat crowded in a corner, snarling with a high whining sound. The stick thudded again and again on its body, but at such an awkward angle she could get no force to her blows.

Then suddenly, desperate, it flung itself out and in one almost invisible flash of movement, jumped at her and ran up her skirt on the underside. Roie felt its sharp claws clinging to her bare leg. She screamed and screamed, beating with the stick at the bulge under the cloth, nearly mad with terror and horror that swamped her like a wave.

"Dadda! Dadda!" she shrieked, and Motty joined in and shrieked too.

She thrashed with the stick. Sometimes the blows fell on the rat and sometimes on her leg, and all the time she felt the cold scaly body slithering and scrabbling for a foothold on her flesh. Then with a thump it fell to the floor and crawled a little way and faced her, squealing on a high-pitched note.

"Beast! Beast!" sobbed Roie.

The rat knew it was helpless and cornered. Its hindquarters dragged and it did not try to crawl away. It stood there, almost with its paws up begging for mercy. A dark ruby of blood quivered on the end of its nose.

Roie hit it once and it collapsed. She hit it again and again, until its pelt peeled away and a sharp white splinter of bone stuck out of its shoulder. Still she went on hitting it mechanically, till it was a red squashed mass in the middle of a thick pool. Then she stopped, trembling, realizing almost with shock that there was no need to hit any more.

She saw the fleas jumping off the body, like tiny black seeds struggling in the sticky blood.

Then she stumbled to the bed and lay down beside Motty, shaking so much that her teeth chattered. Motty crooned to her, patting her cheek with her soft, suede-like hand, marking with her fingers the streams of sweat that ran down her mother's face. So they were when Charlie came home.

"I got angry," was all Roie could say. "I shouldn't of. It bit Motty, and I got angry."

Charlie put them both into bed. He sponged the wound on Motty's cheek with iodine, and cleaned up the floor. He brought up a hot drink for Roie, but she was already asleep, her face fallen into the bluish hollows of exhaustion.

He stood for a while looking round the poor room, the worn oilcloth, the walls rippled with the tide-marks of old rains, the furniture whose every crack was infested with the black crawling cities of the ineradicable bugs. He looked at his child, only one of the hundreds of children maimed or marked with rats, those scavengers whose very presence in a modern city was an affront and a disgrace. He knew now that they must get out of it, no matter the obstacles, no matter the circumstances, they would have to get out of this to some place where the air was clean and the houses fit for human living.

He threw open the window, and there was the scrabble of claws on the iron roof, and the flashing of shadows over the high brick wall. They were waiting out there, as the other had waited, for darkness and silence. Charlie shut the window and fastened the catch so that no one could open it till he could nail some fine wire-netting over the entire window space.

"As soon as the baby's born we'll go," he promised Roie, who lay sunken in sleep as in a stupor.

Then suddenly he remembered the man who had slept through it all, the father who had not heard his daughter's screams when she needed him most. He ran down the stairs and into the bedroom, seizing Hughie by the shoulder and dragging him upright.

"Open your eyes! Open your eyes!" shouted Charlie, shaking him till his head wobbled back on his shoulders.

"Wasadoing?" mumbled Hughie. His eyes rolled open, laggardly, so that the whites showed. There was blank incomprehension on his face, and a breath as though from the mouth of hell came from his lips. "Wasadoing, boy?"

Charlie dropped him back on the bed. He left his eyes half open, but he took up the rhythm of his snoring almost where he had left it off.

The younger man unclenched his fists almost by force. He stood for a little while staring down at Hughie's face, feeling sick and ashamed for what he had been going to do. He went outside and walked up and down in the cramped dark square of yard, trying to recover his self-respect.

Roie went to the hospital the next morning. She woke feeling heavy and unwell, and it was not long before she felt the old familiar pain, a little ripple, the gentle opening of a door. It made her happy, and she began to smile as she dressed, showing Charlie and Mumma the bruises on her leg where she had hit at the rat.

"I won't go to work," said Charlie. But Roie laughed.

"I'll be all right. Don't forget, I've had practice."

And Mumma, too, shooed him off, fussy and important in her anxiety, and assuring him that if three women couldn't attend to getting the girl into hospital, then the world wasn't worth a mallamadee.

She bustled off downstairs, her lips already forming the syllables of prayers to the Blessed Mother, for this was plainly women's work. Roie put her arms round her husband, feeling that it was for her to comfort him now.

"It's not like having the first one, Charlie. I know what happens, now."

Charlie had never thought of the black abysmal terror of the young girl in parturition, to whom every normal phase of birth is a shock and a catastrophe. She put her soft cheek against his chin.

"I love you, Charlie."

"Not more than I love you."

"Wait," she said. "There's another pain coming, a big one."

He held her in silence, seeing the blood flee from her cheeks and the blue appear under her eyes as though by magic. He felt the ripple in her body, and the answering shudder in the child. It was the closest he had ever felt to her; the nearest approach he could make to the mystery proceeding within her.

"Good-bye, Charlie."

He worked all the morning through, against the shuttling clatter of the flatbed, where the shiny sheets flopped out with hypnotic regularity.

"Any phone calls for me?"

"Nope."

The hours went on, flat-footed hours that came in wearily and trudged out bowed and laden with his anxiety.

"Any rings for me?"

"Nope."

It was nearly twelve when he looked up suddenly and saw Dolour, bewildered and flustered by the machines, threading her way towards him. He searched her face for news. She mouthed something, but he couldn't hear. He thrust his face at her.

"What's the matter? What's up?"

She looked at him dumbly, and he took her by the sleeve and led her to the door.

"She isn't too good, Charlie. The baby isn't going to be born for a long while."

"I'd better come?"

"Yes."

Outside her lips began to tremble, and she gasped, "I mustn't cry here, I mustn't cry here", pushing up her glasses and pressing her fingers against her eyes. He put his arm over her shoulders.

"Don't you worry, Dolour. Nothing's going to happen."

"It's all right for you," she croaked. "She isn't your sister."

He looked at her with such pain that she was silent, and so they went to the hospital.

Mumma was there in the waiting-room, sunken into a queer shapeless heap like a clay statue that has been out in the rain. The beads slipped through her cold fingers, but the prayers she murmured were unheard by her own ears. So they waited.

The sounds of the big hospital went on around them, the soft trundle of trolley wheels in the corridor, a muffled laugh, the rubbered tread of nurses, the clinking of cups and bottles.

Sometimes they talked, reassuring each other of the excellence of the hospital, and how even the big specialists sent their private patients here if they foresaw any trouble.

But mostly they were silent, lost in a deathly quiet that seemed to retard the dragging feet of the passing moments.

At five Hughie came in, wild-eyed, dirty and tousled. He said in a hoarse whisper, "What's wrong? I read the note you left. What's wrong?"

"They're operating on her," said Mumma. "She's got a good chance."

At the words Dolour gave a loud snort of agony. She threw herself down beside Mumma and hid her face on her mother's knees. Mumma stroked her hair mechanically, and unheedingly.

A sister came into the room, and they stared at her with dilated eyes, as rabbits at the approaching rabbiter.

"The child's alive," she said. "It's a fine healthy little boy."

"Michael," whispered Mumma.

Charlie was on his feet. "What about my wife?"

The sister had a gentle face. She had seen so much trouble and pain, and it had given her a tranquil strength that could be communicated to others. She put her hand on his arm.

"I think you should all go home. Your wife is still under the anaesthetic, and it may be some hours before we can give you any good news. Go home and have something to eat."

Dumbly they went.

What happened that night and the next morning? Speaking about it in after years they could never remember what they had done. Gone to the church, yes . . . and Mumma had cooked something, and they had tried to eat it . . . and they had sat round for a while, talking about other things. Somehow the interminable hours had slipped away, somehow. Now and then Charlie had gone out and rung up on the street phone, with all the gossips leaning over their gates and clucking sympathetically.

"No change?"

"No."

Mumma got Motty from Mrs Campion, who had had the child all day, and washed some of the dirt off her. The child suddenly took on a great significance, and they all stared at her as though they had never seen her before.

"Mummy coming home soon?"

"Yes, and she's got a present for you, a little brother."

So they talked, and hid their frightened faces, and tried to be ordinary, so as not to upset each other.

"She was so happy this morning."

"When she comes home she ought to have a holiday."

Mumma seized on this eagerly. "Yes, you can put the baby on a bottle, and I'll look after it, and you and Ro can go to the beach like you did for your honeymoon. It did her so much good last time."

Then, all at once, they were back at the hospital, and Father Cooley was there in his surplice, with the purple stole over his shoulders. As he came out of the room they looked piteously at him. Hughie's face was pulled into long vertical lines like a bloodhound's, and his hair stuck up stiff as a brush, it was so long since he had taken a comb to it.

"Did she speak to you, Father?"

"She's still unconscious."

"Couldn't she make her confession?" stammered Mumma.

"She ain't never done anything wrong," growled Hughie, turning his face away.

During this time Charlie and Dolour said nothing, standing and staring at the priest as though he were a stranger.

A nurse came out of the room. "We're ready now, Father."

"We shoulda brought Motty," said Mumma.

"It doesn't matter," said Charlie. They went into the little room with its shrouded lights, the spindle-legged high bed, the strange sharp smell of anaesthetic, and the wax candles seeded with flame. It was a nightmare in which not one, but all of them participated. Who else was there? A doctor perhaps, two nurses, but they saw no one but Roie lost in the whiteness of the bed.

They had washed away the sweat of her long agony, and brushed the hair she had torn and tangled. They had taken away the bloodstained clothes and her depleted empty body was wrapped in a clean white nightdress. Her hands lay upon the counterpane, quiet and at rest. It was hard to tell that they had writhed and beaten and scratched the skin from each other only the day before.

She was a stranger to them all, already withdrawing into the mystery they could not comprehend.

Clumsily they knelt around, while the priest, old, fat, often rash and reckless in his judgments—the clumsy old exile from a land he had almost forgotten save as a legend—cast off his earthly traits and significances and became the bearer of God and God's mercy.

"She coulda been saved," burst out Hughie in his anguish. "Rotten dirty doctors—"

"Sssh!"

Roie did not know anyone was in the room, yet she was acutely sensible of the feelings in her hands and feet. She felt the cool smoothness of the oil on the feet that had walked in foolish and evil places, and on the hands that had been careless and impatient so often. Now it was on her eyelids, and she struggled to raise them and see. But there was no battle left in her. Her spirit, finding those doorways closed, turned away and went to the portals of the ears. But the oil was there, too, the gentle seal of the oil against the sounds of the world.

She lay within herself, in a silence so dark and deep she wondered at it.

Yet sharp and clear she saw once again the things her memory had kept in its subtle archives—a wagon-load of cherries, a dog run over, the smiling face of Lick Jimmy, the chattering machines at the box factory where she had once worked. And she saw, too, the pale young face, and dark eyes of Tommy Mendel, whom she had loved, long ago, and felt again the bitter sorrow and guilt of the loss of his child.

The old days came crowding up around her, insubstantial, and yet part of the fabric that was fraying and tattering as the seconds ticked past. Not one person stood out above another, not Charlie, or her mother, or her children. They were all part of her life, which was unravelling like a ragged banner, and blowing out on some incomprehensible wind.

Suddenly, like a trumpet's sharp blow on the ear-drum, realization came to her. She was dying. It was no dream, no imagining. She was leaving the pattern of her life, the common pattern already experienced by a million, million women, and Charlie would have no part in what she was, any more.

She screamed, "Charlie! Charlie!" but her husband, his face upon her hand, heard it only as a whisper.

A great agony of grief and yearning seized her, a terrible longing for him, his hands, his eyes, the touch of his mouth and warmth of his body. She was part of him, and he of her, and the pain of this last and most terrible amputation seized her in its grip and burst with her through the dissolving dark.

13

IT was hard to remember afterwards. They had stared dumbly at the doctor as he explained what had happened. But what were technicalities to them, caught unstruggling in the simplicity of death like a fly in syrup? With throats aching and eyes burning they looked at all these strangers who were trying to be helpful and kind, and when they said anything at all it was disjointed driftwood from the confused stream of their private thoughts.

"It was only yesterday she said good-bye to me."

"Twenty-four ain't old enough."

"It isn't fair! It isn't fair!"

Hughie sat with his face as red as a beet, his eyes jammed shut and his lips pursed out to stop them trembling, saying nothing; but in his heart he was yelling, "Oh, God, it's me that ought to be dead instead of my little girl. Maybe it was that fright she got, and me lying down there stewed as a pig and not lifting a finger to help her. Oh, God, I wish I was drunk. I wish I was drunk."

It was dusk when they left the hospital, and on all their lips was the taste of Roie's, smooth and cool and waxy. They peered bewilderedly into the blue dimness where the scanty constellation of lamps already glimmered. Dolour pressed close to her mother like a dog, or a little child. She had made no sound, but she was breathing quickly and loudly.

"Maybe we ought to get a taxi, Hughie."

He looked round despairingly. "I dunno."

They waited for a long while, but no taxis stopped, so they set off walking down the windy hollow street. After a little time Dolour stopped, and shaking, clung to a fence.

"I can't go no farther." She broke into violent sobbing.

"We can't go giving in to it, lovie," said Mumma in a voice so strained it did not seem like her own. But in their bewilderment, their astonishment and defencelessness, there seemed nothing else to be done.

Suddenly Charlie said, "I'll be home later. I want—I'll be home later."

Without waiting for a reply he strode off along Murphy Street. He did not feel himself moving. Rather, the street flowed past him, the lemon-yellow windows, the shadow-striped balconies, the cats that whisked over the broken-toothed fences. He felt the pavement under his feet, the cold air on his cheek, and that was all.

Soon he was in Oxford Street, blinking at the flood of light. For a long time he stood aimlessly watching the trams crawling like beetles up the hill and rattling away around the corner. The crowds milled about him, and somewhere a newsboy droned like a bee.

He could not stand there for ever, so when a tram came along he swung aboard, hunching like an old man in a corner of the great, clumsy, open-sided thing. Time meant nothing to him. Staring out the doorway, with the light and the dark rushing past alternately—here a pedestrian's pale face, there a half-lit balcony, a palm-tree, a running dog, a man pushing a barrow—he was aware of nothing.

Soon the city was left behind, and the harsh smell of the sea washed into the tram like a tide. Awaking like a man from sleep he saw patches of sandhills, creamy in the dark, and low scrub that clothed the land like sparse fuzzy hair. He stared at this for a long time, and then, all at once on the right there reared up cubical and monstrous, like blocks of darkness, the smokestacks of Bunnerong. They were the chimneys that empowered Sydney with light and energy, built away out here on the coast because of their dowry of ash and smoke. They seemed to him ominous and sinister, and he turned to the sole remaining occupant of the compartment and asked, "Where's this?"

"La Perouse, boy."

He recognized with astonishment that the man was coloured, and remembered then that La Perouse was the aboriginal settlement that clung, ignored and forgotten, to the proud hems of Sydney. In the shabby little houses there was light, and sometimes the sound of a radio, or the bell-like laughter of a half-caste girl. He stood and listened to the intermittent hum of living behind those walls, then he went up on the hill and down to the low sandstone shores of Botany Bay. It was almost dark there, and the sea below but a breathlessness in the darkness. It tossed out its edges, scroll after scroll that unfolded across the terraces of rock and tinkled away down the crevices in irregular music.

And there were stars, too, a vast white webbing just without the eye's range, as though the Milky Way had overflowed its boundaries and flooded to the horizon.

Charlie stood there and looked at nothing at all. He was acutely conscious of the structure of his body, of the bones mounted and subtly balanced one upon the other, of the latchings of the foundations of his skull. As though he had never heard it before he heard the tremendous shaking of his heart. Thus he waited, like a man who has received a stupefying blow, and is waiting for the reawakening nerves to shout the pain to his mind.

"Roie," he said, questioningly, stiff-tongued, and as though that were the signal, the pain that hung about him converged, dropped, and drowned him in a terrible grief that flung him to the ground, with the whole weight of the world pressing upon his back and shoulders.

In that moment his life was completely ended. The centre of his world had gone, and life itself become illogical. His very existence was a contradiction and betrayal of the death in his heart.

So he lay, motionless, while the dew settled imperceptibly on his clothing and dripped down his hair.

The impossibility of what had happened made him feel that perhaps he had gone crazy, that he was imagining it all, that any moment he would wake and find Roie beside him, laughing at him.

And then, remembering her like that, the pain grew worse until he thought that he would go mad, with the knowledge of his empty room, his empty bed, the realization that all was for ever wasted; her body that had comforted him, her breasts that had fed his child, her womb that had been the doorway of his physical immortality; her voice and smile, and little yearnings and contentments, everything that she had been, all gone, lost for ever, dwindling away to its component atoms. . . .

"Roie! Roie!"

Surely she must speak to him, whom she had loved most of all. He looked into the sky, into the windy wastes of stars that would be so alien and frightening to a girl who had spent her life in little crowded streets and rooms where there was not space to turn round. Where would she go, where could she go, in those vast meadows of darkness where a million, million years stretched between one beacon and the next?

"Why didn't You take me, too, so I could look after her?"

She had never been anywhere by herself since he had married her, and now she was alone.

Then he thought with joy of death, and in a false and unreasonable eagerness jumped up and ran to the low cliff-edge, stumbling over the grass clumps, whispering that he had not thought of this before. He began to scramble down the rocks towards the soft sibilance of the water, then, as though a hand had arrested him, he stopped. Somewhere across the wasteland from one of the little houses there sounded the wail of a child, and almost with shock Charlie remembered Motty, and the boy, the new-born.

It would not matter. They were so young, and Mumma would look after them as long as she was alive.

But the moment of piteous exhilaration was gone. He knew he could not kill himself, not only because he had children to hold him back, but because his own life, though his spirit had suffered so mortally, was mysteriously left to him.

He would have to live, no matter what it cost him.

He climbed back to the top of the cliff and sat there, bowed, drenched with dew, throughout the night, lost and dazed, unable to think, to plan, to do anything but suffer.

The stars were swallowed up, and like the great hoop the Milky Way swung over beneath the water. The light, the world's first, crept up the sky, leaped the ragged islands of New Zealand, and saw that the Australian coastline reared like a wall. It lapped it, besieged it cliff and bay, and drew it upon the dusky sea like a monstrous golden boomerang.

Charlie saw an old man coming over the grass towards him, leading a goat. The man was an old aboriginal, bent at the knees and the elbows into a comfortable workaday shape, and the goat was a fleecy nanny with striped, insolent eyes.

"You up early this morning, boy," he greeted. "Bin fishing?"

Charlie shook his head, unable to trust himself to speak, wishing that the old fellow with his pleasant squatty nose and his deepset bloodshot eyes would go away. He looked down and saw that his clothes were soaked and dank, covered in grass-seeds. Even his shoes had been scribbled across by the gossamer trails of snails that had crawled over him, mistaking his stillness.

"You look bad, son. Bin on the booze?"

"Yeah."

It seemed the easiest way out of it.

"You like to come over to my camp for a cup of tea and a wash-up? Boy, you look a mess all right."

Charlie went with the old man to a little humpy built beside the road. On a bench outside were rows of carved boomerangs and peculiar little shoes and trinket boxes made of shells, for sale to tourists. The old man and the goat went inside, and the goat made itself comfortable beside the fire, staring all the time at the stranger with its inimical eyes.

"Sit down there. You shibbering."

Charlie sat down docilely. The hot tea, sticky with goat's milk and brown sugar, made him feel a little better. He washed his face in the tin dish, outside the door on a box, and turned to the curved sliver of mirror propped up on the ledge.

"I got a comb somewhere, too. Boy, you bin on a bender all right."

The old man's face was full of kind brotherliness. He was delighted to have someone to talk to so early in the morning. He walked round Charlie, brushing at him with the flat of his hand, and clucking anxiously. He did not treat the young man as a stranger at all.

Looking in the glass, Charlie knew why. In the night age had crept upon him, sharpening his bones, stretching the flesh into haggard pits and furrows. Bloodshot and sunken, his eyes looked out of sallow hollows. His great-grandmother had been black, but looking at him now one would have said he was a half-caste, come to the right place at La Perouse.

In the brilliant, blinding light of that new day, he knew with pitiless reason that he would have to go on. There was no dodging anything, not the loneliness, or the pain, or the frequent agony of the long solitary nights, or the responsibility of his children.

Nothing could be avoided except by death. Though Roie was gone he would have to live.

He thanked the old man for his tin dish, and his hot tea, and the comb with the gapped teeth.

"You come back again some time. Me and you go fishing," promised his host in his soft, sibilant voice. "You just ask for Angus McIntosh."

"Yes, I will," said Charlie.

14

A WEEK after Roie's burial Dolour lifted her head from the pillow and knew she would cry no more tears. She was emptied of emotion. A vast coldness spread outwards from her heart until even her flesh seemed chill. She said, "I'm going back to work, Mumma."

"I wish you didn't hafta, darling," said Mumma painfully. "But I'm that short with Hughie off work and everything."

The scalding tears gushed out again, and she quickly turned away to the sink, her swollen red hands trembling amidst the grimy suds.

"Oh, Lord," she prayed, "don't let me give into it. It'll get better some day, just like it did when Thady disappeared, and Ma died. I got to keep me end up so I can look after the baby when it comes home."

So she struggled through the days, waiting for the healing that was so long in coming. There was little help from the others. Hughie, after his first fierce grief, had been continually drunk, and yet in his drunkenness there was no surcease from pain. He sat at the table with the tall bottle before him and his head in his hands, and now and then his blurred babbling ceased and he ran into the bedroom, rooting frantically amongst the old clothes that were jammed into boxes and suitcases under the bed until he found something of Roie's—almost anything. Once a stubbed shoe, another time a grubby powder puff or a bit of blue ribbon with a tarnished medal on the end of it. The sight of these things seemed to drive him into madness. He would weep and whimper over them, his head on the table, and his gnarled hands knuckling into the wood in his agony.

"Roie! Roie! Tell me it's all a dream!" he would cry, grasping at Charlie's shirt as he passed. "Tell me I made it all up meself!" And he would in his stupor pretend that Roie was coming through the door, stumbling to meet her and clasping the empty air, until Charlie's throat ached as though it were constricted with iron bands.

And at other times Hughie would follow Motty round, as she went her way, heedless as a bird of the suffering that surrounded her, for in a few days she had accepted the story that her mother had gone to heaven and would come and get Motty some day soon.

"It ain't no good, Hugh," said Mumma pitifully, her heart aching for him even more than for herself. "Nothing's going to bring the darling back again. We got to go on living without her, that's all."

And she looked pleadingly at him, longing for the comfort and sympathy that he had never given her, and which she was now denied again.

Hughie's face crumpled like a child's, and he cursed Mumma for putting into words the inescapable truth. He made a sweep at the table and knocked over the bottle, jumping on the fragments and smashing them into topaz gravel. Then he crawled into his bed and slept the sleep of the emotionally exhausted, his face sunken into the grooves and pits of an old, old man's.

The hospital had kept the baby for a month, the other women giving their plentiful milk with sympathy and generosity to the motherless child. Mumma went up often and looked through the glass at the smudgy red face, fast asleep with lids folded like poppy petals, or wide awake and yelling.

"Come with me, son," she pleaded with Charlie. "You can't blame the baby for it."

"I don't blame it," was all Charlie answered, but he would not go with her.

Mumma knew everything about babies, but nothing according to the clinic. Dutifully she listened to the sister's advice, and painstakingly laboured through the booklet of directions given to her. But to Mumma directions were only for bottles of medicine and tins of condensed milk. You couldn't bring up a little live baby that way. Mumma knew that what babies need most of all is love, and this she was prepared to give for twenty-four hours of the day. In addition she brought out of her memories of her own childhood the story of the bit of a black goat that had supervised the weaning of herself and her ten brothers and sisters.

"A nice old nanny she was," said Mumma, "and we kept her at the bottom of the yard. I remember her coat, just like a dog's, short and shiny. And a raggy scrap of a tail, and little sharp feet. And talk about milk! She didn't cost anything to keep, either; she just ate all the rubbidge."

"Wouldn't be possible to keep her in our little yard," said Hugh. Mumma fired up at once.

"I don't see why anyone has to know about it," she cried. "Only Lick Jimmy, and Mrs Campion on the other side, and they wouldn't let a yip outa them when they knew the milk was for the baby."

So they asked Lick, and Mrs Campion. Lick, who had been brought up with a water-buffalo putting its shaggy head over the mud threshold of his long-ago provincial home, thought nothing of a goat in a Surry Hills backyard. "I give you all sclapee," he promised, and Mumma, with delighted thoughts of the richness of milk from a goat fed exclusively on specked fruit, nearly cried.

As for Mrs Campion, she said heartily that no bloody health inspector would hear from her, and beside, the smell of goat would sorta clean up the smell of tomcat.

So it was that Anny came to live with the Darcys. She had belonged to a mate of Hughie's who lived up the north line where there was more room. She was young, glossy-pelted, in milk to her first kid, and her neat sharp hoofs clattered contemptuously on the cobbles of the yard. She looked round in amazement, chewing rapidly all the while, so that Hughie said, "Gawd, don't she remind yer of Grandma!"

Anny looked the yard over thoroughly, bent a cold yellow eye on Motty, who had wandered delightedly to interview her, then stood on her hind legs and began stripping the dead fans off the phoenix palm.

"There!" sighed Mumma in relief. "She's taken to us."

Anny took to them with her whole heart. She ate their washing, chewed up the picture books Motty left about, and walked into the kitchen whenever she felt like it. Because the little yard was no place for a healthy animal, she soon began to smell, and she filled the whole rear of the place with an elusive odour, which clung to Mumma until even Mrs Siciliano, who could not live without garlic, twitched a nostril when she came near.

"He'll have good bones," thought Mumma to herself, "and lovely little teeth, like Thady had."

Real excitement possessed her when she thought of the child. It was like having one of her own again. She looked at

141

F

Charlie, and the old jealousy raised itself. Fiercely she resolved that the baby should grow up loving her better than its father.

"Because he won't pull himself together," she argued self-defensively. "A whole month gone, and still you can hardly get a word out of him. And he's that stubborn about Motty."

For Mumma had wanted to re-arrange the house, putting herself and the two children in the upstairs room, and Charlie downstairs with Hughie. A curious streak of unreasonable cruelty in her gentle nature argued that she had put up long enough with broken sleep from Hughie's drunken rip-roarings, and since she was taking the responsibility of the children from Charlie's shoulders, he ought to pay for it some way. But Mumma did not know she felt like this.

She said, "You can't work all day at your job and then come home and be up with the little one when he's got wind, or teething, Charlie."

"I can look after him," said Charlie. The anguish of his confused and jangled feelings made him long to lash out and shut up this old, interfering, and yet eagerly kind woman. But he forced himself to speak quietly.

"He'll need a bottle at two in the morning," cried Mumma desperately and untruly.

"I'll wake up all right," said Charlie.

Suddenly Mumma exploded. "Oh, it's all right for you, thinking it's so easy!" And she voiced what had been troubling her for so long. "You'd sleep all night and let the little thing howl himself sick, you're that cold and unfeeling."

Charlie said nothing.

"Your wife dead for a month, and I ain't yet heard you say her name," blazed Mumma. "What's it matter to you, with your heart like a lump of concrete and your face all shut up so that a body's got no idea of what you're thinking?"

Dolour came in from the laundry where she had been painting the old tin bath for the baby's use. "Mumma, what's the matter with you?"

She put her arm round Charlie's shoulders, looking accusingly at her mother.

"How do you know what Charlie feels? I suppose you think a person has to go round behaving like Dadda before he feels anything. You ought to be ashamed of yourself, Mumma."

Mumma looked at her daughter aghast. In every family quarrel, Dolour had been on her side.

"It's all right, Dolour," said Charlie. She saw his face was thinner now, his skin so sallow it made his eyes look yellow. Any good looks he had had were gone. He looked sick.

Dolour had never thought of Charlie as a young man, or even as a man. She had been jealous because Roie loved him more than she loved her sister; she had disliked him because he was impossible to aggravate or provoke; now, for the first time she became aware that the flesh under his shirt was warm, that she could feel it burning against her bare arm.

He was young, not ten years older than herself. He had been kind and good to her many, many times, and she had been ungracious and ungenerous in her reception of his kindness. She had taken it for granted, as they all did, that Charlie would cope with any domestic crises, that he would hump Hughie into bed when he was drunk, fix the laundry tap, sole and heel their worn shoes. She could hardly remember what it had been like before he had come to live with them.

Before the startled look on the girl's unprevaricant face, Mumma was puzzled and angry. But the moment for accusation had gone, and she said humbly, "I'm sorry I didn't put a tooth on it, Charlie. You were a good husband to Roie, and I'd be the first to have a piece of anyone who said you weren't. It's just that I'm all on edge."

"Yeah," said Charlie. He went upstairs and sat on the narrow bed with his head on his hands. It was as bad as ever. He was like a man with an incurable illness. Now, after all these weeks, the pain was so severe that he could not bear to be alone. Like Mumma he knew that one day he would feel differently, that he would live and enjoy life once more, but he thrust that thought away, feeling it disloyal to his wife.

Motty came up to him. She thrust her head between his hands and looked at him unwinkingly.

"You got a headache, you poor man?"

With a groan he buried his face in her soft neck. "I got an awful headache, Motty."

It was impossible to sit still. He put on his coat and went downstairs. Mumma was astounded.

"You're not going out, Charlie? Not when the baby's coming home this afternoon?"

"I'll be back in time."

It was a compulsion with him to live in his memory, a fierce unavailing attempt to make Roie alive once more, if it were only in mirage. He stood on the Quay, looking at the oily water. Here they had stood together waiting for the Manly ferry.

143

The ferry swished in, and he went aboard, into the sun-dappled saloon, looking for the seat where he and Roie had sat that day they went on their honeymoon. He sat there alone, closing his eyes, trying to feel the warmth of the little blue-clad figure with the bead waterlily on her bodice.

"Roie, can't you speak to me, darling? Just a word, just a word to say you're all right. My sweetheart, my darling! Where are you?"

The ferry musicians came sawing and squawking past, and he fled from the thoughts their blithe disharmonies brought him, lapsing into dullness and mental silence. What was the use of it all?

He had not been to Narrabeen since Roie and he honeymooned there. Four years ago, and he had not taken her anywhere much. Narrabeen had not changed. A solitary figure, he wandered along the empty miles of sand, unmarked by any footprints except the tiny triangular ones of the seagulls who, scarlet-legged, frosty-winged, yelped in anger at this intruder. Now the tide was coming in. The long clear sheets of water, curling at the edges, slid swiftly and silently over the smooth sand, and from afar out beyond the breakers came the sonorous bass of the swelling tide, a prolonged note on a vast organ.

Here they had pelted into the water. Here Roie had screamed and pranced like the child she was. He suddenly wanted to see that little pink house where they had lived for that enchanted fortnight, and he clambered up the dunes, over the rippled sand where every ripple cast a black wave of shadow.

The house looked shabby now. The stucco was faded and stained with mildew, and the garden wild and rank. Even the shell borders of the little path had disappeared. The whole charm and delight of the place had vanished.

He turned away, confused and despondent, and saw in the hollow of the dunes below two lovers lying, still as statues, the dark head pressed against the fair, half-asleep in the pool of shadow. As he looked, the girl opened her eyes, and saw Charlie standing there. Over her fair, flushed face a look of resentment and anger came, and she held the boy's head against her so that he, too, would not see their secret paradise had been overlooked.

Their absorption in each other, their innocent happiness, was almost too great for Charlie to bear. He plunged away down the dune and caught the bus back to town, defeated, despairing.

Meanwhile Mumma had gone up to the hospital and brought

144

the baby home, a little mummy swathed in the good Australian way in woollens and shawls, though the weather was stifling. Its small, surly red face glared out of the woollen cap that had slipped ludicrously down over its invisible eyebrows. Mumma looked often at that face, feeling slightly timorous, for it was many years since she had had sole control of a baby.

"You're not going to be a naughty boy for your nana?" she asked placatingly. The baby blew a bubble of milk, and made a glunking, sinister sound. His eyes stared unseeingly, in the fixed glare of indigestion.

"Oh, baby," sighed Mumma. She folded him closer to her breast, and, half-suffocated, brought almost to boiling point by his wrappings, Michael Rothe stoically endured until he reached home.

Motty and Dolour waited at the door. Motty, streaky-faced, ominous of demeanour, chewed a grass stalk with steady champings. Already she hated the baby. The mystery of her mother's disappearance, the equal mystery of the strange baby's arrival in the household had left her with only one clear thought—she was going to bite it.

This she did. Michael had hardly been laid in Dolour's soft and delighted arms before Motty climbed on the step and bit his cheek so hard that a purple ring of toothmarks was left on the tender skin.

"You little skrimshanker!" shouted Dolour, hauling Motty away before she amputated her brother's nose. The baby roared so loudly Mumma was nearly deafened. Motty screamed with fury, and Dolour scolded. In the midst of it all Charlie came in the front door, and Anny came in the back, marching up the hall, a piece of potato peel poking out of her mouth like a tongue. Motty stopped yelling and looked at Anny's potato peel with delight.

"Ain't she a bloody old hardcase?" she chuckled. Now it was Mumma's turn to roar.

"Oh, what do you expect?" asked Dolour angrily. "Dadda talking the way he does, and Motty hanging over the gate all the time. What do you think she learns out there, prayers?"

"I'll slap her," said Mumma reluctantly, looking furtively at Charlie to see if he were taking any notice of the baby. She sighed, and went off to make ready a bottle.

Charlie had hardly looked at his son. The noise, the smallness of the passage, so low of roof, so close of wall that it seemed to be crowded with women and children, made him wish with a sick urgency that he had not come home. He stood there indecisive, alien, hating himself and everyone else, while Dolour tenderly took the hot bonnet from the child's fragile face, exclaiming at its downy hair and the softness of its cheek. Her heart swelled with pity for this little one, and for Roie that she should never have seen the child for which she gave so much. She said harshly to Charlie, "There's nothing you can do, Charlie. Go and have a rest. It's that hot."

He said, not looking at her, "I want the kid to sleep in my room."

Dolour nodded. "I'm going to take Motty in with me. I'll watch out Mumma doesn't . . ."

She had no need to finish the sentence. Almost unnoticed she had ranged herself on Charlie's side against Mumma's fierce maternalism.

Charlie went out on the veranda, sitting on the gas-box in the corner under the ragged shadow of the vine, hiding himself from the curious stares of passers-by. The whole world seemed poised on a pivot, palpitating in the heat. From the sky like grimy glass came the smell of dust, speaking mutely of the drought-bitten hinterlands, of the cattle-skulls gaping out of the soft-sifted soil, the deserted towns half drowned in sand, the earth grinning and cracked, and the very flesh and blood of the continent whirling out in a cloud to the sea, and nobody caring a tinker's whether it did or not.

But there was something else, too, an expectancy, an awareness, which even he in his numb apathy could not help but feel.

After the unbearably hot day, the old men on the balconies were snuffing the air and saying, "Here she comes!" The southerly buster, the genie of Sydney, flapped its coarse blusterous wing over the city, a hearty male wind with a cool and spirited breath. The women undid the fronts of their frocks, and the little children lifted up their shirts and let it blow on their sweaty bottoms. Even the dogs crawled from the oven-hot shade of parched trees and hung out their tongues like banners in the cool. Now there was movement everywhere, the trees tossing their arms upwards, the torn shop awnings undulating, and the scattered papers on the road taking flight, leaping upwards in gleeful tackings, up, across, over the roof and round the garret chimney, until like a ragged flock of cubist birds they disappeared into the rents and ravines that the southerly had torn in the high far roof of cumuli. Doors slammed, windows rattled, and Lick Jimmy's clothesline spun round like a top.

146

And the birds, too, exploded into the sky. There was no telling where they had come from. They pelted out of the dusky sunset, no more than black dots, as feckless, as disorderly, as swift as insects bursting from a hedge. There were starlings in a loose-flung flight, like a cast net; a rocket of sparrows, and then, far up, the strong-winged, disciplined webfoots, the ducks with necks outstretched, the heavy geese, and the wild black swans; they passed up there where the colour and the light were fading from the after-sunset, leaving behind them the eerie sound of their voices, discordant, forlorn, like distant bugles.

Up the path came Hughie, his feet turned well out so that he would not fall over. He sat down beside Charlie without a word. He reached into his back pocket, and a silent, venomous struggle went on with the cloth. At last, breathing triumphantly, he managed to get the bottle out.

"Have a drink."

The stuff stung like turpentine. Its odour came up into the back of the throat and hung there like a thick and choking curtain. But it crept into the blood and made the rest of the world draw off and hesitate, a little unreal.

"Have another one."

So they sat, while the saffron faded from the sky, and inside the close and musty house Mikey wailed feebly for his dinner.

15

DOLOUR knew no other way to hide her sore heart, so she plunged into work, and in a little while she was so adept at managing the shop that Mrs Drummy was content to leave her to it while she worked at her dressmaking. In spite of Mr Drummy's S.P. activities, the Drummys were so plentiful, and so reckless, that there was invariably one of them in hospital with his leg strung up to the rafters, or trotting about wearing a chin-warmer of plaster. So Mrs Drummy always needed money. If it wasn't one thing, it was another; there was Bernadette learning typing and shorthand at a business college in town, and young Michael frightening the wits out of his parents by saying he felt the vocation stirring in his heart, and them knowing it cost a thousand pound or more to make a priest out of a boy.

So Mrs Drummy sewed, roughly and hastily, slashing out patterns and fitting cheap and unsuitable cloth over the lumpy contours of her clients. An endless parade of bottle-shouldered, down-at-heel women trailed through the shop to the sewing-room, and between the clangs of the bacon-cutter Dolour heard scraps of sentences, and words that had come loose from their moorings: "She's that high-stomached . . . got one hip bigger than the other . . . me bust has gone down something awful . . . petersham ribbon and a few stiffeners . . . green's me colour . . . they pulled down her house and stuck her in a tin shed out at the housing settlement, and her only two weeks from her time."

It was much cheaper for most of those women to get Mrs Drummy to run up a frock on her machine than to buy one, for hardly any of them were stock size, bearing the imprint of too many children, too frequent scones and tea, and bad, damp houses. Also, it was that nice to choose your own colours.

Dolour learned a lot about colour from those customers of Mrs Drummy's. Her mind, coming out of the numbness that follows pain, wondered why they chose hard, insolent blues,

148

jam-label greens, and sometimes even red, which had no relation to their faces or hair, or to anything they wore. It was a
long time before she realized that they had a peasant gift for
looking at a garment as a garment, and not as a part of a
person's entire appearance. When they looked in the glass
they saw the dress, perhaps, or the hat, but never the two as
part of a whole.

"It suits," they often said, not "It suits me", which would have
meant something altogether different. No, it *suited*. It satisfied.
It was a little bit of contentment in a discontented life. It
meant that, even though you had a husband who belted the
daylights out of you every week-end, you still had a dress that
pleased you. There was something deep and primitive there,
and Dolour remembered Grandma telling her of the red woollen
petticoats that the village women wore, tucked up above legs
that, when peat-gathering in the cold wetness, were as pink
as a turkey's.

"It was a consolation," said Grandma, "to have such a petti-
coat, a warm thing to think of, even though the baby had the
whooping cough, and Himself digging up the seed potatoes to
eat."

Dolour had expected to find those days in the little shop lean
and sorry ones, but somehow in the bitter loss of her sister her
ambitions and their frustrations were almost forgotten. She was
kept so busy she did not have time to think, for Mrs Drummy
appeared to help only at lunch time, when the hungry crowd
banked up four deep at the counter, squawking for milk and
sandwiches.

Speckled all over with odds and ends of cotton, as though
she had been caught in some unique pastel snowstorm, she
would rush out and take charge in her own muddled but com-
petent way. When things became really hectic, Mrs Drummy
ordered down reinforcements from Heaven, and often Dolour
heard such things as: "Saint Teresa, three egg and one ham, be
at my side. St Anthony do thou me guide. What was that about
the pickles, Joe? No cauliflower. Right-e-oh, Joe. Oh, Holy
Mary, me feet are that cruel today I can hardly put up with
them. No, dear, the foundry boy wants them in a box, and six
warm pies. That's the style. And you got his milk? Ten half-
pints. Dear Lord, and the kids'll be in soon and the lunch not
even in the oven having a warm. St Francis Xavier, pray for us."

There was something good about that little shop, bursting
with its commonplace opulence, its eager air of rubbing shoul-

ders with everyone, like a scrubby, friendly cat. And it gave Dolour a sense of power to be able to put an extra lick on top of the ice-cream cones she put into the dirty little paws that stuck pennies over the top of the counter.

Shyly she watched the young men who came in, their slender necks protruding like stalks from the collars of their Frankie Sinatra jackets, their knobbly wrists invariably ending in hands that were dirty and stained from the factories and machine-shops where they worked. Dolour felt sorry for their hands until one day, handing the bags of cakes across the counter, she saw that her own were greasy and grey. No matter how many times she washed herself, she couldn't keep clean. The cases of soft drinks, sparkling from the factory, were dumped in the alley an hour or two, and when she went to bring them inside to the refrigerator they were frosted all over with glassy black dust. At the back of the Drummy shop a chimney pointed an enormous blackened finger at the sky. It was so tall that rain-clouds trailed their ragged plumes over it in winter, and on the days that the dank, dirty city frost lay on the soggy ground the starlings vanished into its smoke like midges, looking for warm copings upon which they could huddle awhile. It was no wonder that Mrs Drummy's clothes rope, slung between her shop and the next, twenty feet up, was harsh and hairy with soot.

Mrs Drummy loved cleanliness, a thing that Dolour had never known much about. She wiped up water as soon as it was spilt, and not in all her life would she have polished up a grease-spot with a wad of paper and left it at that. Every Saturday she cleaned the windows, and as she left one side slippery and shining, tiny clots of soot came from nowhere and settled upon it in an impalpable velvet bloom.

Furtively, Dolour began to imitate her, washing her overall every night, and ironing it in the morning before she left. And now, instead of dipping her head in the tin basin of sudsy water, and rubbing it dry, she washed her hair long and lovingly, sneering at the black water with a triumphant sneer, as though she had temporarily defeated the dirt of Surry Hills.

Mumma scoffed at her, but in private she boasted to Mrs Campion over the fence. "She's got the nice ways of the nuns," she bragged.

Often, now, as she came home from work, Dolour found Motty playing in the street, the seat of her pants black and wet and filthy from the gutter, her hair in tangled witch-locks and

150

on her face the look of a mutinous angel. Motty fought silently, viciously scratching and biting, using her toenails as well as fingernails, occasionally spitting out a word straight out of the back alleys. In some extraordinary way she had retreated within herself, and nobody could communicate with her real self. Her father took little notice of her, Dolour was away all day, and Mumma's attention devoted to the baby, so Motty, like a little wandering cat, walked by herself.

"You shouldn't let her out on the road," expostulated Dolour, holding the wriggling child between her knees and looking carefully through her hair for "things". "You know Roie wouldn't like it."

"I know," sighed Mumma, "but Mr Reilly leaves the gate open, and Charlie don't seem to care, and she does look after herself, Dolour, you can't deny it."

"She's only four," said Dolour. "There!" she pounced. "She *has* got things in her hair! You've been wearing other kids' hats!" she accused the sulky Motty, who stuck out her tongue and jerked her hips in the immemorial gesture of contempt. "Kerosene on your head tonight, young lady!"

"They'll go away," said Mumma comfortably.

Dolour snorted. In some strange way it seemed as though the place were falling to pieces without Roie, as though she had been the gentle binder on the toppling walls of their family. With the hopeless, angry desperation of the young, Dolour watched Motty run wild, and, even worse, Charlie's complete apathy to life. On the surface he seemed the same, but to her acute and sensitive vision he seemed to be rotting away within. All that had ben strong and admirable in him had become hollow, melancholy, and completely negative. She watched him, and was angry, and did not know that the ancient fatalism and defeatism of his aboriginal blood was being thus mysteriously manifested in him.

But in his grief Hughie felt drawn to Charlie as never before. He was like an old dog, tolerated, kindly treated, and then suddenly admitted into the inner friendship of the master. It was good, when Mumma was nagging, and the domestic turmoil of the place overpowering, to go up to the attic and know he would be welcomed. His heart, opened up, with the warm air of human contact blowing through it, healed a little.

"A man don't want women round him all the time," he said. He held up the bottle to the light. A curdy black sediment clung round the shoulders like a moraine. Hughie shook his head. "Gawd knows what they put in it down at Delie Stock's. A coupla shovelfuls off Bondi Beach, be the look."

So they drank, and the dead marines mounted up in the corner, where Roie's clothes had once hung. After a little while the lagoons and islands in the kalsomined walls merged into a marbled pattern, and the curtains became a weaving film of light, in and out, in and out, so hypnotic, so dizzying that Charlie could not take his eyes from it.

Hughie's voice washed back and forth with the sound of surf, sometimes hollow, sometimes like the little voice on the other end of a long-distance telephone.

"Put a hump on himself like a ferret . . . shaping up to me . . . I let loose with the old one-two and he fell on his ombongpong . . . me father came from Kerry . . . often he told me about the little cows . . . big as them St Bernard dogs . . . wish I had a cow . . . it was that long ago . . ."

The bottle on the table gathered into itself the rich heavy light of autumn, the sunset that gilded the curly edges of the wooden shingles on Lick Jimmy's roof and turned to yellow flags the shirts that flapped on his line. Charlie stared at it, stupid, unable to think or dream, unable even to distinguish between the sounds below, Motty screaming with rage, the baby thumping a spoon on the table, Dolour clattering about the yard in the too-big shoes she wore in the wet.

It was like the time between sleeping and waking, suspension in a world of no thought, no feeling, no anything. Charlie fell into it as he would have fallen into a deep pool, with complete emotional exhaustion. Hughie's voice was no more than the humming of a blowfly in a corner. There was nothing in the world. Although his pain had dulled and blunted, the pulse of life had not come back. The night would never be a time of contentment any more; the day would never bring the good hard normal joys of work and fulfilment, and hope that things would be easier sometime.

All at once a hideous localized emergency filled his brain with stupid alarm. He got to his feet and, pushing Hughie aside, lurched down the stairs. The fresh air struck him like a blow, and the yard spun round giddily. The distance from the door to the drain lengthened to a hundred yards. He let go the door and staggered towards it.

The sound brought Mumma from the stove, where she was leaning with her forehead pressed against the mantelpiece, stirring at a pot. She looked interestedly out of the window.

"He'll bring up his liver and all its trimmin's in a moment."

Dolour was setting the table. She slapped down the forks with angry vigour.

"Trust him to do it right on teatime. I dunno how you've put up with him all these years."

Mumma went on stirring. She said, with a tiny shade of triumph, "It ain't your dadda. It's Charlie."

Dolour stood frozen. She went to the window. Within reach of her hand was Charlie's face, deathly yellow, his eyes closed, and streaks of sweat running down his cheeks. Dolour could have reached out and wiped those streaks away, or pushed up the dark curly hair from his wet forehead. As she stared, her mouth open, dumbfounded, his head drooped, and she saw the back of his neck, young, clean, and in some extraordinary way submissive, to what she did not know.

"He's drunk," said Mumma complacently.

A terrible fury against her mother rose in Dolour's chest, suffocating her.

"Charlie doesn't get drunk. He never gets drunk. What are you talking about?"

"He can't hold it like your father," said Mumma.

"Charlie?"

"Yes, Charlie," said Mumma angrily, turning and facing her, the spoon dripping on the floor. "Why not Charlie? He's a man, ain't he?"

"What's that got to do with it?" blazed Dolour, trembling with shock and disgust and anger. She heard Charlie begin to be sick again.

Mumma went on stirring. "It's natural for men to get drunk when they're upset. You might as well get it into your head right now."

This time there was no mistaking the complacency in her tones. In Mumma's simple heart a great problem had been solved. Charlie had not shown what were to her the orthodox signs of grief at the death of his wife, and she had resented it. Now that he had, he was established in her approval and sympathy.

"That's not true," cried Dolour. "You've always been jealous of Charlie because he isn't like Dad, and now—now he's going the same way you're glad!"

She rushed outside, and there was Charlie, white-faced and shivering, walking slowly towards the door. She waited till he was within reach, then she hit him as hard as she could across the face. He looked at her, dazed.

"How can you do it?" she cried. "Don't you see what Dadda is? Do you want to be the same as him when you're old?"

He rubbed his cheek slowly.

"Oh, Charlie," cried Dolour, not knowing what to say, and choking over the words that did come out, "Surry Hills is full of fellows who—it ain't fair to Motty or Michael—you got to pull yourself together somehow."

He said thickly, "What do you say 'ain't' for, when you've had a better education than any of us?"

She heard his slow footsteps lurching heavily from one step to another, until they reached the landing and vanished into the sound of a slammed door. Dolour stood in the yard for a long time. Mumma stuck her head out of the scullery window.

"If you've got nothing better to do than stand around on your big flat feet, you can come in and feed Mikey."

"Oh, shut up!" said Dolour.

It was beginning to rain again. The saffron faded from the sky, and strong and pungent rose the smell of wet and rotting vegetables from Lick's shed. The house seemed to draw into itself huddling under its misshapen roof as though it were afraid of getting damp. Dolour ran the tap hard over the drain and went inside, depressed and melancholy. Her hand still stung, and shame and dejection filled her soul. She looked at the room, the crumbs trodden into the floor, the chairs with their seats pushed down into terrible hernias, the plaster blotched with old grease marks where her father had thrown his dinner at the wall. Motty sat at the table, her hair like Medusa's locks, her little beautiful hands thick with grime. Mikey crawled around her chair, napkins bunched behind him in a wet grey bustle, his wrinkled little legs red and raw from their chafe. With a sob Dolour picked him up. He had the sickish smell of the unwashed baby, the smell that hangs like an aura over a hundred thousand slum houses.

"Mumma," she began. Desperately she struggled for words, but there were none. Her mother's broad, patient back was there, the rhythmically stirring arm, the feet planted at right angles to bear the weight that had become wearisome with the years. How could she expect her mother to understand? Dirt was dirt, and life was life, to be plodded through patiently, uncomplainingly, doing what you could and not bothering your head about the rest. And her mother was right. Her method was logical. Mrs Drummy wore herself to a shadow trying to defeat dirt; her mother accommodated herself to it. But what about Motty? What about the baby? As she thought these things, Motty suddenly jabbed herself with the fork, and from her red rose lips burst the words, "Bloody basket!"

"Oh, Motty," chided Mumma, "you mustn't say them things."

"Once," thought Dolour, "she would have clipped my ears, if I'd said that."

Yes, once Mumma would have minded, but now it was different. She was tired of battling against things without making an inch of headway. It was the same with Hughie; it would have been the same with Roie. The slums would have sapped her, too.

"But Charlie ought to be different," thought Dolour in anguish. "He wasn't born here. And I'm different. I am! I am!"

But deep down within her she knew that she was doomed from the start to become just like them, worn down like a stone with the flow of her environment. For how did you get away from it? What were the first steps? Did you have to break every bond of emotion and warm family love before you could become like other people and lead a life wherein cleanliness and quietness and privacy were intrinsic, and not luxuries? A lump in the back of her throat hurt. "I could get a job somewhere else, and board out. But I wouldn't want to leave Mumma, and the babies, and Charlie." At the thought of Charlie a flush of shame stained her face. "He'd never look after the kids properly. And he might get married again and some rotten woman would knock them around, just because they weren't hers. Oh, God, why do You make it so hard for everyone?"

Desolately she knew that the elder people of that house were finished already, that all volatility of spirit was gone, and there was no one left to pull them together except herself. Motty was a little larrikin; in all her brilliant beauty there was no grace or gentleness or kindness; nothing but the piteous brazen fearlessness of the slum children, like little lion cubs snarling at a world that had already shown itself inimical. With a shaking of the heart Dolour could see Motty as she would be thirteen years hence, another Suse Kilroy, a fragile, brittle creature with no more morals than a butterfly, resentful with a deep and bitter resentment against the life that had been begrudged her since conception.

"You didn't ought to have hit Charlie like that," said Mumma.

"No," said Dolour, "I didn't."

They heard the merry footsteps of Hughie on the stairs and

down the hall, and with a sigh Mumma shovelled his dinner on a plate and stuck it in the oven with another plate on top of it. Puffing Billy's oven was peculiar to himself, a bulging stomach ornamented with a tongue-shaped latch and hinges as big as handfuls of knuckles. While one side of the oven tray was red hot, a fly was dawdling about the other side, which explained why Mumma's scones were always either burned black, or semi-liquid.

Hughie was feeling good. The warm generosity that drink and companionship always lit in him burned high. He wished he could corner Mr Reilly in the hall so that he could whack the little fellow on the back, and pour a drink into his herring guts. For Charlie, stretched like a log on the bed, was no longer of any use to Hughie.

"Funny how a fellow that age can't take it," he ruminated as he floated down Plymouth Street, remembering how when he was Charlie's age, not yet married, free as a bird and with twice as much kick, there wasn't a pub in the north-west whose threshold hadn't some mortal wound from his boots as he was thrown out. Hughie felt sorry for Charlie and his drab life.

But he was too late to get in for a drink at the Foundry. As he arrived he saw the beefy great lump of a publican clank the doors together, and the clots of customers dispersing in the twilight. As though he had been a balloon, and it pricked all of a sudden, Hughie's high spirits leaked out of him. The air was chilly, and he had no coat. The blister on his heel, where one of Mumma's catastrophic darns had rubbed off the skin, spoke up shrilly.

"Gawd!" groaned Hughie.

There was nowhere to go except home, and his soul cringed at the thought. He wandered down Coronation Street hoping to meet one of his mates, but there was no one to meet except an occasional stranger hooked around a post, waiting for the feeling to come back to his feet. A flood of kids gushed out of Jacky Siciliano's fruit shop and fled up the street, leaving the footpath miraculously littered, all in an instant, with peanut shells and banana skins. Jacky Siciliano's broom appeared, with Jacky close behind it.

"Some day I catch-a those little devils and beat off their bum-as," he threatened with a broad grin. Then he leaned on his broom and said sadly, "You know, Hughie, what? Tomorrow my little girl, my Tonetta, get married."

156

"You don't say," said Hughie, in spite of himself interested. "Why, she's only a kid!"

"Sixteen," said Jacky Siciliano proudly. "She marry ice-cream."

"Yeah?" said Hughie, puzzled.

"She marry Jupiter Giaquinto, the ice-cream," explained Mr Siciliano.

"Yer don't say!" Hughie remembered Jupiter's father, a tiny wrinkled Italian like a sausage left too long in a shop window, trotting about with a wheeled box containing pink, green, and chocolate ice-cream, and followed by three or four small sons, each with a tray of cones slung from his shoulders.

"Jupiter, Mars, Mercutio, and Venutio," remembered Hughie, and all at once there was Roie swinging on the gate, a big girl of twelve with short white socks and a hole in her bloomers, chanting the names at the four little happy Italian boys. Abruptly he barged away from Mr Siciliano, his head down, knowing that if he thought about it the pain would be too great to bear. She was on every street corner; she leaned out of windows shaking tablecloths; she hid in the bottle; she was written all over Coronation Street, and he could not get away from her.

"Hullo," said someone, and Hughie glanced up, opening his eyes wide so that the tears would not fall out. There, sitting on the verandah of the little yellow house, was the girl Florentina.

At the sight of her Hughie felt so strange a shock that he wanted to be sick. It was as though the years had fallen from him, and left him naked and shivering, or as though the familiar old world had changed and become something quite new and alien, and a little terrifying because it was so. The wine in his stomach curdled and water rushed into his mouth; he was dreadfully afraid he would be sick before he could get away. But all this passed in a moment so short the girl did not notice it.

"How's that little girl of yours?"

"Eh?" For a second Hughie gaped at her, then he remembered Motty. "She's the same little devil."

He went on staring. She had been in his mind for so long, deep down, almost lost under all the worry and sorrow, but still there, with her deep Assyrian hair, and the eyes that were sombre even when she smiled.

"Florentina." Once he said it he felt silly, and a dark red stained his skin.

"That's right. You going anywhere? Then come in and have a drink."

Dumbly he followed her into the little room that opened off

the veranda, a room strange and mysterious to Hughie with its half-seen pictures, its dusty darknesses, and its smell of scent and wine. Almost under his feet unrolled what appeared to be a black mat. It flashed white eyeballs at him, and white teeth shone in a mouth as dark as grapes.

"It's my sister's little boy," explained Florentina. "Go on, Lex."

She stirred him with her foot, and the boy vanished silently from the room. Hughie looked at her, not understanding anything, only wanting to be sick, and wanting to cry because of his loneliness, and growing old, and the way the wine was acting up.

This was the way he fell in love, when the last years of his middle age were disappearing like sticks on a stream, bobbing ever onwards like sticks on a stream in spate, with him grasping after them with one hand, and with the other drawing the coat tighter round shoulders that felt the autumn chill. He had forgotten youth, and long forgotten the enchantment of love. Once or twice it had happened to him, but the years that stretched between were so many that his infatuation hit him with a strength that knocked him dizzy. The loss of his daughter and all its shifting and opposing tides became so identified with his finding of this other young creature, with the same slender arms, the same heartbreaking, mysterious sense of youth, that he could not distinguish one from the other.

But now it was only a beginning. He went home in a daze, and there was Mumma, crossly washing up, slamming dishes about and slinging her hips from side to side with a fury that had been impressive in her youth and was now only ludicrous. He stared at her, appalled that he should be married to this old woman.

"If you had my bunions," she said reproachfully, "you wouldn't have me standing around for hours waiting to put yer dinner on the table."

Hughie told her what she could do with her bunions with such viciousness that she turned round and gaped. He stamped into the bedroom, and Mumma timidly went to the door.

"Don't you want yer dinner?"

He put his face into the pillow to get away from her, her red hands rolled up in her wet apron, her face puffy from the stove, her teeth showing snaggled and yellow behind her half-opened, astonished lips. He wanted to yell, "Shut yer mouth! Get out of here! Go and cut yer throat!" but he knew it would be no use. Mumma would be with him until he died. So he said nothing. Mumma went back to the dishes. Slowly she watched the grey greasy suds ride about her swollen wrists. And it had been a nice dinner, too. She looked at it forlornly sitting there on the plate.

"I dunno."

Suddenly she attacked Puffing Billy, dragging his lid off and stirring savagely amongst his half-digested clinkers.

Puffing Billy decided he had had enough. "Tachah!" he remarked. He spat through every crevice, enveloped Mumma in a choking fog, and gave up the ghost. Mumma gave him one look, threw down the poker, and marched out of the kitchen.

For a long time Charlie lay in a stupor. The air was so chilly that the sweat, drying on his body, made him colder than stone. He was aware of the chuckling croonings of his son being put to bed, of Mumma's hands pulling a blanket over him, but he could not even mumble acknowledgment. The hours went by in half-unconsciousness, with no memory, no pain, no grief. He fought off returning sobriety, knowing it would bring so much to hurt. But it came, anyway, and he raised himself on the moonlit pillow, looking at the empty one beside him.

He shaped in the air the slender contour of her cheek, her little chin, the shell shape of her sleeping eyelids. He stroked her long soft hair, dark as darkness itself, remembering all the times it had lain like silk on his soft chest.

"Roie, my girl."

Then a terrible despair seized him. He sat upright and looked at the room, blocked with black and striped with moonlight, the angle of Lick Jimmy's roof standing like a gallows in shadow on the wall. He smelt all the smell of that slum attic, the wet in the wood, the dirty nappies on the chair. A kind of horror seized him. What did it all mean? What was he doing there? He sprang out of bed, walking aimlessly about the room, his mind a chaos of despair. The little confines of the wall stayed his step in either direction. God was nowhere. Roie was nowhere. He was lost and destroyed and there was no way of recovering himself. He flicked on the light, going automatically to the cot where the baby slept. He looked at the puffy pink face with the bubble of milk on the cheek as though he had never seen it before. He listened to the tiny sound of the child's breathing with wonder. For this Roie had died, for this Motty was motherless, and he was alone.

Yet with clumsy hands he pulled the blanket up about the

baby's neck, and turned the cot a little to shield its eyes from the light.

"What am I going to do?"

There was a little tap at the door. It hardly penetrated the thickness of his thoughts. The handle turned, and his gaze went to it, incurious.

"Charlie, can I come in?"

Dolour was bundled up in her old rain-spotted winter coat, the hem of her nightdress drooping about her bare feet. Her pale mouse face looked at him anxiously.

"I'm sorry I woke you up, Dolour."

But before he could say anything else her face crumpled up piteously like a child's, and out of her closed eyes two big tears squeezed.

"Oh, Charlie," she sobbed, "ain't it awful!" She turned away, hiding her face with her hands. "I'm sorry, Charlie," she said when she could speak. "I know no matter how bad I feel you feel worse. I'm sorry, Charlie. It's just that sometimes I feel I can't bear it if I don't see her soon."

"I know."

They stood looking at each other in the bald light, the great pain between them, the pain that was different from Mumma's and Hughie's because it was young and uncomprehending and impatient. The tears came into Dolour's eyes again. She gulped them down in her throat. He put his hand under her chin and she tried to look at him with her red eyes.

"You look a bit like her sometimes."

She tried to smile. "I won't ever be as pretty as Roie."

From somewhere a little comfort had entered her heart. She went over to the child, picking a bug from behind his soft crumpled ear and squashing it without a qualm under her bare foot.

"Filthy brute, feeding on my Mikey." She slipped her hand under the blankets. "You've let him get wet again, Charlie."

"I can't keep up with him," said Charlie. For a little while all the pain and terror had left the room. He watched with greedy relief the calm commonplace movements of the girl changing the baby and tucking the blanket down. She stroked the downy cheek.

"Gee, he's nice. Wish you'd let me have him in my room."

"Haven't you got enough with Motty?"

"I love kids," said Dolour. She blushed. "Anyway, Motty and Michael aren't just ordinary kids. They belong to me, too."

She gathered up the soiled napkins from the chair. "You want to go to sleep, Charlie. You're looking that peaked lately."

As she passed Mr Reilly's door she could hear the stealthy rustle of paper. He was doing up his parcels again, at two in the morning. The light went off in Charlie's room, and Dolour went quietly into her own. For a little while she hung out the window, breathing in the knife-sharp air. The sky was freckled with stars, blacked out here and there by the squares and angles of buildings. Dirty Dick sat humped on the fence.

She turned away. Her fingers traced the line that Charlie's had.

"Do I really look like you, Roie?"

A little peace stole into her heart. It seemed that Roie could not be lost as long as someone looked like her.

16

ONE day Mrs Campion barked alluringly at Mumma as she was hanging out the clothes.

"Jer hear about Lick going! Poor little stinker! It's not going to be the same street without him."

Mumma gaped. She was not one to gossip, but she always kept her ears open. Mrs Campion, reading her face, was delighted. She reached over the fence and gave Mumma a puck in the chest.

"You mean they're going to pull his place down?" gasped Mumma.

"Naow! He's going back to China!"

Fancy! Mumma waddled inside and sat down to have a think about it, wiping her face meantime with her apron. It was bad enough to think of Lick Jimmy going away, but worse to think of strangers next door, for in Plymouth Street, where the houses were built so closely that your neighbours could spit in your pockets without even trying, it meant a great deal to live next door to amiable people.

"Nasty kids maybe," said Mumma gloomily, visioning dead cats thrown on her roof, and mud on her washing, and maybe a bait slipped to poor Dirty Dick. Or perhaps there'd be a father who'd take a fancy to Hughie, so that he'd always be nipping in with half a bottle, and there'd be rows, and she'd be dragged into it, and life in the backyard would be unbearable. Mumma felt very vexed with Lick, for what was the use of going back to China at his time of life, and with a war on, too?

"He'll hardly put his foot to the ground before they'll be lopping his head off," thought Mumma angrily, for her Chinese history had stopped back in the days of the Old Buddha.

She put the baby in the pram where he lay, blinking in the sunshine, the light glistening on each separate hair on his downy head.

"Nana's little dotie," said Mumma admiringly, tickling him under his lowest chin, and he broke into a loud tuneless song.

showing his new teeth like tiny shells. He had eyebrows now, like dark feathers, and his grubby face was of a glossy waxen texture, like Victorian mantel fruit. Mumma thought nothing of this. She was dead scared of fresh air blowing on babies. They swallowed the wind, she said, and belched themselves blue in the face for days afterwards. They had to be well-wrapped all the time, and taken outside only when necessary. In Mumma's babyhood, in the emigrant days of fifty years before, babies had always been kept in a room with a fire, where they could get a good warm, and when croup and whooping cough carried them off like feathers on a gale, it was the will of God and nothing else.

So with her anxious love she swaddled and coddled Mikey, and only Mikey's solid Irish constitution defeated her.

She pushed the pram down the street to do the shopping, and the parcels mounted up and up until Mikey's eager inquisitive face appeared like that of a bodiless sprite over a heap of groceries. Almost nobody knew that Lick was leaving, and she found a quiet pride in being the bearer of such interesting news. So the story went from fence to fence, and everyone remembered how Lick Jimmy had always given the kids attention instead of serving the grown-ups first, as other shopkeepers did, and how he was never a scrooge with the specked fruit. And Mumma remembered how he'd given Roie all that awful bright pink silk when she got married, poor little fellow, not knowing much about the colours a girl could wear, and how he'd made Dolour kites when she was smaller, and he'd always remembered to give her and Hughie a pot of ginger for Christmas, though he was a heathen, and felt different about the holy day from everyone else.

Plymouth Street was full of a warm feeling about Lick Jimmy, and for a little while all the Sicilianos' customers forsook them and dealt with him, much to his grave amazement. They asked him a great many questions about his trip to China, but Lick, who had never troubled to learn much English beyond weights and measures, and how to make sure he was getting the right money, let it all flow over his head and smiled gently and chirped, "What else, please, eh? You wantee palsnip? You wantee cabbagee, ony lempence, velly cheap?"

"When are you going, Lick?" pleaded Dolour, who had loved him best of all, and could not imagine the street without his soft shuffle, and his bowed blue back plodding along behind a heaped wheelbarrow as he came back from the markets.

"Ahhh, soon," promised Lick.

"You might have told us before," said Dolour, almost tearfully, for Lick was bound up with so much of her childhood that she felt he would be taking the spellbound years back to China with him.

But Mumma often thought of how cold China was, for she had read about it in the *Far East*, and slowly there came the idea that it would be nice to give Lick a little something to remember them by. Timidly she broached this to Hughie, and as she expected Hughie's chair crashed back on all fours from its tilted position and he guffawed, "Who ever heard of giving a Chow a presentation? If you want to give anyone a present, you can give me one."

"He was kind to Ro," was all Mumma said, "and now he's going away."

Hughie was silent. Another one to go away—Thady, Grandma, Patrick Diamond, Roie, and now Lick. Almost violently he said, "You can have the chicken feed this week."

The chicken feed was the shillings and pennies in Hughie's pay envelope, the sixteen shillings he kept for himself, except on those occasions when he really got drunk, when he helped himself to the housekeeping money as well.

So with that, and the money Dolour scraped up, and the little bit Mumma scrooged out of the house money, they bought a cardigan. Mumma, doubtful, had chosen a dark blue guaranteed to make Lick's complexion look like aged soap.

"Bit herring-gutted, ain't it?" asked Hughie critically.

"He's only little," said Dolour.

"True enough," agreed Hughie. "He's got a behind on him like a two-year-old child."

"Never mind the behind," snapped Mumma. "It's the shoulders I'm thinking of."

She marched into Lick Jimmy's shop. Though he was going away Lick did not seem to be making any effort to clean up. The same old calendars showing Eastern pin-up girls with high-necked gowns and thread-thin, crimson lips, spotted the dusty walls. The strings of papery garlic swung in a curtain behind the window, and on the counter his cat suckled five blind bullet-headed kittens in a crate half-full of lemons. There sat Lick Jimmy, peacefully smoking his pipe, his shapely hands, with long thumbnails like transparent horn, placidly shelling peas.

Mumma did not know what to say, so she put the parcel on the counter and blurted, "This is for you, Lick."

164

Lick looked at the parcel. He smiled, shook his head, and gave it back to Mumma.

"Velly nice," commented Lick, "but no money."

"What say?" asked poor Mumma.

"Lick got no money," said Lick.

"I'm not asking you to buy it," cried Mumma, light breaking. "It's a present." She jabbed Lick in his skinny blue chest, then poked herself in her abundant black one. "From us, see?" She took a deep breath, then spoke his own language. "It's a plesent, Lick."

Lick did not understand. He tried to read the meaning of the mystery in Mumma's face. She seemed to be cross, and he did not know what he had done, so nodding and smiling and mumbling he took the parcel and put it on the shelf amongst the wilted celery and leprous cucumbers he had put aside for the pig-man. Then he said doubtfully, "You wantee somesing? Spud? Pummikin?"

Mumma was deeply disappointed. She had pictured Lick putting on the cardigan and beaming all over, for once acting like an understandable human being.

"It's because you're going to China, see," she tried again.

Lick beamed. "Lick come from China all li," he agreed happily. He looked round for something to please Mumma, and fished a passion-fruit from a box.

"For bubby," he said, and Mumma, a little mollified, returned to her own place, where Dolour was impatiently awaiting her.

"Well, how did he take it? Was he thrilled?"

"He was so grateful he could hardly say a word," said Mumma thoughtfully.

Nobody knew just exactly when Lick Jimmy was leaving, but Mumma kept a close watch from her upper windows, and there came a day when he hung out on the line a collection of patched quilts, sacks stitched together, and archaic blankets, and beat the blazes out of them with a broomstick.

"There now, he's going to pack," she said, satisfied. A few moments later she was rewarded by the sigh of Lick toddling out with a brand new high chair, painted a bright glossy blue. She couldn't call down the stairs fast enough for Dolour to have a look.

"I suppose he's taking it back for his grandchildren," said Dolour.

Mumma was determined that Lick wouldn't get away without

her saying good-bye, and she and Dolour watched the shipping news for those vessels coming from China.

"Here's one," said Dolour one night, and her gloom deepened as she heard excessive activity in Lick Jimmy's house that night. A jumping jack bounced in a shower of sparks across the yard, and through the veiled windows they could see all sorts of twinkles and sunbursts.

"He's telling all the devils they ain't got tickets," chuckled Hughie.

Next morning Lick went out early, and all the Darcys hung out of their windows and waved to him. He seemed dumbfounded, trotting down the street and turning round at intervals to see if they were still watching.

"I wonder where his luggage is?"

"Work yer head. He's sent it by carrier." They watched the little figure dwindle to a matchstick in the glossy sunshine.

"Well, that's that," declared Hughie, melancholy. "Now I suppose we'll get a load of Greeks, pelting us with fish-heads."

They all went off to work, and Mumma was left alone to cope with the two children. Motty had a bad cold, and went whooping about the house, whingeing between whoops and clinging to Mumma's leg like a limpet.

"Mother of heaven, won't you let me to meself for a minute, lovie!" exploded Mumma. Then she picked Motty up and cuddled her, saying, "Ah, I've forgotten what it is to be little, Motty, so you mustn't be hard on me if I'm cranky sometimes."

Heavily she climbed upstairs, Motty on one arm and Mikey on the other. Sometimes Mumma felt very tired, but since Roie had died she had had no time for "the change". Life went on over her head, but she was too busy attending to other people to notice its passing.

As she went past she gave Mr Reilly's door a kick. There was a steady rustling going on inside as though Mr Reilly were having a lovely time unwrapping parcels, but at the thud of her toe against the door the rustling ceased with the abruptness of a mouse that hears a footfall.

"I beg yours, Mr Reilly," she called, "but I'm going to put the children to sleep, so please don't make any noise if you don't mind."

Behind the closed door there was the silence of death.

Mumma put the baby down with the bottle of milk, and tucked him up.

Wearily she undressed Motty and put her into Charlie's bed,

where she squirmed and whined rebelliously. But Mumma's big rough hand had motherly magic in it. She patted Motty's back wth a monotonous, hypnotic rhythm, humming meantime a song her ma had sung to her long ago, a song that had come over on the convict ships, and was old long before that:

"Now, all you young dukeses and duchesses!
Take 'eed of what I do say.
Make sure it's your own that you toucheses,
Or you'll meet me in Botany Bay."

Now and then she stopped tentatively, and Motty opened a threatening blue eye.

"Ah, yer little tripehound. All right, then:

"With a tooral-i-looral-i-addity,
And a tooral-i-ooral-i-ay!
With a tooral-i-ooral-i-addity,
Oh, I'll meet *chew* in Botany Bay."

Now, out of the sultry heat of the early morning came rain, and with the soft rattle on the roof Motty went to sleep. The baby was already fast asleep, a trickle of milk on his chin. The attic was dusky with the dimness the clouds had brought, and gratefully Mumma stood at the sill and breathed in the coolness. She watched the beads of quicksilver that streaked across the cranky-paned window, the raindrops bowling along the telephone wires, and the damp, sooty birds that huddled together under cornices and clung upside-down to the guttering. The houses across the road looked shut-up and unwelcoming, with their closed eyes, and even the doormats taken inside. Mumma forgot all about the big wash awaiting her downstairs, the unswept kitchen, and the dishes still lying on the table. She gazed unseeingly at late workmen going past on bikes, with tool-kits on their shoulders under rain-capes, so that they looked like a great many hump-backed little Frankensteins.

"Oh, Roie, darling, is it going to be all right? I get that worried about Motty, and her the little firebrand she is. Do I look after them the way you'd want, and will I live long enough to see them able to watch out for themselves? Look after them going over roads, darling, and other places where I can't be. And if Motty gets the whooping cough and the baby gets it, too, make that Charlie let me have him by my bed so I can see he's covered at night."

So she prayed, shutting her eyes and trying to find Roie in that dim quiet room, longing to have her arms round her daughter, to feel her reassuring flesh.

"Oh, if only I could have my life over again, with you a little child, and Thady my baby."

She felt the panic of sorrow rising in her heart, and she gabbled Hail Marys to still the flood, for there was too much housework to be done for her to give way. Then all at once a most extraordinary occurrence drove every other thought out of her mind. Two taxis drew up outside Lick Jimmy's, and every possible kind of Chinese personage tumbled out, holding newspapers and umbrellas over their heads, and talking at the tops of their voices.

"Glory-lory-ory!" said Mumma.

First came Lick Jimmy himself, squeezed up as narrow as a bookmark by the buffeting he'd had in the cab. He galloped in and unlocked the shop door. Mumma was by now paralysed with astonishment. She tried to fit the facts together, and every second piece was left over.

Lick Jimmy was very delighted about something. He pranced out again and held one of the lop-sided umbrellas over two young men who, laden down with suitcases, rolls of blankets, an empty birdcage, and a large basket, followed him to the shop. After them came a stout middle-aged man, very prosperous, and with a certain critical air as he peered through his horn-rimmed glasses at his surroundings. Then came two pretty girls, with hair so sleek that not even the rain dulled its paint-like gloss. They wore Chinese gowns, and one carried a very fat small boy with basin-cut hair and a smart English style tweed suit.

In the Irish way, watching a good spectacle by herself was not enough for Mumma, so she ran out and thumped on Mr Reilly's door.

"Come and look through the window, Mr Reilly! You've never seen such goings-on!"

The sepulchral silence of Mr Reilly's room was unaltered.

"Quick, or you'll miss it! It's the fun of Cork."

She gave a last despairing kick at the door, but Mr Reilly said not a word. She rushed back in time to see a third taxi arrive. It contained nothing but luggage, a large frying-pan, a bunch of artificial flowers, and a box with the head of a live white fowl sticking through the battens. The middle-aged man paid off the first two taxis with a baronial air, and clucked round the third, making sure that no chickens or new-born puppies were left in it. Then the second taxi heaved once more, and out of it climbed the oldest Chinese woman in the world, a mere morsel of a black-clad creature with a face as big as Mumma's hand, so scribbled over with years that it no longer looked like a face at all, but a piece of vellum, creased many times. Painfully she hobbled on her stumpy feet to the door, and was received with assisting arms and loud cheeps of welcome.

"I suppose they forgot her," ruminated Mumma.

The door of the shop slammed, and almost instantly there was a deafening burst of crackers. Windows flew open upstairs, and the fowl gave a death-cry.

Mumma could no longer see anything, so she went downstairs, pausing on her way to kick Mr Reilly's door and call out reproachfully, "You're a fine one. You've missed the sight of a lifetime."

She muddled through the dishes, thinking excitedly, "Maybe they're going to take the shop over. Maybe he leaves for China tomorrow."

But she had to know for sure, and as soon as possible she had a peep to see if the shop was open. And it was. Mumma took her string bag and went in. The rain had stopped, and the road was steaming in the sunshine. Already one of the girls was scrubbing the shop step, but at the sight of Mumma she and the bucket wafted out of sight. Lick Jimmy and the young men were engaged in incredible activity behind the counter, knocking in nails and jerking them out again, and talking all the time at the tops of their voices. All Lick Jimmy's gravity, his solemn and remote air had vanished. His little lemon face had broken into smiles, and he showed his snaggle teeth right to the cheekbone.

Mumma had to ask for onions four times before he gave them to her, giggling to himself. The young men, subdued into silence by Mumma's presence, stood shyly at one side. Their clothes sat curiously upon them, their slender necks unsuited to the stiff collars of the Western breed. Like Dolour, Mumma liked Chinese, and shyly she peeped at their beautiful wrists, their eyes set gently in the flat of the face, the russet blush in the creamy cheeks.

"When are you leaving, Lick?" asked Mumma. "Tomorrow?"

Lick nodded vigorously. "All flamlee now!" he giggled, his eyes, which were beginning to turn a little blue with old age, crinkling up with utmost pleasure.

Mumma couldn't make head or tail of it. Just then the smallest stranger, now visible as an incredibly fat young godling of eighteen months, with eyes like black glass, and a body completely naked except for Lick's new blue cardigan, which trailed on the floor like a State robe, appeared from behind the screen. Mumma was dumbfounded. In two seconds she had added up all the little sacrifices contributed by Dolour and Hughie and herself towards the "plesent" for Lick, and the sum was ingratitude.

"I've a good mind to ask for it back!" she exploded, and marched back into her own house, leaving the onions and the three Chinese all looking at each other bewildered.

Mumma was very upset indeed. More than that, she felt a fool, and all day long she fulminated against herself, and the Chinese, and Dirty Dick, who invariably occupied the place where she next wanted to put her foot. But it was not until Dolour came home that she could express herself fully.

Dolour was delighted. She rushed into the shop to fetch the onions Mumma had forgotten. After a long time she returned like a whirlwind, crying, "You are a dope, Mumma! Lick never said he was going home to China at all. Mrs Campion must have got it wrong. All he meant was that his family was coming from China."

"All of 'em?" gasped Mumma.

"No, just some of them." Dolour began to count on her fingers. "The old lady is Lick's missus, and the big fat joker is their son, and the two young men are his grandsons, and the girl with the smallpox marks on her face is his granddaughter, and the other one is his granddaughter-in-law. She's married to the grandson with the scar on his chin. And the little boy is their son, and his name is Loger Bubba."

"What?" gaped Mumma.

"Roger Bubba," giggled Dolour. She pranced round the room. "Isn't it fun? And none of them can speak English so as you can notice it."

"How did you find out, then?" said Mumma suspiciously.

"Oh, we made signs," replied Dolour carelessly.

Mumma whacked Puffing Billy turbulently across his waistcoat with the poker. "He took that cardigan for false pretences," she said, and for three days she believed it.

The Lick family settled down peacefully in the little shop in Plymouth Street. Though Lick had kept it as clean as his old sinews had permitted, still they found more dirt, and for days the house seemed to smoke clouds of dust. They crawled out on the roof and slapped mats furiously, talking all the time, and laughing their heads off. They washed their hair in the backyard and sat round endlessly combing it with quince-seed lotion, while they yelled witticisms to those in the house, and those in the house shrieked them back.

Mumma had grown up with noise. The Campions were so close that Mr Campion's drunken roarings sounded in their very ears, and the night his batch of home-brew burst its bonds and bottles, the Darcys had felt the fusillade keenly. So Mumma did not notice the rowdiness of the Licks. They were clean, and minded their own business. They never squizzed through the fence, or lit fires when the wind was blowing Mumma's way.

"It's real homelike with them around," admitted Mumma grudgingly, and indeed it was impossible to feel lonely. Mr Bumper Reilly lived within the house, but might not have been there at all. The Lick family lived outside of it, but they gave off like a glow the atmosphere of congeniality and family warmth.

Very soon Motty was wandering in and out of their household, and Loger Bubba was coming as far as the Darcy doorstep. Loger Bubba, that worshipped Eastern godling, shocked Mumma.

"He doesn't wear nappies," she confided to Dolour. "And he needs to."

But Mumma really didn't mind. She just followed Loger Bubba round with a floor-cloth, waiting for the worst.

17

BECAUSE of her dark glasses, and because she was not pretty, only the queer boys with long noses and pimply chins came Dolour's way. She swung violently between hatred of their raucous voices, their empty heads and right-angled elbows, and understanding of their awkwardness. Half-educated, with minds that revolved round amusement parlours, girls, and timid bets at the S.P. shop, some of them would grow up into that repulsive product of the slums, the middle-aged larrikin, standing over weaker men for money and drinks, dodging work wherever possible, praying for a depression so that they wouldn't have to work. But the majority would just become ordinary working men, unambitious, garrulous, who would spend all their days spilling out of foundries and factories and garages, and spilling into pubs and mean little houses; who would always do even the most fundamental things, such as eating and fighting and making love, in the most unskilled manner; who would never learn anything from those who had gone before, and never want to. They would grow old without knowledge or complaint that they had never really had any conscious life at all.

Dolour learned a few things about them, that it was their nature to give any girl a try, that romance with them was just a word you heard on the pitchers, that it was pansy to have good manners. She understood why all these things should be, but before their inner minds she floundered. What did they think about? How did they get the way they were? Didn't any of them want to be sailors, and see the world, or save some of their money and go elsewhere to live, or talk about something that was real and lasting instead of superficial and ephemeral? Did they wake up in the night and yearn for love, as she did, of abiding and tender love, and not something that was composed of dirty blankets and a bug-ridden bed over a squalid street?

Again and again she looked at Charlie, sunk in his quietness, growing older and shabbier, drunk often, hardly ever taking part in a conversation with anyone, and wondered piteously what would become of him. For she felt that he hadn't been like those other boys when he was younger, and it seemed a contradiction of all her fierce faiths that he should have so surrendered to life now. Maybe all men were the same at heart, living for the flesh, and the moment.

But she denied that passionately, in church, on the street, to herself at night-time, feeling that she could not be alone in her longing for the pure and dignified things of life.

So she went on, a child one hour and a woman the next, seeing the world often as a bright and lovely place with every possibility of great happiness for those who searched for it, and sometimes as a bog that crawled and seethed with hidden dreadfulnesses. Then the walls of the houses would seem transparent to her eyes, and she would see other Kilroys beating their wives and their daughters; mean, dirty women blowing their noses on their aprons, and letting their children play round garbage tins heaving with maggots; women who suckled their children to three years old in an effort to prevent another conception, oblivious to the ill-nourished and imbecilic look of the child; fathers who violated one daughter after another as they grew to the age of twelve or thirteen years, and mothers who stood by and allowed it; grimy-fingered old hags up dark alleys who would abort you with a crochet hook for ten shillings— all the commonality of sin was laid before her in the streets. She saw the reverse of the tapestry, hidden, unfinished, grotesque, thinking it was peculiar to Surry Hills, and not knowing that the whole world was the same, if you wanted to look for those things. In these bad times she did not see any of the good and heroic things that were going on about her, the tubercular mother fighting to feed her children, the kindness and generosity of the poor to the poorer, the old man tending his blind and crippled friend on the park bench, the returned soldier with no legs, sitting in the window whittling wooden toys, as un-bitter as a bird. She did not see that for every sin in Surry Hills there were a thousand heart-warming words and deeds.

There was nobody to ask. Mumma wouldn't know, and Hughie would be embarrassed, and Charlie wasn't the right one. Sister Theophilus would do her best to help, only Dolour didn't know what to ask. She couldn't even find the words to ask Father Cooley, in the darkness of the confessional. What was it she wanted to know? A million things, and yet they all added

G

up to a reassurance from some grown-up and trustworthy person that life was beautiful and noble, as she had once believed it. Perhaps Roie could have told her, in her halting way.

One day she heard from the younger Drummys that Sister Theophilus was leaving St Brandan's. She could hardly believe it, for Sister Theophilus was the bell-tower, the foundation stone, the polished floor, the hum of prayers, and the sweet spiralling smoke of the Gregorian chant. She had been there twelve years, and that was nearly all of Dolour's life.

"It won't be the same without her," said Mumma mournfully, pausing with a half-peeled potato in mid-air. "I remember the first day I took you to school, and you bawling so loud I could see your tonsils."

"Yes," said Dolour softly, remembering the awful moment when Mumma's head, going away down the sloping street, disappeared bit by bit behind the wall, until it was only a tuft of brindly hair. Then Sister Theophilus, so tall that it was years before the child knew her as anything but a long brown skirt and a pair of shabby polished shoes, took her by the hand and led her along the polished corridor.

"You've got warm hands, and a silver ring," said that small Dolour.

"Yes, darling."

"And I've got pants that button up," boasted Dolour.

Long after Dolour could remember things about Sister Theophilus. Often she had fallen over and barked her knees, and was taken into the convent kitchen to have them bathed. She remembered the dark-green linoleum, and the red from the fire reflected in ruddy pools, a round clock like a plate, and a diminutive lay sister standing up on a box to stir the saucepans at the back of the range. And all the time the reiterated, halting notes of "The Jolly Farmer" coming from the music-room at the back of the convent.

And once, too, she had a terrible cold that took chips out of her ribs every time she coughed, and Sister made her sit on the veranda and drink hot cocoa, which she took sacramentally out of a cup with no cracks in it. Of all the things and people connected with her happy schooldays she best remembered Sister Theophilus, her grace, her dignity, her warmth and maturity, and now she was going.

"You oughta go round and say good-bye," said Mumma. "I would meself if it wasn't for the toes sticking outa me shoes."

For days Dolour thought about this, but somehow she felt

174

herself a stranger now. The two years that had risen between her and her school days had thrust her willy-nilly into a too-soon maturity, and she felt long grown up. Besides, she used lipstick now.

She shrank from going into the school, into the old scenes, and hearing whispers from the children who had once known her, and answering kindly questions from the nuns. Besides, what would she say? She was too old to blurt out her feelings, too young and brash to put her thoughts into the right words. And soon it was too late.

Mrs Drummy, rushing in from one of her numberless visits to the church, gasped out, "What do you think, Dol? I just saw Sister Theophilus and that poor dear old Sister Beatrix going off to the station with some luggage."

Dolour stood with the wet cloth clutched in her hand, and said nothing, but kind Mrs Drummy, always ready to put the sentimental touch to things, said, "Why don't you hare off to the station and tell 'em good-bye, love?"

Once Central Station, and Plymouth Street, and all the network of veins that ran between them had been one great cemetery, and even now, so tradition said, the trains thundered over the rotting bones of those old nameless ones who had died in their fetters and been buried without tear or trumpet in an alien land. But there were no unquiet ghosts in Central, only tremendous cavernous spaces, and echoing bells and whistles and voices, and the ceaseless clank of pennies in the public lavatories, and the great indicators presiding over all, like the dials of some incalculable machine. Dolour stood beneath them bewildered, pushed and shoved by the battling crowds, wondering how she could hope to find the sisters in this wilderness.

But she forced down her confusion, and made her brain work sensibly, for they were going to a southern town, and there was only one platform they could be leaving from. Yet when she reached the platform there were so many porters driving beetle-backed little trucks with long snakes of luggage-laden trolleys behind; so much noise and battling, and suitcases left in the way; so many screaming children besmearing their grandpas with kisses and toffee apples; so many old ladies already dying for a cup of tea, and them not in their seats five minutes, that Dolour wondered why she had come. Then she saw them, tidy and quiet in their black mantles, with mittens covering their hands, and their small polished suitcases sitting sedately by their polished black toes. Dolour had often theorized about the contents of those suitcases. Hughie reckoned a pair of sand-shoes and a spare set of pyjamas, but Dolour thought privately of a nightie with long sleeves and a high neck and perhaps a toothbrush and a starched white handkerchiew.

They were so quiet, so self-contained, speaking to each other so rarely, that she hesitated shyly and uncertainly, wondering if it would be good manners to go up to speak to them, or whether they'd be allowed to answer, and what she would say if they did. Her heart yearned over Sister Theophilus, sitting by the elderly Sister Beatrix, a little pale and grave. As never before the ordinariness, and yet the difference, of these women came to her. All her life she had loved the nuns, for the ordered regularity of their lives, so foreign to her own, and now in her near-maturity she realized what she had loved most of all.

It was their womanliness. They had not been shut away from the world. Their locks were all on the inside of the wall. They had shut away the world from them; all its rowdiness and dirt and self-striving and self-adulation was no more to them than the hum of traffic in the distance. Yet there in the cleanly un-cluttered convent they had developed as women and human beings. The rub of character against character was there, the instinctive antipathies and impatiences. The difference was that they subdued all these things to live in amity with each other. This was the secret strength she had sensed in them. They had sacrified all things that the world loved most, but the greatest sacrifice of all, the most wearing, the most subtle, the most fretting was continual self-discipline, hour by hour, minute by minute; the unremitting watch on themselves lest they give way to irritation, weakness, or any shadow on the perfection they set themselves.

The nuns did not see Dolour lurking in the chaff-dusty shad-ows behind the weighing-machine, with her eyes glazed and her mouth open, but other people did, and smiled, thinking her some Protestant girl with a terror of the "robes".

The whistle blew, and before Dolour could awaken from her dream, the nuns had said good-bye to each other. A swift pres-sure of the hand, and a kiss on Sister Beatrix's old red cheek, and Sister Theophilus, together with three of the strangers from other convents, had gone into the carriage. She jumped out quickly from behind the weighing-machine, thinking, "I'll wave as the train goes out. She'll see me. She'll just think I came too late", but as the nuns on the platform turned, she shrank back again, a shy smile trembling on her face in case Sister Beatrix saw her.

But Sister Beatrix, her face scarlet as a beetroot, and her mouth set even more grimly than it had when she was trying to teach fractions to Dolour and thirty other boneheads, was stumbling along, a young nun on each side of her, and not noticing anybody. Even as Dolour's mouth opened to say, "Good afternoon", Sister Beatrix's face crumpled up for a moment and tears rushed down from behind her glasses. Then she was borne away. Dolour was so astounded by this revelation of grief and pain of parting that she did not notice the train slide away, switching its long black tail round the corner, its wail floating back like a banner of smoke. She had not known that nuns ever cried, particularly Sister Beatrix. She had not known that twelve years of living and working together could make Sister Beatrix feel about Sister Theophilus as she felt about Roie.

Mournfully she walked up into Surry Hills again. Here and there were empty spaces where houses had been demolished. Where the dank cellars had sweltered, and the rock faces sweated in the darkness, the sun now shone, and the blue convolvulus, the periwinkle, and the tasselled ragwort blew. And here came again the dispossessed, the honey bee, coming from nowhere to the earth where no flowers had grown for so long. Here and there stood an idle steam shovel, drooping its sardonic jaws like a prehistoric monster frozen in the act of chewing the cud. But Dolour hardly noticed.

She knew that at least she had one thing in common with Sister Beatrix. In Sister Theophilus she had lost a friend and protector, almost invisible, who could never be replaced, and who had left her alone in a world she would have to face for herself.

All day she was sad until Harry Drummy asked her to go to Luna Park with him, and every other thought fled her mind. She rushed frenziedly home to see whether Mumma had ironed her blue floral, and she had.

"I'm going to have a bath," decided Dolour. It was an important decision, for bathing in the Darcy household was fraught with both danger and adventure. Since they had been using the old tin tub to bathe the baby in, they had been climbing into the wooden wash-tubs, a difficult business, for the tubs, with their chewed, pitted bottoms and slanting sides were never made for the comfortable accommodation of the human body. Hughie, who had developed an astonishing liking for baths

177

lately, always ended his ablutions with a curious bruise on the base of the skull, where he had thrown his head backwards and almost fractured the bone on the grim beak of a tap. Charlie never spoke of his experiences, but he usually looked clean, so apparently he managed all right. And Mumma accepted the inevitable and point blank refused to endanger her life by jamming herself into so small a receptacle; she much preferred to "have a rench" with a nice basin of hot water.

But Dolour made it a ceremony. She had hardly entered the laundry and kicked the block of firewood against the door before the whole dank, soap-smelling, candle-lit place was transformed in her mind to a beautiful bathroom like those you saw on the pictures. She dreamily heaved bucket after bucket of steaming water into the deep wooden box of the tub, occasionally plucking out a splinter that floated to the surface. The stone floor was already covered in lagoons from the leak in the pipe, and everywhere the candlelight winked at itself.

"I've got mirrors all over the wall," she murmured.

She took off her clothes, sniffing curiously. Suddenly she leaped at the wood-box, hauled out the spitting Dirty Dick by his repellent scruff, and dropped him haphazardly out of the window. It took all Dolour's imagination to transform the smell of wet tomcat into that of expensive bath salts.

"When I get out I've got my lovely pink—no, lilac dressing-gown to put on. It's satin," she thought, her knees jammed up against her chin, and her neck crooked forward so that the tap wouldn't peck her. It was hard to admire herself in such a position, but at least she could see that her legs were smooth and hairless. By an acrobatic feat she tilted up her toes and warmly appraised her toenails.

"When I'm rich I'll polish them. And I'll wear slippers with very high heels and lots of feathers on them."

Languidly she soaped her neck and chest. It was very difficult, craned forward like a striking hawk, and the knobs of her backbone kept bumping on the hard tub. All at once she had a wonderful idea. She leaned forward and tried the water in the copper. It was still hot. She hopped in. The water came up round her chest, for it was a huge, antiquated copper built to take the washing for a family of twelve. By kneeling she had very much more leeway than she had had in the tub.

"I'm in a sunken bath," she decided. "And there are lovely green plastic curtains hanging all round me."

The next moment the door crashed open, and Hughie blund-

178

ered in, blinking at the dimness and roaring at the top of his voice. Dolour's green curtains disappeared even faster than they had come.

"Some silly galoot's gone and left a candle burning in here," yelled Hughie amiably. "Want to burn the house down, I suppose, and me in it. I suppose that would satisfy the dirt on yer liver." This last to Mumma in the kitchen, where she had ventured to remonstrate with him on his midweek merriment.

Dolour shouted, "I'm in here, Dadda! Go on, get out!"

Hughie lifted the candle like a wavering star and stared at the empty tubs. Dolour, shocked and furious, cowered down in the copper. A pleading note quavered in her voice.

"Go on, Dadda! Clear out, will you? I'm having a bath."

Suddenly Hughie spotted her. His eyes sparkled with mischief. He leaned an unsteady elbow against the doorway and said conversationally, "Well, now!"

Dolour squirmed. "Aw, go on, Dad!"

"That's a fine idea you've got there," said Hughie agreeably. "But tell me, what are you doing to keep your crankcase off the hot bottom?"

"I'm sitting on the soap," said Dolour, surlily.

"Ah, it's you that's got the brains," approved her father. He came a little closer, and Dolour bent herself into the shape of a depressed S and sank into the water to her chin.

"What's that you've got on your head, may I ask?" asked Hughie politely. Dolour gave a squeal of despair.

"Mumma, come and take him out! Mumma! Gosh, you're awful!" she cried to Hughie. "I bet other girls' fathers don't come into the laundry when they're having a bath. Mumma!"

"Tell me what you've got on your head then," wheedled Hughie. There was a moment of explosive silence, then his daughter capitulated.

"Me bloomers."

To keep her hair from getting wet she had thrust her head through one leg of her bloomers and twisted the rest of the garment into a knot at the side. Under this macabre headgear, which came down to her eyebrows, Dolour's eyes shone ferociously. Hughie nearly had a fit. He rolled from side to side, kicking the door wide open so that the laundry was fully exposed to the kitchen. Dolour was afraid that at any moment Charlie would come in to see what all the noise was about.

But Hughie, who wouldn't have hurt her feelings in a million years, couldn't resist pulling her leg a little further. He began to gather bits of firewood.

Dolour whispered, "What are you going to do?"

"That water looks a bit cold, me darling. I'm going to heat it up."

He thrust the wood into the firebox and began ostentatiously blowing. Dolour squawked.

"Here, have a heart! You'll boil me! You brute! You devil, you know I can't get out! Mumma!"

"We could slip in a few onions and carrots with you and there'll be a first-rate stew," said Hughie helpfully, sitting back on his heels and grinning happily into the anguished face of his daughter.

"Mumma!" bawled Dolour, and Mumma, upstairs with Mikey, heard the call and pounded down the stairs with the sound of thunder. She seized Hughie by the arm and jerked him from the room, slamming the laundry door so that the whole house trembled.

"You're shook for something to do that you've got to tease the poor kid like that, Hugh Darcy, and her so modest!"

"Take some of the starch out of her," protested Hughie, still with a twinkle.

"You've got to remember she isn't a child now. She's nearly eighteen, and a young woman," scolded Mumma.

The laundry door slammed back, and Dolour, bundled hastily into her clothes and still wearing the bloomers on her head, exploded into the kitchen. Mumma hid a grin at the hauteur with which she tried to sweep past Hughie.

"Don't take it so hard, love," chuckled that sinner. "I used to change your nappies when you were little."

"Oh!" Dolour fled up the stairs, with a horrid chant of, "I used to change your nappies!" following her all the way.

Down at Circular Quay Harry Drummy waited for her, draped mournfully over the rails in the peculiarly filleted manner of his kind, and eyeing off all the good sorts who were pushing and screaming their way on to the Luna Park ferry. He was game to bet a peanut to a deener that Dolour wouldn't turn up in a pair of them grouse shorts that showed all the fellers what she had and they couldn't get. He couldn't make out why it was he was always stuck with drack types like Dolour Darcy, then, rubbing his hand over his grievously nubbly chin, supposed it was because he had pimples. But she had had pimples, too, when she was younger, and he made up his mind he'd ask her what she'd done to get rid of them. Just as well she didn't have them now, or the pair of them surely would look tricks moting around together.

Yeah, there she was, in a warby kind of a blue dress, and low-heeled shoes. Not an ankle-strap in a cartload, for her. He looked critically at her legs. She coulda worn them, too. And them dark sun-glasses she wore! Gawd! Bitterly Harry recriminated against the heavens that gave him hickies, and girls that no one else would envy him.

A sick feeling entered Dolour's heart when she saw Harry standing there, his hands thrust into his pockets like packages, and a little, saliva-stained fag stuck on his lower lip. Of all the nice boys going to Luna Park, tall, brown, bright-eyed, jolly-looking fellows, she had to draw this droob.

Then she thought that it wasn't his fault he was a drongo. You had to be fair. He didn't want to have pimples, or a thin neck, or that hair all snowflaked with dandruff. Perhaps he would grow out of it some day, and then she'd be glad that she'd been tolerant with him when he was young. Anyway, he had asked her to go out with him, and they could have a nice time if she wasn't too critical.

"Why don't you take off them black windows?" he snarled in answer to her hopeful beam.

For a moment she hesitated, for her eyes were still shy of light, and she had worn the glasses so long that they were a protection for her soul.

"O.K." She took them off, and showed the long, colt-like eye-lashes that had mysteriously grown while her eyes had been bad. She blinked in the wind, and saw Harry looking at her and blushed.

"You know," he said in surprise, "you ain't half as funny-looking as you were a while back."

"Thanks. Pity I can't say the same for you."

She flounced on to the little water-beetle of a ferry that rocked and reeled with the weight of screaming teen-agers who besieged it. Girls with the faces of flowers and the voices of pee-wits clung close to the slick hips of sailors who had hooked their caps on the corners of their heads; compact family groups stood bracing their legs, long and short, against the onslaughts of the younger passengers; an occasional oversea serviceman stood, the whole weight of Empire pressing on his uniformed shoulders, while his eyes roved shyly amongst the unattached girls, who, in twos and threes, giggled and shrieked and rubbed their blue, goose-pimpled legs, for the evening was chill.

Soon they had shuffled alongside the ramp that led to the fantastic, shoddy fairyland of Luna Park, and Dolour and Harry were borne along in the rush for the gates, excited and half-suffocated by the smell of scent and sweat and plain old human-ity. The hot-dog man, his face glazed red as a clown's with high blood pressure, warbled monotonously, "*Carm* an getcher dargies! *Carm* an' getcher dargies! Mustid dor ter*marter*! *Carm* an' getcher li'l' red dargies!"

With sparkling eyes Dolour and Harry gazed on the arena, and their feet jiggled in time to the merry-go-round, which swung in pallid green circles to a syrupy, steam-punctuated waltz.

"I go for the Big Dipper meself," cried Harry with boyish gladness. "Oh, boy, that Big Dipper! You have a milkshake before you go on, and when you come off you spit up half a pound of butter."

"Oh, you!"

Face pink with anticipation and excitement she looked at Harry. She had forgotten about her eyes, and they rewarded her by forgetting about their sensitivity. Her long hair blew out on the sea-wind like a black flag, and the blue dress, blown close to her body, showed curves Harry hadn't known she pos-sessed. He thought, "Gee, she ain't so bad!" A tiny tingle of excitement ran over him, and he haw-hawed coarsely, not know-ing what else to do, or how to express the half-comprehended instincts that filled him. He was delighted and flattered when a passing soldier reached out and pinched her on the thigh. She shrieked, and Harry growled perfunctorily.

"Wantjer big ears flattened?"

"Who's gonna 'elp yer?"

"Ah, pull yer 'ead in!"

Honour was satisfied. Almost with pride he pushed her into one of the Big Dipper cars. Round and round they rode the tilting horizon, deafened by their own shrieks and the shuttling clacket of the machinery, suspended above the jewelled round of the amusement park both sideways and upside down until they were finally decanted in the throes of terrible sea-sickness. They clung to each other, breathless, shrieking with senseless laughter, and praying.

He thought, "Gawd, I could puke quicker than wink."

She thought, "I'd be all right if I could sit down for a moment."

182

They smiled at each other brightly. Harry took her arm, more to support himself than anything else, and they strolled away uncertainly. But after a few moments, so great was the youthful resilience of his digestive tract, Harry felt better, and he slid his fingers up her arm until they rested against the slight curve of her bosom. A wary prickling ran over Dolour. She wanted to jerk free, but she felt a little shy about doing that. Harry was a good Catholic boy, and not like those other louts at the pictures, and he had his hand there most likely by accident, and she might hurt his feelings if she pulled away. So she left the fingers there, feeling uncomfortable and cautious and indecisive, all of which Harry interpreted as acquiescence.

He thought, amazed at his own dumbness, "I shoulda given this sheila a go before." But he said, casually, "How'd a hamburger go?"

"There," said Dolour triumphantly to herself, "it was just an accident," and for some reason felt just a little disconcerted.

The blue fumes from the grill wafting over them like grease-laden incense, they waited in the queue of hungry hands that reached out for the hamburgers, each cosily nested within its half-burned bun in a posy of greasy onions and rusty shredded lettuce. Harry champed with bits of onion falling out of his mouth, and he finished by opening wide and throwing the last corner of bun into it with bear-like dexterity. Dolour tried hard not to watch, but it was too fascinating. A deep melancholy, which had been in her heart from the very beginning, welled up and nearly overcame her.

Forlornly she followed him into the little boat that bobbed at a doorway, ready to take passengers through the River Caves. It was cool and quiet and damp in there, and the noise of Luna Park sounded like the muffled squawking of magpies. The light slid silver and unearthly down the concrete stalactites and the silky, chuckling water. Her yearning for romance rose up again, and she thought, "Poor old Harry." He snuggled up against her, his long angles trying to accommodate themselves to her shorter ones. His hair brushed her cheek like a greasy mop, and he smelt of brilliantine and onions, but then, she did, too. She had a wild impulse to start talking about something to distract him, but he looked so pathetic and homely, and she knew no other girl would ever let him kiss her. Anyway, at least it would be an experience, and there were lots worse than Harry. She opened her eyes and saw a green, corpse-like face leaning over her, swallowing.

"I wish he was someone else so I could slug him," she thought. His soft wet lips descended on hers, and she peeped through her lashes a moment to see him looking cross-eyed and concentratedly at the top of her nose. She shut her eyes quickly, trying to imagine the kiss different—exciting, wicked, enthralling, or even merely pleasant. But it wasn't. It was like kissing a wet hamburger.

"God," gasped Harry, "I could go for you!"

He was amazed at the effect the kiss had had on him. He wanted to get her by herself in some dark place and forget all about everything and just be himself. For a long time he had envied those mates of his who just had to look at a girl and she'd fall into their arms, so they said. Although he had had lots of furtive back-alley experiences, hot and frightened and uncomfortable, they'd all been with little tarts who'd get behind a back fence with any boy. Yet here was Dolour Darcy, with the reputation of being cold as an eel and a bit of a nark as well, plainly falling for him like a stone. He was about to go further, eagerly, when the boat shot out into the light, and with a wrench of anger and frustration he realized that he'd have to wait.

Dolour was feeling noble that she'd let Harry kiss her, particularly since it had been so ghastly. And even though it was only Harry, she was flattered that he could go for her. He might have looked a moron, but he had good taste, was what she felt, though she did not think it. She smiled encouragingly at him, longing with a great longing to hear him say something romantic, or tell her she looked pretty, or that he liked her dress.

Harry was having trouble. He swallowed once or twice, wanting to change the subject and regain control of himself, so he blurted out, "How did you get rid of your pimples?"

"I went to Sam Gooey," said Dolour wanly.

The evening never recovered its lustre. It was the same as all the others when she had gone out with neighbourhood boys and known that she was not a success, and, even worse, could not persuade herself that she wanted to be a success with them.

No matter how much she tried to blame it on the boys and their gaucherie, she could not help feeling that the fault lay within herself. Some deep humility made her search her own personality for the trouble, for it was plain that most girls got on all right with boys, and not because they were all Suse Kilroys, either. In books and films there were plenty of girls who went out with boys and had a good time, with no awkward silences or feelings of discomfort.

"I wish I was prettier," yearned Dolour. "It would be different then."

Her heart went out to Harry, apologizing because she couldn't feel romantic about him, and thanking him because he could go for her. He put his arm round her and squeezed, raking his sleeve buttons painfully across her hipbone. Their feet jockeyed urgently for the same place, then Harry squashed her to his chest and kissed her again, there in the darkness behind the fairy-floss stall, where there were lots of other clotted figures doing the same thing. For the first time Dolour felt a pleasant kinship with these figures. People who saw her and Harry wouldn't know that she was putting up with it just to be nice. They'd think she was just a girl getting kissed by her boy-friend.

"Poor old Harry," she thought remorsefully, and kissed him back, getting the flavour of hamburger with renewed poignancy.

"Christ," thought Harry, "she ain't so bad. And I ain't so bad, neither." He snuggled up closer to her, his cold damp nose poking in her ear. Dolour resisted a desire to struggle. "What about clearing out?" he asked hoarsely.

"Where to?" she asked cautiously.

"I know where there's a party on. Like to go to a party?" He thought, "I ain't ever walked in to Shirley's place yet with a sheila of me own. Give 'em a shock."

Dolour was delighted. It was like the stories you read, where the girl went out to dinner and then on to a night-club. Going to Luna for a hamburger and then on to a party wasn't so different.

"Is it someone I know?" she asked eagerly. But she hadn't ever met Shirley, who lived in the second house on the right, by the biscuit factory in Pump Lane. She felt a little shy, wondering if her dress were nice enough, or whether her nose were pink from the cold wind. But Harry's kisses, catastrophic as they had been, had bolstered her self-confidence, and all the way over on the ferry she submitted to his cuddles and assured him, in answer to his reiterated inquiries, that they would have real dinkum fun at the party.

Harry was choking with excitement and confusion and delicious anticipatory guilt. His mentality was such that it was totally unable to cope with any but the simplest problems of life, and that was the way he liked it. He suited himself. Consequently he was shocked that Dolour had been under his nose for so long, and he hadn't done anything about her. Of course she wasn't what any fellow could call a whacko-the-diddle-O piece, but she was a girl. And kid she didn't know what it was all about! It was true what the blokes said, the quiet ones were the hottest, and he'd find out how high she could send the mercury tonight.

On the other hand, if she'd just been stringing him along, he could leave Shirley's early, before the fun started, and she'd be none the wiser!

But Harry had miscalculated the time. Shirley's mother, who worked as a late-shift waitress in a fish café near the railway, started at six o'clock, and Shirley had had two clear hours to get wound up.

The tall old house was all in darkness, cocking its gable roof rakishly at passers-by, and wearing its chimney like a top-hat.

"Round the back," said Harry confidently. Dolour's feet slipped on glassy tiles as they felt their way through the pitch darkness, which was filled with the sharp smell of woodsmoke from neighbouring chimneys. She was a little shy and nervous, thinking of all the strangers she would meet. The house had a basement, a yellow-lighted well beside the steps. Two cats erupted like rockets out of the well, and rushed screeching past Dolour's legs. By the time she had collected herself the basement door had opened, and she and Harry, blinking and dazzled, were inside the big cavernous cellar, which seemed to be full of young people, great splodges of black shadow, a naked globe strung over a nail on a serpentine flex, and a gramophone belting out a raucous dance tune. The first person she saw was a girl she'd been to school with, Connie Croucher, and even though she'd never liked Connie, the pleasure of seeing a familiar face amongst all the strange ones was great. She waved gladly, and was astounded when Connie looked dismayed, and melted into the crowd as though she'd never been there at all.

"What's up with her?" she asked Harry indignantly, but Harry was tugging at her sleeve, trying to introduce her to Shirley, a small, round, fat-faced girl with catlike eyes, which she considered were like Ava Gardner's. She narrowed them now at Dolour, protruded a wet lip and crooned, "Make yourself at my place, love." Dolour disliked her on the instant. She felt four sizes bigger than Shirley, with great, long, hanging arms. Besides, Shirley wore the tightest red sweater in the world, and smelt slightly of plonk. Dolour looked closely at her. Shirley was tot-

186

tering on the brink of being properly stewed, and she was no older than seventeen.

"Here you are." A glass was thrust into Dolour's hand, and almost instantly a tall pimply youth in a king-sized Frank Sinatra jacket, whirling past with a girl in his arm, snatched it from her grip and poured the liquid down his throat. "Catch it, Minnie." He tossed the glass back to her, and Dolour, flustered, missed, and it splintered on the stone floor. Shirley broke into a shrill flood of complaint. Most of her expressions would have been welcomed by the Kidger into his select vocabulary. Coming from her round, childish, scarlet bud of a mouth, they sounded fantastic. Suddenly she spat at Dolour, "What are you grinning at, you big gollion?"

"I wasn't grinning," gaped Dolour feebly, then rage flashed out of her, and she cried, "You dirty-mouthed little ape, you can keep your rotten party."

Shirley's face crumpled like paper; she emitted a little wail and whimpered, "She hasn't got no reason to come here slinging off at me. I didn't ask her. And I ain't a nape, neither."

Dolour was overcome by her own rudeness. It was true, she hadn't been asked, and there was no reason why she shouldn't have left quietly without insulting her hostess. But there was no time to say she was sorry, for Shirley was borne off, weeping winey tears, in the arms of the boy in the Sinatra jacket, and Dolour herself was pushed down into a chair, and a red-hot saveloy was placed in her unresisting hand. Somebody lifted up her hair and nuzzled the back of her neck, and shuddering with nervous titillation she glared round into a bold, long-nosed, currant-eyed face which smacked its lips and whispered, "Hullo, silk pants. What you got that I ain't got?"

"This," snapped Dolour, and she jammed the burning saveloy into her admirer's vest pocket, beside his dazzling yellow silk handkerchief. She jumped up and looked round for Harry, but Harry had disappeared. In that hollow, dirty grotto of a place, smelling of damp and old timber and cats, she couldn't even see the door. The candles were guttering down in their bottles, the electric globe was a blinding hoop of brilliance, somebody was being sick in a corner, and extraordinary things were going on in the shadows. Dolour felt her heart stick in her throat. For a moment she felt she was asleep and dreaming the sort of dream she would try to forget in the morning. Paralysed, she stared, unwilling to look, and yet unable to take her eyes away. Shrieks of laughter came from the alcove near her, and Shirley

187

appeared momentarily, her sweater pulled over her head, so that she staggered blindly this way and that.

"Gimme another boll soda water," she was yelling, "or I'm a goner."

"My God," giggled someone near her. "Don't she know it isn't grandma's day any longer? And her just out of hospital after the last!"

Clutching her soda water, trying to drag off the cap with her teeth, Shirley was pulled off into the dark by another boy. Her sweater flew out into the middle of the floor like a scarlet bird.

An arm slid around Dolour's waist. It belonged to Harry, who was pressing up against her with a curious mixture of defiance, trepidation and persuasion on his face.

"Come on, kid," he whispered. "Be in it."

"Harry," she said, hardly hearing him. "They're—what are they doing?"

"What we ought to be doing," said Harry, and everything left his face except a hot glazy-eyed eagerness, and he slid his wet lips over hers like a slug. Dolour was a strong girl. He was bigger than she, but she shoved him away, spitting her loathing and terror, and stumbling over a couple on the floor, she groped along the wall for the door, which had melted into the cobwebs and dust. Harry seized her.

"Don't be mad, what's the harm in it? Everybody does it. I'll look after you. Gawd, why don't you break down and be human!" He was ashamed and a little frightened, but he had to disguise it by roughness. Dolour fought him off, sobbing with rage and shock, and some of the others, with shrieks of joy, saw their unequal battle. In a moment she was surrounded by a ring of half-lit faces, so young, so fresh, so unmarked by corruption that for a moment she thought it must have been a hallucination.

"Come on, be in it, chick!"

"Where did you find it, Harry?"

"He got it outa a Sunday-school book."

"Christ almighty! It's a virgin, that's what it is!"

It would not have been so shocking if they had looked bad, but they didn't. They were just ordinary boys and girls from sixteen to twenty, that you might meet on the street any day of the week. They were healthy young animals, cynical beyond belief, amoral, shameless, and for all she knew all young people were like that. Harry was like that—Harry, from a good family like the Drummys, and a Catholic boy as well. Maybe it was a common thing to sneak into each other's houses in the absence of parents, and indulge in the wild, incredible promiscuity that can only be approached with a mature body and an immature mind. She stared at them wildly, wanting to be sick, and with a deadly fear creeping over her. But they meant her no harm. She was the canary in the cage full of sparrows, and they couldn't help teasing her. She was funny to them, and they began to have fun with her, pulling up her skirt to see her legs and holding her hands so that she couldn't protect herself. She was that comic object, the one virtuous person in a degenerate gathering.

Harry stood by, terribly ashamed of Dolour, more ashamed of his friends, not knowing whether to laugh or protest in case he was lumped in with her. Suddenly she got her foot free, and the long-nosed boy received such a kick under the chin that his jaws clopped together with a loud loose sound.

"I ought to fix you for that, you bitch!" He seized her by the front of the dress, which ripped out in his hand. "And I'll do it in front of everyone, too!"

"Leave her alone, you bastard!"

Harry, plum-faced, boiling over with his uncatalogued emotions, spun him round and lashed at him so amateurishly that everyone laughed. They fell on the floor, struggling like two beetles, and while they were doing this some of the others pulled down Dolour's dress and wrote a filthy word in lipstick across her bosom. Then they opened the door and pushed her out into the dark, amongst the squalling cats and the icy wind, and the strange obstructed darkness of the yard. Her glasses had been smashed, she had lost her purse, and she was physically and mentally on the verge of collapse. A moment later Harry, dishevelled, his nose dripping red, hurtled after her, with a chorus of good-natured mocking obscenities following him. She ran away from him, hysterical with relief and disgust, wanting to be sick. She barged into the side of the house and struck her face stingingly upon the corner. Harry took her arm to lead her up the dark path, but she ripped it away and ran, stumbling on the dew-wet tiles, and finally crashing through the gate into the dim street. She heard a passing woman say, "That little swell Shirley Hubis! I wonder her mother don't tumble to what goes on behind her back!"

"I didn't know," appealed Harry, rushing through his pockets for a handkerchief. He blew his nose with his fingers, sending a shower of ruby drops through the air. "Honest, Dolour, I didn't."

Dolour tried to get away from him, but she was too distressed to run. She leaned over a fence and was deathly sick, not caring at all that he was watching.

"You won't tell Mum?" he pressed anxiously. "Dinkum, I hadn't the faintest that they'd go on like that."

"Oh, go away," gasped Dolour, and grumbling and disturbed he went, to stand on the corner and watch until she moved into Plymouth Street. He thought, "By God, if she opens her big mouth I'll tell the world she was right in there with the rest of them. I'll put her pot on, the bitch, thinking she's so holy. I'll tell every feller I know she's easy, and she won't be able to go down the street without having the acid put on her." But underneath he wasn't really frightened that she would tell. The habit of minding their own business was too deeply ingrained in the young and the old of Surry Hills. Pulled up as witnesses by the police, they preferred a fine or jail rather than have their heads kicked in as top-offs when they came home. He watched a little longer, then decided he'd go along to Siddy Doust's place to clean up a bit, in case the old woman got the wind up when she saw his bloody nose.

Dolour's feet were weighed down with lead, and she shivered spasmodically, holding up her torn dress, and keeping to the shadows so that no one would see her dishevelment. Now that the terror was over, she was numb with the reaction from shock, her common sense and sense of direction so destroyed that she would just as soon have crawled into a dark doorway and huddled there all night as gone home. Nothing was real any more. In a sense, she felt the same as she had after Roie's death, as though the world had stopped.

All at once she saw Charlie, walking unsteadily in front of her, and at the sight of his shabby familiarity her numbness thawed. "Oh, Charlie!" she cried, and in a moment was in his arms, crying loudly like a child, not caring that people might hear, or that he might not want her there.

"What's the matter, Dolour?" He let her put her face on his shoulder and sob, soothing her as he might have soothed Motty, feeling an aching compassion for all her pride and independence that had vanished in the stress of some crisis he did not know. "What's happened, darling?" The word slipped out of him unnoticed, for he had never held any crying girl in his arms except his wife. He saw the bruise on her cheek, and as she moved, the torn dress, and the beginning of the obscene word upon her white skin.

"Dolour! Who did that? Did something happen to you?"

190

Now he was alarmed. She shook her head. "No, nothing happened. Only—Charlie—oh, Charlie, people aren't all bad, are they?"

Out of her great need, out of her shattered ignorance and assaulted innocence she begged him whom normally she would have been too shy to ask. He was a little drunk, but because he understood her he didn't ask any more questions, but answered hers, "Most people are good, Dolour. No matter what they tell you, or what you see, most people are good."

"And people can love each other, and it isn't terrible and filthy like—" She could not continue, but began to sob again.

He knew what she wanted to know, but although he sought desperately he couldn't find words that satisfied him. "No, Dolour, no!" He felt her stop sobbing, though her face was still hidden. He did not know what provoked this tumult, but he knew that her need was desperate, that he had to tell her plainly, without any obscuring delicacy. "What's between a man and a woman was meant for marriage. Otherwise it's like a picture jagged out of a frame, all wrong, and hard to see the right way."

"I want to see it the right way," whispered Dolour.

"Lots of people have wrong ideas, but you mustn't get them. There's nothing more wonderful than to love a girl and have her own you and you own her, because it's not only your body that matters then, but your soul and mind and everything you've got." He had never said anything like that before; the words were torn out of his own experience, and for a moment an echo of his terrible grief trembled on the brink of his consciousness, but he ignored it. "Dolour, don't you ever let anybody tell you any different. That's the way God meant us to look at it, and because people smear it all over with their filthy paws doesn't make it change." He was floundering again. "You believe what you know is true, and some day you'll find that you've been right all along."

She was quiet now, almost drowsy, the physical strain of her experience expressing itself. His arms were warm and sheltering. He was not Roie's husband, he was not even a man; he was just a human being older and wiser than herself, who had given her the rope when she was drowning. She thought, "All along he's been there, and I didn't know."

She did not know that her innocence, like Mumma's, was intrinsic, that she could not help her violent reactions to those things that affronted her chastity. She only knew that after she'd thought about this, after the shock and horror were all gone, and

191

she was able to look Harry Drummy in the face again, she'd be able to think about Shirley's and not feel soiled. Shirley would slip into her right place, as she, Dolour, had slipped into hers. What Charlie said was right. It was what she had always felt. Life was good, and love was beautiful, and she would not mind any longer keeping aloof from everyone rather than waste herself on love that fell short of perfection.

But just now she wanted to sleep.

"You can't let Mumma see you like that," said Charlie. "I'll go in first and talk to her in the kitchen, and you can sneak upstairs and fix yourself up."

Mumma was unsuspecting. Anyway, she was worried, for Anny was sick. Mumma had her in the kitchen, lying on a sack in front of Puffing Billy. The devilishness had died out of her golden striped eyes, and her feet were cracked and hard. She hung her head, with long silvery streams of spittle looping to the floor.

"What's the matter, Anny, eh?" Charlie smoothed the dry, rough coat. Anny made a feeble attempt to bite him, then struggled up and limped into a corner of the kitchen. Dirty Dick appeared momentarily, like a smelly ghost, and slunk across the floor. A brief twinkle came into Anny's despairing eyes, and she lifted a back hoof and got him fair and square in the ribs.

"I'm afraid she's going to die, Charlie," said Mumma mournfully.

"I could take her down and let her loose in the park," suggested Charlie. "The poundkeeper would find her and she'd get a good home."

Dolour came soundlessly in. She had changed her dress, and scrubbed the word off her chest. There was nothing to tell of her experience except the blue welt on her cheek.

"You're that late," scolded Mumma, "and what on earth's the matter with yer face?"

"Cracked it on a swing over at Luna," lied Dolour.

"Gallivanting around when I'm worried outa me wits with the kids yelling, and your dadda as drunk as an earl, and Anny gone sick on me," complained Mumma.

"Poor Anny." The goat had been dry a long time, and there had been no need to keep her cooped up in the backyard, except that Mikey loved to play with her. It seemed to Dolour that their treatment of Anny was typical of the spirit of Surry Hills. They could have sold her, or given her away. She could have been bred again and provided milk for some other child. But they just didn't bother. They just left things as they were, as Mumma left the curtains torn, and Hughie left the floor unmended, and Charlie allowed Motty to go her own sweet way. It was always too much trouble to do things immediately; far easier to take a risk on the future. So Mumma let her teeth rot in her head, and Mrs Campion just didn't bother to get her children inoculated for diphtheria, for they mightn't ever get it, anyway. Laziness was the core of the slum. Dolour grasped after this thought, but her brain was too fatigued, and it skipped out of her reach. One day she would think about it. And she was just as bad, for she hadn't bothered about Anny, either, accepting her unquestioningly as a part of that little, imprisoning yard, as thought she were a clothesline.

"She needs fresh feed. She'll be all right," said Charlie, stroking the animal's delicate hairy nostrils.

"Poor Anny." The tears rolled down Dolour's cheeks. They were the reaction to her experiences that evening, but there was no bitterness in them any more.

"I never seen such a fuss over an old goat," scolded Mumma, but her glance was sympathetic, and together with Dolour she watched as Charlie took the limping, stumbling animal down the dark street to the shelter of the park.

18

IN all that great village of Surry Hills, which clung to the proud skirts of Sydney like a ragged, dirty-nosed child, there were little eddies and pools of streets and blocks, peculiar to themselves, like towns within a town. Mumma knew all the women in her street; she knew whose children had things in their hair, and who stayed longest in confession, and quite often why. She knew all the little shops in Coronation Street, and which ones were good for tick, and which weren't, the measly-minded vultures. But out of her locality, in the next street but one perhaps, she felt strange, with the people looking at her, and the women criticizing her.

So Hughie, when he went to Florentina's house, felt that no one round there would recognize him. He had been in the pub on the corner, but that was all, for there were no friendly faces of old mates there, and the barmaid had aloofly ignored his uplifted finger. Two blocks away from his own street he was a stranger. Not that the possibility of discovery had ever occurred to him for a moment. His life outside the doors of his home had always been his own; he had gone his own way and come back when he felt like it, and always found Mumma still there. He would have been amazed at the idea that it was any of her business what he'd been doing.

Now, in the lop-sided dream that had arisen out of the incomprehensible alchemy of his own mind and body, he rarely thought of Mumma at all. She was part of Number Twelve-and-a-half, Plymouth Street, dirty, monotonous, hardly animate. Dolour was a prating voice, cheeping away in the distance, barely heard and never understood. And Charlie, sullen, silent, growing thinner and older and sallower by the day, was just a stranger who appeared sometimes to keep him company with a bottle. He came into the house and went out, blankly, his mind so filled with the girl that he could not think while he was working, or laugh with his mates, or do anything in the world wthout entangling his thoughts about her.

Sometimes he would stand in wonder and look at his thick, unsupple hands that were weathered and beaten, scarred and battered. How could they be worthy of the shoulders soft as suede, the dovelike softness of the throat of Florentina?

He was bemused with her, walking gape-mouthed through life, unable to think or plan. It was like waking up, and finding he had only dreamed he was middle-aged and fettered to a life of no more value than ashes. She was the glass of water in the sand, the rain at the end of a burning day. She had given him back his youth, and like a drug he had to possess her to preserve the illusion.

It did not matter that she was a prostitute. In Surry Hills and other places like it the curious inversion of the moral law that made the policeman an object of contempt and the basher someone to be looked up to and respected, accepted the harlot as a commonplace. The reputable people of Surry Hills were too proud to be snobbish with the disreputable. They felt themselves on a level with everyone else. The grocer on the corner was a good, church-going fellow, but mean and dirty with his children; the chromo next door got her money easy in dark doorways, but she was always ready to shout you a feed when you were down and out. It all balanced when you came to the end, and God alone knew whom He was going to ask inside when He had the lot of you clamouring outside the walls of Heaven. So when a prostitute got old or tired, there was almost always someone ready to marry her, and later on, when she had a houseful of nice kids, and the same troubles as everyone else, hardly anybody remembered her youth except with good-natured tolerance. So Hughie accepted Florentina, because he had to, for his passion ignored everything but its food. If she had been diseased he would have accepted her just the same. His was the frantic monomania of a man who will rape the woman he wants rather than be frustrated of her; but being Hughie he begged and prayed instead, when he had no money, that she be accessible to him. It was only in these moments that a tiny corner of his soul, almost hidden in the darkness, hated itself because of the humiliation of grovelling to a girl young enough to be his daughter.

But Florentina was always accessible. Lazy, good-hearted as an animal, she would never have turned down any man because he didn't have enough money. Besides, in some subtle way, Hughie fed her ego. She would have been content to loll and watch him, and often she felt an indolent resentment at Seppa for continually holding out her hand.

"You're mad," said her sister, the thickset Italian woman, standing before the glass and plucking fiercely at her black moustache. "If you want an old man hanging around, why don't you pick one with money?"

Florentina hardly heard. Lying on the unmade bed, dreamily watching the rain, she murmured, "Aw, he's that mad about me, Seppa. He's like a dog. Honest, he is."

The other woman snorted. "And you'll get about as much from him."

Florentina rolled over. "Aw, shut up, Seppa. I bring in the dough, don't I? You ain't losing anything."

The black boy sidled into the room, his chocolate eyes rolled askance at his mother for fear of reproof or a blow. Out of the mirror her face glared at him, "Out the back, you black bastard!"

Florentina reached out an arm as the boy skittered past.

"Ah, don't be such a bite, Seppa! Ain't his fault he's black. He was got on a dark night, eh, Lex?" She nuzzled her face into the child's slender neck, soaking up his adoration. "Here," she put a chocolate into his mouth. "Go on, Lexie. You better go before your mumma chips an ear off you."

The elder woman looked at her with disgust in which jealousy struggled to show its head. "You make me sick, Florrie. You're like a bloody cat, purring and stretching whenever anyone strokes you."

Florentina laughed. Her sister slammed out the door, and she relaxed in the dimness, her ears lulled by the gurgle and splash of the rain, the swish and roar of passing cars, the sucking patter of feet on the road. Her mind was a stream that flowed silently, placidly, deeply and narrowly. Like a flower, benevolent, beautiful, unrelated to morality or inhibition, she bent this way and that before the wind, and thought nothing about anything.

She had grown up in the shadow of the great markets, her road strewn with blue-mouldy oranges, yellowing cabbage leaves, and apples brown-sugared with decay. There she had knelt, black-curled and angel-faced, coaxing out the lost kitten cowering beneath the wagon, or feeding broken sugarcane to the children who were not so fortunate as to have for a father a man in the wholesale fruit business. She could not remember when she was a virgin, if she knew the word. She dreamed her way through life, floating along on the stream of her own

196

drowsy intelligence, her own human-kindness, passing from one man to another and not being polluted by any of them. As long as they were kind to her, she did not mind who they were. When she was sixteen her father died, and she went to live with her sister Seppa, who had been on the streets a long time, and there she stayed, happy, incurious, waiting for life to happen to her.

Minutes or hours passed, half in sleep, half in waking dream, when there was the sound of wet boots on the balcony and a bang at the door.

"Push it. It ain't locked," called Florentina sleepily. Milkman, iceman, or customer, it did not matter to her. "Watcher want?"

Hughie stood there blinking in the dimness which, even after the dull grey of the streets, was that of a cave. He was at once abashed and excited at the sight of the girl on the bed, and dragged something out of his pocket. He wanted to say something significant and memorable, but he only growled, "You can have this."

"Gee, love!" She took the bangle, a streak of yellow light. He had bought her a present, and almost nobody ever bought her a present. Affection for him flooded her easy heart. "Ain't you a duck!" She tried it on, twisting her dark wrist this way and that to catch the light. "Don't it shine, Hughie! Just like a Christmas tree with all that stuff on the branches." She put her arms round his neck.

"Where's the kid?" mumbled Hughie.

"Oh, I dunno. Around. You don't want to worry about Lex. He never sees nothing."

Over his shoulder she could see a plate of apples on the table. "Gee," she thought, "I'd like a pear. I could go for a pear, one of them brown winter ones. Hope Seppa remembers to bring home the garlic. Last time we had stew there wasn't none, and it ain't the same somehow. When he's gone I'll get up and wash me hair. I'll do it right up with a lot of curls and a green ribbon round it like that tart I saw down town last Satdee arvo. I need a new dress, too. That blue one's nice but the colour's all gone funny where I spilt the wine on it. I better get out tonight and get meself some money, Seppa picking on me all the time like an old hen, think I never brought anything in to the house. That's a nice cop on the beat along Oxford Street. Never said a word to me. I sure do go for them blue eyes, like sparks. I could wear me new bangle with a new dress. I think I'll get green after all. Green makes Seppa look like an egg-yolk. Gee, she's getting fat, poor Seppa, must be all them spuds she eats. Hope she remembers the garlic."

Hughie lay with his face in the pillow, spreadeagled, trembling. She looked at him pityingly, and got him a drink. He gulped the red-hot spirit gratefully. He said, not looking at her, "You shouldn'ta let me."

This remark, which rose mechanically like a bubble from the submerged reef of Hughie's moralities, always left Florentina silent, not knowing what to say, for nobody else ever said it to her. She lifted the glittering bracelet and held it to her cheek.

"I sure do like you a lot, Hughie."

Hughie groaned. He sat with his head in his hands. He knew he would have to have money, lots of money, if he were to continue in this frail precarious heaven.

"I'm sick of this place," he said hoarsely. "Working me guts out for nothing. We'll go to Melbourne. You'd come to Melbourne with me, Florrie?"

"I sure would like to go to Melbourne," said Florentina meditatively, staring into the kitchen, where she could see the white eyeballs of Lex blinking in the shadows. Melbourne's the place where you can make money, all the girls said, just like Brisbane during the war. All them swank hotels, and me going in with a high-class feller, and one of them strapless evening gowns like the movie stars wear, and me hair long with a silver ornament in it, just here. But Seppa wouldn't ever leave Surro, and I sure would miss little Lexie. When Hughie's gone I'll light the fire in here and me and Lexie'll finish up the chocolates and have a good warm.

"What's that, love?" she asked Hughie.

She wondered what he'd been talking about, but it didn't matter, anyhow, for there was Seppa, stumping in, streaming with rain, a kit of food in each hand. She glared at Hughie, and Hughie, grabbing his hat, muttered, "Well, I better go through."

"Hope you don't get too wet, duck."

He plunged away into the silver sheet of the rain, and Florentina turned to her sister eagerly, "Bet yer forgot the garlic!"

Hughie battled up Coronation Street, cursing the people who hissed past in big cars, water swinging up in grey circles from the wheels. The rain squelched up in his shoes and bubbled out through the rotten stitching on the uppers. He felt nothing, thought nothing except of what obsessed him. He did not even think that he had been physically unfaithful again. Unfaith meant nothing to him, for his marriage, with his past, had disappeared in his mind. He could only think of himself, a man with no name, no trappings, no responsibilities, nothing except manhood. Yet his physical unfaithfulness did not bring any content, nothing but a deeper and wider hatred of life, of himself, and all the things that he knew. It bred confusion, and Hughie's mind was not made to cope with confusion.

As he skipped across the muddy road before the onslaught of the trucks the money in his pocket jingled. He had just enough there for a few drinks. The bangle, shoddy and all as it was, had taken all his pay. He wondered indifferently what Mumma would say when he told her there wouldn't be anything for the rent and the housekeeping this week, and bitter gall came up in his throat as he thought of her, and that intolerable house, and the yelping clamour of the children.

Well, she didn't have much to complain of. She had Dolour's money, and Mr Reilly's rent, and whatever Charlie would bring in.

"Let bloody Charlie keep the place for a while," growled Hughie to himself. "Wake him up a bit."

All at once he saw in a fruiterer's window a pale yellow pyramid of marmalade oranges, the ironically christened poor man's oranges that starred the winter orchards. Their skin was so smooth and shiny, their pith so plushy, their juice so tangy that they might well have been little wild grapefruit. But they were so bitter that they made Hughie's face screw up wryly at the very sight of them. Dolour loved to eat them, going round chewing at them, oblivious to the looks of loathing on the faces of her family.

"I'll get the kid a dozen."

But he only had enough money for a few drinks, and what use was it trying to carry a paper bag in this weather? Ten steps and the oranges would be bouncing all over the road.

"I'll get them again."

But he knew that it was a toss-up between the drink and Dolour, and the knowledge that she didn't have a chance was so cold, so bitter, so self-contemptuous that he swallowed hard as though someone had hit him, and plunged into the steamy maelstrom of the pub.

So it went on, for week after week, until one day Harry Drummy said to Dolour, "Aw, come on, let's go to the pitchers tonight."

"Go and get your head read", retorted the girl furiously. "I wouldn't go out with you again unless I had a diving suit on."

Harry was piqued. He'd been a bit sick of her frigid silence over the last months, and anyway, she'd brought it on herself, the way she'd led him on.

"Pretty choosy, ain't yer?"

Dolour sulkily slammed the milk bottles into the refrigerator, trying meantime to think up something smart.

"So bloody stuck-up no one's good enough for you. Pity yer old man ain't a bit the same way."

Dolour wiped the wet cloth energetically down the counter, flicking the crumbs his way. "What are you babbling about?"

Infuriated, the boy picked the crumbs off his shirt. "About that wop chromo your old man knocks about with, that's all."

Dolour stood with her mouth open. "Go on, you're mad." She dipped the cloth into the bucket of water.

"Oh, am I! I seen him down at her place meself. That yellow place on the corner of Elsey Street."

Suddenly Dolour could stand the sight of his hateful, jeering, pimply face no longer. She blazed, "Don't you say things like that, you dirty-minded jerk!"

Mrs Drummy popped out of the inner room. Her face was anxious. "What ever's the matter, love?"

Dolour was silent. Her lips trembled.

"I just happened to mention her dad and Florentina, that's all, Mum," said Harry, injured. "Thought she knew all about it. Isn't as though it's a secret."

Mrs Drummy looked from Dolour to Harry. "You shouldn't of told her," she said weakly. "It's uncharitable talk."

All at once Harry got mad. "Swanking around the way no feller was good enough for her. Why doesn't she look at her own family?"

Dolour hardly heard him. She appealed to Mrs Drummy. "It isn't true, is it?"

Poor Mrs Drummy didn't know what to do. She said cautiously, "Well, dearie, I'm not the one to say it is or isn't. You know my friend, Mrs Croucher, she lives next to Florentina's, and I seen your father myself going into Florrie's place, but you know how it is, maybe he had to go on business or something."

"Business!" guffawed her son. Mrs Drummy turned on him like an infuriated rabbit. "You get to the back of the shop, you big yob! And keep your nose out of Dolour's business. If I hear you slinging off at her again, I'll knock you bandy, honest to goodness I will!"

Harry marched out, trying to look haughty, but beetroot red at the back of the neck. Dolour's face was white. Mrs Drummy stood on tiptoe and put her arms round her.

"There, you don't want to get upset, dear. You know how men are. You can't trust any of them, not even the old boys. Don't I know what my Bert would get up to if I took my eye off him for a moment. Anyway, it mightn't mean anything. Just like I said, there's lots of things your father could go there for."

"What, for instance?" asked Dolour bleakly. Mrs Drummy floundered.

"There isn't anything," said Dolour. She took off her overall and folded it mechanically, staring at nothing. "Dadda! And he must be about fifty."

"Well," said Mrs Drummy helpfully, "he's a strong, healthy man."

Dolour's face crumpled. "Oh, stop it! Stop it!" she cried, and with a look of unutterable disgust, she grabbed up her things and ran out on to the street.

Dolour was trembling with fierce hatred of her father and fierce love of her mother. She felt sick with passion. For a long time she stood at the open window of the attic, unable to think or plan to do anything constructive. The disgust in her heart was a huge indigestible lump that completely demoralized her. How could he! She said it over and over again, grasping the sill so that the splinters went into her palm.

"How could You let him?" she cried passionately, putting her head on her hands and crying bitterly. She had often felt shame before, for her father drunken on the street, for her mother's shabbiness, for her own poverty in school, lack of clothes, of shoes, of threepences to give to the basketball fund or the bazaar. But this—to have everyone laughing at them because silly old Hughie Darcy was making a fool of himself over a prostitute.

She tramped up and down the room, face crimson, her eyes getting painful with the tears, imagining herself going down and facing Florentina and telling her to get out of the district or she'd kill her.

"And I would, too! I would! I would!"

And then her mind went off at another tangent, and she saw herself taking Hughie aside and talking to him sensibly and calmly, telling him of all her mother had been to him, and putting before him the wickedness of what he was doing. But she knew that she couldn't possibly do any of these things, that she was helpless, her hands tied before this inexplicable manifestation of adult character.

She felt that it wouldn't have been so bad if her father had fallen in love with a decent girl, whose very decency might have lent some romantic aspect to the affair. But a prostitute! And falling in love! Dolour castigated herself bitterly for using the expression, for what did love have to do with it? She felt as though she were sucked down in a current of evil, the old feeling that it was there, invisible, all-pervading, a dreadful miasma that she could never escape.

She forgot that she had loved her father, that he had been kind to her, and generous often, that he had been her protector when she was young, and her unnoticed guardian since she had grown up. All at once he became a man and nothing else.

"I'll run away," she babbled. "I won't stay in the same house with him."

And she imagined how all these weeks people had been coming into Drummy's and going out and jerking a thumb and saying, "That's 'er. That's his daughter," forgetting that the same thing had happened so many times that it was hardly more than a subject for idle gossip. But to Dolour she was the centre of all the scorn, the laughter, and the jeers. She made up her mind that her mother would never learn the truth from her, wiping her eyes and blowing her nose with such savagery that Mr Bumper Reilly, snoozing in the next room, awoke with the trembling conviction that it had been the trump of doom.

That day Mumma was feeling very happy. She sat on the step, Mikey on her spread lap, rocking gently back and forth, and enjoying the savour of the stew on the stove and the warm mellowness of the sunshine with equal pleasure. Now and then she turned Mikey over and listened approvingly to the wind bubbling out of him. "Was it at you, Mikey?"

There were very many things for her to do. The tubs were half full of nappies that she had started to wash and forgotten at some interruption. Motty had not been washed all day, and her legs wore socks of dirt. And there were pants to be patched, and a shirt with the elbow out, which Mumma had looked at helplessly a dozen times and then put away in the pathetic hope that Hughie would forget about it. But in spite of all these things Mumma just sat and enjoyed the sunshine, and played with the little boy. She knew that Motty was happy, dirt or no dirt, and as for the nappies, well, another hour in the tub would do them a world of good. She buried her face in Mikey's fat neck. "Wouldn't your mummy have loved you?"

At the thought of Roie tears came into her eyes, but they were not sad tears, for in the way of things the sorrow had been blunted, and now she could speak freely of her daughter and remember things about her that made her happy instead of grieved

"He kisses your pitcher every night, darling," she said.

She put the baby down in the yard, and went inside and yelled up the stairs for Dolour.

"What are you doing loafing up there when I'm run off me feet with the work?"

In an instant Dolour had forgotten all her love and passionate defence of her mother. She protested, "You are not. You've been sitting down there ever since I came home."

She flounced into the kitchen and surveyed the desolation with despair.

"What a pig-sty!"

Mumma was angry, because she was guilty. She made a backhanded swipe at Dolour. "Talking about your own home like that!"

"Well, what else would you call it?" flamed Dolour. The two women looked at each other with real, though evanescent dislike.

"Well, why don't you get down on your knees and give it a scrub, seeing you're so fussy?" demanded Mumma scornfully. She gave Puffing Billy a kick in the teeth. "Let me tell you a few things, young lady. You're too big for your boots, that's all. You always did have ideas bigger than your stomach could hold. Just because you've got a better education than any of us, forgetting that your poor father slaved to give it to you."

Dolour was scarlet with emotion. "Don't you poor father me. I'd like to see him fall off a tram."

Slam! Mumma's heavy hand hit her across the ear and almost knocked her flat. Bells ringing, drums beating, Dolour collapsed into a chair.

"Don't you talk about your father like that! It's a pity the nuns can't hear you, and them thinking so highly of you."

Dolour began to cry, talking in a loud high voice through her sobs so that hardly any of her words were intelligible.

"I hate him! I hate him! Oh, I wish I was dead!" She rubbed her ear, which felt as though it were swelling to the size of a plate. "I'm not the one you ought to hit. Why don't you have a go at his girl-friend? You're so smart with your fists you ought to have a go at Jack Hassen."

And so she sobbed and hiccuped her way through childish threats and inanities until Mumma seized her by the shoulders and cried, "What are you babbling about?"

Dolour had gone too far, so she said defiantly, "He's got a girl-friend, that's all. Everyone knows about it."

Mumma's mouth hung open, her face as pale as soap.

"Don't you dare say such—"

"I'm not daring anything," said the girl sullenly. "He's been knocking around with her for months." Then she began to cry again, her head on the table amongst the pots of jam and the torn tea-towels and bits of tape and old receipts that Mumma had left there when she was cleaning out the dresser. "Oh, Mumma, I didn't mean to tell you."

"You ain't sure?" asked Mumma. She searched her daughter's bleared face. Dolour nodded.

"Mrs Drummy said so. I guess that's what he bought the new shirts for."

There was a long silence. Fearfully Dolour looked at her mother. She stood there stirring the stew, round and round and round, looking at nothing. She said, "Do you reckon Charlie knows?"

"I dunno. I dunno who knows. Oh, Mumma, isn't it awful? Everyone laughing about it. He's an old man!"

"Mrs Drummy don't gossip," said Mumma finally.

They were silent a little while, then Mumma said, "The baby's out there in the yard, and Motty, she's out in front, with a dirty face."

"I'll go," said Dolour, anxious to escape, and she went out and found Motty, and took her into the yard, where she kept both children quiet, listening all the time for any sound from the kitchen, fearful and a little in awe of what might happen.

Mumma, left alone, showed every sign of a person suffering from shock. She stood so still it seemed she could hear the very ticking of her body, staring straight ahead of her and not seeing a thing. For a while she wandered aimlessly about the kitchen, putting on saucepan lids and picking up scraps of food, wiping her vegetable knife with detailed care. She could not think. Her mind was like an empty room, with many things in it, but none moving.

After a while she did the thing she always did when great trouble came to her. She put on her old brown coat and went down the road to the church. She must have gone along the street, perhaps even spoken to people, but she did not know it. She came to herself as she dipped a hand in the conch shell full of holy water at the door.

There was nobody in the church, for it was a busy hour. Mumma squeezed in between the seats and knelt down. The coolness of the place, the homely dust on the great arching beams, the comforting red glow of the sanctuary lamp was there. Always they had brought her peace before, but now they did not even register.

For Mumma had never considered Hughie with another woman. He was hers, and she was his, for better or worse, and although she had always had the worse end of the stick, that was marriage, and nothing could be done about it. Mumma had the true, traditional Irish regard for matrimony; in itself it was an important and significant and holy thing, and this very holiness made possible all the things that had been done in its name in Ireland and other places where people almost strangers, with no passion or magic between them, had become husband and wife and been true, and raised children, and died at last lamenting each other.

Mumma knew that marriage, the sacrament, was more important than the people committed to it, and thus she had never imagined, not even for a moment, the possibility that she should look at another man, or that Hughie should look at another woman.

The horror and shock of it lasted for a long time. Then, like a stirring in that empty room of her mind, came the grief, the terrible humiliation that she had loved and worked and suffered for this man, and now, at the end, had been thrown aside. She had put up with his drunkenness, his fecklessness, his complete disregard for her happiness and comfort, and the poverty he had brought with him. Yes, she had been the injured one, the one who had borne, and not complained, and yet she was to be discarded, and the worst of it was that Dolour knew it. This was Mumma's bitterest knowledge. She did not know why; she only knew that her most intrinsic dignity had been laid waste.

Mumma tried to awaken her wild Irish anger, but it was crushed, silent, and unwilling to give even a wag of its tail. The grief and the shock, appalling in their pain, surrounded her, drowned her, and her spirit sank beneath them in a despair that not even she had known before.

She knelt there a long time, a shapeless clod in the gathering shadows; thick red hands over its eyes, skirt trailing in the dust of the kneeler, and the patched soles and run-over heels turned up to the gaze of any passer-by. Out of that hour of pain came many, many thoughts. She had given up her name for that man. Along with all the other things she had carelessly and indeed even joyously given up had been her own patronymic, and yet Kilker had been a name that had fought its way through the

206

famine, and the black plague, and the Troubles, and survived to travel steerage to Australia nearly ninety years before. An unbeatable name it had been, yet she had thrown it away at Hugh's bidding, put it on a shelf and never so much as took it out and gave it a shake and a kind word.

And her own name, her baptismal name, what had happened to it? She was a stranger to it. No one ever used it any more. She was a nonentity, a creature who had entered marriage a person, and within a year was nothing but Mumma, an institution.

"Where's it all gone?" cried Mumma's soul. "Where's me hair that was so curly, and so pretty, and the way me complexion never got a spot on it, and the bust that made even a five-bob blouse look like the front of a ship? Where's the times I went out with Roie on one hand and Thady on the other, and Roie with the great ribbon in her hair, and Thady's legs so fat and round that everyone smiled? Oh, God, what have You done with all the years?"

And Mumma's memory stumbled from tumbledown shanty to bug-ridden residential, to evil dirty cottage; up lanes she'd nearly forgotten, to countless gates where she'd waited for Hughie, dreading to see the stammer in his step as he came up the road. And she saw the red geranium she'd once grown in a pickle bottle, and the little canary that had choked on a bit of banana, and the lovely hat with the flowers she'd worn for her wedding.

And Thady came into her thoughts, playing marbles on the footpath, the way he'd been before he'd disappeared; and Roie, kicked and bleeding the night she'd told her Mumma she'd been going to have Tommy Mendel's baby.

Oh, there were many things. Mumma stared straight into the face of God and they rushed through her mind, pell-mell, like birds flying—the great sadnesses, the disappointments, the endless anonymous monotony of her life that was no more than a passage and a buffer for the other lives about it.

"It makes you wonder what a body's born for," she said.

She got up. Her bones seemed to have set into a clumsy, bowed shape, and it was hard to genuflect. She stood for a moment on the steps, blinking in the last of the sunlight. The street flowed past, almost unseen, and it was with difficulty that she brought her thoughts and her eyes to Mrs Drummy, coming up the steps.

"Why, Mrs Darcy!" said Mrs Drummy. "You ain't got your hat on."

Mumma put up her hand, and there was her bare, tousled head.

"Neither I have," she said in a tone of incredulous wonder. She looked bewildered at the other woman for a moment, then her lips began to tremble and she put down her head and hurried away.

2 O

NEVER again at any time did Mumma mention Hughie and Florentina. Like Patrick Diamond, who had ignored his cancer, so did Mumma ignore this incredible eruption in her married life, hoping that because it was ignored it would go away and stop bothering her.

Before her dignity, her silent, self-contained dignity, Dolour felt childish. Her anger flickered out into doubt and uncertainty, her disgust into bewilderment. For what was it all about? Dolour did not know. Hughie was just the same to them as he always was, coming home tired and dirty-faced, ready to snap their heads off till he'd got his boots off and had a snore-off on the couch. He still yelled at Motty one moment, snatching her up and cuddling her extravagantly the next. When he was drunk he still hung tearfully over Mikey, trying to ease the pain that came when he thought of Roie, and he always thought of Roie when he was drunk.

She and Mumma stared at him as though he were a new man, and the mystery was that he was still the same old Hughie. Had he been like this all the time, faithful to them in his way, and yet running off in his mind after other women? Dolour was so confused that she felt sick. For the greatest puzzle of all was how a man could have a wife and family and go on living with them, and yet love another girl.

For to Dolour's mind the issue was clear-cut. If you loved someone you went away and joined your life with theirs. You could not travel two roads at once.

Sometimes she hated her father so much that when he brushed against her she shrank away, and the moment afterwards yearned for him when he looked puzzled and hurt. For Hughie, in his confidence that nobody knew about his association with Florentina, acted as though he were innocent. In effect he was innocent, and would be until found out.

So he looked at Dolour and said wistfully, "You're getting

that cranky. Why don't you turn in that job and get a better one?"

"We need the money," she answered coldly and obstinately.

"You ought to go to night school," he said with unwonted timidity. "I know how you feel, and you having to leave school and everything when you was getting on so well."

"Maybe I don't want to go to night school," she said, and turned away.

"Next year I'm on to a better job down at the factory and I could shout you to a course in typewriting and shorthand or something down in town, like Gracie Drummy," he pressed eagerly.

Both Hughie and Dolour knew very well that any extra money he might earn would go the way it had always gone, but once the thought would have pleased her as much as the act, and she would have thrown her arms round her Dadda and given him a hug.

But now she did not say a word, leaving Hughie bewildered and affronted.

Just as he had ceased to be Dolour's father, to become a man, so did he become a man to Mumma, who had for twenty-five years looked on him as that anonymous humdrum creature, a husband. At night as he lay snoring on the far side of the bed, she crept over and put her hand on him, feeling his flesh that was still warm and smooth, and his shoulder still strong and shapely. She felt almost sinful as she did it, quick to alarm at his snort or snuffle, ready to roll away to her side of the bed to pretend sleep.

"What did you have to do it for?" Her thoughts went round and round, wondering what was the matter with her that he went looking elsewhere. She was old, of course she was, but so was Hughie, and Mumma could see nothing but unnaturalness in a middle-aged man's chasing after a young girl.

"It's just as if I got sweet on a young feller like Charlie."

At the very thought an embarrassed giggle came out of Mumma into the darkness, and Hughie grunted inquiringly. Mumma lay as still as a mouse, hoping he would not awake, and yet longing for him to do so, so that she could have it out with him, furious denunciation and denial, abusive admission, and perhaps forgiveness. For Mumma knew that even if there were no repentance there would be forgiveness.

She thought sometimes of Dolour's outburst about the kitchen being dirty, and how the girl spent all her Saturdays scrubbing and washing, and she thought, "All very well, but after twenty-five years of married life it's as much as you can do to keep yourself clean."

Suddenly doubt entered her mind. Giving your face a lick with a wash-cloth, and a bit of a rinse round the neck and armpits wasn't the way the advertisements in the papers spoke of being clean. He could talk, anyway. Him with all his new shirts. They didn't hide the grey in his whiskers. And as for that Florentina, all them Italian girls ran to fat, and got hairy round the face. But Mumma made up her mind that she would smarten up a little, just to show Hughie what he didn't have the sense to appreciate.

Hanging out the nappies—for Mumma was too bothered to train Mikey otherwise, and so he was still using them—she pondered how she should do it. She hauled on the dry sooty rope, and away up between the walls flew the clothesline, the nappies flying like signal flags from some unimaginably drab battleship.

"That's the way it is," said Mumma, watching the soot, like bits of black lace, sifting down out of the paint-blue sky. There was a flicker of movement in the open doorway, and Mr Bumper Reilly's little face appeared for a moment, upside down like a mirage. Mumma squinted until she realized that he was peering round the side of the door. Delicately she went inside, and not till a scamper of creaks on the stairs told of a mission accomplished did she go outside.

"He's no company," sighed Mumma.

She got the mirror, a thing she hadn't done for years, and for a long time looked at her face. It seemed to her that she was fading away. It wasn't sickness, or thinness of body. Rather were her bones sinking into each other, joint upon joint, so that her frame was forced outwards into a squatness it surely hadn't possessed when she was young.

"I'm not going to be a neat old woman like Ma was," mourned Mumma. "And I ain't got the skin she had, that white you would have thought she was a lady."

For a while she thought of her Ma, saying a little prayer for her rest, and then remembering that rest was the last thing Grandma would ever have wanted, and changing the prayer in a hurry to, "Make heaven to her liking, dear Lord."

She was still there when Dolour came in for lunch, dragging a shrieking Motty by the hand.

"I found her down the road with her pants off. She was carrying gravel in them, and throwing it at motor-cars," she said giving the turbulent one a shake.

"Watcher doing, Nana?" asked Motty, opening wide her tearless eyes.

"Looking at me teeth," said Mumma sadly. She rolled up her lip for Motty's inspection. Dolour shuddered.

"Jeepers, what an awful-looking lot of clothes-pegs. Why don't you get them out?"

"I was thinking of it," said Mumma. "A person can't look their best with a mouthful of old snags."

Dolour understood instantly. "I can just see you with a lovely set of white teeth," she said. Enthusiasm filled her. "I'll pay them off for you, Mumma. Gee, you'd look nice. Fatter in the face."

They looked at each other like conspirators. Dolour burst out, "Show him a few things! You don't have to depend on him to buy new teeth for you."

It had been so long since Mumma had good teeth that she couldn't remember what she looked like with them. They had started to go when Roie was on the way, and by the time Dolour was born they were crumbling like old monuments. It was a long time since she had had a toothache, for the nerves were all dead, and the teeth just lay like yellow stumps in the gums. But she hadn't forgotten her childish horror of dentists, ever since a drunken dentist in her childhood had planked her down in a chair and, holding her jaw in a steely grip with one hand, crushed a molar to pieces in complete disregard of her hysterical shrieks.

"I think maybe I'll wait till the weather's colder, so I can wear me coat," she said uncertainly, looking at Dolour hopefully.

"No you don't," said her daughter. "You're going as soon as I can get an appointment for you."

"Me shoes are that awful," protested Mumma, and they argued back and forth across the lunch table, Dolour holding Michael on her lap and poking spoonfuls of vegetables into his mouth. He was a remarkable eater. He would obligingly eat all his dinner and then, after his junket or jelly had been amiably taken, eject an unsullied mouthful of pure carrot. Now the food oozed out as fast as she put it in, and she scraped it up and determinedly put it back again.

"Want to grow up a squib? Want to be as thin as a stick of celery?"

212

Mumma sighed. Roie wouldn't have bothered to make the child eat. But Michael went to Dolour when he tumbled from his chair, cried for her, "Do-Do-Do!" when he was sad, and laughed at her approach.

"You'd think she was his mother," said Mumma privately to herself. "She's that queer, interested in babies at her age."

But she had been the same way, doting on all her small brothers and sisters until they'd been carried off by colic or whooping cough, and lamenting over them until a new one had come along, for Grandma had been indefatigable.

Motty decided she had had enough, spat out a bone, and dived for the door.

"Hey, where are you going?" asked Dolour.

"Out," replied Motty briefly. She remembered a child down the road who had a string of red wooden balls, and Motty considered that it would be easy enough to take them off him. At the thought she bunched her filthy, scratched little fists.

"You come back here," commanded Dolour. Motty spat juicily at her, and ran.

With lips grim Mumma rose and went after her. Most of the time Motty was entirely out of her control, but she did not admit it in front of Dolour. Dolour sighed. She went on feeding Mikey, kissing the back of his soft neck and murmuring words that meant nothing except that she loved him. So they were when Charlie came in, pushing open the door half apologetically as though he no longer had any place in that house. When he saw the sleek dark head bent over the fuzzy one, his heart stopped for a moment.

"Why, Charlie, what are you doing home?"

"Breakdown. Thought I might as well come home." He sat down, wearily.

"You finish giving Mikey his milk and I'll get some lunch for you. I gotta go back soon."

From the stove she watched him covertly as she lapped an egg with the sizzling fat. He stared at the child sucking at the mug as though he had never seen it before.

"I hope he notices that Mikey has a dimple," thought Dolour. "I hope he sees that his hair goes up in the front like Roie's, and his chin's like hers. Gosh, I don't know why he isn't interested in Mikey." Aloud she said, "I'll take him now. You eat something."

Once she would have been uncomfortable alone with Charlie, looking for things to say, or excuses to leave the room. But now she sat companionably silent, buttering him a piece of bread, pushing the salt along before he needed it. Furtively he looked at her, wondering how she was content to stay in this place that once she had rebelled against, wondering what she thought of when she was alone.

Dolour said, "You ought to go away for your holidays this year, Charlie. You look rotten."

He did not answer, and she burst out, "And no wonder, leading the sort of life you do, lying around all the week-end half stewed and never taking any interest in anything. And I'll bet the last time you were in church was at Roie's funeral!"

His eyes blazed at her. "Oh, shut your trap!" He pushed the plate away and he and Dolour glared at each other over the baby's soft hair like two dogs. Dolour felt a pang of pleasure that she had awakened him from his apathy. In her mind she quickly revolved whether it would be better to backtrack like Mumma, or attack tooth and claw, like Grandma, but before she could decide he said, "I'm going away for good. Perhaps that'll satisfy you."

The words were ordinary ones, but as though they had been in a new and magic language, a door slammed shut in Dolour's mind and she knew what she felt about this man. He had been the barrier to all the world about her, the last fence to protect her against its coarseness and cruelty, the last link she had with delicacy and sensitivity and self-respect. She recognized that she had bitterly opposed his downward path not only on his behalf, but on her own, because he had represented all that was stable in her unstable life.

"How can I do without you, Charlie!" cried her heart, and tears gushed into it, and she bent over to hide them. She said in a strangled voice, "I don't know that I blame you. You ain't —haven't ever fitted into this place."

"I've lost myself somewhere," he said with difficulty. "You know."

"Yes, I know."

"I thought if I cleared out of it, it might be easier. The kids won't miss me. Mumma'll look after them. I'll send her their keep."

Dolour was silent. Then she said, "Money isn't all a father gives to his children. And Motty needs someone all to herself, even if Mikey doesn't yet."

"Motty?"

"Haven't you noticed?" asked Dolour painfully. "Motty isn't

the kid she was when Roie was here. She's the cheekiest kid in the street. Mumma can't do a thing with her. And neither can I."

"But Mumma—" Charlie was astounded.

"Mumma can't look after kids the way she looked after Roie and me. She's old now. She says God will give Motty grace in His own good time, but what she needs isn't grace but a good hard switching three times a day." She looked appealingly at the man. "I dunno how to put it, Charlie. Mumma loves Motty and Mikey, but as long as they're happy she doesn't care about keeping them clean, or putting warm clothes on them, or watching out they don't play with kids that have the measles—or anything." Suddenly the tears came to the top. "She's on the street all the time and I just can't forget the way Suse Kilroy grew up, or the way Thady disappeared. There's such awful men wandering around and—" She gulped. "I suppose you'll say I've just got an imagination."

Now he was confused, appalled that he hadn't thought of this before, ashamed that he had had to be told, guilty that he had been going to leave these children without a thought for their future except physical provision.

He said, "I'll go out for a while."

Dolour rose, too. "Don't go to the pub, Charlie." Then she blushed and grinned. "I sound like Mumma talking to Dad. I guess it runs in the family. Go on, get drunk, and see if I care."

He said wonderingly, "You do care."

He saw her for the first time as a young woman, and not as a child who looked a little like his dead wife. She was grown-up. She was old enough to have borne the child she carried, she was old enough to get married and go away and never be there for him to talk to any more. He had forgotten that there was nothing to keep her there, while there were two children to keep him. He said, not knowing what else to say, "You're a good kid."

Dolour's eyes fell. "I'd better get back to Drummy's." Inside herself she was saying, "I'm not a kid. I never will be any more."

Right up to the last moment on the Thursday when Mumma had her dentist's appointment she maintained the illusion that she was going, alluring Dolour along by frequent references to herself as a sight for sore eyes with her glittering double row of new teeth.

"Do you think I could have a tiny speck of gold, about ten bob's worth, in the front ones, darling? It looks so tasteful." And,

"After all, a body hasn't been able to smile properly in the last ten years, what with the awful spectacle it's been, and the cold air playing jip with the aching ones."

Dolour eyed her with suspicion. She had her doubts of Mumma's glibness and careless courage. "I'm going with you, you know. Mrs Drummy's given me the afternoon off."

Mumma looked at her like a trapped animal. She hadn't quite decided which excuse she thought best, but she hadn't banked on Dolour's presence complicating everything.

Dolour said grimly, "I'm going to press out your dress now."

"It's got egg down the front," protested Mumma feebly.

"How on earth did you get egg on it?" demanded Dolour angrily.

"I dunno," faltered her mother. She flared up momentarily at the expression on Dolour's face. "Don't you look at me in that tone of voice, young lady, or I won't go at all!"

"Oh, won't you?" said Dolour, tipping up the shiny black bottom of the flat-iron and touching it with a sizzling wet finger. Mumma stamped after her. "No, I won't, if I don't want to."

"All right," said Dolour. "Stay home and look awful and have Dadda run off altogether with his girl-friend." Mumma went pale, for that had not entered her mind. Dolour stretched out the dress and rubbed at the egg stain. "And then you'll have to go to work in a café washing greasy dishes all day."

"You stop that talk," quavered Mumma. She pressed her hand to her face. "Oh, me nerves are all jumping and bumping fit to kill. I'll go next week."

"And what a fool you'll feel when you remember that you could have had the whole thing over by then," said Dolour, clouds of steam from the wet cloth rising around her. "You go and get your stockings on."

Miserably, talking to herself, condemning Dolour one moment and proudly thinking how much the girl thought of her mother the next, Mumma dragged up the stockings and jammed her feet into the boat-shaped shoes.

"Oooer!" she began, and then, hopefully, "Oh, Holy Mother, me bunions are that bad I could cry."

"Probably your bad teeth poisoning your whole body," returned the hard-hearted girl from the kitchen.

Mumma scowled. "It's a grand lot of sympathy I'd be getting from you, my girl, and me in me death agony."

"Here you are, put it on," said her callous daughter briskly, "while I do my hair."

Mumma snatched the dress, hating it, and then remembering she had worn it for Roie's wedding, and holding it to her breast tenderly.

"It's one thing I'll never send to the ragman."

Upstairs she could hear Dolour bumping about, and a sudden glint flashed into her eyes. With great agility she climbed on the bed and groped about in the clots of dust on top of the wardrobe. There was her navy hat, approximately the shape of a jelly-mould, and trimmed with a flute of pink ribbon. Ordinarily she loved her hat, but now she detested it. Cunningly she tipped it over the back of the wardrobe, where it fell down into the mouldy darkness on top of all the other things that had accumulated there throughout the years, for the wardrobe weighed two tons, and could not be moved by anyone except a giant.

Giggling, Mumma continued to get dressed. When Dolour came down she was rubbing her nose with a powder puff and saying docilely, "I suppose I'd better take a lot of clean hankies."

Dolour was delighted. "I'll fix that. You do look nice, too. Now, where's your hat." She sprang upon the bed and rooted round in the well of the wardrobe. "That's funny." She pulled open the door, and half a dozen garments fell out and engulfed her. "You're going to have gas, and it'll be over and done with before you know it," she cheered, fighting her way out of the clothes, and diving into the musty depths of the wardrobe.

"Gas!" sneered Mumma silently, looking with real enjoyment at Dolour's heaving form as she struggled with the fifty old shoes, cardboard boxes, and fallen, dust-stiffened garments on the wardrobe floor.

"It's not here," said her daughter, redfaced and puzzled.

"Well, I dunno," said Mumma. "I musta wore it last Sunday."

There were not many places in that room for a hat to hide. Dolour peered under the bed, snorting at all the dust and papers which had been swept under there. She came forth snorting with Motty's shoes.

"There, I told you she didn't lose them."

"I wonder where it could be, dearie?" cried the false Mumma. "We're going to be late if we can't find it soon."

Slowly Dolour went over the room to the shelves in the corner, then whizzed round to face her mother.

"Hah!" she cried. Mumma wiped the expression off her face

217

with lightning speed, but it was too late. Dolour stalked towards her. "You hid it!" she accused.

Mumma decided to brazen it out. "Be that as it may or isn't," she proclaimed, "I ain't going without me hat for no one, so if you can't find it you can wait till next week to get me teeth out."

"Oh, you're a heart-breaker!" raged Dolour. "After I went to all the trouble to get you an appointment, and got the afternoon off and everything! I could murder you!"

Mumma sniffed triumphantly, but she had reckoned without the spirit of her daughter.

"All right," cried the girl. "You can't go without a hat, but I can!"

She yanked the dark felt sailor off her head and planked it down on Mumma's amazed and tousled head. It curled up at the sides, and made Mumma look like some exotic type of long-haired padre. But she was too angry to laugh.

"You're coming if I have to drag you every foot of the way."

Mumma peered into the glass. "I won't go. I wouldn't be seen dead in it."

"You'll be found dead in it if you don't pull yourself to-gether. Think you're smart, don't you! You're just like a kid!"

Mumma had two pink patches in her cheeks. A fine and glorious temper was working up in her, but before she could frame it in suitable words, Dolour jeered, "You're just scared, that's all. You're frightened. And you're supposed to be Irish! Oh, I'm ashamed!"

Before this insult to the nation Mumma folded up her lips so tightly they disappeared altogether, so that she looked like a missionary about to thunder hell and damnation. She took up her withered little purse and marched out, Dolour following her and silently giggling. At the front door Mumma's brief rage flickered out.

"I want to go to the back again," she appealed.

"No you don't," said Dolour inexorably, and she marched her Mumma down to the tram stop. It was a lovely afternoon, and Mumma should have been glad to have the children off her hands for the afternoon, for Mrs Campion was looking after them, and had promised not to feed them any rubbidge, but she wasn't, she was too mad. By the time she reached the dentist's, the loathsome white-tiled place with its smell of antiseptics, and the clink of instruments sinisterly penetrating the bright bareness of the waiting-room, she was in a lather of fear, her eyes sticking out, and her fingers boring holes in her handbag.

Dolour watched her sympathetically, but she knew that at the first sign of weakening Mumma would be up and off like a hare.

"You don't want to be frightened," she said kindly. "Remember how brave you used to be when you brought Roie and me here to have teeth out."

Mumma gave her a look that seared her to the bone. Just then a patient tottered through from the surgery, a blood-red handkerchief pressed to his mouth. Mumma reared up on her chair.

Dolour forgot all her psychology. "Gee, it'll all be over in a minute or two, Mumma, and it won't hurt. And you will look lovely with your new teeth, honest."

Mumma nodded voicelessly, and when the nurse appeared she followed her without a word. Dolour relaxed. She fished in her pocket for her rosary beads, and began mechanically to say Hail Marys for her poor mother with the funny hat on, hoping the dentist wasn't the hairy old shocker he had been in her day. Though the door was closed, she could hear the clink of glass on porcelain, and the slight sound of the gas apparatus.

"Don't let him hurt her," prayed Dolour. "She's that upset with Dadda and everything."

The next moment there was a loud masculine exclamation, the crash of a breaking glass, and a shudder of the door as though someone had tried to come through it without bothering to open it first. Dolour jumped up, just in time to catch Mumma as she hurtled through, bug-eyed and yellow-pale, but still with all her teeth.

Behind her appeared the red angry face of the dentist, and a flustered-looking nurse.

Mumma's face twisted up like a child's and tears popped out of her eyes.

"I ain't going back in there," she sobbed. Dolour looked apologetically at the dentist.

"I had hardly begun to examine her teeth when up she bounced out of the chair," he expostulated. Dolour patted her mother's back. Suddenly she seemed so small, so old, that the girl gave up all hope of new teeth for her.

"She's had a lot of trouble," she whispered.

All the way down the stairs Mumma kept sobbing, but deep down in her soul she was crowing. Dolour wiped the tears off her face and pulled the awful hat down further over her forehead.

219

"Me teeth are jumping like grasshoppers," moaned Mumma. "Oh, I can't face the tram."

"We'll walk then," soothed Dolour.

They passed down the crooked lanes where the slattern houses leaned close as though gossiping about dark secrets. Some had sandstone steps, cunningly placed out in the footpath to trip the drunken or shortsighted. They were worn down almost to the road level. On the balconies sat old people, sunken-mouthed, hair tightly drawn back, taking the sunshine into their brittle old bones. There was a smell of age everywhere, and of stones that had soaked up the dankness and mouldiness of winter and were now opening their pores and giving it back.

"You're ashamed of me," lamented Mumma.

"Course I'm not."

"My feet hurt that much," said Mumma in excuse. Dolour sighed, for Mumma seemed to hurt in so many places.

"When I get my next pay we'll buy you a nice new pair of shoes," she said.

"What about the coat you was saving up for?" asked Mumma hopefully.

"That can wait."

Suddenly they came upon an extraordinary thing. It was a patch of blue sky where it had no business to be at all. In this place the skyline had not been seen for eighty or ninety years, and yet there it was, bright and bare between two goblin houses that looked forlorn and surprised because they had nothing to lean against.

"That's what they do to yer," proclaimed Mumma sorrowfully.

A heap of rubble lay where the old house had once been, and its squat shape was imprinted upon the aboriginal clay that had not been seen by the eye of man for so long. And now they saw that the houses on either side were empty-eyed, staring at the sun for perhaps the last time.

"Yairs," said a woman leaning over a near-by fence. "The whole terrace is coming down. Next month we go out on our heads, and my father and mother lived here before I was born."

"Fancy," said Mumma sympathetically.

"Old Mrs Farrell lived in that place," said the woman, pointing with her thumb to the empty space. "Blind, she was. Knew it like the back of her hand. Now they've pushed her into one room out at Lilyfield. Fell down the stairs the first day. Doesn't know a soul to give her a hand with the cooking or shopping. Here we all took an interest in helping old Mrs Farrell.

"Well." She booted a rooster back into the hall as it came striding through the house to freedom. "That's progress for yer, love. That's progress."

Mumma and Dolour went silently on, Mumma with a vast dread pressing on her even more painfully than her bunions.

Dolour said, "But it might be years before they get around to Plymouth Street."

"I dunno why they can't leave us alone," said Mumma dully. "I ain't ever heard anyone out Surry Hills complain about the way they lived."

Now it was sunset, and a breeze awoke in Redfern and came leaping up the gutters, bowling the bits of paper before it. They turned into Coronation Street, a bedlam of noise, with the trams crashing and clanking round the corner, their flanges reverberating against the points as though they hated them, and the wires overhead singing on an infinitely high note. Mumma stopped before the window of a ham and beef shop, where Mr Kontominos, in the midst of clearing his window for the day, was resting amongst the pickled cucumbers and the sausages cleaning his nails with his long fork. He ducked and smiled at them.

"Oh, look at the nice brawns," admired Mumma, looking at the glazed pink circlets of heterogenous meat. "Your Dadda would just love one of them for tea."

"Let him go and run after his own brawns," snapped Dolour.

Mumma was abashed. She wanted very much to go in and buy the delicacy, but she felt that after her carryings-on this afternoon, she had better pull her horns in a bit with Dolour. Dolour spied some tomato sausages sitting in the window-corner.

"Oh, isn't that the stuff Ro brought home one day? Charlie liked it, didn't he?"

Before Mumma could object, for it gave her the repeaters, Dolour had darted in to get some. Little Mr Kontominos was just about to close up. He was a small, sweet-faced Greek whose hair had slid backwards over the crown of his head in an orderly retreat from life. He seemed to be worried, going to the door to peer up the street.

"What's the matter, Mr Kontominos?"

"Big trouble," he muttered, and was wrapping up the sausages when all at once there was a roar and the trampling of many feet. Dolour found herself being pushed towards the door. The sausages were thrust into her hand, and the shilling plucked out of it, and Mr Kontominos's door banged behind her, and the bolt crashed into its socket. Bewildered, she shrank into the doorway, looking at the mass of fighting men who surged about in the street.

"Mumma!"

But where was Mumma? Panic-stricken, Dolour tried to get out of the doorway, but a bottle crashed at her feet and a splinter stuck into her ankle. The next moment two threshing figures reeled against her, and the tomato sausages were squashed into a pink blob against her chest. She shoved, and the two figures toppled out into the stream of the main battle and were swept away.

What the fight was about nobody, not even the contestants, could have said. It had started with somebody spilling somebody else's beer down a third party's coat in the Thatchers' Arms down the street, and before the police arrived four hundred men and women were involved. Now the police were here, and the majority of the crowd had turned on them, determined to prevent their arrest of anybody at all. Blue forms, crushed by superior numbers, shot up off the ground here and there, and whistles cried piercingly for help that never came.

An old woman, who had been tottering down the street with a little billy of milk, was knocked down and trodden into the pavement, and Dolour heard the shrieks of children dragged away from their mothers and lost amidst the forest of hostile legs. Ever an anon, above the roar, could be heard the blithe pipings of old men who, safe up on their balconies, leaned over rails and exhorted everyone to 'ave a lash.

"Mumma!" roared Dolour, reverting to the strong-lunged terror of her youth, and as though in answer she saw the red face of Mumma, far out on the stream, with one arm jammed above her head, and the little withered handbag still clutched in it. Dolour flung herself into the crowd. Blows flew past her face, and now and then she came hard against a pair of men locked like wrestlers, crudely trying to kill each other, and not making the slightest impression. Now a punch on the shoulder thrust her hard back against a fat lady who shrieked and jabbed her in the stomach with her elbow. Mad with rage, Dolour stamped on a foot, but it didn't belong to the fat lady, and the anguished face of a friend and neighbour swept past her on the tide.

At last she reached Mumma. Mumma was spent and gasping,

222

squashed so hard on every side that she had almost popped out of the top of her corsets.

"Oh, Dolour," she gasped, "I'm going to faint."

Frantically Dolour held up her head above the crush, for she knew that if Mumma slipped and sank beneath the trampling feet she would be killed. Sobbing, sweating, she pushed off the wild faces, beating men in the chest and slapping women off Mumma until all at once she was jammed in a corner against something hard and metallic. The sound of a key in a padlock was lost in the chaos of screams, oaths, and crashing glass, for already the brighter spirits in the crowd were smashing the ends off bottles and using them as wicked weapons. The metallic bars behind her parted, and a hand rudely dragged her and Mumma inside the shelter. The same hand ruthlessly thrust back a little ragged man, who scrambled to follow them, and the grids clanged together.

"Quickly."

Half-dead, Mumma and Dolour staggered into a dark shop. In the show-cases dimly winked brassy gold and shoddy silver. The old-clo' smell of the pawnbroker's establishment was there.

"Oh, Mr Mendel," sobbed Mumma, "I'm on me last legs."

The old pawnbroker took them into the room behind the shop. It seemed to be furnished in untold luxury, with a carpet smooth under their shoes, and a polished table which showed not the usual film of bloom, but gentle reflections from a red-shaded reading lamp.

"Jeepers, lookut all the books!" gasped Dolour, her eyes wandering in awe over the shelves. There was in this room the smell of old leather, of floor polish, and a strange, sweetish tobacco.

Mumma fell into a chair. Even in this moment of stress Mr Mendel's noble white hair was neatly brushed, his black silk coat falling in classic folds about his gaunt frame. Though outside bodies crashed against his thoughtfully grated window, and hoarse yells and imprecations filled the air, he took no notice whatsoever, pressing brandy on Mumma with a courteous air as though she were his guest and nothing else mattered. Anyway, brawls had occurred outside Mr Mendel's shop so often they were merely a part of the occupational perils of his profession.

Dolour became aware that her leg was bleeding profusely. Her torn stocking was blackened with blood, and a great slow gout was bulging over the side of her shoe. In a moment it would fall on the carpet. All Dolour's fright, her anger, her physical stress, her terror for Mumma's safety, became concentrated on one small point—she could not let her blood soil the beautiful blue carpet. She held her ankle, not knowing what to do with it, pressing her grubby handkerchief against the wound.

"It's nothing," she said, embarrassed. "A bottle hit me. It's just a bit of a mess."

She giggled, abashed, as she saw, hovering in the farther shadows of the room, another man. He was a pale, fattish fellow, with dark and sullen eyes, a soft white neck, and a look, deep down under unfamiliar contours, of familiarity. Dolour's gaze fastened on him piercingly. In a moment she was twelve, with short socks, and shoes with henpecked toes, and there was all around her the gaudy rowdiness of the Paddy's Markets—and Roie—and she was looking at a scarlet shawl on an old-clo' stall.

"Tommy!" she cried, and then was unsure, and turned her face away and blushed. She was aware that a most extraordinary change had come over her Mumma. Lying back in the chair, smelling strongly of brandy, and still looking pale she was, but the next moment her face flushed darkly and she turned her head as though by compulsion and stared at the young man.

"My nephew Tommy," said Mr Mendel, motioning the young man closer. He limped forward diffidently, not wanting to show himself, and yet putting a bold front on it.

"Hullo, Mrs Darcy," he said.

"How are yer?" said Mumma, not wanting to know at all.

"Gee, Tommy Mendel!" marvelled Dolour. "I'd forgotten all about you. You went clean outa me mind."

"Thanks," he grunted.

Dolour stared at him, trying to find the slender, delicate boy he once had been in this sickly-looking fat young man. He could not have been older than twenty-six or seven, but he looked well into his thirties. His belt was stuck out a little over a balcony of stomach, and she had grown so much in stature that she thought he had grown shorter. Tommy stared covertly back, trying to place the tall dark girl as the stumpy-legged, loud-voiced child he remembered. Disconcerted, he looked at Mumma.

"How's old Ro these days?"

Mumma's face was sickly. "She's been dead over eighteen months," she said. Dolour stared angrily at Tommy, whose life had gone on without his knowing that Roie was dead, or hardly caring that he knew. He was astounded.

"My God, what knocked her off? She couldna been more than twenty-four!"

Cripes, Roie! The first girl he'd ever had. He remembered her soft hair and the way her eyes glimmered in the dark, and her soft-lips, not knowing how to kiss, but wanting to. That kid! Dead as a doornail. Dead as she ever could be. Tree shadows, and the cool, needley grass, and trams casting yellow flares across the grass, and Roie crying and not knowing how to say no. And now she was dead for all that time, the way he well might be next year with his chest, and the way coughs hung on, tearing the guts outa him all winter. And the bad taste he had in his mouth when he got up, and his bell burning like acid after he'd had a drink, the way he might have been an old bastard instead of only in his twenties.

He stared at Mumma, waxy with shock and fear, and Dolour thought, "I was wrong. He does care. I remember him going out with Roie. He musta liked her, even though nothing came of it."

"Get some water and some cloths to bathe the girl's ankle," said old Mr Mendel curtly, but Mumma heaved to her feet, crying, "Don't you touch her, you—you—" To see her mother there, her face puffy and scarlet with rage, her eyes glittering, defeated by her inarticulateness, struggling for words to express an emotion Dolour couldn't understand, appalled the girl.

"Mumma, what ever's the matter?"

Mumma seized her by the arm and began pulling her towards the door.

"Not that way," said old Mr Mendel quietly, guiding Mumma towards the back entrance. Mumma struck his arm down, pushing rudely past him, and dragging Dolour willy-nilly, so that she had time for no more than an appealing, bewildered glance at the old pawnbroker before she was stumbling down the steps into the cool quiet of the clean cobbled yard, where a frangipanni-tree bloomed whitely in a mist of fragrance.

"Mumma, he was kind to us!" she cried, but it was no good. Her mother pushed her through the gateway, and the gate slammed like a final word.

"You must be mad!" cried Dolour furiously. "Acting like a lunatic! I'm going back in to thank him."

Then she saw to her dismay that Mumma was crying like a child, her face screwed up, and the tears pouring down without any effort to stop or hide them.

"My little girl!" she sobbed. "My poor little girl!"

225

And she went on sobbing and lamenting in words that had no meaning, and sentences that had no relation to each other, till even in that locality where people fought and screamed and made love publicly, women came to scullery windows and men looked over back fences to see what was happening.

At last Dolour managed to get her up the lane which abutted on Plymouth Street, and there, Mumma, exhausted by her grief, subsided a little, hiding her face on Dolour's shoulder and saying, "You'll be ashamed of me, but it's been bottled up that long."

"What has, Mumma? Tell me what's the matter," whispered Dolour, unutterably distressed.

"That feller," said Mumma, and in the bitterness of her soul she burst out with that which had been a secret in her heart for seven years or more. "That Tommy Mendel. I hoped and prayed that I'd never have to lay eyes on him again, and now I have I feel just as bad as I usta."

"But what's he done?" whispered Dolour.

"If it hadn't been for him maybe Roie wouldn't have died," said Mumma, and she gave a great gulp and forced down the sorrow that was rising like a flood in her chest once more. "I've tried to forgive him, and I've prayed for him, but somehow when I saw him there to-night, large as life and not even caring what he'd done—I coulda spit in his eye," ended Mumma forlornly.

A chilliness seized Dolour, a feeling that forbade her even to speak.

"He got around her, and she had a baby by him," blurted Mumma, unable to go any longer without sharing her trouble. "And before it came them sailors caught her in the street and kicked her, and it died."

"Roie!" breathed Dolour, trembling. "Roie!"

"I thought you mighta guessed, when she was so sick," said Mumma, "but anyway you're big enough now to know what she went through, and it wasn't her fault, neither, poor little innocent, thinking she was in love with him", and she wandered off into comforting denunciations of Tommy, not noticing Dolour's silence as they went slowly between the tall bare fences and the swinging, dilapidated gates.

"The doctor didn't say that was the reason things went wrong at the birth, but I always felt it mighta been. Oh, Roie! Roie!" and Mumma broke down and wept miserably, her feet hurting, and her dress all torn with the brawl, and the hat feeling like a barrel-hoop on her forehead, and her teeth still in, and no hope of nice white glistening ones any more.

"I suppose Motty is giving Mrs Campion what-for," she said, brightening a little. In some strange way she felt relieved, as though Dolour had lifted a load from her shoulders.

Dolour went up to her room, sitting on the bed with Mikey, and not seeing anything. Her last dream had fallen. So even Roie, gentle, delicate little Roie had known the darkness and despair, the unutterable grief and sorrow of disillusionment when it comes in early girlhood.

"Nothing could have made Roie a bad girl," said Dolour to the darkening room.

She had expected to feel disgust, anger, disappointment, anything but what she did feel, an understanding at last of love and its pitfalls for the innocent and trusting, of the agonies Roie had suffered, and that perhaps had made her what she was in her wifehood and womanhood. It had come at last, that understanding, and she did not know that it marked the end of her childhood and the opening door of her maturity. She pressed the child into her shoulder's hollow, breathing in the smell of its flesh, and it was as though she embraced Roie, her sins, and tears, and the anguish of her last good-bye, her defenceless shrinking before the hard and callous world.

"Charlie had the best in the world when he had you," she said to her sister.

In the next room Charlie stood listening, thinking she was speaking to the baby. He wanted to go in and watch her attending to the child, and know that if he spoke she would understand him, and if he was silent she would know why. He had been so long without human companionship, marooned on the isle of his own grief and self-absorption, and now he needed the comfort of her presence, the balm that her quietness would apply to wounds that were healing a little.

For the first time in a long while he stood up straight, as though the load had grown lighter—or he had grown stronger under the load.

2 I

So it was Christmas again, and those that were left were still together, which was the main thing. Down in Pump Lane, and all the way up the crooked elbow of Grace Street were fallen bricks, and fences standing up round nothing at all, a sad confusion to the drunks who went looking for steps to sit on and found only emptiness. But in Plymouth Street the old plane-trees put on their yellow leaves for Christmas, and the houses nodded together as they had done for nearly a century.

"They might get tired of it before they come to us," said Mumma darkly, as she creaked cautiously about the house at six o'clock, with the clear untarnished sunshine splashing on the floor and showing up the dirt something terrible. And although it was the third Christmas since Roie died, and the day brought back memories sharp and sorrowful, Mumma burst into *Adeste Fidelis* and swung open the scullery window letting in a frightful smell that nearly lifted the hair off.

For there was Lick Jimmy standing in his yard burning fish-bones and singing like a tomcat.

"Merry Christmas, Lick," coughed Mumma.

"Melly Clismus, Misser Darcy," chirruped Lick. "Loger Bubba just gone in to see you."

"The dear little fellow," said Mumma warmly, picking up her floor-cloth. But she had hardly reached the kitchen door before a small tornado struck her amidships, and a larger tornado took her by the shoulders and turned her round.

"Don't you look!" cried Dolour.

"If you do we'll kick you in the bottom," cooed Motty. So Mumma waited, with Motty's small black shiny head burrowing into her, and her grubby hands clutching her thighs.

"You can look now. Merry Christmas!" cried Dolour, and there on the table, arranged in a nest of tissue, was a pink woolly cardigan. With sparkling eyes Mumma looked on its softness and prettiness, but she was overwhelmed with flailing arms and enthusiastic kisses. Tears came into her eyes.

"Ah, you're good girls," she said. It was almost like having Roie again to have the two of them giving her a surprise together. "But you shouldn'ta bought anything for me. I don't need anything."

Every Christmas she solemnly cautioned her family not to buy her anything, and every Christmas she hoped they wouldn't take any notice. Then she had a terrible feeling, for as she straightened out the cardigan she saw it was much too small. It hadn't been built for her bottle shoulders and fifty-inch bust, and once her arms jammed into the sleeves they would bend like boomerangs. Her disappointment was so great she nearly cried, but stronger than that was the knowledge that she couldn't let Dolour and Motty know. She stammered, "Me hands are all black from the coal. I'll try it on after I got the dinner going."

"Aw, come on, Gran'ma!"

Mumma didn't know what to do, but just then Hughie came out of the bedroom, his hair sticking up, his braces hanging down his back like a tangled tail, and a yawn unrolling down his face like a blind.

"Compliments of the season," said Mumma shyly, looking at him yearningly, as though expecting that her prayers had come true and he would stump over to her and give her the kiss that would tell her he was her own husband again. But Motty jumped at him and yelled, "What did you get for me? You promised me a doll's pram with a red handle and real wheels."

Hughie looked helplessly at Mumma. He was ashamed to tell Motty that he had never had any intention of buying her a doll's pram, in spite of his lavish drunken promises, so he pulled away from her clutching hands and said, "We'll see about that some other time", and went into the laundry and shut the door.

Motty stood as though he had slapped her face. Her eyes filled with tears and her lip stuck out so far that it nearly cast a shadow. She threw herself at the door, kicking it and wrenching at the knob, yelling, "You're a bloody liar! You didn't get it! And you promised! You promised, you dirty, stinking old liar!"

Dolour and Mumma were filled with dismay.

"Don't you go speaking to your grandpop like that, Moira, or you'll get a belting. The like of it!"

"Look, Motty, look!" Dolour pulled a package out of her pocket. "I got you a present."

Motty glared through her tears. She tore the paper off rudely. It was a string of green beads, each painted in red and gold like a tiny Chinese lantern. Motty clutched them to her breast and howled, "Oh, I told Roger Lick and Betty Brody and Fatso Kennedy and everyone I was getting a doll's pram!"

"He could have got her something," said Dolour bitterly.

Mumma tightened her mouth. "It's her father's job to get a doll's pram, not Hughie's, anyway", and she lifted a foot to land a good one on Dirty Dick's rusty tassel of tail, recollecting his needle claws just in time to draw her foot back smartly.

Hughie sluiced his face over the tub. The water was dank and already warm from the sun-drenched pipes. He spat it out and wished he had a drink. There was a sickish feeling in his stomach, and his head was stuffed with wet paper. He sat for a while on the laundry step, blinking at the blazing sky and swallowing at the poignant smell of Lick's fishbones.

"I coulda saved up for it," he groaned. "Sixpence a week ain't much. Poor kid. I ain't much good to her or anyone else. I coulda pawned something", and his thoughts went dolefully to Mr Mendel's shop where most of his clothing already hung.

"It's going to be God's own misery in the winter," he thought, for he knew that he could never redeem them. Then he forgot all about Motty and the rest and not having a present for any of them, with the worry that was in his mind about Florentina.

He was physically exhausted, and the wild flare of passion for her had almost gone, but he couldn't see that it was his fault. She just didn't take much notice of him any more, that was the reason. Once, above all the others, she had liked him best. But now it was different. He was just another customer, and not a particularly welcome one, either. Always the woman Seppa hung round, scowling, reluctant to let him in. And the black boy Lex dogged Florentina like a faithful hound.

"If she's got someone else, someone special," he thought with piteous ferocity. But the fear of losing her was not as great as the fear of realizing that he was too old and too poor to hold her interest.

"She's only a bitch, anyway," he said, and rose to his feet feeling strong and contemptuous, for the moment above all women and all male weakness. Lick Jimmy's shrunken face popped up above the fence.

"Too much pooey for you?" he inquired, waving with his eyebrows towards the smoke.

"Ah, shurrup," growled Hughie. He stumped inside and there was Mumma teetering precariously on the rickety table, with Motty and her brother sitting expectantly underneath it, waiting for the crash. She was trying to unhook the Christmas pudding

230

from the rafter where it had swung, a shrivelled black cannon-ball, shunned by flies and looked at askance by cockroaches, for the last six months.

"For gawsake," protested Hugh, seizing his wife by the legs, "do yer want to smash at me feet like a cup?"

She wanted to be dignified, but she was too delighted, and she said, "Oh, get out!" and passed the pudding down and lumbered to the floor.

For the first time in a long time a pang of pity entered his heart and he thought, "Poor old cow. She don't get much outa life."

She said appealingly, "You'll come to one of the Masses, Hugh?"

"Say the eleven o'clock," said Hughie, avoiding her eyes by busily examining the pudding cloth for toothmarks. Mumma sighed, for it was a sung Mass, and what with all the getting up and sitting down and forming fours that went on, it was a trial even to a devoted Catholic like herself, let alone Hughie. She had known all along that he wouldn't go, Christmas and all as it was, but she had hoped wistfully that her instincts were on the wrong track.

"Well, we'll get going then," she said, resigned. "Your breakfast's in the oven, don't let the egg get leathery, and the pudding's to go in the pot at half-past nine. And you gotta be careful with Mikey if he's in the yard that he don't eat any broken glass."

"Ah, I've had kids, too, haven't I?" suddenly thundered Hughie, and Mumma backed out, vowing to herself that for all she cared he could sizzle like a sausage for the want of a prayer.

She and Motty and Dolour went sedately into the church, into its brown silence, and with pleasure Mumma sniffed the archaic smell of the incense, which had been floating in invisible clouds among the rafters ever since Holy Thursday. All along the row of brass candlesticks twinkled the stars of the candle-flames, and the altar cloth was starched so stiffly, and ironed so smoothly that the stars were dimly reflected there, too. Even Motty, such a restless, difficult little pagan, was awed. She twisted around and stared up at the choir-loft, and there was Mr Siciliano leaning over, looking with beaming interest at the latecomers. He had once been slender and romantic with hair like black Florentine silk, but now he had an equator, and a bald spot from whch radiated locks grey and straight, except at the ends where they kinked desperately in memory of the old days. Mr Siciliano had little claims staked out all over church. There was Michelangelo on the altar, and in the front row were Rosina and Violetta in their Children of Mary blue cloaks and over with the Holy Name Society was Gio making big black sparkling eyes at the girls, and towards the back was Mama, with Tonetta, expecting a child herself, helping her to keep an eye on Julio, Albertino, Redempta, and Van, who was named after Mama's favourite film star.

"This next bambino," thought Mr Siciliano, "we call him Finito, and perhaps God tak-a the hint."

"Yoo-hoo, Mr Siciliano!" cried Motty benevolently.

"Sssh!" hissed Mumma, and Motty's protests were drowned in a wild moo from the organ as it chased the choir into full flight.

"Look, there's Daddy!" cried Motty, dragging at Dolour's arm. She looked, amazed, at Charlie's dark head, away over in the transept beside a pillar, as though he had slunk in a side door so that no one would see him. A warm, glad astonished feeling filled her heart, she did not know why.

"Well," said Mumma, reluctantly letting some ironic remark pass by just because of the season and her circumstances, "I won't say it ain't time."

"*Et-a in terra, pax-a hominibus!*" cried Mr Siciliano's harsh soaring tenor, which all the years of shouting "Fin-a broccoli, lempence da punch! Two-a pob da grapis!" had done nothing to impair. In between the triumphant phrases he scowled at the basso, Mr Dugan from the fish and chips, who was booming away like a bee, fighting with the organ for the lowest place, and the contralto, who sounded as though she were singing down a bottle. But the good hearts were there, and Father Cooley, moving round the altar and trying not to bellow when he genuflected, so bad was his back, felt proud of his people, especially when they joined in the singing. It was strange, those labourers and shop people and ordinary down-at-heel house-wives, singing the archaic and hallowed music of the Church, which had once run in square notes along monkish paper.

"Oh, Lord," prayed Father Cooley, "the times have changed, but their hearts haven't, and there's so much good in them I feel small."

He raised his eyes to the dazzling brass doors of the Tabernacle, and was rewarded by the reflection of his youngest altar boy, Michelangelo Siciliano, dangling his rosary beads from his ear.

After Communion Dolour sank into herself, shutting the doors one after another until she was deep in her own heart, wondering, asking, answering. The great problems that had once seemed such insuperable obstacles to her rose again, but her piece of mind was not disturbed. The mysteries remained, but she saw them as mountains to be climbed later, not now, when she was too young and too small. From somewhere patience had come. Once she had wept because the great miracles of religion were all repulsive when she looked at them closely. Calvary was a butcher's block, and Joan of Arc a charred skeleton, and who'd be able to look on Stephen, the beautiful young man with his blue Israelite eyes pits of bloody dust, and his brains trickling over the broken stones? But now it was different, and she couldn't understand why.

"I've grown up," said Dolour wonderingly.

Somewhere in her heart she found her sister, for in possessing God she possessed all the dead. She felt as though Roie were only standing in a dark room. Or perhaps she was the one in the darkness, unable to see the bright figure lost in the light.

"Roie," she whispered. And, all at once, with a shock not of shame or guilt, but only of astonishment that she had not consciously realized it before, she said, "I love Charlie."

A blush burned up from her inmost depths and she buried her face in her hands. "Roie, I love Charlie!"

Now it was all explained, her loathing and terror of the wicked and vulgar and ludicrous things in her life, her amazement that love did not seem to be the joyous and cleanly thing she had dreamed. She had matched all those boys with him and they had fallen short; she had stacked all her own experiences against the sweetness Roie had known with Charlie, not knowing she had done it. All men were not like Charlie, but she hadn't known why until now.

She had never heard of anyone loving a dead sister's husband; she did not know whether it was wrong or impossible or foolish. She only knew that he did not love her and probably never would. At the thought of the battles unfought, the sorrows unexperienced, the years to be travelled, alone, uncompanioned, tears sprang unasked into her eyes, and she stared at the altar and hardly saw Father Cooley lifting his hands laboriously and blessing them in a voice which suddenly sounded old and tired.

"Never mind," whispered Mumma, and her warm hand gave Dolour's arm a squeeze. "He'll realize he's doing wrong and come back to us after a while."

Dolour blinked away her tears and nodded and smiled, knowing that Mumma was talking about Hughie, for whom she had prayed and yearned all through Mass.

Outside little Ryan Street a small crowd had collected in the hot sunshine that beat down and ran like honey into every crack and cranny. Mumma and Dolour and Motty stood there gawking with the rest.

"What's 'appening?"

"Oh, it's crool! Who'da thought it, eh, and her with the stren'th of ten when it comes to bashing johns over the ned."

Mumma's new hat, a grey straw with a lovely bunch of poppies and sweetpea and those little blue cornflowers that nobody ever saw nowadays, was as tight as a nut on a bolt, but she stood as though it were a crown, conscious of her Christmas newness, and the white shine of her soul. For once Motty had stayed clean, and for the moment her little face looked up out of her white sun hat like an Italian angel's, as richly coloured as wine. Mumma held her hand so tightly that Motty was compelled to direct her energies in subtle directions. She sneaked a piece of red chalk out of her pocket and began furtively to draw cats on the skirt of a woman standing in front of her.

In the shadowy depths of Mrs Stock's house there was a crash and a frightful torrent of blasphemy as someone fell down the stairs.

"I remember the time old Mrs Purcell had the stroke up there," breathed someone, "and the coffin got wedged on them stairs. Had to take her out, all stiff and cold, before they could get it down."

"Glory-ory!" gasped Mumma. "You're not telling me that Delie Stock's dead?"

But the next moment a flustered ambulance man, red in the face, with a great streak of dirt across his white coat, appeared, and behind him in the stretcher was Delie herself, half sitting up and haranguing the stretcher-bearers with the full of her tongue.

The little crowd backed into a compact heap, it was so strange to be seeing her, the immortal, the indestructible, getting shovelled into an ambulance as though she were an ordinary old woman.

"Go on, get out of here!" croaked Delia, vermilion patching her floury-white cheeks, and her dark eyes, sunken with pain and sickness, coming to life for a moment and shooting sparks. "It ain't a monkey-show. Who're yer gawking at? By God Almighty, I'll move yer meself!"

And she heaved on the stretcher and the blanket fell off, showing the rest of her clad in a fancy pink silk nightdress splotched all over with spilt food and medicine and God-knows-what, and the hem of it pitch black from long trailing in the dirt.

"Lie still, madam," said the second ambulance man, pushing her gently down again. Delie erupted like a volcano, screaming curses, then all at once she shrank into herself, clutching her chest and coughing hard as though there were something sharp stuck into her chest-wall. Tears came into her eyes, whether with coughing or emotion none could say, and suddenly her face crumpled up and she sobbed, "I ain't coming back, you know. I ain't coming back here any more."

"Now, now," soothed the man, motioning his companion to lift the stretcher into the ambulance.

"Now, now me big black foot, you starched bastard," sobbed Delie. Out of the doorway of the ambulance, looking like a raddled, sick old bird in all that white-enamelled austerity, she looked at the crowd with a yearning, longing expression. They were nothing to her; she had battened on their menfolk, starved their children, lured and bullied their daughters. She had fed them filthy liquor and taken them down every way she knew, but they were Surry Hills to her, the little scuttling beetles who had looked up to her as their spokesman, who came to her when they were in trouble. They were her people, and she would never see them again.

"Well, here's mud in yer eye," she croaked. An old woman in the crowd darted forward and squeezed her foot, which was all she could reach.

"They can't kill you, Delie, never you fear," she cried. Delie brightened up amazingly. The warmth of the crowd's feeling touched her in that chilly place where she had gone since she learned that her heart would never get better.

"Carm on, give us a kiss, you old ratbag."

The old woman's puckered lips touched her cheek as she bent forward.

"That's more like it." Her gaze took in the crowd. "There's ten cases of bombo in me backyard, and youse can split it up between youse."

The ambulance door clicked, and amid a ragged cheer Delie Stock left Surry Hills.

"God bless 'er," said Mumma. "She's a bad woman, but she's done more good than a lot who'd like to think God's got a pair of wings on the hook for them."

235

She spotted the red hieroglyphics on the skirt of the woman near by and, full of horror, dragged Motty away and up the street before she was discovered.

"And you just after going to Christmas Mass and seeing the little Baby in the crib and everything," she scolded. "Just wait till the Sisters get you in their dear kind hands when school opens," she added pleasurably. A look of inward absorption came over Motty's face. She had inspected the Sisters minutely as they filed into church, and it seemed to her that they had stomachs to be kicked just like anyone else.

It was still early, and so Mumma hissed over the fence to Mrs Campion for her rabbit, which Mrs Campion had been keeping on the ice for her. Mrs Campion was busy cooking, her blouse undone nearly to her middle, her red face downy and dewy with sweat.

"Gawd," said Mrs Campion, lifting up an arm and scratching under it lingeringly. "You oughta see what the family give me for Christmas, love. A lovely fur. Real rabbit. It's that warm I nearly 'ad a fit when I tried it on for size." She sighed with pleasure. "Watcher get?"

"A pink cardigan," said Mumma complacently. "The high-class sort. Only it don't fit. Too small. I dunno what musta come over Dolour."

Mrs Campion sympathized. "Never mind, love. It just goes to show you don't look as big as you are."

"No," agreed Mumma, the thought dawning pleasurably, and she pulled in her middle as though to prove to Mrs Campion that she was right.

"And 'ere's yer bunny," said her neighbour, swiftly handing the frozen red corpse over the fence. Mumma whisked it into a tea-towel and waddled inside. Nobody in the house would eat rabbit, but Mumma reckoned that well-covered in gravy they wouldn't know the difference. She hurriedly dissected it and hid it underneath the roasting fowl from which delicious odours rose in such profusion that Mumma's breakfastless stomach burst into a soprano song of praise. Chook came only once a year, and Mumma loved it.

She was happy. She went again and again to look at the pink cardigan, and the box of face powder, ostensibly from Motty, and the green hankies from Michael, which she loved as much as if Mikey himself had toddled out, a spare napkin under his arm, and bought them himself. Mumma didn't expect anything from Hughie, for he never gave anyone anything, but she did think Charlie might have come across with something. She went about her cooking and table-laying steaming gently about this, for Charlie, even though he was off work such a lot, must have had a little bit put aside, and he could have spared a thought for his mother-in-law who wore her feet to the bone looking after his children.

"I can't stand the mean ones," she confided to Mikey, who was trotting about with a mouth full of pumpkin seeds, which he spat out one at a time with an effect like shot. He was a beautiful child, his hair still silvery white and his eyes sparkling like blue beads. He grinned and Mumma melted.

"I didn't get anything for him, either, comes to that," she admitted, "but that's different."

It was no good. Though she tried to be sober for Roie's dear sake, the happiness of Christmas overcame her, and she sang loudly as she went about her work. As she was dishing up, Hughie popped his head in the door.

"Course you know Mr Reilly's coming to dinner," he said.

Mumma couldn't believe her ears. She looked in dismay at her husband. "Hughie, you didn't oughter! Not without telling me!"

"It sorta popped out last night when I was having a drink with him," confessed Hughie, a little shamefaced. "Poor little cow, up there with not a soul in the world to call his own."

"You got no right," burst out Mumma. "You know I like to keep Christmas dinner in the family. I suppose you'll be asking Lick Jimmy in next."

Hughie didn't know what else to do, so he got angry. "That's a nice thing to hear from you, just back from Communion and everything. You can sling off at me being tired out and missing church, but I got more feeling for that poor lonely little bastard upstairs than you or any other holy moses in this house."

He slammed out of the door, and Mumma stood upset and undecided, feeling that perhaps he was right and she was mean. A hotness came over her at the very thought, and she put the plate of food she had just dished up into Dolour's hands and said, "That'll be for Mr Reilly, then."

"What about you?" protested Dolour.

"Oh, there's plenty here yet," said Mumma falsely and mournfully, and she scraped the last few dried peas out of the pot and added potatoes and a few shreds from the rabbit's bones, and splashed some gravy from the pan over all. She could have cried as she saw the little, forlorn heap of food in the middle of the

237

I

plate's white desert, and she resolved to leave it just like that, just to show Mr Bumper Reilly that he couldn't come bursting into the middle of other people's Christmas dinner without depriving them. Then, as she heard his timid squeak outside the door, her natural generosity overcame her, and she hastily spread out the food over the plate, arranging the potatoes so that it would look as though she had as much as everyone else.

Mr Reilly was shaved to the very bone. He had been up since six o'clock preparing for this great event, and his collar, though unironed, was as white as paper. His little pug face had shrunken until a saucer could have covered it, and out of it his weak eyes looked apologetically.

"I brought along a little something, Mr Darcy, for your kindness," he said, tendering a long parcel. It was two bottles of the cheapest, most potent port, which he had bought out of the remains of the six pounds he had earned the previous week when the Council, out of the charity of its heart, had put old-age pensioners to a week's sweeping of paths and weeding of parks. The rest of the money Mr Reilly had put towards an interesting purchase which he intended to use at the very end of his life.

"I don't want any of your porpoises' coffins," he often said to himself, his little chin trembling with pride.

"God keep the man!" roared Hughie now, and he kissed the bottles resoundingly on their cool smooth sides.

Mumma sniffed. She slapped down the last plate and said gallantly, "Well, merry Christmas, Mr Reilly, I'm sure."

At the sight of the steaming food Mr Reilly's eyes watered, and a piercing arpeggio sounded from under his waistcoat.

"And plenty to fill that little tin-can, too," said Hughie cordially. They all sat down in the dizzy heat, with Motty sitting between Dolour and Mumma, and fixing baleful eyes on Mr Reilly, who dropped his gaze to his plate. He was terrified of Motty. She reached out with her short legs as far as she could, but Mr Reilly had tucked his underneath the chair. Dolour gave her a sideways glare, which Motty understood perfectly.

"You take them away from me and I'll cut holes in your stockings," said Motty, her brown paw flying protectively to her beads.

Dolour did not dare to look at Charlie for fear she would blush, but he kept stealing looks at her, wondering if she were cross with him for something. He had a present for her, and he didn't know how to give it to her. For the first time he felt self-conscious with her.

Mumma, standing her knife and fork up on their feet, beamed round the table. She was so hot she felt she would pop, but it was Christmas, and the pudding was hubble-bubbling in the pot in the most satisfactory manner. With a sigh of relief she turned to her meagre helping.

"Criminy!" Hughie dived into his plate and held up a leg dripping with gravy. "I can just see this bolting across a paddock with a pack of dogs yelping after it."

Mumma blushed guiltily, and Mr Reilly cheeped helpfully, "Some fowls have tremenjus shinbones."

Mumma flared up. "And some people never know when to be grateful."

The suppressed resentment in her soul surged up through the happiness, and she yearned to crack Charlie over the head with a plate for not giving her anything, and tell Mr Bumper Reilly off good and proper.

"Ah, shut up!" snarled Hughie. "Here." He poured out a cupful of the port and shoved it at Mr Reilly, who snorted it down to drown his embarrassment. He had already been shouted a couple of beers that morning, and the port hit them and gave off an umbrella-shaped canopy of smoke. The fumes rose to his head, and he saw Mumma's face as a full red moon, sinister and unpleasant.

"And don't you go listening at my door, neither," he said challengingly, choking down a mouthful of seasoning and almost hearing it sizzle as it struck the burning lake in his stomach.

Mumma was shocked, as if a mouse had snarled at her. She rose from the table, taking her plate with her, and Charlie suddenly broke his silence and said, "Oh, sit down, nothing's the matter."

"I beg yours," said Mumma haughtily. "You're a nice one to be complaining about anybody, and you so tight-fisted you couldn't even buy anyone a present."

Mr Reilly gulped down another cupful of port, and Hughie kept him company.

"Oh, Mumma," protested Dolour, "how do you know Charlie hasn't got you anything?"

For she had helped him to choose a gift for Mumma, and was terrified in case Mumma alienated him before it was given.

"Insulting a guest," shrilled Mr Reilly suddenly. "Owww!" Motty had managed it at last, and her hard-toed little shoe made a chip in Mr Reilly's brittle shin. "You little hell-cat, you want your bottom heated."

Mikey, who had been gazing from one to the other with trembling lip and wide open eyes, could not bear the angry voices any longer. He began to howl like a wolf, and Dolour picked him up and hugged him tightly.

"You ought to be ashamed of yourself, Mumma," she hissed, and Mumma waddled out to the scullery with the air of an affronted queen. There was a great washday smell, the clang of a dropped lid, and a chump from Puffing Billy, then the pudding appeared, a steaming black boulder of a thing, strangely depressed and gibbous, and exuding a limp smell of wet dates.

"Strike!" gasped Hughie. "It's a sod!"

And so it was. The water had got to it, and it lay upon the plates in crumbling slabs. But to Mr Reilly's starved eyes it looked rich and rare, and he wolfed it greedily.

"You'll bomit if you eat like that," prophesied Motty darkly.

Her lips compressed with her hunger, and the great disappointment of the pudding that had been made with such high hopes, Mumma sat down.

"There's six threepences and four sixpences in it," she said, morosely, and brightened a little when there was a murmur of approval at her generosity. Motty began to gobble furiously. But the first find was made by Mr Reilly.

"Now you'll have good luck all the year round," said Mumma begrudgingly.

Mr Reilly brought the little silver thing close to his eyes and beheld the image of some old Roman saint who had hung up his head on a gate-spike some nineteen hundred years before. It was a holy medal, which Mumma had put in by mistake, and sick with rage and disappointment and port Mr Reilly rose to his full five foot three and proclaimed, "I'm an Episcopalian."

"Be careful of your language," flared Mumma.

"Don't you speak to my missus like that," cried Hugh, the pudding suddenly acting within him in a dreadful fashion, and he leaned across the table and snatched at Mr Reilly, who jammed his chair back and squawked with courage that amazed himself, "Keep your rotten Christmas dinner!" and made for the door. It was so exhilarating not to be frightened that he turned at the door and yelled, "And don't think I don't know you snoop through the keyhole when you think I'm not noticing!"

Hughie choked down another cup of port and began to rampage round the room, sick with remorse at poor Bumper's hurt feelings, and furious at his unpardonable breach of the laws of hospitality. Mumma sat answering up bravely for a while, and trying to eat her pudding. Finally she gave it up and cowered in her chair, tears running down her face, for the dinner had been awful, and the place just not the same as it had been when Roie and Grandma were there.

For a while Charlie took no notice, for he had found out that fights in that house boiled up quickly and ebbed just as fast, except when some outsider put his spoke in. But after a while he grew sick of it. He jumped up and thrust Hughie out of the room. Hughie had been a valiant fighter in his day, but he was like clay in the stronger grip and longer reach of the young man, and all he could do was to pick up the depleted pudding as he was borne struggling past, and whang it at the fence, where it dribbled in a wet black star instantly covered with a swarm of rapturous ants.

Hughie was livid. The humiliation of being marched out like a misbehaving child, and by someone who wasn't even a member of the family, went to his head where it formed an explosive mixture with the beer, the port, and the orange cocktail he had been surreptitiously slugging all the morning.

"You shoulda left him alone, Charlie," wailed Mumma as a boot thudded against the locked door. "Oh, he'll perform now! And I went to Communion this morning and now I'm angry, and me tongue with wicked words tottering on the tip of it."

Hughie's distorted face appeared momentarily at the scullery window, as he jumped up and down trying to catch a glimpse of Charlie. Motty shrieked with delight, and the baby hid his face on Dolour's shoulder.

"Come on out here and I'll smash yer black face in!" roared Hughie, and then, to some invisible onlooker, "And you, too, you ice-slinging bonehead, come on in here and I'll pull out your tripe and feed it to the cat!"

"That's Mr Campion," shuddered Mumma, "and him sixteen stone if he's a day."

"I'll go out and shut him up," said Charlie, but Dolour put her hand on his arm.

"You know it's no use. He'll get over it if he doesn't think anyone is listening." She struggled for words. "Mumma, Charlie's bought you an electric iron for Christmas."

"I wouldn't use one of them dangerous things," said Mumma sulkily, and, remembering her manners, added reluctantly, "Not that I don't appreciate the thought."

"That's a nice way to put it," cried Dolour, suddenly losing her temper. "I don't suppose you realize how much electric irons cost! I suppose you think Charlie didn't save up for weeks to get it for you. Don't say thank you, will you?"

"Oh, what's it matter?" asked Charlie. He pushed his chair back. "I'm going out for a while."

They heard the front door slam. Dolour's lips trembled. "You make it so pleasant for him, don't you?"

"Getting awful careful of his feelings, ain't you?" sneered Mumma hotly, and was too angry to see how Dolour turned away to hide her face. Meanwhile Hughie, having insulted one neighbour, had turned on Lick Jimmy, and they could hear him trying to climb the fence and falling back on the garbage can, his voice rising to a scream of fury, "Rice-eating magpies, ain't yer never heard of the White Australia policy? Yi, yi, muckakili!" he chanted in hideous travesty of Lick's language. Mumma flushed scarlet.

"That's the end!" she declared. "I'm not having him insulting poor little Lick after all he's done for us. That finishes it. I'm going to get a policeman."

Dolour sighed. It was Mumma's grand gesture, and never carried out. Mumma would no sooner have put Hughie or anyone else in the cold cells on Christmas Day than she would have jumped off the Bridge. She bolted down the passage out into the street, and Dolour resignedly began to stack the dishes. It was just another fiasco to her, and she burned passionately to be out of it and away from it for all time.

Now, in all her life, Mumma had gone for the policeman only four or five times, and had always taken great care not to find one. But this time there was one just outside in Plymouth Street, standing dutifully in a shady doorway, wiping his neck with his handkerchief and longing for the evening. It was too late for Mumma to draw back. He had heard the shouting voice, and saw her distressed red face. In less than no time she was waddling up the road beside him, trying to keep her anger up to fever heat, and feeling nothing but a Judas.

Meanwhile Dolour had gone into the yard. "You'd better shut up. Mumma's gone for the cops, and she means it!" she threatened.

Hughie couldn't believe such treachery, but all the same he climbed down off the fence, mumbling, "I can't stand a bar of a Chow." He bolted inside, and, not waiting to take off his boots, shot into bed and pulled up the quilt, closing his eyes and pre-

242

tending to be asleep, for in spite of all his bravado, Hughie didn't like the cops.

"I been sick in bed all day, d'yer hear?" he bellowed at Dolour. "I been sick in bed all day, or I'll beat yer brains in."

"Poor Gran'pop," crooned Mikey, sticking his elfin face round the door. "Poor Gran'pop want basin?"

While Hughie was a mere recumbent statue, Mumma was coming up the path with the policeman and a failing heart. She didn't want to put Hugh in, God knew she didn't, but with the day all spoiled, and the rest of it already booked up for his arging and barging, she felt she couldn't bear it.

"I'm getting old now," she sobbed. "I ain't just up to it."

"Don't worry, missus," said the policeman kindly. "A night in the cooler will do his blood pressure a world of good this hot weather."

He marched down the hall, and just as he did the door over his head opened, and Mr Reilly, who had been chewing over his wrongs, and repenting his retirement from battle just when things were going so well, bounded down the stairs, leaned over the rail, and screamed, "Come on out here, Hugh Darcy, and I'll turn yer long snout inside out! Let me finish what I begun, and the cats can clean up the rest!"

The policeman's calm hand settled comfortably into the back of his collar.

"Come along, me boy," he invited, and Mr Reilly, mentally paralysed by the miraculous eye of the police force, went down the passage as quiet as a dove under the appalled eyes of Mumma, and disappeared down the street before she could get a twitch out of her tongue. Mumma tottered towards the kitchen door and met her daughter.

"Dadda's in bed, quiet as a mouse," whispered Dolour.

"I got a policeman," confessed Mumma, awe-stricken. "And he's gone and taken Mr Reilly."

Their hilarious shrieks rang out, causing Hughie to pop his head over the bedclothes in bewilderment.

Mumma's eyes glistened. "I'll bet he's left his door open!"

"Mumma!" warned Dolour.

"Oh, ain't I?" retorted her mother. "After I've wore me head to the bone wondering what's in them parcels of his."

She lumbered up the stairs, and Dolour darted after her.

"It isn't fair, Mumma. It's his own business. Gee, you're mean."

"It's not going to hurt him, me knowing what's in his parcels," cried Mumma, slapping Dolour's hand off her skirt.

Full of triumph she pushed through the door she had not seen open for two years or more. "Ha!"

The small attic room was half full of parcels, big and little, tied with rope and string and tape. They reached almost to the ceiling in the corner. Mumma and Dolour gaped at each other in a wild surmise.

"You mustn't, Mumma," cried Dolour. "It's not honest."

"Go on out then if you're so finicky," jeered Mumma. "You don't have to look."

She picked out a large, oddly-shaped parcel and began to untie the string. Several others crashed down about her feet. The odour of old food and dirty clothes wafted round them. Behind a hanging tea-towel Dolour could see a solitary sausage on a plate, black with flies. In a saucepan on the gas-ring was something clotted and brown. It crawled with ants. Distressed at Mr Reilly's undisguised poverty, Dolour looked back at her mother, who was avidly taking the paper off the parcel. Inside was a squashed shoe-box. Mumma looked at it a little timidly.

"Maybe there's a bit of body in it," breathed Dolour. Mumma took off the lid, and Dolour craned forward to look. Inside was an old brassière, a cotton slip with torn blue lace, and a blood-stained handkerchief. The two women stared with popping eyes.

"Maybe he *has* killed someone!" twittered Dolour.

Mumma pointed a shaking finger at a tiny parcel on top of the others. "What's in that one?"

"Looks like a big toe," said the callous Dolour. She dragged off the paper, and there was revealed a baby's shrunken sock.

"That's Mikey's!" said Mumma indignantly. "I missed it in the wash when he was round about eight months, and gave Anny a kick in the ribs for eating it."

"I'd like to know what else he's got," cried Dolour angrily. "What about that blouse of mine that someone snowdropped off the line, and my new red belt that I blamed Motty for taking out in the street and losing?"

"You want to look for them?" said Mumma righteously.

"No," admitted Dolour sullenly. "And he can have this, too, if it makes him happy. Mikey's too big for it, anyway."

She wrapped up the sock and put it back, and Mumma arranged the shoe-box unobtrusively underneath. Not speaking to each other they went downstairs, and washed the dishes in silence. Now and then vast questions rose to the tops of their souls like bubbles, but for some reason they did not speak about the parcels again. If anything, a certain respect for Mr Reilly, unique in his eccentricity, had stolen into the house, and the very air was tinged with it.

Late in the afternoon Hughie, who had succumbed to his rage and his mixed cargo, awoke, and Mumma told him what had happened. Feeling righteous, he went down and bailed Mr Reilly out, and Mr Reilly, piteously confused about the whole business, and pathetically grateful for such a good friend, begged his pardon for creating such a commotion, and sneaked upstairs to have a good lie-down.

Christmas had been a bad one for Hughie, and there was an indigestible lump inside him not caused entirely by Mumma's cooking.

He came now to the blistered yellow house in Elsey Street, his body sticky with sweat. The hairs on his legs tingled with discomfort, and at the back of his neck the cuts from his holiday haircut stung with the salt. As he raised the knocker he felt again, with amazement, the lack of interest in this house, in Florentina, even in himself. On the surface there was a mechanical repetition of his old eagerness, but underneath, and not too far underneath, there was the deep fundamental exhaustion he had never felt before. It was not only physical, it was moral and spiritual. After all this time of walking in an unreal world, of impatiently thrusting behind him all his real life, he was beginning to drag back to that world—or perhaps it was sucking him back into its tide.

"Well, what do you want?" The woman Seppa did not come fully into the light of the door; in the habitual way of those who always expect unwelcome visitors, she stood in the shadows to one side.

"She in?"

"No, she ain't."

They stared unwinkingly at each other like two cats on a fence. Hughie hated her—her moustache, the thickness and greasiness of her skin, the knowledge that she was what Florentina would grow into. In her the younger sister's tidal drift had become a fixity of purpose, a gimlet-eyed commercialism. Seppa did not bother to wear bright clothes. Her sense of economy told her that men would come her way whether she decked herself or not. She detested Hughie mainly because Hughie detested her, and made no attempt to invite him in to wait. In the dimness behind her he saw the white roll of the black boy's eyeballs.

"Hi, there, Lexie."

245

"Hullo, Mr Hughie."

"You get out back there," ordered the woman. She tried to close the door. "Florrie's out, and she won't be back for hours. Want to make something of it?"

"She's gone out with Topper. Topper's living here now," chirped up Lexie eagerly. Seppa's eyes glinted expectantly. She hoped Hughie would say something, and juicy phrases of abuse rolled round her tongue in anticipation. But to her disappointment he merely looked stupid and blank and remained silent. A dull apathy soaked him. All he wanted was to take off his shirt and undo his shoelaces and have a cool-off somewhere.

"Ah, you got no guts."

The door slammed. Hughie dawdled off up the road. It was surrendered to the sunshine and the somnolence of after-Christmas dinner. Here and there a group of old men clotted a shady balcony, cheeping over old times and hooting on their withered noses with saxophone sounds. A ragged urchin stood outside the closed doors of Drummy's squeaking on the glass panes with a sixpence and hopping from foot to foot as the pavement grew too hot for him. Hughie tried to feel angry, or disappointed, but he couldn't. Deep within him there was some depressive area of emotion, like the buffer depression that runs before a cyclone, but he could not find the energy to examine it. He came to Delie Stock's lane, and along into its furry black shadows he went, feeling sick with the heat and the food and the bad liquor. He peered through the palings, seeing a sliver of the Kidger's bent roach back, then another of his lolling pale face, and yet another of a dirty hand clutching a bottle with the neck knocked off. Hughie raised himself cautiously above the fence.

"Hey," he called, "any chance of getting a boll?"

The Kidger came out of his trance and made a feeble gesture. The yard was a wreck. Little Ryan Street had taken Delie's parting largesse. They had stormed into the yard, broken open the cases, and snatched every bottle. They had even lifted off the lid of the copper where she did a bit of private adulteration, and dipped out the nauseous mixture with cups and peach-cans. A dim, broken sound of revelry from the end of the street showed that it hadn't all gone yet.

"Come on in and help yerself," said the Kidger. His hair was matted as if he had poured syrup on it, and his face was the face of a corpse. Out of his bright pink shirt, streaked all over with spilt wine and vomit, his neck rose long and pallid, like a duck's.

"Gawd, you look in a bad way, boy," said Hughie, eagerly going in. The Kidger suddenly dropped the bottle as though it were hot, and began to cry like a child, without raising his hands to his face or doing anything to mop up the tears that welled stickily out and dribbled on to his unspeakable shirt.

"Poor Delie, she ain't never coming back," he babbled. "She's got it that bad in the chest."

"Ah, yer don't want to take it so serious," soothed Hughie, looking covertly round the yard. He saw a bottle sticking out from under the woodheap and cracked off its top. A blast of methylated air nearly blew his hat off. He inhaled thankfully.

"Tell me about it," he invited, sitting down beside the Kidger and expertly blowing off the glass splinters.

"I been with her for fifteen years," mumbled the Kidger, wiping his eyes on the back of his sleeve. "I been her useful for that long I don't know what else I can do."

"Wish someone would give me a chance to get me claws on to the business," said Hughie dreamily. "Christ, what's she put in this?" he added, spitting out a mouthful of froth.

"Lemme whiff it," blubbered the Kidger. He took a forlorn sniff. "You got some of the lemon essence lot there."

But the distraction was too slight, and he staggered across the yard and lay down on the woodpile like a yogi, sobbing to himself and picking incessantly at the shedding bark of the logs.

Hughie kept on drinking. He wanted to feel big, and by the time dusk fell he was beyond all measurement.

When Charlie came home the house was quiet, so quiet he could hear the ping-pong-pang of the iron roof complaining under the sun. He peeped into the stifling bedroom and there was Mumma, a shapeless hump in her slip, snoring beside the starfish figure of his daughter. Mumma loved to camp after dinner, but she didn't often get the chance.

He went upstairs and there was silence there, too. He stood on the landing for a while, then he went into his own room and got the little parcel, turning it over in his fingers and wondering if it were the right thing to get for a girl like Dolour. Maybe she would have liked some scent, or a bright scarf. Roie would have.

Feeling diffident, and in some strange way pleased and a little excited, he looked in her half-open door. She was asleep, and

247

it was typical of her that on that burning day she had taken Mikey to bed with her, his pink puffy face squashed on her arm, and his naked body gently shining with sweat.

Charlie thought, "I'll put it over there, and she'll see it."

But instead he stood there looking at her, defenceless in her sleep. He felt guilt because she was defenceless, and yet he was unable to look away. It was almost the first time he had looked at her because she was Dolour, and not because she looked like her sister. All at once she awoke, alarm and surprise on her face.

"What's the matter, Charlie?"

Stammering, he held out the little figure. "I got this for you. I was going to put it on the table."

"Gee!"

Dolour slid her arm out from under the baby, and cautiously got off the bed. Barefooted, flushed with heat and sleep, she pushed back her hair and eagerly took the parcel.

"Oh, Charlie . . . I didn't expect . . . you shouldn't have bothered . . . it must have cost an awful lot!"

It was a little bone carving of a Chinese water-seller with a yoke bearing two swinging buckets. His feet were bare, his trousers rolled up, and under the conical hat his goat-tufted turnip of a face was so cheerful, so completely indifferent to the troubles of this world that Dolour laughed with glee. Charlie smiled with relief.

"Oh, Charlie, I love it! I'm going to call him Ah Grin. How did you know I liked little Chinese things?"

"I've seen you with Loger Bubba," he chuckled. Dolour had almost forgotten what he looked like when he was happy. Holding Ah Grin in her hand she looked at him, forgetting that she didn't wear her glasses now, and that what she felt was plainly written in her eyes. She thought, "Oh, Charlie, I'd like to put my arms round you and tell you—" She dropped her gaze and said, "Nobody else would ever think to give me anything like this. It doesn't seem to fit in with—" She made a small despairing gesture around the small, ugly room, whose bone-bare cleanliness only emphasized its ugliness.

"Dolour, why don't you leave home?" he asked impulsively.

"Oh, I dunno." She flushed. "I suppose I will some day, when the kids are bigger."

"How old are you now?"

"Twenty in March. Why?"

"It's funny, a girl of your age so interested in someone else's

248

kids," he said, half-tenderly, half-jokingly, watching the blushes chase each other over her face and wondering why.

"Mumma needs a hand. Anyway, it doesn't matter much. I'm too old to get any more schooling. I'm only good for shop-work and the factories and I might as well be here as anywhere else."

"You'll be getting married one of these days," he said, and was amazed to feel all at once an extraordinary anxiety grip his heart. Like a child she dropped her head, but not before he had seen the tears in her eyes. "Why, Dolour, what's the matter?"

"Nothing," Dolour said, trying to pull away from the hand under her chin. "Nothing, Charlie. Honest."

"You don't like the little Chinaman," he accused. "You'd rather have had something to wear."

"Oh, no, I wouldn't. I love it. I'll always keep it," she whispered, terrified lest he should pull her closer and she would not be able to bear it.

"Then what's the matter? Are you in love?"

Almost at once he saw he had hit her in a vulnerable spot. She jerked her chin away from his fingers and said, "Of course I'm not. You've got a nerve!"

But it was written plainly in her flushed face, her angry, resentful eyes and trembling lips. She was not old enough, or experienced enough, to dissemble, and, more than that, the honesty of her nature would always make her face transparent to those who wished to read it.

But this was not what shocked Charlie. He was appalled to find that this was what he had been unconsciously looking for in her ever since they had spoken of Motty's future in the kitchen. He didn't know what to say, standing there like a fool, his arms hanging at his sides, not knowing whether to put them round her, or to say something, or just to go away and leave her to her tears.

"I'm sorry," he said. "It's none of my business."

"No, it isn't," she cried, and he went out, knowing that she would cry and then pick up Mikey and comfort herself with him.

He sat on his bed a long time, staring at the wall, his mind a confusion, and a deep shame waiting to engulf him. For he didn't know whether Dolour was to him just a young girl, whose sympathy and youth and virginity had called to the starvation within him. For four years his adoration for his wife had expressed itself in unbroken companionship and tenderness and frequent passion, and never been rebuffed or discounted, and when Roie died his body had sickened and hungered. It was

249

not through desire alone, but for a much subtler reason. The tongue had been taken from the nightingale, the white paper from the poet, the eyes from the seeing man. His had been the rich and contenting routine of husbandhood, broken like a snap of a thread, so that his soul had been thrown willy-nilly into solitariness.

And Dolour, the passionate, mutinous child, the soft-hearted and mercurial girl, and now the young woman secret within herself? What could she see in him, who had perhaps once been lovable, but now was only driftwood, a man whose courage and spirit had no fixed abode? It was only her romantic imagination, her sympathy for him, her love for his children that she had extended to include him, too. So he argued with himself, and did not notice that in all this time he had not once thought of Roie as a part of his life, only as a part of that which had gone.

The cool wind sighed up the street blowing the heat away like a monstrous balloon until it floated out to the Tasman and was absorbed in the ragged clouds.

Hughie rose and reeled down to Elsey Street again. He waited a long time, shivering in the wind, with his lumbago prickling like a fiery belt and his eyes watering with the intensity of his glare. Hughie did not know why he waited. He just wanted to be sure. Of something. His lips were dry and cracked, he was sobering up with unpleasant quickness, and his stomach rumbled that it needed hot food to keep away a chill.

"Ah, shuddup," said Hugh to his midriff.

During the time he waited he had a hundred arguments with unseen and inaudible persons, plunging down into the muddied well of his emotions and coming up with false and furious reasonings. The bitterest taste in his mouth was the wry, ironic one of the knowledge that he had to spend the last and most exultant flame of his mature life on a prostitute. Rich men could have girls clean and decent in themselves. They could have girls privily, and know that no other hand would touch them until they came again. But he had to fall in love with a woman who had been on the town since she was fourteen. He had never been anywhere in the running; all his life he had been sixth-rate, failing in crises, sickening in emergencies, flying to the bottle when he was needed. There was in him the unconquerable ability to be missing at the right moment. So it was typical that he should spend his passion and infatuation on a little bit of street flotsam.

And now she had a pimp, somebody to pick and choose her men for her, to batten on her earnings, and finally, when she grew old or diseased, to pitch her out. And in the incredible, fantastic way of women, she would take it. At the thought of this man, this Topper, whose shadow had been over his life for some time now, the most terrible murderous jealousy rose in Hughie's throat and nearly choked him.

About eleven o'clock he saw the girl come along Elsey Street with a man. She walked slowly, her head down, and her manner weary. For a moment Hughie's heart melted, then he remembered that she had never been his; she had never been anyone's, not even Topper's. She was largesse to all the world, and like fairy gold she melted from sight as soon as she was given. The man with her was big and young, but like a fox terrier giving challenge to an Alsatian, Hughie took no notice of the other's size. He wrenched at the fence in his maniacal rage, and a rotten paling came away in his hand.

"By God," said Hughie, as though God Himself had given the weapon. As Florentina and the man came closer, he stepped out of the darkness to meet them, standing there motionless, the paling down in the shadow beside his leg.

"Well, how'd yer make out tonight?" His voice was thick, and the smell of wine hung round him like a cloud. He might have been any abusive drunk. The couple walked on, ignoring him, and after a moment of shock and resentment Hughie ran after them, a squatty figure against their tall slenderness. On the wall his shadow showed like a gorilla's, with one long deformed arm hanging to the ground.

Florentina said something to the young man, who leaned against the wall, his face still unseen, but his shoes twinkling in the lamplight. Hughie found his eyes fascinated by them. He loved fine clothes, suits that fitted like a glove, ties that hooped out in a blaze of colour, stickpins with lumps of red and blue rock in them, but he never wore anything but old hand-me-downs from Joseph Mendel's. The sight of the shoes maddened him even more.

"Go away, Hughie," said Florentina. "You don't want to be bothering my friend."

Hughie spat out a filthy word pregnant with his scornful disbelief. Neither Florentina nor the young man took any notice of it; they had heard it fifty times a day all their lives. A flood of blasphemy poured out of his mouth, aimed at the girl, but rooted in his own misery, his realization of his failure, his complete and utter futility.

Florentina half put out a hand to Hughie, but the stranger struck it down with a casual, un-self-conscious viciousness. Hughie looked at her with such hatred on his face that, bewildered, she backed away. She walked off quickly, and Hughie galloped behind, continuing to abuse them both in a voice that grew louder and thicker until it awoke the echoes in the empty allotments and caused a window to clang upwards and a voice to yell, "Put a sock in it, can't yer?"

Suddenly the young man left Florentina and came back. In the lamplight his face showed lean and ratlike, with pale protruding jaw and keen, zinc-grey eyes. It was the face of the petty racketeer, the black-market tout, and the successful man of unobtrusive criminal affairs. He had a pleasant, persuasive voice.

"Look, mate, sling yer hook before something falls on yer head."

It was all Hughie needed. His common sense had long fled, and he had rushed on towards this moment like a river rushing towards a ravine. He raised the paling and jabbed the young man in the belly, intending to crash him over the skull with the other end as his head came down. But the rotten thing snapped like a carrot, and he stood defenceless.

"She's a whore!"

"Sure, pally."

The street tipped up and hit Hughie on the back of the head. Quick as a cat he bucked out of the way of the boot that flashed towards him, but the wine slowed his legs, and the young man leaped on his back, twelve stone of larrikinism that had cut its teeth on such brawls. He seized Hughie by the back of the neck; his long sharp fingers stabbed in on either side of the windpipe, and he ground the older man's face into the pavement, up and down across the gritty asphalt, until a thick trail of blood was smeared across the footpath. People came out on the balconies, blinking in the light, and leaned over the rails to watch.

"It's a bloody shame! He's only a little feller!"

"Ain't he got go in him, but! He oughta be on at the Stadium."

Hughie got one boot in the young man's side and gave a desperate downward rip towards the groin. As the other fell back with a whistled groan, Hughie leaped on him, half-blinded by blood, savage as a tiger. But he was too old. In a second he

252

was underneath again. Their skulls met with a sharp crack, and Hughie's teeth closed on the other's ear. It was good, warm and rubbery, and with delight he heard the grunt of the man as his teeth went through. Like a dog he dragged at it, then his dentures flew from his mouth, shattering on the street. An anguished curse against God went up out of Hughie's heart. He struggled for the gouge, but the strength ran out of his limbs like milk, and his heart swelled up and hit him under the chin. The light was blotted out, and a fierce agony exploded against the side of his head. He lay hardly conscious, aware of the boot crashing into his side as he might be of a drum beating a long way away, his mind pulling up the darkness like a blanket until he lay lapped in its shelter.

The young man flipped his hand, sending a rain of blood-drops across the street as he dabbed at his ear. He went to Florentina, who stood against the fence, half awed, half fascinated, lifting her eyes to his with the unquestioning docility of a child's.

"You and your old bastards!"

His fingers closed over her arm, thrusting downwards between the two bones. She squealed in torture. He looked at her closely while he thrust deeper, relinquishing her with a laugh and striding ahead to fit the key in her door. Florentina followed after, looking backwards covertly at the sprawled figure under the light, her eyes dim with the tears that would never be shed. A moment or so later she would have forgotten why she wanted to cry.

Most of the people on the balconies went inside, after Hughie had lain still for more than five minutes. They knew that sooner or later he would get up and stagger away. Anyway, the excitement was over.

When he opened his eyes the street was empty, save for a dreadful old ratbag of a woman with bare blackened feet sticking out from under her long skirt. She was squatting beside him chewing at nothing at all, and staring at him with eyes filmed with white.

"You got that much of a belting from that Topper," she said. "You better come into my place and I'll give you a drink."

Hughie rolled over. His ribs felt like an iron cage that had been heated. They pressed against the flesh with a hooping, outward movement that he could hardly bear. He tried to get up several times before he succeeded. An old arm, hard and strong as a stick, hoisted him to his feet, where he stood sway-

253

ing, the light in the wire-protected globe fuzzing like yellow fur.

Suddenly he was sick, an awful blood-streaked convulsion that made his stomach feel even worse.

"Gawd, he's torn yer guts loose from their moorings," remarked his witch-like companion with eager interest. She put out her arm to support him, but with a groan Hughie avoided it and staggered up the street. He heard her calling after him, "Hey, you forgot yer tats! Don't you want yer teeth?"

It was endless miles to Plymouth Street, which seemed to lie on the other side of the city. By the time he reached his own dark gate he was whimpering with the pain and exhaustion, and the fearful, irrevocable humiliation.

"Well," he gasped to the bright sky, "You got Your own back."

Mumma was in the kitchen, pottering about soaking porridge, and wondering what it was she had forgotten. He reeled past her, hideous in his mask of dirt and blood, and she stood there yellow-faced, not saying a word, holding the saucepan in her hand. He managed to get into the laundry, and Mumma, listening, heard the scrape of a match, and then his sobs. The tears ran down her own face as she listened.

After a while he felt better and, lifting up the candle, he stared at his toothless face in the mirror. The blood came straight from his savaged heart, and what hurt most of all was the realization that the steps could not be retraced, that he could never recapture his youth any more, that time was final, and not all the human pride or anguish in the world could gainsay it.

He lay beside Mumma in the darkness. He would not touch her, and she would not touch him, yet each felt the bodily warmth of the other. They breathed the same air, and that was all. Mumma tried to be triumphant, to be hard and revengeful, pleased that he was beaten and bruised, proud of herself that she had been silent and not reproached him ever. But all that her heart could cry was, "Oh, Lord, let it be next week, or next month soon, so that we can forget it all, and be like we usta!"

2 2

Almost with a shock Dolour watched Lick Jimmy's papery fingers putting the jar of purple immortelles into his window. So it was winter again. Once the seasons had been to her as the slow turning of a book's pages, each with its unique delights and troubles. But this last half-year had gone like a dream, and she realized with an ache that it was because she had grown up. There were so many things to think of that she hadn't noticed the bed-bugs sluggishly sidling into cracks and crannies for their cold-weather hibernation, or the wet-stains on the walls growing green-velvety with renaissant fungus, or Mikey in the house all the time because he couldn't play in the flooded yard. It was winter again, and at the thought the piercing, dusty wind whipping up Plymouth Street seemed to gain an added shrill bitterness.

And Lick was older, too. He had always been old, but since his family came to keep him company he had settled contentedly into his years, allowing the plum bloom to creep over his kind, diamond-shaped eyes, and the frost into his stiff black hair, which he kept covered now with a little flat tweed cap, like a lid. He had shrunken against his own brittle bones, so that his blue coat flapped, and sometimes even his shoes fell off, which made him giggle gleefully.

"Oh, Lick," thought Dolour sadly, "why has everything got to change?"

Yet she did not want to go back to the old days, for she had not loved Charlie then. It had happened to her, and secretly, tenderly she hugged it to herself, feeling her womanhood flower and her heart open day by day. It was a mystery she could not comprehend, for Charlie had been there with them so long, and in all that time there had been no love for him latent in her. It had come unbidden, like a child into the womb, and as though it had been a child she cherished it, for it was all she had. Charlie would never love her, for she could find nothing in herself to love.

255

As her eye trouble had disciplined her to the limits of her fortitude, as the loss of her ambition had taught her to look further than the moment and at the same time to make the best of what she had, so did this unacknowledged and unreturned love make her conscious of the divine principle that it is better for the soul to love than to be loved. Yet the bitter consciousness of the loneliness that would be hers if he left them, the jealous terror in case he should marry again, and her continual battle against sin in relation to him were always with her, so that she dreaded her solitary hours and the thoughts they bred. Sometimes they came upon her like darkness itself, shrouding all her brightness and hope, crushing her beneath a despair she could hardly combat. Was it to be like this all her life, empty of all she most wanted? No husband was to be hers, no children; she could never pour out her whole being in adoration of another. Her sweet saps were to be curdled, her bloom withered, and all for nothing. She thought, desperate, "Oh, Roie, you were luckier than I am! It was worth it to die, to have what you had!"

And at other times the temptation came to her to belong to Charlie in dreams, for she could belong to him no other way. She lay in her bed and listened to him moving in the next room, her body crying out with incredible, insupportable longing for his hands in her hair and his lips on her throat, so that she got out of bed like an old woman, walking up and down the room with her hands against her ears, tormented beyond control, and yet piteously determined that she would not sully him by sinning with him in her thoughts.

She did not know that he sat in the darkness and listened to her footsteps, wanting to go in and speak to her, longing to wake Michael so that she would hear the child's sleepy whimper and come in to see what the matter was. He hated himself for his thoughts, calling her a child, and knowing that she was not, telling himself that she was only infatuated, and knowing that might have been true of anyone but Dolour. For a long time he had not known what he himself felt about her, but now he knew, and the knowledge was bitterer than the confusion.

He had thought that in his emotional instability he had identified her with Roie because she looked like her sister, that his body wanted her because of their propinquity, and his mind because she was the only solid and understandable creature at which he could grasp But that was not true. If he had never met Roie he would have loved Dolour as she was now. He knew that God had picked her up gently as a child, saying, "This one I will teach the inner meaning of life", and put her down softly on her own feet to go her own way, knowing that her idealism was not that of the escapist, who shuns realism, but was strong and untainted enough to come hard against the utmost brutality of evil and retain its integrity. Charlie knew that whatever happened to Dolour she would not be conquered, but his heart bled at the griefs that still lay before her, dreading that she might fall into the hands of some man who would savage her instincts and blaspheme her innermost sensitivities. Charlie had faith in God's care of Dolour, but he wanted to be there to make sure.

He fished under the bed for the bottle there. It fell and bumped across the floor, and Charlie stood ashamed, grinning wryly, knowing that Dolour would have heard. He let it lie where it was, thinking, "It's all in the frame of mind, anyway. It doesn't make me think clearer, or feel better, or get things straighter." But a moment later he had persuaded himself that as she'd believe he was drinking, he might as well be doing it, and he fumbled round after the wine in the darkness, and found it with the gratitude of a man finding a lifebuoy in a desolate sea.

It was six months since Motty had started school, and in all that time not one day had passed without her causing a commotion. She was small, a pocket-sized girl, yet what could one do with a pocket-sized girl who could transform herself into a spitting, shrieking, biting, swearing tiger at will? From the moment she got up they bolted the door lest she should run out and disappear, and so, frustrated, she hid. Mumma's back ached with dragging Motty out by the leg from under beds and behind chairs, while she screamed blue murder. Taking her to school was a trial of strength, for outside the gate she sat down hard, pulling back with her strong little arms and digging in her heels, so that she had to be dragged every inch of the way by brute force.

The sisters had never seen anything as bad as Motty before. They had struck wildcats, but Moira Rothe was a werewolf. In the schoolroom she rampaged at will, tearing up books, slapping her companions, and throwing herself on the floor purple with rage and suffocation. Even when she was subdued by force she put up the sort of fight Dirty Dick would have put up if matched with a lion. A grown-up could crush her only by sheer weight and strength, reducing her to a panting, tearless, glittering-eyed little animal at bay, with no words, no defence or excuse, nothing but hate.

"I never in all me days seen a child like her," wailed Mumma to Mrs Campion.

She was an outlaw, and she tore Dolour's heart to pieces. She felt that it was her fault, for alone of them all she had realized the way Motty was heading. She should have made Mumma send her to school the year before, instead of letting her get away with, "Oh, she's only a baby. You don't want her in there bothering her head with reading and counting at her age." She should have managed, some way, to get her into a kindergarten, instead of allowing Mumma to let her run the streets.

Motty's treatment of her brother was that of a sultana with the lowest rank of black slave. Still, he trotted after her adoring her visibly and audibly. He and Loger Bubba liked to play together, sitting placidly in the sun conversing in Australian-Chinese and pressing gifts on each other. Motty liked nothing better than to storm in, kick their games to pieces, and crash their heads together. She was kind to nobody except Dirty Dick, and he and she treated each other with a sort of silent, mutual respect, understanding each other very well.

Mumma tried everything with her, affection, indulgence, force, bribery and corruption. Mrs Drummy said that St Joseph did wonders with difficult children, and Mumma tried him, but Motty left him standing. Some days she vanished directly after breakfast, and not all the searching up and down streets and in neighbour's backyards brought to light a shred of her. For all they knew she was kidnapped and raped and murdered and her body stuffed down a sewer. But when sundown came Motty would turn up, filthy, exhausted, and ravenous as a wolf.

"Belt it out of her!" growled Hughie, but belting never did a thing with Motty. Sometimes after she had been given what-for with a strap she would crawl under the table, and Dolour would cautiously lift the cloth to see her squatting against the wall, Dirty Dick in her arms, the pair of them staring fixedly into space, pondering perhaps on the incomprehensible cruelty and dictatorship of adults in a world that seemingly was not made for children.

Then Mumma would weep a little, filling up a kettle or stirring a pot meanwhile, for she never had time for weeping as a separate process. "Oh, I done my best, honest to goodness I have, and I'm at my wits' end what to do about her."

258

"Perhaps we could take her to a doctor," suggested Dolour helplessly, for how would you get Motty to a doctor when she didn't want to go, except by tying her hand and foot with ropes and heaving her into a taxi?

"Maybe she's a bit wrong in the head," said Mumma, blessing herself for fear she was right. But Motty's eyes were brilliant with intelligence. It wasn't her head that had gone wrong, and Dolour knew it. But it was no good trying to explain to Mumma.

"It's that black blood in her," said Mumma, "making the child into a savage."

Acid words rose to Dolour's lips, but she did not say any of them, for Mumma had an opinion inside her head, which was tantamount to saying that she had a billet of hardwood resting snugly against her frontal bone. She thought, "It isn't the drop of black blood that makes her that way, for where could you find anyone gentler than Charlie? She was all right when Roie was here, and she'd be all right still if Roie had lived."

She put her arms round Motty, expecting a forearm jolt in the face, but instead Motty gave her a quick hug, and wriggled away, as though embarrassed. Yet often in the middle of the night, when Motty woke frantic with nightmare, Dolour would take her into her own bed and cuddle her till light came, with Motty clinging like a bear, choking with sobs that shook her to her calloused, dirty little toes.

"What's the matter, Dolour's girl? Aren't you happy? Tell me and I'll fix it up. Would you like to go away with Dolour and live somewhere else, in the country, with lots of room to play in, and trees to climb and dogs to play with? Would you?"

But Motty wouldn't answer, and Dolour knew that the dark hid a face that was tightly shut-up, like a book, hiding God alone knew what jealousy and loneliness and piteous rebellion against a world too big to be managed. So she would talk on, half to herself, "Soon they'll be pulling this place down, and then we'll have to go. And if Nana and Grandpop won't come, you and I will go away somewhere, and Mikey, too."

So she spoke to comfort the child, forgetting that she herself had never walked across a paddock, or touched any horse except the baker's weary old mare, or heard the sea boom at night, or watched the wind shake silver out of the gumleaves.

The worry of Motty was so great that to some extent the pain of her love for Charlie was ameliorated, for she didn't have time to think about it.

It was a bad six months. Something seemed to have happened

to Twelve-and-a-half, Plymouth Street. The old simple, warm contentment was gone, and there was nothing left but uneasy anticipation of worse things to come. Mumma's bunions were playing up something cruel with the cold and the wet, and Mr Reilly caught a kidney complaint and there was no getting into the lavatory for anyone else in the house. And Hughie, though he made a brave attempt to be as he had always been, had all at once become an old man.

"And no wonder, with his teeth gone west, and him not doing a thing about it," scolded Mumma.

For his face had fallen in round his toothless mouth, and the ruddiness had drained out of his skin, leaving it sallow and baggy. But he couldn't be bothered to get new teeth, all that money, and going to the dentist and having his moosh stuffed full of concrete to get an impression, and all the rest. He just couldn't be bothered, but chumbled uncomplainingly on Mumma's tough steaks and gangster chops, and learned to smoke a cigarette without sucking off the end.

The doom was on the house, and at night the old planks creaked and croaked to each other, "Ninety years, and you and I remembering when the Surry Hills were green, and the wild swans nested along the swamp in Coronation Street." And, "This house stood by itself then, and where the Licks live, and the Grogans and the Brodies, the orchard stretched, full of loquat-trees where the pink parrots held parliament."

It was almost a relief when the Casements, in the boarded-up shop on the corner, got their removal notice. Perhaps it wasn't so bad for them, for they were elderly folk, with their children long since flown, so that they wouldn't have to put up with getting the kids to a new school, and disagreements with new neighbours over who bashed whom. But Mrs Casement was distraught. "I'm too old. I'm too old," she kept saying. "I've bin here forty years, and me curtains won't fit any other windows." To get Mrs Casement out of her house was like digging up an old tree. She was so used to ducking her head under the dwarfish doorway to the bedroom that for the rest of her life she would do it whenever she saw a bed. She liked the little yellow window over the stairs, and the white fleur-de-lys in the dangerous, slippery tiles in the backyard. The clothesline was just her height, and she'd never be able to find another window-sill with a dip in it that just fitted her pot of mint and parsley.

"And where am I going to hang me canary in me new kitchen, wherever it's going to be?"

She sat in the doorway complaining and weeping a little at the sympathy of her neighbours, enjoying her temporary fame in a miserable way, for it wasn't often that she had the chance to be the focus of Plymouth Street conversation. Nobody took much notice of old Mr Casement, who was pottering around the yard, his chin shaking, and a terrible churned-up confusion in his mind. He wanted to cry, but what with all the women coming in and out, bringing batches of scones and cups of tea, and biting his wife for something to remember her by, he couldn't find a place to be private in. Already he felt his roots becoming dry and shrivelled, as though he'd be dragged out of his own soil and thrown on a heap of weeds in the sun. He was much older than his wife, and he didn't know what he'd do if they sent him to Hargrave Park. For this was the terror of most of the evicted people, that they would be sent to the squalid housing settlements where worse slums had been created than any the Council had pulled down.

"Them little army huts," thought Mr Casement in panic, "and people fighting and screaming and banging on walls, and pinching the washing, and Jessie expecting me to go in and tell 'em off. I just ain't up to it these days."

He went again and again and looked at the spot on the ground where Keithie, their youngest, had crashed off the wall and broken his skull, and him only four and a bit. For thirty-five years Mr Casement had grown candytuft on that spot, and not allowed anyone to walk there, and now they were going to come and trample it all over, and tear it up with steam shovels. At the very thought Mr Casement's eyes filled with sticky, difficult tears, as though Keithie were going to be killed all over again.

"I wish I was dead," he moaned, and didn't know that a fortnight after he left Surry Hills he would be already buried, his soul shocked out of its fragile shell by the violent disruption of routine.

The Casements had hardly gone before the men arrived to pull the shop down, and they pulled it down with such ease that it was a wonder to those watching that it had stood up so long. Mumma and Mikey stood in the crowd, curious and morbid, to see Mrs Casement's living-room exposed to view, like a doll's house. Down came the wallpaper, striped with scarlet roses and lettuce leaves. Up came the floor that was most surprisingly black in squares where Mrs Casement hadn't bothered to clean under the furniture. A window fell out and crashed in a million diamonds across the candytuft, which was now a green slimy smear over the tiles. The plaster shot up in spurts of white smoke, sprinkling the heads of the crowd like a dying benediction. The workmen, stripped to their brown middles in spite of the winter wind, sat astride the beams sucking tea out of enamel pannikins, while the sun filtered down through the naked roof on rooms it had never seen before.

"They had bugs awful bad," said Mrs Campion mournfully. "I guess it's one way of getting rid of them."

Mumma picked up a piece of red-rose wallpaper and sneaked it into her pocket. She was going to keep it in memory of Mrs Casement. Unhappily she went home, wondering, sick with trepidation, not knowing whether to curse or pray.

"I suppose they mean it for the best," she said drearily.

She couldn't be bothered cleaning up the kitchen or getting dinner ready, so she made a cup of tea, and was still drinking it when Hughie came home. They didn't look at each other, but Mumma poured him a cup and sugared it heavily, listening without criticism to the drainpipe noises he made as he drank it.

"Won't be long before we get the boot, too," said Hughie gruffly.

"What do you reckon they'll do with us?" quavered Mumma.

She snorted into her tea with her worry and distress and anger at all the interfering boneheads who couldn't leave decent people where they were.

"We'll make out," said Hughie. "We've always made out."

She looked at him blindly and hopefully, and for the first time he saw her not as the girl she had been, or as a dumpy, rather dirty middle-aged woman, but just as a person whose exterior didn't matter much. Roie had gone, and Thady had gone, and some day soon Dolour would get married and leave them, and he'd be alone except for Mumma, sticking around as she had always stuck around, wanting to make things comfortable for him, and not much else.

"It ain't been much of a life for you," he said, uncomfortably looking down at the syrupy pool in his saucer.

"No, it ain't," thought Mumma, remembering herself in childbirth, and Hughie crashing in drunk and lying across her feet until the midwife pulled him off; remembering hungry days, and ashamed ones, and days muddied with sorrow and annoyance and humiliation. The words were there, ironic, acid, waiting to spill out and encompass him, to burn him down to the ground like an old building.

It might have been the greatest feat in the world, to force back those words and say nothing, but it wasn't. She looked at him, and she knew there was no bitterness in her heart, no resentment, nothing at all but a trembling hope.

"Ah, well, we're still together, Hughie," she said.

Like summer, withdrawing into the upper air, leaving her warmth and mellowness half as a reality, half as a memory, Hughie felt his youth leave him for all time, unregretted. He was strong yet, a healthy, hearty man, with plenty of kick in him, and, Hargrave Park or not, he'd give them all a run for their money. They hadn't been kicked out of Surry Hills yet; it might never happen, and even if it did, they could always come back. It was a free country.

"We ain't licked," he said, and crammed half a scone into his mouth. "No, we ain't licked yet, old chook."

"You will be," said Mumma, "if you don't get yer tats in and stop golloping."

"Ah, shuddup."

He came over clumsily, and put a buttery kiss on her cheek, and Mumma thought, "Ah, I don't mind where we go, if only he's with me. But You've taken Your time with him and me, Lord, and no mistake."

C H A P T E R

2 3

As though the dust rising from the Casements' fallen dwelling were the dust of an implacable, pursuing rider, Charlie knew that he must shake himself out of his apathy and do something. Motty could not go on as she was; he could not go on as he was. Before the next Christmas perhaps the pattern of their lives would be broken, and he had a desperate desire to aid his destiny a little, not wait for it to happen to him as though he were a log of wood or block of stone. But he had forgotten how. Faced with decision, the old confusion of thought and spirit overcame him. He knew only one thing, that he could not live in the same house with Dolour any longer.

He listened at walls for her voice, and her light footstep on the floor. He watched her covertly as she washed the dishes or swept the yard, seeing how in this little while she had become beautiful, with a wistfulness he had never noticed before. Once perhaps, before his marriage, he could have borne her continual presence, but not now, when he was fully a man, accustomed to the physical expression of love as an accompaniment to the spiritual.

Could he go to her and say, "I love you, and I want to marry you, but it is forbidden"?

For Charlie had thought of something of which Dolour was ignorant, that according to the Church they were within pro- hibited degrees of relationship.

He had to go away before it was too late, and he had spoken to her.

Now, as never before, Roie seemed to be closer to him, as though she had put her sister in his way. He walked the streets, and she was with him, not loving him less, but more, so close that he could have put out a hand to touch her.

"Roie, what'll I do about Motty if I go?" he asked.

The two ends of the rope were there—Motty to keep him, and Dolour to send him away, and the bitter thing was that he knew Dolour was the only one to coax Motty back to a normal childhood. He laughed with the irony of it, and then suddenly, on an impulse, went up the worn, lop-sided steps of the church and into its stillness. He had not been there since Christmas, and he had not even bothered to work out the riddle why, since he believed that God was there, he had not come near Him. Now he felt dirty and unshaven, a spiritual tramp, as embarrassed as though he'd gone to see the nuns with ragged clothes and hair down the back of his neck. He was uncomfortable, looking at the Tabernacle half apologetically before the sensation was swamped in his misery. He sought for Roie in that presence, knowing she was there somewhere, but feeling himself too coarse and corrupt to touch her.

"What'll I do, darling?"

She was still his darling. His simplicity was too close to earth for him to confuse the two loves. What he felt for Dolour was not what he had felt for Roie. His adoration for the dead girl still lived, its colours a little dimmed, its perfume a little nostalgic. It had made him what he was, and was part of him for all time.

Again he had the impression that Roie had given him Dolour, and again and again he came against the stone wall of why, why, why, when it was impossible, when he could never marry her according to the laws of the Church, which for Dolour was the only way. He could feel himself getting exhausted, falling into the ready panic that called for drink and stupor to alleviate it. There was no way round the problem, and no one to ask about it.

He became aware then that for a long time a curious sound had been the background to his thought and, startled, he focused his attention upon it. It was the creaking of boots, up and down, up and down. He raised his head, and there was Father Cooley marching up and down the aisle with his head bowed over his breviary, but for all that looking like a policeman on the beat. Now and then a Latin mutter, strongly tinged with Galway, escaped his lips, and as though apologetically his eyes looked up under their grey bristly shelves and fastened on Charlie's. Father Cooley looked weary and old; the broad heartiness had left his frame, and Charlie suspected that under the concealing flow of his soutane he was thin and a little bowed. Actually Father Cooley's back was so bad he wanted nothing so much as to give in, bend over like a safety pin, and limp away and lie down with a hot-water bottle, for which weakling thought he condemned himself to another twenty-five turns up the church, not skipping the corners. He reckoned another three looks at young Rothe would do the trick, and they did.

"Can I speak to you, Father?" asked the young man, and Father Cooley shut his breviary with a business-like air.

"You can that."

The visitors' room at the presbytery looked like a parlour, and so it was, bare-floored, drab, smelling slightly of cabbage, and with a picture of the Pope looking cadaverous and eager-eyed over the mantel. Father Cooley sank gingerly on to a chair, suppressing a cry of pain as his lumbago stabbed him like a tack. He thought, "Holy Mother, I've left me flannel off. No wonder it's at me."

Charlie said, all thumbs with nervousness, and the need to blurt out everything, and yet with the feeling that Father Cooley was a priest, and not a man, "I wanted to ask you about Motty—Moira, my little girl. She's . . . hard to manage. I thought perhaps you'd give me some advice."

"A beautiful child," said Father Cooley immediately. "I remember her well. Bit right through my trouser leg the first time I met her in the playground."

Charlie was uncertain whether Father Cooley was chiding him, or pulling his leg. He looked diffidently at the priest, and the priest's blue eyes twinkled back, so that Charlie laughed. Father Cooley felt relieved. He hated the ice-breaking business, and couldn't understand why these people felt there was any ice left on him after all these years of attending to their intimate spiritual troubles. So he took the Irish way, and gave Charlie a prod.

"Your face isn't one I see at mass every Sunday."

Charlie shook his head dumbly.

"On the other hand I've frequently seen it down the street with the wrong sort of look on it. It wasn't like that while your wife was alive."

"I don't feel the way I did when she was alive," said Charlie, and was amazed when Father Cooley became very angry, stamping up and down the worn bit of mat in front of the fireplace, saying, "And why should you? You're older, you've got more responsibility, and you should have more sense, too, and yet, God help you, you've fallen down on the job." Charlie was dumbfounded. "Oh, you've not come to me before, and your mother-in-law, poor woman, hasn't asked my advice either, so you can take that look off your face. But I've got eyes in my head, and the sisters have been having their troubles with

Moira, and I can tell you I've been wondering when you'd wake up to yourself." He suddenly levelled a stumpy finger at the young man. "I'll tell you what'll happen to Moira. She'll go the same way as plenty of other children in this locality, into a reformatory. She's an uncontrollable child already, and the blame for it is at your door."

"I've always been kind to her. I've always provided for her," defended Charlie.

"Kind to her! Is that all a child's wanting? Do you think she's a kitten, perhaps? Oh, it'll do for some children, and little harm will come to them, but not for that tempestuous little creature." He was silent, rubbing his leg fiercely, as though Motty's bite still pained him.

Charlie burst out, "Well, if it's my fault, I want to fix it up. God knows I don't want Motty to grow up the wrong way, but what can I do about her?"

"Do something about yourself first," said the priest. He slapped his breviary down on the table. "Ah, it's bad enough to see these poor lads about here cracking like rotten sticks when misfortune hits them, but it's worse to see a man who's had a better start in life sliding into the backwash as though he hasn't an ounce of courage or fortitude in his whole body."

Charlie thought, "How do you know what sort of a start in life I had? Would you call knocking around the bush with a half-crazy bagman a good start? And how would you understand how I felt when Ro died?"

But Father Cooley didn't give him a chance. He saw he had Charlie pinned, and he went after him like a bulldog. "You're falling to pieces like an old book, and the worst of it is that you're feeling sorry for yourself as the pages fall. Who are you to be sorry for yourself? You're young, and healthy, and your life's hardly begun. Buck up and get hold of the pieces and pull them together, and maybe your children will feel you're not just a column of air for them to grasp."

"I thought of going away," muttered Charlie.

Father Cooley snorted. "So, you're going to pass the buck entirely! Mrs Darcy's going to have the care of the little ones, I suppose, or Dolour, hardly more than a child herself."

"I've got to go," said Charlie desperately.

"And why, may I ask?"

Charlie blurted, "I've fallen in love with Dolour."

Father Cooley was silent. He went up and down the mat a few times thinking, "So this is at the bottom of it, not the child's welfare." Then he said, "And what about Dolour? Does she think the same about you?"

"Yes, she does," said Charlie. "I haven't said anything about it, but I know she does."

"I suppose you would," admitted the priest, with a twinkle which he quickly suppressed. "Well, she's a fine girl, a good girl, and old enough to know her own mind. You've been thinking of marriage, then?"

"She's my sister-in-law," said Charlie, astounded, thinking the priest had forgotten.

"That's true, she is," said Father Cooley thoughtfully. He ruminated, "Now, here's a fine excuse. Shuffle off the children, be the martyr, off into the wide world with the head bowed and damn Mother Church for her stony heart."

"So, if I can't marry her I can't stop in the same house with her," said Charlie, his eyes asking "You're enough of a man to understand that, aren't you, even though you're forty years older than me, and long forgetting the cry of the flesh to be comforted?" He went on, "I just want to know what to do for the best, Father. I've got myself so muddled up I don't know what to do."

"The Sisters tell me she's grand with the children," commented Father Cooley meditatively. "Perhaps that's what the little one wants, a mother of her own, and not the feeling that there's no one in the world to belong to."

"You'd think they were her own the way she's always working for them," said Charlie. A wild rage against the frigid and implacable laws of the Church filled him. What right had they to keep him from Dolour, and Dolour from him, and Motty and Michael in their separate places? Anybody else, and he could go away with her and marry her in a registry office, and no one would know the difference. But he knew that wasn't what Dolour would ever do, not even if she had to spend the rest of her life alone. And it wouldn't do him, either, there was no real use in fooling himself. He had not been a good Catholic for a long time, but the ticklish conscience of the Catholic was there, never sleeping, never to be destroyed, always ready to raise its obstreperous fist and jolt the drugged or dreaming spirit back to life.

"It would be best for you both, not regarding the affection between you. She's a grand girl, and too good for many who'll be after her. The kind of girl who would make something of her life, given half a chance," said the priest. His pain caught

268

him with an iron grip across the loins. He thought, "If I don't sit down I'll fall down, and if I sit down, I'll never be able to straighten out again."

"Yes," said Charlie dully. "She's made for better things than she's got here."

"I suppose," said Father Cooley, keeping the wince off his face by a great effort, "you could forget all these bad days and leave the grog alone if you had such a woman to think of."

Charlie said nothing. Rub it in, he thought, but I don't need you or anyone else to tell me I've turned the game in these last years.

"And the children, you'd take them away, and they'd have a chance to grow up in the atmosphere children need," went on the priest pleasurably, as though he were planning, and not merely babbling on about an impossibility. "It's no life here for children. Even when the old place is pulled down, and the new Surry Hills built, there'll still be streets for them to play in, and the city smoke, and the criminal element always waiting to show its nose like a rat out of a hole. For there's people here who will make slums wherever they go. They won't be different, even though the shape of the house is changed." He could see the wonderment on Charlie's face, the resentment at the salt in the wound, so he said hastily, "It would be a fine thing for all four of you, but there's the impediment. We've got that impediment whichever way we look at it."

"That's right," said Charlie.

Father Cooley contemplated him. "I'll give him a little more rope," he decided, with a flicker of mischief. "I suppose you're thinking the Church is hard in matters of this sort?" he asked.

"It's all just a question of law, isn't it?" said Charlie angrily. "I'm no relation to Dolour. Marrying her sister didn't make me her brother. I can't see what'd be wrong in it no matter what way I look at it."

"Ah, there could be things that make it wrong," replied the priest. "You must remember the Church has lived for longer than any of us, and has had plenty of time to think about things. She doesn't bother to make her commandments just for a whim, or just to let her children know she's holding the whip."

Charlie sought for words, but he could only show his despair on his face.

"On the other hand," added Father Cooley suddenly, "you'll go a long way before you find an old lady who hasn't collected a great deal of commonsense throughout the years, and the Church is no exception."

He became aware of the silence in the room, of the young man's yellow eyes looking at him, waiting like those of a watchful dog. This is where he'll show himself, thought the priest, and went on, gently, "If you'd come to me earlier I might have been able to save you a lot of anxiety by explaining that very often a dispensation can be obtained in such a case as this. But no, that was too simple. You had to leave it unsaid, and worry yourself to a rag, all because you didn't have the gumption to come and ask the man whose job it is to know most about such things."

And he went on grumbling and scolding, watching Charlie furtively from under his eyebrows, and feeling his heart melt as though it were under the burning eye of God Himself to see the flush under the dark skin, and the whole expression change from bewilderment and anger to one of hope and exultance, chasing each other swiftly and excitedly until a torrent of questions burst from the young man's mouth. Father Cooley thought almost with pain, "Ah, Lord, do me a favour and make it come out right for him, and the young girl, and the little devil with the bite like a dingo." He held up a hand.

"I'm not saying we'll manage it. I'm saying it's possible. But I feel, myself, that with things as they are, and especially with the children needing a proper family life. . . ."

"We'll go to the country," said Charlie. "I was brought up there. There's plenty of jobs I can take a hand at. Or I could find a place with a small-town printery—"

"Whist-a-whist! It's not me that has the say. The case has to go to the proper authorities. I'm only the man who'll present it to them. I'm the go-between."

"Father," said Charlie. He stood up, wanting to say many things, unable to express any of them, feeling an almost exhausting relief and eagerness, and an urgent desire to get away by himself and think about it.

Father Cooley cautioned him, "Don't say a word to the girl yet. It'll be a week or so before I can get an answer for you. Don't talk to anyone about it except God." He sat down painfully at the desk. "Now, let's get the facts down."

Charlie stood staring at the bristly white back of Father Cooley's head, trying to read the thoughts therein, and feeling, no matter how much he tried to control it, that all would be well. His mind leaped out to Dolour, probably putting Mikey

270

to bed now, leaning over his cot with her soft hair falling in a curtain down the side of her cheek. In his mind he took hold of her by the shoulders and turned her round saying, "Oh, Dolour, I'll love you the more because I loved Roie. There's no conflict between you and her, and couldn't be, because you know how I felt about her, and I know how you feel still. I'll take you away and we'll start again, with the children. There's so many wonderful places to see in this country, beautiful places to live where the trees grow, and the lakes and rivers run, and the sea is always to be heard even on the quietest night. You don't know what life is yet, Dolour, the way you've been shut in here by the greyness and the dirty buildings, and the people living the lives of parrots, squabbling and screaming because they're unhappy and discontented and don't know it."

He was suddenly aware that the priest was speaking to him, and with a wrench he brought his thoughts back to the old man, who declared crossly, "There's plenty of time for that later."

Charlie flushed and grinned.

"And now," said Father Cooley, "doubtless you'll be wanting my company in the church."

Charlie opened his mouth to say, "I'm not ready. I haven't examined my conscience. Next week—tomorrow—" but Father Cooley went to the cupboard and got out his purple stole, and with the air of one laden down with broom, bucket and scrubbing brush, briskly led Charlie back to the church and the confessional.

Charlie spent the days in an agony of anticipation and terror lest something should happen and Dolour should change towards him. He could not show his feelings in case the permission for the marriage was not given, and yet he could not altogether hide them. Sometimes he grabbed Motty and held her to him saying, "Things'll be different for you, sweetheart", and kissed the insolent, darkly suspicious look off her face, receiving either a hug or a blow in exchange. Or he followed Michael round, laughing at his quaint and stolid amiability, so that Mumma nudged Hughie and whispered, "What's up with him now? Taking notice of the kid! And he's not drunk, neither."

Dolour noticed the difference with a pang, thinking that perhaps something important had happened to him which would change the course of his life and therefore hers. But he was no different towards her, except perhaps to avoid her glance.

She stood looking after him and wondering, hardly noticing Hughie standing there with a brown paper bag in his hand.

"Lookut I got, Dol."

He grinned, and with his toothlessness looked like a shabby old leprechaun, so that she marvelled how it was she had ever hated him. For the signature of his lifetime of hard work was on him, on his calloused hands and his strong bent legs and his tousled head, and she wept inwardly to think she could have begrudged him the little pleasure he had found in being drunk and rumbustious.

"Oh, Dadda! Fancy you remembering I like poor man's oranges!"

"Saw them in Lick's window," boasted Hughie. Something sad and fugitive came into his eyes, shadowing their blue and devilish glint for a moment. It was almost as though the sharp aromatic smell of the oranges had made him remember something better forgotten.

"What's up, Dad?"

"Nothing. It's just that me liver goes all goose pimples when I think of eating them things."

She laughed. He looked at her admiringly. He liked Roie's sort better, just big enough to get into your arms, and the shy timid look to her. But Dolour was someone to be proud of with her straight back, and the way she looked you in the eye no matter if you was the Pope himself. He thought, "The right bloke had better get her, or I'll stiffen him out, as God's my judge."

To cover his embarrassment he said, "Watcher know? Just seen young Charlie coming out of the presbytery. Suppose he was having a couple of pints with the Father."

He rolled off, roaring with laughter, gathering up Mikey and Motty on the way, and, one under each arm, bore them shrieking with joy into the sun-striped backyard.

"Whatever could he be doing in the presbytery?"

The mystery of it bothered her all through teatime, and she couldn't help stealing glances at Charlie as he sat silently eating. He didn't seem to be cast down. It was only now and then that she felt she detected an air of intense excitement about him. But what had he to be excited about? What had he been doing?

It was with relief that she finished the dishes and went to her room, sitting on the bed and brushing her hair, still thinking and puzzling. She was there when Charlie came in. He pottered about, looking out of the window and picking up Ah Grin and putting him down again. Dolour watched him with an aching heart.

"What's wrong, Charlie?"

"Dolour, remember we had a talk once and I was thinking about going away?"

With cold hands she put down the brush. "Yes, I remember."

"Well, I've made up my mind. I'm going to go. Outback."

She was not old enough to hide her feelings, but she tried, looking at him and saying in a voice which quavered a little, "I guess you'll be happier somewhere else."

She tried to say more, but the words wouldn't come. To her helpless shame tears welled into her eyes. "I'm an awful crybaby, aren't I? I don't know what's the matter with me lately. I guess—I guess it's because I'll miss you."

"You'll stick by Motty and Michael as long as you're around, Dolour?"

A little irony came to her face. She'd be around. He wasn't tied by his love or anxiety for the children, but she was, and would be until she was earning enough money to take them away with her somewhere. But what would she do without Charlie? It was no use trying to be brave. The pain was as great as if her heart were pulled in half. The emptiness, the fruitlessness of her coming years, magnified beyond calculation by this shock, fell upon her and crushed her, and so she looked at him, not knowing it was all written on her face in letters an inch high.

He wanted to encompass her in the tenderness he felt for her, but this was not the place. Not this squalid room where Mumma or Hughie might burst in upon them at any moment. He said, "You and I haven't ever been out anywhere together, Dolour."

She was astounded, blinking back her tears in puzzlement.

"Let's go out for a walk tonight. A tram ride. Something."

The strangest feeling stole into her heart, more delicate than she could describe, more poignant than she could comprehend. It was like the quiet time when the great instruments rested, and the players waited, patiently, for the conductor to raise his hand, and the music to flow.

But she did not say anything but "I'd like to, Charlie."

2 4

HERE on this long low shadowy shore, first of the coast to be seen of white men's eyes, the coarse grass blew, bleached and melancholy.

Botany Bay.

Name of glamour, name of grief! A great round harbour, it rose up out of the dusk into the light of the moon, a sheet of pewter. The wind blew from the city behind and, meeting the cold breath of the sea, it funnelled upwards with a sound like a vast sigh. Perhaps it was the same sigh that had come from those rotten leaking ships that had limped into that bay a hundred and sixty years before . . . the sigh of the exiled felons who would never see home any more.

"It looks like the end of the world," whispered Dolour. She whispered because there was heaviness in the air, an uneasiness that weighed on the heart. It was as though a very thin and palpitating tissue divided this night from the past. The cry of the convicts was all round them, the heartsickness of the innocent penned with the guilty, the weeping of women who had stolen food for their children and would never see those children again.

Dolour wanted to cry "It's all right! It's all right! Sydney wouldn't be the same if it hadn't been for you!"

She wanted to show them the city behind her; the stony forest, the fantastic lichen that crept from the moonlit shores out over the foothills, here and there poking up a shoot in the form of a radio tower, a brazen-scaled steeple, there dwindling away into the earth-hugging film of the little slum houses of the 'Loo, or Surry Hills, or Erskineville. It was like a sea, this city. It had bays and peninsulas; it broke in a foam of tumble-down cottages about some massive sandstone outcrop. It receded like a defeated wave from the northern hills.

It was a strange memorial to the forgotten and defiled, yet everywhere they had left their mark upon it. Sydney's cobble-stones were worn with the tramp of chain-gangs; her road cuttings still bore the scars of their chisels, and the walls of those cuttings were still streaked with the rainbow slime that the thirsty convicts had licked long before.

There was no convict blood in Dolour, yet she felt a fierce pride in these, the wicked, the hating, and the hopeless who yet had been the components of a miracle. It was right that this wild and brilliant land, this last, lost fabulous continent should have such a beginning in all that was best and worst, and most passionate and vital in mankind. For the felons, in spite of starvation and flogging and despair, had survived. They had survived.

The wind was colder now. It blew her long dark hair across her face and Charlie's, and at that subtle touch he put his arms round her, kissing her as though he were a starved man. He had not had a woman in his arms for three years; with joy and gratitude he felt once more the delicate lyre-shape of hips and thighs, the slender waist and broad arch of the breast fashioned so precisely for life and life-giving.

"Dolour," he said, "come with me when I go."

She was silent. She bowed her head on his shoulder, trembling.

"What's the matter?" he asked. "Don't you want me to love you?"

She had no words, but the beat of her heart drummed over and over again, "Thank You, God."

He looked at her face in the moonlight, her features that had changed in his memory from the smudged contours of girlhood to strength and beauty, with broad planes and winged eyebrows, and eyes that lay deep and calm in darkened sockets. He had been familiar with that child, but the woman was a stranger. He knew nothing of her deepnesses, only that he loved her.

"Charlie."

She opened the top button of his shirt, rubbing her cheek against his chest. He laughed.

"Roie used to do that, too."

Dolour felt that she should pull away from him, that she should be hurt or dismayed. But she could not feel any of those things.

"Is it only because you miss Roie?"

Down below the water chuckled on the sandstone ledges and tinkled off with the sound of a thousand waterfalls. "No."

A little pang of jealous pain caught Dolour's heart. In spite

of what he said, she knew that she was second-best. She had
wanted most of all to be first-loved, and best-loved, but that
was not to be hers. Then it was all swallowed up in a burst
of love for Charlie, for her sister, and their children, and the
children she herself would bear.

"Roie is part of me, and part of you," she said. "This won't
make any difference to what we both feel for her."

She knew the poor man's orange was hers, with its bitter rind,
its paler flesh, and its stinging, exultant, unforgettable tang.
So she would have it that way, and wish it no other way. She
knew that she was strong enough to bear whatever might come
in her life as long as she had love. That was the thing, the backbone of endurance itself, and she who possessed it needed no
other weapon.

She kissed him, timidly at first, and then answering antiphon-
ally his love, feeling him tremble, and confiding her trust in him
by her very defencelessness. So this was passion, not the shoddy
imitation of it that she had feared and witnessed, that blas-
phemed the fundamental nobilities of life, but passion that
walked hand-in-hand with innocence, a magnificent delight that
encompassed all tenderness, all self-sacrifice, all richness of
giving.

"Roie knew," she thought.

They walked up from the city, through the dark alleyways
where cats sprang hissing from the garbage tins and the walls
glittered with their crowns of broken glass. Here and there a
drunk lay in a doorway, or a woman showed a pale face from
a balcony or dim-lit window. Music spilled across the street like
the yellow light that spilled from the tall corner-lamp slung
in its archaic wrought-iron bough. But mainly there was silence,
as though already Surry Hills felt its doom, and down in the
earth the old grass-roots were stirring, ready to clothe this soil
with the verdure that had been there a century before.

They came to the top of Plymouth Street and saw, where the
old ochre shop had stood on the corner but a week or two
before, a square of stars. There was a sharp clatter of falling
bricks as a stray dog slunk across the allotment, and then silence
once more.